BLOOD
FOR POWER

BLOOD FOR POWER

BOOK 3

AN APOCALYPSE LITRPG

SCOTT W. JAMES

Timeless
Wind

First published by Timeless Wind Publishing LLC 2024

First edition

Editing by Jennifer Ehrhardt. Proofread by Lorne Ryburn.

Cover art by Macarious.

THE STORY SO FAR...

The world ends when the System arrives. Lucas, the protagonist, is given the class of Blood Reaver, which favors speed, ferocity, and striking from the shadows. He is informed that his world has ended and that his apartment building has been converted into a 100-floor tower filled with traps, monsters, and loot. He starts on floor 100 and has one year to reach the bottom and escape before the tower self-destructs.

At the end of book 1, the Goddess Samara coerces Lucas to accompany her on a short trip beyond the tower to train. Book 2 starts with Lucas being transported to her home planet to begin training to better use his abilities. Samara is a goddess with blood-based powers, and very much wishes that Lucas will pledge himself to her service. This would make her his patron in the Tower and would allow her to offer him more assistance on his journey. But Lucas politely refuses. He does not wish to be beholden to anyone.

After a week of training, Samara hosts a dinner party in which various gods and their sponsored Tower Climbers attend. Here, Lucas meets Roan, a mysterious god of shadow and manipulation. Roan is sponsoring more than one Tower Climber. Hugo has already pledged his service to Roan. Daisy, a pale woman with dark hair and shadow powers is distrustful of everyone, but she has also pledged herself to Roan. And she's not happy about it.

At this party, the Officiator, the representative who controls the Tower, makes an appearance. He tells the Climbers that they have one hour to find the portal and escape the planet or they die.

Lucas, working with Daisy and several other Climbers, finds a way through the portal. He lands back in the Tower on a small, deserted island, with a gift from Samara—a Blood Reaver's Cache Bracer. It can directly store and summon blood with its gems, allowing Lucas to weaponize his offensive abilities without first needing to draw an enemy's blood.

Several monsters are fought on this island. Eventually, Lucas is picked up by a passing pirate ship and taken back to town. Once there, he reunites with Hugo and the others, and joins them just as they are about to attend an important meeting.

Many other Climbers also attend this meeting. Soon it is revealed that the meeting is an auction held by the Officiator. However, there is only one item for sale. The map to the Golden Door. Whoever opens the Golden Door first gets a head start on the next floor, along with a special legendary item. Any non-Climber residents in that party will be allowed to leave the Tower completely.

The auction begins, and Lucas succeeds in winning the map. But there is a catch. As soon as he takes possession of the map, a countdown begins. The Climbers only have four days to reach the Golden Door before it disappears for good. If no one is able to reach and open the Door in time, then the Tower goes into permanent lockdown—condemning everyone inside to death.

Upon gaining access to the map, Lucas becomes a target. Each Tower Climber wants the map for themselves. Therefore, groups form and work to try and take it from him. Ultimately, Lucas and his friends manage to escape and board a ship and set sail across the sea.

They have to fend off enemy Climbers and multiple monsters. When all are conquered or driven away, Lucas receives a Class evolution option for something called the Scarlet Beast. Its description troubles him and he rejects it, but the thought of it won't leave his mind. He needs advice, so he turns to another god, Yakeshi, who has mentored him in the past.

Yakeshi is a peerless swordsman. Previously, he warned Lucas to never drink the blood of sapient creatures—lest he turn into a monster himself. However, Lucas broke this rule by drinking Anders's blood in a place cut off from the Tower. Still, he is confident that he can hide this from Yakeshi and decides to contact him.

Yakeshi summons him to another planet. He is in the middle of hunting a monster and has decided to show Lucas firsthand the fate of a blood drinker. Together, the pair track a series of killings to an abandoned warehouse. There they find a Scarlet Beast. A man whose addiction to blood has corrupted him and turned him feral. The transformation has enormously enhanced his strength, toughness, and speed.

Only Yakeshi's presence saves Lucas's life here as the god quickly disposes of the creature. He once again warns Lucas not to drink the blood.

The duo are about to leave when they discover the Scarlet Beast had kept a prisoner. It was Damian, another Tower Climber and an ally of Lucas and Hugo. Damian discloses that he was captured while doing a job for Roan. Lucas is surprised by this, but Damian makes it clear that he has not pledged his service to Roan.

Hidden explosives within the warehouse are suddenly detonated. Yakeshi protects all of them, but is troubled by the development. The Scarlet Beast couldn't have set it up and he realizes that someone is trying to send him a message.

Lucas wants to know more, but the god refuses to elaborate and asks if Lucas is ready to pledge fealty to him. Lucas refuses and is sent back to the Tower.

After returning to the Tower, he and his group encounter a new hostile alien faction. A humanoid fish species called Shrikon. After defeating one of the fish, Daisy opens up to Lucas about her past. She reveals that Roan has stolen her last name and many of her memories from before the System integration. She claims it is punishment for a crime she doesn't even remember committing and bitterly hates Roan for it.

They resume their search for the Golden Door. It is revealed to them that a key must also be discovered to unlock the Door. During their travels, they are overwhelmed by Shrikon enemies, and eventually captured. The group is taken underground by the Shrikon and presented before their leader, the Sea King.

Several of Lucas's group are then forced to fight Shrikon one-on-one solely for the King's entertainment. Lucas is pitted against the King's strongest soldier, who is known only as The Captain, a skilled Shrikon warrior who possesses a Legendary sword and shield. With these skills and weapons, Lucas is brutally defeated in combat, but is spared from death.

The Sea King decides that the Tower Climbers would provide a worthy contest to the rest of his people. Each Climber is separated from the others and deposited in an isolated part of the island. They are given a five-minute head start before the Shrikon begin hunting them.

Lucas manages to evade them and, in the process, meets a strange new alien. He looks like a terrifying killer, but he is polite and introduces himself as Tanver Vhar. Parts of the Tower floor glitch out around him, and Lucas realizes that he is not supposed to be in the Tower. He also learns that Vhar is an S+ Grade being who is only one step down from being a god in terms of power.

Vhar tells Lucas that Blood Reavers are rare in the Tower and explains that the Officiator gave him the Class to shake things up with the gods. Lucas wants to know why Vhar is confiding in him. Vhar avoids the question and instead suggests that Lucas take the Golden Door's resident offer and simply leave the Tower for good.

Lucas refuses the offer, as he cannot leave his friends behind. Vhar is pleased with his answer and says that he sees potential in him.

The pair part ways and Lucas continues fighting monsters and exploring more of the island until he is eventually reunited with Hugo. At this point, Lucas is feeling strong and has gained several new abilities that allow him greater control over blood.

Tired of being hunted, he and the others decide to take the fight back to the Shrikon directly. He faces The Captain for a second time and defeats him in battle. Lucas claims his Legendary D-grade sword and a bracer for his other arm that can dispel shadow magic.

Lucas and Hugo move forward to confront the Sea King. But as they enter his throne room, they are surprised to see Tanver Vhar and the king having a friendly conversation. Vhar encourages the king and Lucas to fight since it is revealed that the king holds the key to the Golden Door.

Lucas enters the fight feeling confident, but soon realizes that he is dangerously outmatched. The Sea King is close to killing him when Tanver Vhar calls for a timeout. In this brief intermission, Vhar asks Lucas if he's willing to do whatever it takes to win. Lucas confirms that he is. So Vhar forces him to drink a potent cocktail of sapient blood.

Lucas's levels rise quickly and his Class is forcibly evolved. He has become a Scarlet Beast! With nothing on his mind except feasting on blood and claiming his next kill, he attacks the Sea King with wild ferocity. Lucas's power grows even further as he consumes the king's blood until he's drained and dead.

Lucas immediately searches for his next meal and quickly spots a small bird trying to hide behind a pillar. Because his mind is clouded, he does not recognize Hugo and moves to attack his friend. Only Hugo crying out his name in fear is finally able to break through Lucas's trance and stop the assault.

Hugo's familiar voice becomes a lifeline for Lucas's humanity and he uses it to claw his way back to sanity. His Class, however, devolves back into that of a Blood Reaver, greatly impressing Vhar. Lucas is furious with the alien for almost causing him to kill Hugo. As a consolation, Vhar offers him a portal directly to the Golden Door.

Lucas and Hugo reluctantly walk through the portal and arrive at the Door. They are not alone however. At least fifty other Climbers are there waiting for them, including the rest of Lucas's friends, except for Damian.

The Climbers are tired of fighting. They just want Lucas to open the Door so that they can all eventually progress to the next floor.

As soon as Lucas unlocks the Door, he is faced with a Golden Elevator. The Officiator is standing nearby and appears to congratulate him on opening the Door and winning. Unfortunately, this proves to be a trap as Tanver Vhar ambushes and kills the Officiator.

The death of the Officiator prompts multiple gods, including Roan, Samara, and Yakeshi to appear within the Tower. Yakeshi wants to kill Vhar for what he's done, but Vhar has taken over control of the Tower. He warns the god that fighting him will no longer be so easy. Vhar then brags that he could not have achieved this alone, and Roan reveals that he has been secretly assisting him.

The other gods are outraged by Roan's betrayal, especially Samara who swears that she will destroy him. Yakeshi warns Roan that a tribunal will be called against him. However, the god is indifferent to both threats.

Vhar then uses his new control over the Tower to forcibly expel every god except Yakeshi and Roan.

Thus far, Lucas has considered Yakeshi to be a good mentor and was leaning toward selecting him as a patron and making a formal pledge. But Roan discloses that every time there is a System integration, one of the gods is chosen to select the planet. He explains to Lucas that it was Yakeshi who chose Earth, Yakeshi who killed billions of his fellow humans and condemned him to the Tower.

Lucas feels angry and betrayed. Yakeshi tries to explain himself. Meanwhile, Vhar exposes to the god that Lucas has drunk human blood. To Yakeshi, a Blood Reaver that commits the act can never be anything more than a monster that must be destroyed. He exits without a word and the bond previously shared between them is now irrevocably broken.

Roan informs Lucas that Yakeshi and Samara will both try to kill him in the future for his betrayals. Seeing no other option, Lucas agrees to pledge fealty to Roan in exchange for the god's protection and assistance. A brand forms on Lucas's hand to show that the new bond with Roan has been forged.

Immediately afterward, all the Tower Climbers at the Golden Door except for Lucas, Hugo, and Daisy suddenly drop dead. Tanver Vhar had used his control over the Tower to kill them in order to test the Tower's security.

Roan is taken aback by Vhar's choice to kill so many, but ultimately accepts it. Hugo, on the other hand, is stunned and devastated by the death of his friends. Lucas feels the same and quickly flies into a blind rage as he advances to attack Roan and Vhar.

Roan activates the brand on Lucas's hand, delivering excruciating pain in an attempt to subdue Lucas. Once the pain subsides, the god tells him that he will continue to climb the Tower.

Lucas and Hugo are in a daze as Daisy escorts them to the elevator. Once inside, she slips Lucas a scrap of paper and says goodbye to them both.

The book ends with the elevator doors closing on the pair and Lucas reading Daisy's note, which simply says, "I know how to beat them."

CHAPTER 1
LOSING AN ARGUMENT TO
A WASHING MACHINE

ALMOST EVERYONE we knew had just been killed.

The golden elevator doors closed and Hugo and I traveled down to the next floor. Just like that it was over.

Neither of us knew what to say or how to react. Neither of us knew where we were going or what we'd find once we got there.

It was nauseating.

I tightened my fist around a slim piece of paper. It was my lifeline. The one thing that kept me grounded. Just six little words hastily scrawled out that offered me a tiny bit of hope.

"I know how to beat them" was what the note said.

Them being the gods that had invaded my world, killed most of humanity, and then enslaved the rest of us, forcing us to run through a series of life and death challenges. Them who murdered innocent people that I cared about.

In my darkest moment, it was Daisy who'd slipped me the note. Another survivor of the massacre on the previous floor.

But if she knew how to beat the gods that controlled our lives, then why hadn't she done so already? There must be more to her plan. More pieces that needed to be assembled. She might have the knowledge but not the means to beat them.

I had to find her on the next floor down and learn everything she knew.

Soft Jazz elevator music played out of the speaker in the top corner. It had a calming quality to it and I could feel myself getting swept away by the comforting sounds.

Hugo flew up to the speaker and ripped out the cables with his talons. The music abruptly halted.

"Is that meant to be a joke?" Hugo spat. "Playing music after what just happened?"

"I was actually enjoying it."

The music started up again, despite not being connected to anything.

Hugo groaned.

"Magical jazz speaker notwithstanding, how are you doing?" I asked.

"How can you joke after what just happened? I'm so angry that I feel like I'm going to explode! Why aren't you more upset?"

He was hopping around the floor to try and burn off his excess anger, but it wasn't working.

Despite my calm outward demeanor, I was upset. I'd walked into this elevator shaking with rage. But undirected anger would just turn inward and I'd start blaming myself for the recent events. And it wasn't me. The gods were to blame. I hated them for what they'd done, but expressing those feelings now could be our undoing. We had to be patient. We had to get stronger and wait for the right moment to strike back.

I showed Hugo the note. His beak fell open in shock and he stopped bouncing.

"Does that mean—"

I cut him off. "Not out loud."

He nodded and put two and two together to figure out who had handed me the note. Some of the tension in his body loosened as he relaxed.

Then he pecked my hand hard enough to draw blood.

"Ow!" I yelled.

"You ass! I've been stuck in this gold shit box losing my mind and you had that note the whole time?"

Abashed, I reeled back.

He was right. It was selfish of me to retreat into my mind and leave him alone to try to process what had happened.

"I'm sorry. I should have shown it to you as soon as we were alone."

He harrumphed. His way of reluctantly accepting my apology while also saying that I still had to make it up to him.

A few minutes of silence passed until he noticed I hadn't healed my hand.

Hugo scoffed. "Oh get down off your cross, and then tell me you have a plan."

The pain was minor compared to what I was used to. It was also well deserved, but I took Hugo's point.

I reached for the magical healing blood that I stored in a gem on my bracer. I quickly closed up the wound.

"The plan is the same as before," I said. "I don't know how long it will take Damian or Daisy to reach the next floor. So we should focus on getting stronger until we can find them again."

Hugo agreed with me and we stood in silence for about fifteen minutes until we realized the elevator ride was taking far longer than it should.

In that time, we ran through a lot of emotions. It was cathartic in a way. We raged, we mourned, and even laughed a couple of times before settling into boredom.

Strangely, it was Hugo who moved on the fastest. Maybe it had something to do with his age or his physiology, but I could see him quickly returning to his old self.

Suddenly the doors opened up into a carpeted hallway with a single door at the end of it. A tall, rakish man in an all-black suit was leaning against the door. He smiled warmly at the sight of us, like we were old friends. Like he hadn't just murdered people that I'd cared for.

The anger I'd been working so hard to keep under control was threatening to bubble up again.

"What are you doing here?" I asked, a little more sharply than I'd meant to.

I forced myself to take a breath. *This is a marathon not a sprint. Getting free from these gods will require patience.*

"I know you didn't expect to see me again so soon," Roan said. "But I felt that I should explain some things and answer any questions you have. Some changes have been made since Tanver Vhar took over running the Tower, but a lot of other things remain the same. Whereas both of you are now being sponsored by me, I'm here to make your transition to the new regime as smooth as possible."

I tried to go into party chat to talk to Hugo privately and received a strange message:

[Error!]

[Party Chat has been removed]

[Bonded Companion detected]

[Companion Chat activated]

Lucas: Hello?

Hugo: That was weird.

"I see you've activated Companion Chat," Roan said. "And no, before you ask, nobody but the two of you can see what is written in there. When Vhar removed party chat from the Tower, he found the older Companion version underneath it like buried code. It's an old System function that actually predates the invention of the Towers. As such, we have no way of removing it."

I frowned. "You're not in control of the System?"

Roan laughed at the idea. "No, of course not. We have some control over the Tower that interfaces with the System."

"That doesn't feel very comforting," Hugo said.

He was right. It gave the impression that this was too complex for them to handle. 'Some control' made them sound like kids who'd gotten ahold of their parents' car keys and were going on a joyride.

"The Officiator was custom built to run the Tower," Roan said. "But everything it designed is still here and running on autopilot. Other than the party chat feature being gone, the changes you'll experience will be minimal. Oh, and there's also this."

[God Chat Activated]

Roan: See, not all the changes are bad. Now if you ever have a question about monsters, quests, or items, you can use this feature to reach out to me.

"That's being *awfully* generous with your time," I replied.

"Well, I wanted to make it up to you after the whole murdering your friends thing. But the downside is that other Climbers will have access to the same feature with other gods."

"Wait, the other gods are still here?" I asked, surprised.

Roan grimaced. "Unfortunately, we couldn't get rid of them permanently. Again, old System rules and whatnot. We did manage to cut off their sight completely though. Now none of them can find you or see what you're doing in here. Instead, we'll be sending out time-delayed updates of every Climber's progress to those who watch the Climb."

That didn't sound particularly reassuring. Especially since some of those gods wanted me dead. The whole viewer aspect of this also confused me.

It was rarely spoken of in the past, and beyond the gods who directly sponsored Climbers, I failed to see the value in it.

"And all these viewers are okay with you taking over and changing things?" I asked. "What do they even get out of watching this anyway?"

"Some of it is entertainment, some of it is advertising to incentivize people to volunteer, and some of it is research on potential future rivals. Planets would also pay to watch and the Officiator would use those funds to run the Tower."

"So by taking over, you've become rich?"

"*Richer*," he corrected me. "But it's not all sunshine and rainbows. A lot of the money that gets sent to us has to be reinvested into the Tower. You didn't think all the items you received were just created out of thin air, did you? No, experts across an array of fields are hired to make them. Every non-Climber you encounter from this point on is being paid to be here. It's not cheap, you know."

He was starting to make it sound like more of a burden than a prize. So much effort and expense just for a few gods to get first pick of the new System recruits? It seemed unlikely. There had to be more to the story.

"Why create the Tower in the first place if it wasn't profitable until your takeover?"

Roan's smile dipped. "I didn't create the Tower and it's a mystery as to who did. As for why it was created, the reason is simple. Because the System is always expanding and integrating new planets. That is a process even I don't know how to stop. The Tower was invented to slow the integration process down and give newly inducted people like yourself a chance to acclimatize. Things were... let's just say a lot more chaotic before the Tower was made."

The idea of the Tower being the kinder, gentler way of being integrated into the System was a troubling thought. I wanted to ask more questions about the time before the Tower, but I had greater concerns surrounding our safety that needed to be addressed first.

"What's happened to the other gods that want me dead?"

"They're off consolidating power or looking for new Climbers to sponsor. Don't worry, there are no more portal loopholes. You're not going to wake up to find one of them standing over you," he grinned. "Other Climbers can still find shrines throughout the floors and pledge their service to them though. So be careful with whom you trust."

Great, now we had to worry about other Climbers coming after us. At least before when Hugo and I clashed with others, it was because we were a tangential threat to a quest. An inconvenience that was getting in their way. Now we were direct targets.

"How many Climbers could even be left after what happened?" Hugo asked.

I nodded in agreement. All the killing on the previous floor could easily be considered a culling. Sure, there might be Climbers who'd survived by not being there, but I'd be shocked if it was more than a handful.

Roan laughed again.

It was a habit that was starting to feel condescending.

Hugo did his best version of a scowl, and I folded my arms.

"Elaborate," I said.

"The Tower is massive and has many versions of the same floor running at once."

My eyebrows rose. "You're telling me that while I was completing my Golden Door quest, others were doing the same elsewhere."

Roan nodded. "Some completed theirs before you, some after, while you were in the elevator, and some are still trying to complete it right now. Never assume you're seeing the whole population unless you're on the ground floor. There's only one version of that floor and it only opens for a select period of time."

I didn't understand why so many others had to die earlier if I was still competing. It didn't make any sense.

"Why not just kill every other Climber like before?" I asked.

"Tanver Vhar was the one responsible for that. He hasn't pledged his service to me so I don't control what he does. We're in a kind of partnership. There are protocols that prevent a god or someone pledged to a god from taking ownership of the Tower. I needed Vhar to gain access. He needs my ongoing support and protection to not get brutally murdered by angry gods."

"That still doesn't explain why you won't remove the other Climbers," I pointed out.

"Because we're unable to. The Tower is like a highly complex living machine that reacts and adapts to certain stimuli. After I told Vhar not to kill anyone else, he ignored me and tried to do it again. He failed. The option to do what he did before had just disappeared. It is yet another reason why we're hesitant to make changes. But that's an issue for another time. Want to see your apartment?" he asked with a twinge of excitement.

I didn't trust his tone and narrowed my eyes. "You say that like it's changed."

He waved my suspicion away. "Just a minor update when we removed the pay phone. Consider it another gift to help make things easier."

Hugo hopped up onto my shoulder so that he could be face to face with Roan. He was still bursting with energy.

"What about our Grade evolution?" he asked.

"Both of you will receive it once you leave the apartment. But I should warn you, both Vhar and I felt that the Officiator was being too miserly with these rewards. Now every Climber who descends to the next floor will be receiving the Grade evolution process."

"That's not fair!" cried Hugo.

"You turned the prize we fought and bled for into a participation trophy?" I shouted.

"The Officiator would've found another way to even the scales eventually," he replied calmly. "This Tower was, and will continue to be, a training ground. It would have never let you pull too far ahead on your own. That would've made the whole thing too unbalanced and defeat the purpose."

I snorted. "And the purpose is what? Become the best I can be in here so that when I get out, I can be a soldier in your army and expand your territory?"

"No, my plan was for you to be in charge of Earth after you complete the Tower."

At first, I thought he was joking. Putting me in charge of an entire planet? Before the System had arrived, I was barely in charge of my own life. The idea of running a planet was dizzying.

"What about me?" Hugo cried, feeling left out.

Roan shrugged. "Well, I guess you'd be co-chairs of Earth."

"But you'd still own us and the planet," I said.

"I think you'll find that working under me will be more helpful than you realize." He then sighed. "But I understand that our relationship will take time to develop."

I was getting sick of his overly familiar tone.

"Is that what you told Daisy when you took her memories?"

Roan's cheerful expression vanished. His lip curled up and he loomed over us. "Daisy overstepped and saw things that she should have never seen. Things that would have made life a lot more complicated for everyone. She thinks I cursed her by taking her memories, but she has no idea how much worse it could've been."

He opened the door to the apartment and gestured for us to enter.

Whatever had happened between him and Daisy, it was clear that it was a sore area for him. I doubted that I'd glean any more information by pressing the matter, so I dropped the subject and went inside.

The apartment looked relatively the same. There were only two rooms. A bathroom, and a large open plan space that started as a bedroom on the left, became a living room in the middle, and ended with a kitchen. The pay phone used to be bolted to the floor in between the kitchen and living area. Now in its place was a large metal orange box that I quickly realized was a washing machine.

"What do you think?" Roan asked, pointing to the washing machine with pride. His cold anger from before vanished as quickly as it had appeared. Now we were all friends again.

"I don't get it," I said.

Meanwhile, Hugo flitted around the apartment, checking every nook and cranny. "Hmm, dent in the lower wall is still here," he muttered before flying over to the couch. "Yep, there's the stain where I knocked over that soda, and there's where I dropped the TV remote." He came back to my shoulder and declared, "Everything appears to be in order."

"Yeah, we're going to have a talk about our living situation later," I told him.

Turning back to Roan, I asked, "What's the big deal? It's just a washing machine."

Roan shook his head. "This is the greatest washing machine in the universe. It can clean any substance off your clothes and dry them in thirty minutes or less. Say hello to Misty."

He put his hand on the machine and it rocked side to side before stabilizing itself.

There was a black screen on the front above where the clothes would go, with a moving digital smiley face on it.

"Oof, I was having the most wonderful dream," said the washing machine in a woman's voice. "There was a bunch of Valtrexian leather that was absolutely soaked in advanced slime guts. The job was almost too big for me to handle, but I found a way," she said wistfully.

Inwardly, I groaned. This was the last thing I needed right now. The apartment was meant to be a private space for Hugo and me to decompress in. It was not a place for a robot to watch and comment on our every move.

"My mistake," I said sarcastically to Roan. "You've given me a sentient washing machine. However can I repay you?"

"*Excuse me*?" Misty asked. "First of all, my name is Misty, and I am a fully licensed cleaning service intelligence. I find the term washing machine derogatory. Second of all, I don't appreciate your tone. But maybe I should cut you some slack since you look like you spent the last week living in those clothes." She made a sniffing sound. "Actually, scratch that. My olfactory detectors indicate that the real number is at least twice that long."

"I'm guessing you bought this on sale," I said to Roan.

"Or maybe brought it home from the dump?" Hugo added.

"I do not appreciate that sass, young man!" Misty said.

Hugo looked down at his feet. "Sorry."

"Hey, don't apologize to the machine," I said. "We organics have to stick together. We can't let them divide and conquer us."

"Any chance I could convince you to conquer a shower?" she asked. "Because I'm not allowed to turn off my sense of smell due to my programming, and right now I'm wishing my creators had installed a kill switch in me."

"Oh come on. It's not that bad," I said, looking at Roan and Hugo for reassurance.

The traitorous crow wouldn't even make eye contact with me, while Roan just shrugged. "It's not great, and cleaning yourself up before you step onto the next floor would probably be a wise move."

I didn't like to lose arguments, but I wasn't stubborn enough to argue against taking a shower.

I sighed. "Fine. I'll do it."

Roan waited outside and Hugo was in the kitchen demolishing whatever food I had left in my cupboards. Meanwhile, I stripped down and put my clothes into Misty. I closed the door and then frowned. There were no buttons on the machine.

"How do I start the process and do I need to add anything?" I asked.

"I produce my own cleaning fluids and fabric softener. The only thing I need now to begin a wash cycle is an apology."

"I'm sorry?"

"No, it'll have to be more sincere than that."

"Fine, give me my clothes back. I'll hand wash them in the bathroom."

The smiley face on the screen became a frowny face and the door mechanism clicked. She'd locked me out.

I gritted my teeth. I couldn't believe Roan saddled me with a snooty AI as a present. How was this a good gift?

I didn't want to keep arguing. "Alright, I apologize. The whole AI washing—"

She loudly cleared her throat.

"Service," I continued. "The whole AI washing service thing caught me off guard. I'm not really familiar with your kind and I was too hostile with you. Will you please wash my clothes?"

The face on the screen smiled again.

"You bet your ass I can! I'm seeing armored grooves with dried Shrikon blood in them and Abyssal Sharkskin fragments in your boots. Hoo boy, this is gonna be a fun challenge!"

"Wait, you *like* cleaning?" I asked. "So you probably would've cleaned my stuff, no matter what?"

"Yeah probably."

"Then why the hell did we have to go through all this bullshit with me apologizing and begging for your cooperation?"

She giggled. "Dude, I was just fucking with you."

The smiley face winked at me, and I had to turn away before I started looking for a hammer. Roan must have a return policy or a warranty some-where. I'll ask him about it once I've cleaned myself up.

I marched into the bathroom and took my time showering since nobody else seemed to be in a hurry. Muscles that I didn't know I'd been tensing, relaxed. By the end of it, I didn't feel just clean but restored somehow.

When I'd finished, Misty's door was open and all of my belongings had been cleaned, dried, and neatly folded.

It felt too easy.

I put my hand in Misty slowly while wary of another trap. Misty didn't react to me taking my clothes. I got dressed and put my armor back on. It might've been my imagination, but I could've sworn she'd polished my bracers. The black metal seemed shinier than before.

I collected Hugo and headed for the door. It was time for Roan to make good on his Grade evolution process and get us to the next floor.

"What, no tip for my excellent work?" asked Misty as we were leaving.

"Here's a tip," I said. "Friendly service gets rewarded. Laundry hostage takers get the finger."

I flipped her the bird and closed the door behind me before she could respond.

"I see you two are getting acquainted," Roan said drily.

I found myself smiling. It was childish, but I enjoyed getting her back for her earlier snark.

Still, the point of her existence in my apartment nagged at me. Surely there were bigger priorities at play here than getting my laundry done regularly.

I repeated my earlier question. "Why a washing machine?"

Roan didn't appear bothered by my lack of appreciation for his gift. In fact, he brightened up whenever I asked questions and seemed to enjoy answering them. It reminded me of a history teacher I'd once had. She often spoke with passion when giving lectures. The energy she put out into the room would make the topics come alive in my mind and keep me invested for the entire time.

That teacher is probably dead now along with the rest of that class.

Roan looked at me pointedly. "Going forward, you're going to encounter more real aliens living their lives on floors. They have their own goals or quests to offer Tower Climbers. In exchange for their time and effort here, they'll be rewarded. Provided they survive all the way to the end, of course. That's right, no more NPC protection shields either. But almost all of them will have ways of making money outside of the Climbers, which means how you present yourself can matter. If you walk into a store smelling like a dead animal, then there's a good chance they might refuse to sell to you or talk to you about their problems."

"So it's closer to real life in that sense?"

"Precisely, especially when you factor in that a lot of them are traveling in groups. In the future, killing one person could cause that person's friends or family to come after you."

That was good to know. The fact that merchants were unprotected made me wonder how they'd survive when more Climbers showed up. While Hugo and I wouldn't kill an innocent merchant over an item, there were others who'd be far less uncomfortable with such an idea.

Hugo stomped his feet. "Come on, already!"

"What's up with you?" Roan asked.

"You guys have been talking about a dumb washing machine for ages. It's boring. Look at me? I don't even wear clothes. How is that supposed to be a gift to the apartment when half the residents can't use it?"

"You're right," Roan said. "I apologize. Let me make it up to you by letting you go through the Grade evolution process first and make your choices."

Hugo looked up at him, eyes wide. "Wait, we get choices? Hell yeah! I'mma turn myself into a giant crow and Lucas will have to sit on my shoulder for a change."

A new door appeared out of nowhere and Roan explained that this would take us to the Grade evolution room. As soon as it opened, Hugo zoomed inside before I could stop him.

Technically, neither of us knew what a Grade was or how it impacted us. I still had so many questions.

Roan assured me that he'd answer them all in the next room and stepped on through.

"You better not make Hugo a giant bird," I grumbled. "The power would go right to his head. I'd never hear the end of it. Plus, you'd need the output of a small country just to feed him."

I walked through to join the others.

"Don't worry," Roan said. "Half the time the process is completely painless."

Wait what?

The door shut behind me and vanished before I could change my mind.

CHAPTER 2
ARGUING ABOUT EVOLUTION

THE GRADE EVOLUTION room wasn't what I expected.

Inside the large room, a polished wooden floor stamped with a spiral pattern led to red painted walls with tinged gold at the edges. The middle of the room was empty. Old and expensive furniture decorated three of the corners, while the fourth corner contained a fully stocked bar.

This wasn't a place for Tower Climbers to evolve. It was a parlor room.

First a washing machine as a gift and now this? I kept my expression neutral, but inwardly I was irritated by such a transparent attempt at manipulation. If Roan thinks he can bribe me like this, then he's sorely mistaken.

Still, I studied the rest of the room in case I'd missed something important.

Chandeliers hung from a ceiling that contained several frescoes. As I continued to stare at them, the paintings began to shift. Armored knights of old would move back and forth as if in the midst of battle. The soldiers without helmets were the most captivating. The fear in the eyes of the losing side was palpable. As was the rage in those pressing their advantage. I almost felt like I was there.

A sense of dread crept over me. I'd seen both expressions many times since entering the Tower. Hell, I'd worn both myself on several occasions. Usually, it was something one only caught in brief glimpses. But here, they were eternally frozen in a conflict that would never end. It was a stark reminder of my own seemingly endless battle.

"Lucas?" Roan called.

He said my name like he'd already said it several times. I pulled my eyes away from the paintings and went to join him and Hugo.

They were both sitting on an ostentatious chaise lounge. Roan pointed to an ornate empty chair beside them.

I still didn't care for the overfamiliarity, but it felt childish to remain standing.

Once I was seated, Roan gestured at the room and smiled like he was pleased with himself. "You like it?" he asked. "I'm told this was the height of luxury in your world."

I found it to be gaudy and outdated.

"Did you pillage it from a seventeenth-century nobleman?" I asked.

Roan's smile dipped. "What, were you expecting a sterile all-white space like the aliens have in one of your science fiction movies? Because I can change it to that if this bothers you so much."

He raised his hand up, ready to snap his fingers.

"No, no, this is fine," I hastily said.

He seemed oddly proud of this space, and my chair *was* comfortable. If we're to discuss different choices, then this was as good a place as any.

Roan nodded and let the insult go. I was relieved. I'd let my big mouth get away from me. We weren't here to argue about the décor. This process will only move as fast as he allows it to. The sooner I indulge him, the sooner Hugo and I can evolve.

"The furniture is very… nice," I said.

Nice? Good one, Lucas. Looks like you missed your calling as an interior decorator.

Roan nodded again. "Yes, I think so too. I was lucky and managed to poach a few pieces before the System integration could destroy them. I took this room from a Russian oligarch who wasn't using it anymore. Except for the frescoes. Those I brought with me from my homeland."

I glanced back up at the paintings. Huh. I'd been so transfixed by their faces that I hadn't noticed that the blades they held were of a strange design. There were more otherworldly details too. In one, someone wore a glowing amulet that spoke of magic. I had missed these particulars because the emotion on their faces was so mesmerizing and lifelike that I'd just ignored everything else.

It did beg the question of why bring such a thing so far from home?

This wasn't just a Grade evolution room, or a bribe aimed at me and Hugo. This was a personal space for Roan. Was this his way of trying to open up to us?

"Did we really need to come here?" I asked. "Couldn't we have evolved back in the apartment?"

Roan went to the bar to make himself a drink. He was unsure of what to pick and stared at the shelves lined with different bottles.

"No," he replied. "The process can take a while and I wanted to be somewhere comfortable while it happens. Also, it is very difficult and time consuming to move the stones. I actually had to rebuild the whole room around them, so we're committed to doing it here."

"The stones?" Hugo asked.

Roan waved his hand behind him while continuing to assess his liquor collection.

A large part of the center floor split in two and retracted back to reveal a large ring of connected stones on a platform. Each stone had a different symbol carved into it. The platform itself was raised up until it was level with the rest of the floor.

"That still seems excessive," I muttered.

"Evolving is a big deal, hence the sacred stones," Roan said. "It's one of the benefits of being a Climber."

"Hmm, you could've used a smoke machine for a little more pizzazz, but I'll take it," Hugo said.

He jumped up and flew toward the stone ring.

"Hugo, wait!" I shouted.

He landed inside the ring before I could stop him.

I cursed inwardly. I'd swear this bird had a death wish sometimes.

The symbols on the stones glowed blue, and a yellow translucent barrier formed around the stone ring.

"Once somebody goes in, they can't come out until the process is complete," Roan said. "Don't worry, he's perfectly safe in there."

"Didn't you say something before about it being painful?" I asked.

"Wait, what pain?" Hugo squeaked.

"That's only for some of the more extreme transformations. I'd recommend Hugo stay away from those anyway."

"So no giant bird," I told him.

"Aww, I never get to have any fun."

[Grade Evolution Process Has Begun]

"What exactly *is* a Grade?" I asked.

Roan rubbed his chin as he thought about the best way to answer. "Think of your body as a balloon. The stats and abilities you receive are the water that fills the balloon. Eventually there's a point where you reach your limit. The balloon either bursts or ceases expanding. Evolving your Grade means replacing the flimsy rubber with a stronger material. That said, there should be some choices coming up for us to see. Different choices will offer different benefits."

[Hugo, Class: Psychopomp, Level: 93, Grade: F]

[You have three Grade Evolution choices. Choose wisely as this process cannot be undone once a decision has been made.]

"That sounds ominous," Hugo said. "Lucas, I don't like this. What if all the choices are weird? This thing could turn me into a magpie, or worse, a cat," he shuddered.

"Or maybe a raven?" Roan joked.

Hugo gasped. "You take that back! Crows and ravens have a long-standing rivalry. Everyone thinks ravens are so cool since Edgar Allan Poe gave them so much press. But we're the smart ones."

[Transition to Grade E has begun.]

[Here are your choices. Please note that all previous skills and abilities will be retained regardless of your choice.]

Grade Evolution Path Identified! [Path of the Steel Talon] – For those of the avian persuasion, this is an excellent choice if you want to get up close to the enemy. This path focuses on greatly enhancing Strength and Dexterity stats and abilities. It also provides Class upgrades in a similar vein. A great pick if you want to rip and tear your foes to shreds.

Contains:

+5% boost to your Strength

+10% boost to your Dexterity

Unlocks the Piercing Diver Ability

"Woah, this one sounds pretty good," Hugo said.

Roan and I shook our heads.

"It doesn't fit with your fighting style," Roan said.

"Plus, you hate it when you get blood on you," I pointed out.

"Yeah, but look at those stat boosts. Think about how much trouble I could avoid by increasing my dexterity that much."

I looked at the path again. "Huh, I mean that is a lot of points. Maybe it wouldn't be the worst thing."

Roan sensed he was losing me.

"How about we look at the other two options first before making any final decisions?" he asked.

"Fine," Hugo huffed. "But first, what's the Piercing Diver skill?"

Roan hesitated for a moment before explaining. "It allows bird races to build up enough speed when diving in the air. You become almost like a bullet. Your Constitution is temporarily buffed and you blast through enemies."

Hugo's eyes lit up. "Awesome!"

Roan shook his head. "No, not awesome. Stupid. There are so many ways it can go wrong. For one thing, you can't deviate from your path once you start on it. You're like a blind juggernaut when the ability is active. There are so many ways it can be exploited. Lucas, help me out here."

There was something bugging me about the description of the path that Roan hadn't mentioned yet.

"What are Class upgrades?" I asked.

"Oh, that's something you'll unlock after evolving your Grade. It's a chance for you to upgrade to a better Class or improve your pre-existing one."

I pursed my lips.

"And when were you going to tell us this?" I asked, my voice edged with irritation.

He shrugged. "As soon as you asked, or it became relevant. There's only one viable path for Hugo to take, so I wasn't worried."

Well, I secretly was. Especially knowing how impulsive Hugo can be.

We moved on to look at the next path.

"Now this is the path that I think you should take," Roan said.

Grade Evolution Path Identified! [Path of the Twilight Soul Dweller] – A path that many a mage and mystic have ventured down to try and unlock the secrets of the soul.

Contains:

+10% boost to your Willpower

+5% boost to your Perception

Unlocks the Arcane Core Shield Ability

I frowned. I couldn't see it. While this was a magical path, Hugo's current style was very different from this one. This one seemed to be as great a deviation as the previous path, while still being magic based. The description was also vague. I wondered what exactly made this path so special and sought after.

"What's the shield ability do?" asked Hugo.

"It's a form of soul magic that would allow you to protect your spirit summons from spiritual attacks," Roan said. "Those types of attacks do soul damage and have the potential to permanently destroy your spirit summons."

This path makes sense as a choice, but I still wasn't sure if focusing on defense was the right move for Hugo. Especially for a niche area like soul magic that we'd yet to encounter. If Roan was pushing for Hugo to protect himself in this area, then the next question was obvious.

"Are we going to encounter soul magic on the next floor?" I asked him.

Roan remained impassive. "I can't say. I can give you advice if you encounter such a force, but not before then. As a god, even one tied to the running of the Tower, I have to follow this rule. If I break it, then every other god can as well. Then they'll be handing out the secrets like candy. It would defeat the whole purpose of training Climbers."

"The fact that you're favoring this path for me probably does mean we'll face soul magic," Hugo said, surprising me. He was still paying attention. Under the boyish enthusiasm was someone who was taking this seriously and actually thinking about how his choice here could impact our future.

Roan grunted and gestured for Hugo to show us the final path option.

Grade Evolution Path Identified! [Path of the Spirit Keeper] – For those that wish to harness the spirits of the dead, this path will deepen your study of this discipline.

Contains:

+10% boost to your Intelligence

+5% boost to your Constitution

Unlocks the Spirit Vault Ability

"The Spirit Vault Ability is an upgrade to Hugo's pre-existing Spirit Box," Roan said, anticipating the obvious question. "You won't need to physically touch the body of an enemy that you or Lucas have slain in order to claim them anymore. If one of your spirit summons is temporarily 'killed' for lack of a better term, you would then be able to supply them with magic in the vault to self-regenerate. There would also be space inside the vault for future upgrades, including the potential to turn it into a domain ability."

"Yeah, I pick this one," said Hugo.

I nodded. I had to agree this was far and away the best choice.

"Of course, too much soul damage to a spirit summon would still be permanently fatal," Roan added pointedly. He took one look at our faces and then pinched the bridge of his nose. "Look, these abilities aren't always exclusive to a specific path. It is very possible to acquire a Spirit Vault after choosing the Soul Dweller Path. I'm telling you that this—"

"Too late," Hugo said.

He'd already selected the Spirit Keeper Path.

Roan grabbed the nearest bottle of brown liquor and poured himself a drink.

[New Class Options Available]

"Hey, what's with the Class stuff and why don't I feel any different?" Hugo asked.

"You won't change until all your choices have been made. You've also unlocked new Classes to pick from," Roan said. "Sometimes they're better than what you have, sometimes it's better to stick with what you've already got, and sometimes there's an upgrade. Usually there's a handful of options to sort through with one or two obvious frontrunners."

[374 Class Options are now available]

"Oh wow, that's a lot of choices," I said.

"Yeah, is that good or bad?" Hugo asked.

In response, Roan opened the bottle of liquor again and poured until the liquid reached the rim of the glass.

———

Hours passed. Every option had been read, considered, and then reconsidered. We went round and round in circles. None of us could agree on which Class Hugo should pick.

Roan was now lying on the chaise lounge. Several bottles of booze lay nearby. Some empty, some still waiting to be consumed.

I was still sitting in the chair, though now I leaned forward with my head resting in one hand. Periodically, I would get up and pace back and forth to stretch my legs. This deliberation was insufferable. Worse still was that Roan kept offering me drinks which were getting harder and harder to refuse.

Hugo appeared immune to the effects of time and was just as bright eyed as ever when he said, "What about the Chainbreaker Class?"

Roan and I groaned.

"We've been over this," I said. "It's better to steer clear of the physical Classes. I'll handle that side of things while you focus on the spirit stuff. That way we both play to our strengths."

"Okay," he said, sounding entirely unconvinced.

Roan blindly fished for a fresh bottle and knocked over some of the empty ones. He cursed when one of them broke.

"I've never seen someone this indecisive," Roan grumbled. "Usually, the Climber will have an intuitive sense that tells them what the right choice should be."

If there was a patience stat, we could level up right now.

I glanced at the crow, who had a faraway look in his eyes as he scanned the list. "Yeah, trust me when I say that you don't want Hugo making any snap decisions."

"It has to be perfect," Hugo muttered.

Neither of us responded to that. I mean, what was left to say? Each of us had suggested a Class that one or the other two shot down. Hugo wanted a more diverse set of powers and kept suggesting Classes that moved away from his current power set.

After the path he'd chosen, I doubled down on it and wanted him to pick a direct upgrade to his current Class. Unfortunately, that was easier said than done. There wasn't an option called Psychopomp 2 to select. Every choice had a unique name and a description that required digging through just to learn what the Class offered.

There were over thirty Classes that referred to using spirits. None of them listed any of the Skills or Abilities that could be gained from them.

While I knew this might be difficult, I had to say I was a little surprised at how quickly Roan had become frustrated.

"I thought you knew that this process could take a while," I said to him.

"When I said that, I was picturing it taking an hour for both of you." He snorted. "Like this would be simple. 'Sponsor a Tower Climber,' they said. 'It'll be fun,' they said. 'It'll challenge you,' they said."

I shot him a sharp look. "Are you drunk?"

Roan blinked and sat up just long enough to take another swig from a bottle. "I'm getting there. I'm not used to staying in one place on such a mundane task for so long. You might think that by being an immortal god that everything slows down and you gain endless patience, but it's just the opposite. Everything speeds up as I move around the cosmos. It's been a long time since I've stayed so still."

"Who told you that sponsoring Tower Climbers was a good idea?"

He smiled with a look of longing. "The Plenathian sisters. We've had an ongoing intimate liaison for quite some time and... Oh goddamn it!"

Roan shot up and pulled a potion out of his inventory. He downed it and then scrunched up his face in disgust.

"Those things never get easier to drink," he muttered.

"What was that?" I asked.

"Instant soberfication potion. I still don't feel great, but at least my head is clear."

"No, I was asking about the realization you just had."

"Oh that. I just realized that I got played."

"Happens to the best of us," I quipped.

"Damn straight. Been a while since it's happened to me though. They pushed the idea of sponsoring a Tower Climber. Before, I'd rarely seen the point. Tried it once, a long time ago. It turned out to be more like babysitting duty. Not unlike now."

"Well, don't let us keep you," I said. "If something important comes up, we'll use the chat function."

"Nah, I can't go back empty-handed. Now that I'm here, I'm committed. If you fail now, then I'll never live it down. Plus, it would embolden the other gods to move against me more than they are already. No, the only way to beat the sisters is to have it backfire on them."

"How are you going to do that?" Hugo asked.

His eyes twinkled. "I'm going to make you two the best Climbers in the Tower whether you like it or not."

Why does that sound so ominous?

"Of course, I still have to figure out why they wanted me out of the way in the first place," he continued. "Damn, you think you know people."

"Wow, life must be so hard for you," Hugo said sarcastically.

Roan clapped his hands together so suddenly that we both jumped. "You're right," he said. "No more complaining. We'll show them all how wrong they are. So, how far have you narrowed down the Class choices?"

I'd honestly lost track at this point.

"Hugo?" I asked.

"Forty-seven," the crow replied.

"Please tell me he's joking."

I shrugged. "Most of them are magic Classes and a lot of them let Hugo keep his current abilities, making the choice harder. Like Pyromancer would allow him to give himself and his summons control over fire, or Ghostwalker that allows Hugo to become incorporeal and move through solid objects. There are a lot of uses we could think of for either ability."

"What about Thanaturge?" Roan asked. "Pick that one."

I frowned and scrolled through the list until I found it and rolled my eyes. It was literally the first option on the list. I said as much, and Hugo agreed.

"That's just being lazy," Hugo accused.

"It's a direct upgrade to your current Class," Roan said.

"Why didn't you suggest it sooner?" I asked.

"Because you wouldn't have believed me then. You needed to exhaust other possibilities and tire yourselves out before I led you to the water. I just didn't think it would take this long."

I didn't like to admit it, but he did have a point. We would have been far more skeptical if he'd suggested it at the start.

I scrolled up through the list and looked at the first option.

New Class Option Identified! [Thanaturge] – Much like how a Thaumaturge works with miracles, a Thanaturge works with death. While a Psychopomp is a keeper of the dead and a spiritual guide, a Thanaturge claims dominion over spirits. They mold them into whatever they desire.

"It's still kind of vague," Hugo complained.

Roan shrugged. "Fine. Keep looking then. But you should know that others have already made it down to the next floor. They're starting quests, finding unique one-of-a-kind items, and slaying special monsters as we speak." He feigned a look of concern. "I do hope there's something left for you two by the time you get down there."

Hugo looked at me for guidance. "Lucas?"

I tapped my finger against the armrest as I reviewed the other spirit Classes, before making my decision.

"Your current Class has been incredibly powerful so far," I said. "A direct upgrade would be even more so. I think he might be right and that you should pick Thanaturge, but ultimately, the decision rests with you."

Hugo nodded, and we fell silent.

After a couple of minutes, I gave up hope and sighed. He was still undecided. This was going to take all day.

Then the message appeared under Hugo's stats.

DING! You have been upgraded to the Thanaturge Class*

DING! You have gained [Spectral Touch (Uncommon)] – You now have the ability to absorb spiritual energy and deploy a ghostly hand to manipulate the physical space beyond your normal reach.

DING! You have gained [The Bell Toll (Rare)] – This is a psychic attack that forms a hundred-meter radius around you. It magnifies the fear other creatures and sentient beings have for their mortality and causes them to panic. Note: some beings will have ways of protecting themselves from this ability and other extenuating circumstances will alter its effectiveness.

DING! You have gained [Spirit Vault (Legendary)] – The Vault is not merely a repository for spirits, it is your workshop. There, you can not only heal the spirits you control but also experiment with them. At the basic level, these spirits are still magical constructs. As your study of them in the Vault deepens, so too will your ability to alter and improve upon their design.

The barrier around the rings disappeared. Despite looking the same, Hugo zipped out of there like a new bird.

"Oh yeah! This boost feels amazing. I can feed so much magic into my summons now!"

It was great news as we would no longer have to worry as much about when to deploy his spirits. Now he could simply heal them in his Spirit Vault. Spectral Touch and The Bell Toll would also have great uses. The former with Hugo's ability to spy and the latter with crowd control.

I'd wanted him to wait until we got to the new floor to test these abilities, but a green skeletal ghostly hand appeared in front of Hugo. It then floated across the room to the bar before fading away.

"Is its range limited?" I asked.

The bird shook his head. "The farther it went from me, the more magic I needed to use to sustain it. I'm saving what I have left for the next floor. We can experiment once we're in a safe place down there."

Wow, that was a very mature decision. I was impressed.

Roan looked at me. "Your turn."

I felt nervous as I approached the ring. My current Class wasn't exactly a pretty one, and I'd already seen it turn one person into a complete monster. This might be my opportunity for a fresh start. Roan couldn't complain. He'd have to support me no matter what. Plus, if I switched away from Blood Reaver, then Yakeshi wouldn't have a reason to come after me.

I took a deep breath.

Yes, let's weigh the options and see if there's a way for me to get stronger that doesn't put so much of a target on my back.

I stepped into the ring. The stones glowed, and the barrier formed.

I waited, but no System message appeared.

Roan frowned. "This is peculiar. I'm not seeing any options here. I don't know why it's not working."

"That shouldn't be happening," Hugo said, sounding concerned.

"Don't panic," Roan replied. "Just step out of the circle and we'll try it again."

I put my hand out, but the barrier wouldn't go down. I was trapped in here.

Roan's frown deepened. "Okay, maybe panic a little."

CHAPTER 3
OFF AND ON AGAIN

Words like 'trapped forever' and 'dying of thirst' were soon thrown around casually. Apparently, Roan considered my situation more dire than he'd first let on.

He stared at the ring of stones as if some answer would magically jump out at him.

Having none of my own, I was forced to silently wait for his epiphany.

Hugo had no patience for that. He believed that we'd get to the solution through the process of elimination. He kept suggesting ideas that were hardly worth answering. Though Roan kept indulging him. Likely in the hope that the questions would soon stop.

No Hugo, we couldn't just destroy the stones without risking an implosion that could kill me. No Hugo, there wasn't a reset button on the back somewhere. And no, I couldn't just bust out of there using my abilities.

On and on it went. With neither strategy getting us any closer to a solution.

I paced around the ring. Three steps left. Turn around. Then three steps right.

I thought the movement might calm me down, but I was growing more tense by the minute.

"Have you considered turning it off and back on again?" Hugo asked.

"It's not a Wi-Fi modem," I said.

I wanted to say more, but I had to stop. My breath was getting short. The anxiety must be getting to me.

I stopped pacing and tried to slow my breathing. It normally calmed me down, but this time it was only getting worse.

"My heart's racing," I muttered.

"It's just a little hypoxia," Roan said, like it was no big deal. "The evolution ring is malfunctioning. The barrier is up, but it's not supplying you with oxygen."

"What?!"

"Don't worry. You won't choke to death. You'll pass out and gently drift away in your sleep. It's actually quite a nice way to go, all things considered."

"Can we focus?!" Hugo cried. "There has to be something we can do to stop this!"

Roan nodded. He bent down and tapped one of the rocks. All of the glowing blue symbols on them flickered for a moment and then returned to normal.

"What was that? What did you just do?" Hugo asked.

"I tried turning it off and on again," he replied.

I'm going to die in here.

Since entering the Tower, I'd never really felt safe. There was always the possibility of some danger lurking in the background. But I'd never considered that my death might be so pointless and banal. Or that I'd be led to it by the ignorance of a god.

"This is your fault," I accused Roan. "You stole the keys to this place, but you don't know how any of it works. More to the point, you killed the only being who does, and now you're surprised that he didn't leave behind an instruction manual."

"You should stop talking..."

"Hey!" Hugo yelled.

"To conserve your air," Roan finished. "But you're right. There are things about the Tower that I don't understand. This however, shouldn't be one of them. Hugo went through the process without any issues. It must be something about you that set it off."

Blaming me for this wasn't going to work. Not for me, and certainly not for Hugo. Good luck with sponsoring him after I'm dead. You can criticize the crow for a lot of things, but one thing he can't be accused of is being disloyal.

"Or this thing is an ancient piece of junk that breaks down after the first use. What does your partner in crime think?" I asked, alluding to the being now in charge of officially running the Tower.

Roan's eyes flickered to me before settling back on the stones. There was a hardness there. An anger that I'd do well not to press on. "Tanver Vhar is busy and is unable to help."

The god clearly wasn't used to being ignored.

"As for your other idea, the stones appear to be intact."

"The hardware's fine, which means it's a software issue?" I asked. "People have said that my Class is rare..."

Roan made a face and cursed. "Of course, I should have thought of it before. Your Class is on the restricted list. The stones reacted the way they did because to them, you technically shouldn't exist."

"Restricted list? That seems excessive," Hugo said.

"It's about what I could turn into," I said quietly.

Roan nodded. "You've only seen a weak Scarlet Beast that consumed maybe two dozen people. Imagine what one that consumes entire worlds would look like."

He wasn't saying it out of altruism. The gods don't want anyone who stands a chance of challenging their power. I know that they can be killed and there's a way for others to take their place. How such things are achieved is still a mystery. One thing I did know is that Roan had survived longer than any of them.

"You don't sound too worried about me turning bad," I pointed out.

Roan grunted. "You have the brand that seals our contract with me as patron and you as—"

"Slave?" I asked.

The edge of his mouth twitched upward in amusement. "Actually, the original term translates more closely as protégé."

I said nothing. I'd seen the way he treated the other Climbers he'd sponsored like Hugo and Daisy. It wasn't the compliment he thought it was.

"Uhh guys, the oxygen levels?" Hugo said.

Roan nodded and refocused his attention on the stones. "Right, sorry. Got sidetracked."

That was odd. I hadn't gotten worse while we were talking. I checked the blood cache in my bracer and sure enough, the amount I'd held in reserve was almost gone. During the conversation, I'd been unconsciously healing myself. Useful for keeping a clear head, but I'd wasted a lot of air by talking.

I sat down and crossed my legs. I had to avoid using what little healing blood I had left until the very last moment. Keeping myself low to the ground should make things a little easier.

It barely helped.

"Can you make Blood Reaver an approved Class?" asked Hugo.

My head felt faint, and I yawned. So tired. I was struggling to stay awake. Time was running out and yet I wasn't afraid. The urge to sleep just overwhelmed everything else.

It was getting harder to convince myself not to lie down.

"Come on! Do something!" Hugo yelled.

"I already tried that!" snapped Roan. "Even though it allows more people to have access to the Class in the future, I *did* add it to the approved list. But the stones still won't recognize him."

At some point, my head was resting on the floor. I could hear Hugo shouting at me and Roan explaining something that didn't need explaining. Their voices were getting further and further away. My eyes were so heavy that they refused to stay open.

I could feel myself slipping away. I wasn't sure how much time I had left. The blood cache was empty. There was nothing more that I could do.

Then Darkness took me.

———

I awoke to a sharp pain in my hand. More irritated than hurt, I blindly lashed out and heard a startled yelp from Hugo as he hopped away.

I rubbed my eyes and sat up.

"He's awake!" Hugo exclaimed.

"I told you he would," Roan said.

Both of them were inside the stone ring, which meant that the barrier was gone. Somehow, they'd managed to solve the problem while I was unconscious.

I got up and nearly fell. My body was shaky and unstable. I wobbled over to one of the chairs. There was no way I was staying in that ring, fixed or not.

Roan handed me a drink.

"Is this more of your liquor?" I asked.

He snorted. "You couldn't handle my stuff. Do you know how hard it is to get my hands on alcohol that could make *me* drunk? Anyway, this is just regular Earth whiskey."

I took the drink and gulped it down. A comforting warmth settled in my chest that relaxed me.

That was when I noticed that something was off. For one thing, Hugo hadn't said anything to me yet, which was unusual for him. Another was that Roan was hovering nearby, as if he thought I might collapse at any moment. Both were apprehensive in their own way.

I sighed. "So what happened? How did you fix the problem?"

Hugo said nothing, so Roan took the lead. "Technically, we didn't fix it," he said. "After you lost consciousness, I tried a variety of things, but none of them worked. I was about to give up when suddenly the barrier fell. We entered the ring, and that was when I realized what had happened."

I could guess where this was going, but I was afraid of the answer all the same.

"You died," he said.

It hit me harder than I expected. I'd come close to death many times since entering the Tower, but the fact that something in this place had actually succeeded in killing me, made me shiver.

"How long?" I asked quietly.

"Only a few seconds," Hugo said, trying to comfort me.

"It was closer to a minute," Roan corrected him. "But you came back whole. I checked you over myself. Brain function is fine. Or at least as good as it ever was," he joked.

I still couldn't believe I'd died. It had happened so fast.

"How did I come back?" I asked.

"Roan had some special potion," Hugo said.

"A special, expensive, and rare potion," Roan added. "I don't have any more of them lying around, so don't think you can cheat death a second time by coming to me."

"You make it sound like this is my fault!" I snapped. "You put me in this situation."

He waved my concern away. "Don't be such a baby. You're fine, Hugo's fine. Now stand up and get back in the ring."

My stomach went cold.

"What?"

"For your evolution. We never got to yours because of the ring's malfunction. It'll work now, so hop in there," he gestured with his thumb.

"I'm not going in that thing again," I said.

Roan gave Hugo a nod and said, "See, I told you he would make this difficult."

Hugo sighed. "Sorry about this, Lucas."

"What do you mean?"

Tentacles shot out from behind me. They wrapped themselves around my body and bound me to the chair. By Hugo's command, Ostorox lifted me up and carried me back to the stone circle. I was dropped inside and as soon as the tentacles let go of me, a new barrier formed.

"You could've given me a little more time," I groused.

"We've wasted plenty already with Hugo," Roan said. "So come on. Let's see what's available."

Hugo at least looked a little apologetic, though he clearly agreed with Roan.

Fine.

Evolving had seemingly done a lot for Hugo. If the ring worked as intended, then I should have something valuable to gain from dying. But I didn't like the fact that Roan was rushing me. It felt like more than just simple impatience. Was there something time sensitive on the next floor that we had to get to? Asking the question out loud would've been a waste of time since he refused to provide any information, afraid he would spoil any future events.

I sighed. Might as well get on with it.

I brought up my menu and my eyes widened. It went beyond my expectations.

Despite Roan's best wishes, it looks like we could be here for a while.

CHAPTER 4
REIGN OF THE SANGUINE LORD

[Lucas Hudson, Class: Blood Reaver, Level: 110, Grade: F]

[You have three Grade Evolution choices. Choose wisely as this process cannot be undone once a decision has been made.]

[Transition to Grade E has begun.]

[Here are your choices. Please note that all previous skills and abilities will be retained regardless of your choice.]

Grade Evolution Path Identified! [Path of the Peerless Blade Master] – This path is for those who want to hone their craft with a blade until mastery is achieved. It will lead you to the point where any adversary or obstacle can be destroyed with a single cut.

Contains:

+10% boost to Dexterity

+5% boost to Perception

Unlocks the Peerless Mind Ability

Interesting. I would've assumed the path of the sword would've included Strength under its stat boosts. I said as much to Roan, who grunted and said, "It's making recommendations based on your previous choices.

Hugo's was a bit more haphazard because his desires were all over the place. You're a lot more focused in that regard, so the choices will reflect that. Each path you see will be viable for you."

"What's the Peerless Mind Ability?" Hugo asked.

"It provides an analytic framework for fighting that goes above and beyond what Lucas's current instincts can tell him."

"See, that's me staying on topic," Hugo said smugly. "Haphazard, my ass. Wait, that ability sounds lame and boring."

Roan sighed and turned to me to explain. "It analyzes fighting styles, presents weaknesses you otherwise wouldn't have noticed, and gives you superior instinctual counter attacks. It is an *extremely* good ability."

I nodded. "I'll keep that in mind."

"I believe it is also the path Yakeshi chose to go down when he was still mortal."

That did not surprise me. I'd heard the story of how he'd destroyed an entire planet with a single cut. Now he was my enemy. An enemy I had no idea how to survive against, much less fight.

"How do you counter someone with the Peerless Mind Ability?" I asked.

Roan smirked. "If you're thinking about fighting him anytime soon, don't. The best thing you can do is hide. If he finds you, then you try to talk him down. Running should be a last resort that is almost guaranteed to fail. Did you notice how the concept of you fighting him isn't even worth mentioning?"

"I might encounter another Climber with this ability," I said.

Roan conceded to my point and said, "It's simple. Peerless Mind tells you the best thing to do in a fight, but that doesn't mean you can pull it off. There are ways to shield yourself. For example, using shadows to obscure your movements. Another is that you might have a stat or ability that overwhelms your opponent. You can have all the knowledge in the world, but it doesn't matter if you're too weak to execute any of it properly."

It was a lot to think about. Roan stressed that I was decently strong for my level and incredibly fast. He said that despite its counter measures, Peerless Mind would be devastating in my hands.

Based on his description, I had to agree. But that only roused my curiosity further for what the other paths might offer.

Grade Evolution Path Identified! [Path of the Howling Void] – A path that consumes all eventually.

Contains:

+10% boost to Constitution

+5% boost to Strength

Unlocks the Void Storm Ability

I frowned. "That description could've been more helpful."

"Maybe the void ate some of it?" Hugo suggested.

"The Howling Void?" I asked Roan.

"Shadow and darkness are the lesser forms of the void," Roan said. "It is the true absence of light or any other matter. A very potent direction to head down. One that I'm well-versed in."

"Is that the path you walked before you became a god?" Hugo asked.

He shook his head. "No child. There were no paths back then. Each of us alone carved our own journey to power." His eyes hardened as he remembered something. "But that's a topic for another time. Void magic and shadows are my specialty. Lucas choosing this path means I can offer far more items and guidance than I can with any other path. This is the one choice where he could profit the most from having me as his sponsor."

I remembered all the weapons, armor, and knowledge Samara had dangled in front of me, tempting me to join her. If Roan had something similar, then he was underselling it. I'd become a walking armory. Not to mention elevating my shadow powers to their ultimate destructive potential. With enough control, I'd be able to make weapons out of darkness the same way I do blood. And nothing about my fighting style would have to change.

"The Void Storm, in case you were wondering," Roan continued. "Is another Domain ability. Unlike your Crimson Domain that creates a small pocket world that you can pull people into, the Void Storm joins with this world. It is a place that is antithetical to most life. You would be shielded, but any other living thing caught inside would not. The Storm can also be expanded by feeding it power."

"Seems kind of excessive for Tower Climbing and difficult to control," I said, thinking about the innocent people I'd encountered before in previous towns.

Roan disagreed. "You would control the size of the storm and eventually, you could be strong enough to wipe out entire armies with this single ability."

He wasn't just talking about what I could do to survive the next few floors. He was talking about when I reached the peak of my power.

"These are endgame abilities," I realized.

Roan shook his head. "No, they are included in the paths because they are there to aid you along your entire journey. Their strength depends upon your level of power. If you used the Void Storm now, it probably wouldn't even fill this room."

Hugo flopped onto his back and hid his face with one wing. "I've been robbed!" he moaned. "All these amazing abilities and I got offered things like *Piercing Diver*?"

"I once saw a god get killed with that ability," Roan said.

He peeked out from beneath his wing. "Really?"

Roan nodded. "Really. Plus, your Spirit Vault could be something special in the future, once a few expansions are made to it."

"Expansions?" He sat up, suddenly taking interest.

"Forget I said anything. Now, Lucas has one more path to consider before making his decision."

I nodded. It was time to see what the blood path offered me. At first, I went into this certain that it would be the only path for me, but now I wasn't so sure.

Grade Evolution Path Identified! [Path of the Crimson Arts] – Be prepared. More than any other, this path causes suffering. Because what else comes from blood-letting if not suffering? Though the more important question remains. Who will be the one to suffer? A Hemokinetic Master is one with absolute authority over their own lifeblood and those of others. An artist can shape this essential element to their will. What kind of masterpiece will you paint with the blood of your enemies?

Contains:

+10% boost to Dexterity

+5% boost to Strength

Unlocks the Blood Orchard Ability

Roan coughed awkwardly. "I guess you can see which description the Officiator wrote. Though 'Crimson Arts' is a vague, unassuming title for such a potent path. I'm not going to downplay this one. It was placed on the restricted list for a reason, and that reason is power. This would be a great path for you to pick, but you have to also remember why there're no living blood shapers anymore. Meanwhile, beings who have walked the other paths available to you, remain gods to this day. Think carefully about your choice."

"Would it make me less of a threat to the other gods if I took a different path?" I asked.

Roan grimaced and shook his head. "At this point, no. You retain all of your prior abilities regardless of what you pick. So if you picked the void, your Class options would be a blood shadow hybrid."

"And The Blood Orchard?" asked Hugo.

Roan threw him a tired look. "Yes, I was getting to that. The Blood Orchard is an expansion for your Crimson Domain. There, blood trees will grow as your power increases. But the effects vary depending on the type of blood you feed it."

"That's not exactly helpful," I muttered.

He shrugged. "Blood powers are not my forte. I have no idea what would happen if you picked it. Considering what I know of the other options, it is likely to be something powerful though."

This gave me a lot to think about. My current blood powers were already incredibly useful. Would I really benefit from going deeper into this discipline when I could diversify with void powers?

I took another look at the Crimson Arts Path description when suddenly the message shimmered and changed.

[Prior Path Choice Altered]

[Unique Path Detected]

Grade Evolution Path Identified! [Reign of the Sanguine Lord] – As the only Blood Reaver in a thousand cycles to reject the beast's call, you alone have earned the right to inherit this path. By not falling to the temptation of the blood, you have demonstrated mastery over one's desires. This path is that of the first and only blood god. A being who once shared some of his knowledge to create pale imitators through the Reavers and the Scarlet Beasts. All will come to learn in time that the Sanguine Lord rules above all others.

Contains:

+10% boost to Dexterity

+10% boost to Strength

+5% boost to Perception

+5% boost to Vitality

Unlocks the Blood Orchard Ability

Unlocks the Hemorrhage Gate Ability

"So are you going with Crimson Arts or are you going to start taking my advice seriously?" Roan asked.

I'd been busy staring at the new path. I was so distracted that I barely heard him and was caught off-guard when he'd spoken.

"Are you okay?" Hugo asked.

"Yeah, just some new life jitters," I said. "Give me a moment."

That's odd. Roan couldn't see the name change. Was this a secret path? It had an extra ability and stat boosts, which did make it the best path to take. But how would I explain the extra ability to the others?

It was unlikely that Hugo had noticed the change, if only because he would've complained about not getting similar treatment. But I had to be certain that he wasn't just playing it cool for Roan's sake.

"What do you think of the Crimson Arts?" I asked him.

The crow shrugged. "It's been working for you so far. It's like you said before—why change up a good thing?"

So neither of them could see it, and if I wanted to keep it a secret, then I couldn't ask Roan about what the second ability did. The description also gave me pause. It referenced the first Sanguine Lord as being a blood god that rules over others. I had no interest in doing either of those things. Still, this was far too good of an opportunity to pass up.

I selected that path and waited for the Class options to appear.

[Path Choice Confirmed]

[Class Options Loading]

[ERROR!]

[Class Pre-selected]

DING! You have been upgraded to Grade E, Blood Reaver Class.*

DING! You have gained [the Blood Orchard (Rare)] – A tree of blood has now been planted within your domain. Feeding it the blood of your enemies will cause it to grow until it bears potent fruit.

DING! You have gained [the Hemorrhage Gate (Legendary)] – This ability allows you to create portals between the real world and your Domain without activating your Domain Expansion.

The rush of power hit me all at once.

I staggered back a step and my foot cracked the wooden floor. I was now ten percent stronger than before. With my enhanced Dexterity, moving forward felt almost like gliding.

Hugo was right. This did feel incredible.

"Huh, so you're sticking with Blood Reaver? That was fast," Roan said as he read the messages. His eyes glittered at the last part. "Wow. That Gate ability is something else. Hey, can I see your bracer for a second?"

Frowning, I took it off and handed it to him. That Blood Cache Bracer had saved my life a dozen times. It was easily the best item I possessed and one of the few good things I'd gotten out of my prior relationship with Samara.

Roan examined the bracer for a moment. It began to degrade and turn to dust. Within a few seconds, it had completely vanished.

"Hey!" I yelled.

He smiled. "Trust me. I just did you a favor. Samara could've used it to track you. Besides, you don't need it anymore."

He was talking about the Hemorrhage Gate. It could do what the bracer did by summoning blood to me, but instead of drawing from a limited cache, I could draw from my domain directly. He was right, this was something else.

"I have to test it out," I said, excited.

He nodded. "But not here. It's time you two went down to the next floor."

CHAPTER 5
ENTERING THE STRAND

"WELCOME TO THE STRAND," Roan said as the elevator doors opened. We stepped out into what appeared to be an empty desert. "This foundation floor combines the monster difficulties from floors 65 down to 55." He stopped and glanced up at the sky. "Ah, you guys are lucky. We picked a good time. It's early morning. Not too hot and not too cold."

Hugo sat on my shoulder and we both looked in confusion at the empty landscape. So far, this whole place seemed pretty underwhelming.

"Where are the monsters?" I asked.

"Technically, we're outside of the Strand. It's a city not too far from here. Where we are now is part of the wasteland that surrounds the city. It is vast and while it might look desolate, it's actually crawling with monsters and other surprises."

"Are we meant to leave the city to fight them?" Hugo asked.

He shrugged. "You might. With this floor, every person gets a big unique quest that they have to solve before they can progress down to the next floor."

That didn't sound good. The last "big quest" we were involved in kind of soured me on the whole concept. I knew Roan wouldn't be able to tell me anything about it, so I suppressed my frustration and tried to focus on what I could learn.

"How many Climbers are here already?" I asked.

"Hmm, couldn't say."

"What about Daisy? Is she here?"

"Please refer to my previous answer."

"Well, what *can* you tell us?" Hugo asked, exasperated.

"Quite a bit, actually. If you let me continue."

Hugo gestured with his wing for him to go ahead.

"The city is populated by people from other worlds," he explained. "They've been put here and given jobs to do. Most of them are going to be indifferent to, or outright dislike Tower Climbers, so be on your best behavior."

"Why would they dislike us?" I asked. "We're the ones trapped here."

"Because former Tower Champions rule their worlds."

"Ah."

Hugo activated companion chat and a new message popped up.

Hugo: If we win and survive the Tower, are we going to be bad guys?

Lucas: No, we're just doing what we have to do to survive. And if it so happens that the responsibility of ruling the planet is foisted upon us, I'm sure we'd rule with an even hand.

Hugo: Yeah, but how would we decide, between us, who rules what? I don't want to be stuck in charge of the crappy parts.

Lucas: Oh really? Which *parts* might those be?

Hugo: Delaware.

Lucas: What? I'm sure Delaware's lovely.

Hugo: So when dividing up the states, it's agreed that you'll take Delaware.

Lucas: Well, I don't know if I'm *in love* with the place. Look, we're getting off-topic. Let's put a pin in this Delaware thing for now.

"You know I can tell when you're mentally typing," Roan said. "You should probably work on making it less obvious in the future. Some might consider it rude."

"Sorry. It wasn't anything serious." I coughed. "Getting back to it. What's the point of importing aliens instead of using more people from Earth?"

"Eh, they were too whiny about their planet being invaded. We wanted people living their lives. Not spiraling through depression. That's why this time, we're using aliens who chose to be here. Real people with their own real problems. It makes for a more exciting broadcast. Also, they have no protection shields. Anyone can kill or steal from anyone else. Luckily, communities have formed in the city to curtail such behavior."

"Communities formed that fast?" I asked.

"Oh no. The city and its inhabitants have been here for years preparing for this Tower. It's basically home for a lot of them and once this Tower is finished, the city will be moved back to its original world where they can continue to live."

"So if I killed a shopkeeper for their items, the surrounding community will come after us?"

"Yeah, but not in an official System-like capacity. It's more realistic in the sense that this hypothetical shopkeeper would have a family, friends, or customers that would miss them. Those are the ones you'd anger and risk retribution from. But don't worry too much about that. The city still runs on money and from what I understand, you two have plenty of it to spend. Just be polite and focus on making it worth their while."

"You imported whole families here?"

"Of course. We couldn't just import a bunch of merchants. They'd be at each other's throats within six months. Most of the older people you meet will have come from worse places, which means they're grateful for this city and are protective of it."

Roan resumed walking, and we followed him up a sand dune. Once we were at the top, we saw the city below.

The Strand was a big city built with Victorian architecture in mind, with cobblestone streets and gas lamps lighting the way. It appeared to be a dense place with stone and brick buildings tightly packed together. Even from our vantage point, it was difficult to get a clear picture of the place. One thing was clear though. Accompanied by the morning light, the city presented itself as a peaceful, prosperous place.

I glanced back and saw that the elevator we'd used had vanished. I asked Roan about it.

"That's just a temporary one that I made use of. Don't worry, the elevator in the city is clearly marked. You won't have to hunt for it like last time."

Good, because I was also tired of racing for those damn doors.

A patch of sand ahead of us rippled. The ripples intensified and began moving toward us.

Roan took a few big steps away from us. I looked at him.

"What? I can't interfere, remember?"

A giant bug burst out of the sand. It was ten feet long, with mandibles the size of my forearm. It screeched and scurried toward us.

Beast Identified [Junior Dune Pincer (common)] Level 85 – Drawn by the vibrations across the sand, these Junior Dune Pincers go off alone seeking food before they are devoured by their parents. They feed until they grow large enough to rejoin their colony as equals.

I used the Hemorrhage Gate ability. A small red summon circle with sigils inside it formed in the air near my left shoulder. Instantly, a connection was made between me and my domain. There I also felt the presence of a sapling that had sprouted out of the blood. The first tree of the Blood Orchard I'd unlocked. I sensed no power from it, nor any way to harness it, so I ignored the tree for now and instead focused on the bug monster that was rushing toward me.

I formed a blood spike and pushed it halfway through the gate, where it hovered in the air.

"Uhh, Lucas. It's getting kind of close," Hugo said.

The Dune Pincer scurried closer, clicking its mandibles in anticipation of its meal (us). I waited and watched as the front of its body reared up, ready to strike.

I released the spike. It blasted up and speared the bug right in its brain.

The thing went limp and fell over dead.

"That was easy," I said.

DING! You have slain [Junior Dune Pincer (common)] Level 85 – Experience Points and Currency Acquired.

I glanced at Hugo.

"You want its spirit?" I asked.

The crow appeared torn.

"What's the matter?" I asked.

"It's just so gross looking."

"I'm not asking you to make out with it. Just capture its spirit so that it can join your unholy army of the damned. Hasn't it been a while since you took anything?"

"He's right, you know," added Roan. "Despite your relatively decent level, even your strongest spirit summon would've struggled to take out that bug. And that was just a low-level monster for this floor."

"Fine," Hugo said. "Arise," he muttered, sounding bored.

He wouldn't even look as the spirit climbed out of its dead body. It then turned to mist and vanished as the crow added it to his spirit vault.

"There, happy?" Hugo asked.

"Ecstatic," I replied before yawning.

That was odd. I was suddenly feeling a little tired again. I activated a Hemorrhage Gate and reached for the blood inside. I made the connection, but there was no burst of healing energy like there should've been.

I frowned and asked Roan about it.

He shrugged. "I guess once it passes through the gates, it's considered your blood. You can weaponize however you like, but it won't heal you."

I cursed. It's like two steps forward and one step back. The cache had more limited storage space, but at least I could heal with it.

"But why the sudden loss of energy?" I asked.

"Because without enemy blood to replenish you, your magical abilities are finite. Different Classes store power within themselves differently. For you, I think it's your Vitality. So put points into that if you want more magic, or you know, touch the bug's blood." He stared at me. "Unless you have a problem with that?"

Hugo caught on and joined in. "Yeah, is that an *issue*, Lucas?"

I kept my face blank and raised my hand, summoning the blood to me. It poured out of the bug and gently floated toward my outstretched hand.

As soon as the blood hit my fingers, I became revitalized. But more than that, I could *feel* the Blood Orchard. The tree that had sprouted out of the blood grew a little higher.

"Can we go in the city now before more of those things show up?" Hugo asked.

"Oh, there are monsters in the city too," Roan said. "Some will be hidden in plain sight during the day, but most come out at night in secluded areas."

"It's not going to be all bug monsters, is it?" Hugo asked, concerned.

"No, it varies. The city is divided into districts. Each district serves its own purpose, but there will be signposts inside directing you. Just a final piece of advice before I leave. You both have a lot of money on you. I'd suggest going to the market district and splurging on some new equipment. Most of the monsters you encounter from now on will be a lot stronger than that bug."

He turned to leave.

"Wait," I said. "What do we do about the wasteland or this special quest of ours?"

"I'd stay near or in the city unless you have a guide or a map. The wasteland is big and it's easy to get lost out there. As for the quest, you need only to explore. Eventually the quest will make itself known. Though it's unlikely to be a simple one."

"Are you being coy, or do you actually not know?" I asked.

"There Are over half a dozen main quests for this floor that have yet to be claimed. Any one of them could find you."

Sand rippled behind us.

Hugo panicked. "Gah!"

He mustered his new bug spirit summon and sent it after the disturbance. His creature dove into the sand and disappeared. Moments later there was a loud screeching sound followed by a crunch before the spirit summon resurfaced.

I gave Hugo a smug look regarding how effective his new summon was.

"Shut up."

I turned to ask Roan something else, but he'd disappeared. I guessed that was it for the introduction.

The pair of us walked down toward the city. There were no guards posted at the gate, nor any sign of life inside whatsoever. The gate itself was open, inviting anyone to come inside.

I hesitated to go in. The empty openness made me suspicious.

"The place seems abandoned," I said.

"Maybe it's just early?" Hugo suggested. "Want me to send some of my birds into the air to scout ahead?"

I shook my head. "No, let's keep our presence small for now. Keep a low profile until we learn more about this place."

Roan had made the city sound too ordinary, but I sensed a trap. Unfortunately, the only way forward was to step into it.

CHAPTER 6
A SMALL BEAN

Hugo and I continued down the first empty street. We had to walk in the middle of the road as garbage and refuse filled the sidewalk, further contributing to the image that the place was abandoned. Hugo was perched on Norris's shoulder. The goblin spirit summon had his knife out, ready for anything, as they walked beside me.

"I'm just saying that it's a personal preference thing," Hugo said. "It has a lot of nice qualities too."

"I just don't know what I'd be giving up," I replied.

Yes, we were still arguing about this.

"Well, what would you like?" he asked.

"How about this? I'll take Delaware, but in return, I get the Virgin Islands."

The crow nodded. "I can live with that."

"And, you have to take Guam."

He stomped his foot. "Oh, come on!" He paused, took a moment to reconsider, and then said, "Fine. But you have to take the bad parts of Florida, like Herbertsbergville."

"Okay, this is insane. If we start going city by city, then it'll take us more than a year just to decide who gets what."

"Are you sure? Because I'd be willing to take say… Gary, Indiana, off your hands for the right price."

I was taken aback. "Oh my God, you'd really do that? Because *no one* wants Gary, Indiana. Even the people living there wish they were in Detroit."

Hugo nodded. "Beneath these feathers lies a giving heart."

My eyes narrowed. "Wait a minute. Nobody is *that* generous. You're angling for something."

"I want New York. Just the city. You can have the surrounding state."

I threw up my hands. "There it is! No deal."

I increased my walking pace to get ahead of them. This argument was getting us nowhere.

"What? It's not like I wouldn't let you visit!" Hugo yelled after me.

Up ahead, a five-foot-tall goblin leapt out of the alleyway. He hit the ground and dramatically rolled to his feet. He didn't appear to be carrying any weapons under his brown buttoned-up leather vest, simple pants, and boots.

He pointed an accusatory finger at me. "Lucas Hudson! Your end is nigh!"

Some sort of yellow cube device appeared in his other hand. It was enough for the System to consider it a threat.

Beast Identified [Goblin Engineer Dratch] Level: 91 – Dratch has been biding his time for you, ever since you killed his cousin on the roof of the Tower. Here, he plans to avenge his fallen family member and restore honor to his family's name. This is a real sapient creature, by the way. You really want that blood on your hands?

I casually reached for the sword on my back.

"Hey, you got the last one!" Hugo complained.

BLOOD FOR POWER   57

I put my hand down. "Fair," I said, and stepped over to the sidewalk. I leaned against a street lamp and gestured for Hugo to go ahead.

The goblin scrunched his face up in disgust. "I am not here for one of your associates, Lucas Hudson," he sneered. "I came for you!"

"He's actually my bodyguard," I said. "He handles all of my physical altercations so I don't get sued."

Hugo hopped off of Norris's shoulder and flew over to land on mine.

It was an interesting choice. I guessed Hugo wanted to test out his weakest spirit summon first before reaching for anything stronger. I was also curious about the goblin Dratch. Not about his dumb revenge plan. I was ambivalent about whether I'd killed his relative or not. No, it was the device in his hand that interested me. If it was some kind of bomb, I doubted it would be a big one. But the goblin wasn't holding it like a bomb. He gripped it like it was a device of power and significance.

Norris charged at the goblin with his knife held aloft. A beam of white energy shot out of the cube and hit the spirit summon square in the chest. Norris instantly vanished like smoke.

Hugo gasped. "Chuck! He busted him! He's been ghost busted!"

I gave him a look. "*Chuck*? Come on, settle down."

"The emotional impact of losing my first spirit summon warranted a first name basis, Lucas."

"If he really has been ghost busted, then he's probably just trapped in that cube device. Relax, I got this."

Hugo flew up to perch on the top of the lamppost while I drew my sword and walked calmly toward Dratch.

The goblin raised the cube threateningly. "At last, I may have my—"

He blinked and suddenly I was beside him. The arm holding the cube had been severed at the elbow by my sword.

Unfortunately, Dratch had managed to activate the cube before I'd reached him. One last blast shot out toward me as the cube was falling. In a panic, I threw my arms up. The blast hit my other bracer before the cube hit the ground and shattered into pieces.

I was unharmed, but the bracer was smoking. It had dispelled certain magics. I hoped whatever damage it had taken from the device was repairable. I took it off of my arm and a new message appeared.

Item Identified! [Burning scrap metal]

I cursed. It had been completely destroyed. So I tossed it aside.

There goes my second favorite piece of armor.

Dratch saw his bleeding stump, screamed, and tried to make a run for it. I seized him by the throat and glanced at Hugo. "Did Norris come back after the cube broke?" I asked.

"No," Hugo cried. "He's gone for real. The goblin killed him."

"Well, he was already dead, so..."

"He destroyed his spirit then!"

I turned back to address Dratch. "You killed my friend's favorite manservant. So he's pretty upset right now."

"Take his other arm, Lucas!" the crow shouted from the lamppost.

"See? He's crazy. But I'm willing to let you go if you give me some information," I said. "Starting with what was that cube you used?"

Dratch groaned, and I worried that he'd pass out from blood loss, but then his eyes regained their focus. "Please sir, I'm just a little guy who got too big for his boots. Have mercy! I'm just a small bean. It's also my birthday! You wouldn't kill someone on their birthday, would you?"

While distracted by this bizarre display of begging, Dratch pulled a knife from the back of his belt. He moved to stab me with it... so I broke his neck.

DING! You have slain [Goblin Engineer Dratch] Level: 90 – Experience Points Acquired.

"That was weird, right?" I asked Hugo, who flew down now that it was safe.

He ignored my question and asked, "What about the device?"

All he could think about was his lost spirit summon.

I poked at the pieces. It looked like it had been a complex piece of machinery that used magic in some capacity. Whether it had killed the Norris spirit outright or just held it until the device had broken was unclear. The biggest issue was that there was a weapon out here that could easily counter Hugo's spirit summons. To make matters worse, any piece of the device I touched was just identified as its component piece. The System telling me that the copper wire I picked up was copper wire, was less than helpful.

"I guess we now know why Roan was so insistent on you picking that other Class," I said. "Maybe the Arcane Shield would have protected Norris from the blast."

He looked worried. "You think we'll encounter more of those devices?"

I nodded. "I'd bet on it. But look on the bright side. At least you got a new goblin spirit to replace Norris with," I said, pointing to Dratch.

Hugo aimed a wing at the body and said, "Arise, Dratch!"

Nothing happened.

Hugo coughed and cleared his throat. "I said, arise Dratch!"

Still nothing.

"Lucas, it's not working. I can't even sense his spirit, much less claim it."

"It must be related to the device he used."

New Quest Unlocked [Sometimes Dead isn't Better] – Discover what the deal is with the dead goblin Dratch and his mysterious device. This is your main quest for this foundation level.

"That's it?" Hugo huffed. "That doesn't tell us anything."

"We should collect the pieces. Roan talked about there being shops here. Maybe one of them has an engineer that will recognize the design. Do you have a bag I could borrow? There's like a million tiny pieces here that would each take up an individual inventory slot."

"No, I don't have anything like that. Maybe you could use a handkerchief to wrap up all the pieces?"

I shook my head. "Sadly, I left all my handkerchiefs at home, alongside my reading glasses, and my Werther's Originals."

He sighed. "You don't have to be rude."

"And I'll bet you the entire East Coast that you already knew that I didn't possess any handkerchiefs when you mentioned it."

The bird said nothing, so I let his guilt hang in the air as I painstakingly collected every piece from what I was now calling the spirit killer device. Once done, I was able to loot Dratch's body to hide the evidence. Roan had said that some of the city's inhabitants had friends. Better to make it look like we were never here at all.

We continued down the street, turning a corner until we reached a market-place filled with stalls that were being set up. Everyone there was a goblin.

Hugo and I froze.

A few goblins glanced at us before resuming their work. The rest ignored us completely. None of them seemed to care about our presence. Their behavior toward us was the opposite of how Dratch had acted.

"What's going on?" Hugo asked.

I frowned and said, "I don't know."

There was a wooden sign hanging over the market entrance with the word 'Goblintown' hastily scrawled across it in black paint.

Roan hadn't said anything about other cities or towns. Was this still part of the Strand?

At one stall, I tried to ask a male and female goblin couple if we could buy something. Neither of them looked up at me and the woman goblin only grunted.

So they weren't just busy. We were being deliberately ignored. This gave me another bad feeling and so I picked up my pace while trying to keep out of their way. Past the stall owner goblins were a group of male goblins leaning against a wall wearing leather vests similar to the one Dratch had worn.

These goblins stared daggers at us as we passed.

Before I could warn Hugo to keep an eye on them, two of them approached from behind with what looked like tire irons.

I kept walking and didn't turn around, but a dense crowd was forming up ahead. They intended to block us in. I turned around and attempted to backtrack, but those two goblins in our way were either bolder or stupider than the others.

I warned Hugo.

Lucas: Get ready to hold on when I run.

I formed a Hemorrhage Gate and sent a blood whip out. It sliced the two goblins in half. I was able to break out into a run before they even realized what had happened.

After they'd died, I received a new System message.

[The Tree has been sated.]

What the hell does that mean?

More goblins were massing behind us. They were running now too. They poured out of the side streets to join the angry crowd. There were too many to count and too many to fight. Hugo and I did the only dignified thing we could do. We fled.

The goblins working the market stalls didn't try to stop us and as soon as we were outside of Goblintown, I chose to run down an unfamiliar alley and out onto an empty street. We couldn't remain where we were;

anymore backtracking would just put us back in the wasteland. We had to head deeper into the city.

After racing down the street and taking a few more turns, I stopped to catch my breath.

"Okay, I think we lost them," I said.

BOOM!

A piece of sidewalk ten feet to our left exploded. Something from above had dropped down on it. But there was nobody in sight, which meant someone was giving orders from a distance.

They're firing artillery?

"Hugo, crows now! We have to find where the spotter is!"

"I thought you wanted to keep a low profile," he said as I resumed running.

BOOM!

Another explosion only a few feet ahead of us. I skidded to a stop before I fell into the crater the explosion created.

"That moment has passed," I snapped.

Five spirit summon crows clawed their way out of the ground and took flight in different directions. It only took a moment for Hugo to find them.

"There, I got them!" he said. "They're on the roof of an old factory to our left."

I looked and sure enough, there was a factory a few blocks away. It was the tallest building in this area and was more than enough to give away our position.

I grabbed Hugo and raced away, sticking close to walls where we were harder to spot.

We came out on another street only to find it was blocked by carts and debris. I kept running, but it was like we were going in circles. Meanwhile, the noise of a crowd was drawing closer. An angry mob had formed to hunt us.

We went down another alleyway, but it led to a dead-end with a courtyard. There were some houses around and a well for water in the center. Hushed voices could be heard from one of the houses. The angry mob was getting closer.

I went over to the well. It was hard to see how far down it went. From what I could see, there didn't appear to be anything sinister lurking in it.

I hopped into the well and jammed my feet into either side like an acrobat, to hold myself in place. Hugo flew down after me and sat on my shoulder.

The crow sent me a message through chat.

Hugo: What now?

Lucas: We wait.

CHAPTER 7
PROBLEMS AT HOME

An hour passed with us stuck in the well. Nobody else had entered the courtyard since we'd arrived. It was impossible to gauge how long it would take for the goblins to give up their search. Still, we couldn't stay here much longer. The sun was climbing higher, and eventually someone was going to want to use this well for its intended purpose.

To stave off boredom, Hugo and I passed the time by talking in companion chat. It inevitably led to the same topic that was always close to Hugo's mind.

Hugo: So where do you want to eat after this?

Lucas: You think the city has restaurants?

Hugo: Why not? It's a big place. We're still only on the outer edge. If there are merchant shops further inward, then restaurants aren't a big stretch.

Hugo was setting himself up for disappointment. Given their environment, their food source was obvious.

Lucas: Did you see a lot of farmland or livestock outside of the city?

Hugo: No, why... Oh no.

Lucas: That's right. If they eat anything, it'll be the bugs from the wasteland.

He didn't feel like talking about food after that, and we both fell silent.

After a bit more time, my legs were starting to cramp up, and the bird was getting restless.

Hugo: I could send more scouts to check things out.

Lucas: No, they would've seen you summon them. They'll likely have someone watching the sky now.

Hugo: So what's the plan?

Lucas: If it was close to sunset, I'd say we leave when it's dark. My cloak would obscure us, but we can't wait that long. It's early morning. This city is going to wake up soon, and we don't know how the other inhabitants will react to our presence.

Hugo: I say we just go for it now. Sneak to the center of the city and find the silver elevator to get back to the apartment.

It was a compelling argument. I was tired of hiding, and it had been some time since we'd heard anything.

I pulled myself up and peered over the edge of the well.

The courtyard was empty. So far, so good.

We climbed out and were about to leave when one of the house doors opened. A male goblin stepped out wearing a suit with a bowler hat. He was whistling a cheery tune until he spotted us.

Our eyes met. Hugo and I froze. He didn't look like a threat, but what if he tried to call for help? I wasn't sure if I could silence him in time, so I waited to see what he would do.

Slowly and without turning around, the goblin closed the door behind him.

"Why don't you go back inside and pretend you never saw us," I said to him.

The goblin shook his head. "I can't do that."

"Sounds like we've got a problem then," Hugo said.

Archer materialized beside us and drew her bow.

"Not necessarily," said the goblin. "I just came out here for a little peace and quiet. Alerting somebody to your presence would disrupt that."

He took a packet of cigarettes out of his pocket and walked over to a bench on the other side of the courtyard. Archer tracked him with her bow, but he paid her no mind as he sat down.

I got the impression that he just wanted us to leave quietly, but this was the first goblin that we'd met that hadn't attacked or ignored us. Curiosity got the better of me, and so I had to ask, "You don't seem to care as much about our presence as the other Goblintown folk. Why is that?"

The goblin eyed the packet in his hand as if having second thoughts.

"We're not in Goblintown," he said. "I don't live there anymore. This is Ormond Street. It's part of an unincorporated district that nobody else has managed to fully claim yet."

I had no idea what that meant, but he turned away from us like he was done with the conversation. Not wanting to push our luck, we decided to leave.

"I wouldn't go out there if I were you," the goblin said.

"Why is that?" Hugo asked.

"They'll have set up checkpoints to block all the main routes of escape. They'll catch you if you try to leave. This area is dense with a lot of hiding places. They can't search it all, so it's more efficient for them if they just wait for you to make a mistake."

Lucas: Looks like we'll have to wait till nightfall after all. I can use my Umbral cloak to hide us in the darkness. Oh, and put Archer away. It's unnerving the goblin.

Archer dematerialized, and we went to sit beside the goblin.

"I heard another voice from your house. Is that going to be a problem?" I asked the goblin.

"No, I told the wife that I was going out to collect some water from the well. She won't expect me back for at least an hour. I'm Gren, by the way."

We introduced ourselves and I was about to ask him if he knew anything about the spirit killer device when suddenly his house door flew open. A female goblin holding a baby barged outside. Gren muttered a curse under his breath.

She saw us sitting on the bench and her face twisted with anger. "Oh my God. I sent you out for water and this is what you're doing? Making friends with humans?" Before he could explain, her eyes grew suspicious. "Wait, are these the murderers everyone has been looking for? What are you doing just sitting there? Turn them in to the elders."

Gren shook his head. "I'm not doing that."

"But we could use the reward money," she pleaded. "We could get back what we lost."

"I already gave them my word."

"Pft! Your word? You have no honor," she snarled. "You know my mother was right about you!"

She stomped back into the house and slammed the door behind her.

"Yeah, well maybe my brother was right about you, Colleen!" Gren yelled back.

Hugo and I glanced at each other. Both of us wanted to leave and take our chances with the goblins that had weapons. But we weren't sure if that would make things worse. So we just awkwardly sat there.

Gren sighed. "She's probably going to leave me, you know. Not that I blame her. As if getting exiled from Goblintown wasn't humiliating enough for us."

"How did that happen?" asked Hugo.

I threw him a look.

Lucas: Seriously? Don't encourage him.

Hugo: What? It's not like we don't have time. Besides, he might tell us something useful once he's calmed down. He seems smart.

Lucas: How can you tell?

Hugo: His hat.

I'm never getting out of this conversation.

"It happened a few months ago," Gren said. "But another way would be to say that it's been happening my whole life."

Oh Jesus. It was hard not to roll my eyes.

Hugo encouraged him to continue.

"As you may or may not know, goblin trades are family trades. You're born into doing a certain type of work when you grow up. My family were light infantry. I was expected to follow in their footsteps, and I did at first. The night before my first battle, I stayed up all night cleaning and polishing my armor. I guess I thought that the better it looked, the more intimidating I'd be. Stupid me..." he said, trailing off.

"Take your time," Hugo encouraged.

Gren nodded. "Anyway, when it came time to fight the next morning, half of my team were so hungover they could barely stand up. The battle might've still been salvageable if we were against another goblin clan, but we weren't. It was a group of Grayskins. With no sappers or explosives, it would've been a slaughter for us. They hadn't seen us yet, so I proposed that we quietly retreat before we could be discovered. My commander instead decided to shout, 'death to Grayskins!' and charge after them. I did the only thing I could do. I ran."

"You shouldn't beat yourself up for that," Hugo said. "Lucas here runs away from fights all the time."

"It's not that," he replied, his voice tight. "When I returned to Goblintown, some others spotted me and branded me a coward before I could say a word. It was my armor, you see. My clean, shiny armor was what gave me away. After that, it was either exile or death for desertion. So I took my wife and baby and left."

I frowned. "But you're only a few blocks away? That doesn't seem that far."

"It's far enough. I can't see my brother or parents. I can't work with any of the goblin crews. I have to go into the human districts to beg for work. The only thing keeping me sane is these." He held up the packet of cigarettes to us. "You know it's ironic. They give these to soldiers to help with the stress after a battle. I've only been in one battle, and I ran away from it. And yet I'm addicted to these things. You guys want one?"

"Sure," Hugo said.

"No," I replied for both of us.

"It's not tobacco. We call it Serenity Leaf. We grow it ourselves. It temporarily removes all negative emotions when you inhale the smoke. You don't get high off of it. You just feel this kind of calm inner peace."

Huh, that could be useful. Reluctantly, I took one and put it in my inventory.

Item Identified! [Serenity Stick] – Ground up and dried Serenity Leaf wrapped in paper for smoking. The inhaled smoke has a psychoactive effect of creating a calm, inner peace.

Gren was about to light one up and then changed his mind.

"This isn't the time for inner peace," he muttered. "I know I said it's dangerous, but you two should take your chances and get out of here." He stood up. "I gotta go too. I need to be off looking for work before my mother-in-law shows up. Apparently, there are no rules against a goblin in good standing visiting an exile. Not that *my* family would know that."

I was worried he might cry. Hugo must have thought the same because he said, "We've got money!"

Gren looked at us with hope.

"We're not a charity," I said.

He nodded, crestfallen.

Goddamn it.

"But we could do with hiring a guide to help get us out of here," I said.

Gren agreed and led us out of the courtyard. Then he opened a nearby sewer grate and gestured for us to hop in. Hugo and I shared another concerned look.

"What?" asked Gren. "The goblins avoid the sewers. It's the fastest way to bypass their checkpoints."

I took charge and hopped in first. So far, we'd been able to handle everything this place had thrown at us. Why should the sewers be any different?

I landed with a soft splash in water that came up to my ankles. I also decided that breathing through my mouth for this portion of the journey was a wise decision.

Archer jumped down next, with Hugo right behind her, while Gren awkwardly climbed down the ladder rungs. Once he was down with us, he took over as the guide. A task which did not prevent him from continuing to complain about his family.

"Thank God we left before my mother-in-law arrived," he said. "She never shuts up about how great her late husband was. And this was a goblin who died in his very first battle. Apparently in goblin culture, that's more honorable than living to fight another day." He shook his head and snorted. "Corpse piker. What a ridiculous profession. Do you know what they do?"

The question felt rhetorical, and it was clear he needed to get this off his chest, so Hugo and I politely shook our heads.

"A corpse piker hides among the dead bodies of his allies after an initial battle. There they hide and wait until the enemy comes to collect their dead and loot the bodies of the goblins who fell. At which point a corpse piker is meant to go 'ah hah! I've fooled you' and then stab whoever's closest before making a run for it."

"Isn't that also kind of cowardly?" I asked.

He shrugged. "As long as there's blood on the blade, nobody cares."

Hugo: Goblin society is weird.

Lucas: Agreed.

CHAPTER 8
A WONDERFUL EXPLORATION OF THE CITY'S WASTE MANAGEMENT SYSTEM

THE PUTRID SMELL of the sewer wasn't something we got used to. It lingered with us every step of the way, like an unwelcome guest. Though it was more fair to say that we were the unwelcome ones who were eager to leave.

The sewer tunnels were dark, dank, and utterly maze-like. I had no idea how Gren was navigating them. Yet he strolled confidently through the darkness, only stopping briefly at certain intersections to consider the best route.

He had used these tunnels before, which made me wary of goblin patrols. But when I asked him about it, he assured us that we wouldn't find anyone and anything else down here during the day. The extra emphasis he placed on the day part didn't make me feel much better.

"So how is it that you know these tunnels so well if goblins avoid them?" I asked.

Gren shrugged. "I know a few goblins who will still trade with me but are too afraid to leave the safety of Goblintown. The sewers make it easy to sneak in without being seen."

"Isn't that dangerous?" Hugo asked.

"Of course it is. I'm dead if I get caught, but with a baby I don't have much choice. There are certain things she needs for her diet that I can only get from there."

Hugo: Lucas, we should pay him more money for helping us!

Lucas: Agreed. It might be useful to keep a friendly relationship with someone who knows how to sneak into Goblintown.

Hugo: No, not that! I meant for his family.

Lucas: Do not give him all of your money. Roan advised us that we should buy better equipment while we're here, and that's what we're going to do.

Hugo: Have you seen me? I'm already perfect. I don't need to accessorize.

I suppressed a sigh.

Lucas: Look, we'll compensate him well and then check out the merchant stores. If there's nothing there that you want, then we'll return to Gren and give him the rest of your money.

Hugo: Deal.

Since we were paying for Gren's time, I figured that this would be a good moment to learn as much as I could about this city and the strange goblin we'd first encountered with the spirit killer device.

"Say Gren, have you ever heard of a goblin named Dratch?"

He stopped. "Where did you hear that name?"

Gren already knew that I'd killed other goblins before. He didn't seem to care. In fact, he didn't seem to care for other goblins at all outside of his family. So I had to just hope that they weren't related.

"He attacked us as we were entering the city. So I killed him."

Gren frowned. "That's peculiar. I only asked because Dratch too was exiled from the community, though for a different reason than myself. Only the goblin elders know why he was punished. It was quite the talk amongst all of us back then. Everyone was trying to guess what he could've done, but no one ever figured it out."

That wasn't of much use to me. So I pressed on.

"The System said something about him being an engineer? What did he do before he was exiled?"

"He worked on generators in the hydroponics section. Everyone in the crew who'd worked with him back then said he was a stand-up goblin. Always worked hard and was responsible. The only odd thing was that a couple of months before his exile, he became more quiet and withdrawn. That was about it."

"So you don't know about him building anything in his free time?"

"Not that I can recall."

Damn, it looks like solving this quest is going to take more work than I thought.

"What about magic?" I tried.

"Err, no."

"Anything to do with spirits?"

"I don't... think so."

Hugo: Careful, you're practically interrogating him and he's doing us a favor.

Lucas: We're paying him.

Hugo: Just let me try. You're being too harsh to Triple G.

Lucas: Triple G?

Hugo: Yeah, Gren the Goblin Guide.

Lucas: Just ask your questions.

I gestured for him to go ahead.

Hugo sat on Archer's shoulder. He urged her to speed up so that they could walk beside each other.

"Apologies for my companion. He gets testy when he hasn't eaten in a while. So Gren, we're new to the city and were wondering what you can tell us about it."

Gren pondered for a moment.

"Well, I suppose the main thing about this place is that it's broken up into factions. There are three factions that control most of the city. The goblins, the humans, and the Grayskins. As you already discovered, Goblintown is on the lower east side, half of the industrial part of town. The north-east side is mostly abandoned because it gets too many monster encounters. Humans live mostly in the city center and the Grayskins control the entire west side. Humans and Grayskins also have an agreement where they trade with one another and can freely move between districts."

Hugo wanted to ask who the Grayskins were, but it was difficult for him to get a word in edgewise. Once Gren started talking, it was hard to get him to stop.

"Okay so…" Hugo began.

"The problem is the fighting," Gren continued. "The Grayskins are the wealthiest of the bunch. The humans do all right, and the goblins are left fighting for scraps. The Tower compensates the leaders of each faction for how much territory they hold. This was meant to encourage infighting and competition, but the humans and Grayskins figured out a way to sidestep the whole thing with an alliance."

"So the goblins are fighting the humans and the Grayskins?" Hugo asked.

"What? No, haven't you been listening? Goblins and Grayskins are fighting each other. Humans trade with the Grayskins and they tolerate us. When it comes to fighting though, they mostly stay out of it. I think it has something to do with their religion."

"Religion?"

"Yeah, don't know much about it though. I usually steer clear of the holy roller types."

We reached another intersection. A crossroads of sorts, with three directions to go down. Our guide paused, as if trying to remember something.

Gren shrieked and jumped back. A small brown shape floating in the water had bumped into him. The little creature squeaked in response and swam past him.

"Relax, it's just a rat," I smirked.

It darted toward me and I shooed it away with my foot.

Beast Identified [Brown Rat (Common)] Level: 10 – A regular sewer rat.

"See, it's harmless," I said. "Although level ten is impressive. I guess you gotta be tough to be a city rat."

The rat squeaked again, almost like it agreed with me, and then swam deeper into the tunnel until disappearing into the darkness. That should've been the end of it. But it kept squeaking somewhere in the dark. It was quickly joined by more squeaks. Hundreds of them. A cacophony that spoke only of danger.

I drew my sword and braced for it. The squeaks stopped, and a thunderous roar shouted out from the darkness as a challenge. The creature heavily thudded into view.

At first, I thought it was a giant rat monster, but upon closer inspection, it was a monster made up of rats. Thousands of them being loosely held together by some kind of magnetic energy source. All of the rats were still alive, writhing and rippling across the creature's mass. A mass that consisted only of a torso, two arms, and two legs.

It roared again. It was an unnatural voice coming from all the rats in unison.

Beast Identified [A Rat King (Uncommon)] Level: 120 – No, not a fake tourist attraction born from animal cruelty. This here is the real deal. A Rat King is the spirit of a dominant rat. A rat who fought and

bled their whole life. One who's known nothing but violence and dies angry. This angry spirit lingers, gaining power until it can control the minds of living rats. Eventually, it becomes strong enough to build itself a new body. And at this point, all it wants to do is feed and fight.

Gren's face turned a paler shade of green. He turned and ran past me while muttering, "oh crap, oh crap, oh crap," to himself.

Hugo shook his head in disappointment. "I can't believe Three G would leave us like that."

"He did warn us that he was like this. Technically, he's just being consistent. Also, I'm revoking your nicknaming privileges. Three G, seriously?"

"Aww man. Fine, but who takes this one?"

"How about we take turns? One attack each and I let you go first."

Hugo nodded. "Sounds good."

At his command, Archer drew her bow and fired. The arrow went through the mass of rats, killing three and pinning a fourth one to the wall behind it. The Rat King quickly replaced those rats with new ones, seemingly unaffected by the loss. There were even spare rats in the water behind it, ready to replenish its numbers.

Archer moved back, and I stepped forward. We needed something more powerful to take out this creature.

With my sword, I made a vertical slice in the air and a wave of power shot out and down the tunnel. It hit the creature's center mass and blasted it apart in an explosion of blood.

Hugo cheered in celebration, but it wasn't over until I got the confirmation message.

A few seconds later, more rats came pouring down the tunnel so that the Rat King could rebuild its body.

"Huh, maybe Gren had the right idea?" Hugo suggested.

We started to back up as we considered other abilities.

The Rat King's left fist lunged at us, its arm stretching impossibly long, and large enough that it slammed into me and Archer. At the same time. The three of us were knocked back into the shallow water. Quickly, I scrambled to my feet and picked up Hugo.

He sputtered and spat. "Ergh. Now it's going to take forever for my feathers to dry."

I did sympathize, but we had bigger problems.

The Rat King was still growing taller and wider until finally it blocked the whole tunnel. I glanced behind us and saw only a wall. We'd been knocked into a dead-end. This was its plan all along. It was a slow and heavy creature. By trapping us, it took away our speed advantage.

"Alright, no more games. Let's throw everything we have at it," I said.

I went first and launched a series of Air Slashes, hoping to cut us a path to escape. But the Rat King reformed again too quickly. He was tougher than before. The mass wouldn't even break apart now.

My only other thought was to trap it in my Crimson Domain, but that would use up most of my power. If I missed any of the rats, something told me that this thing would just rebuild itself.

After my attack, I had to back off and catch my breath. Hugo summoned Ostorox and threw it at the Rat King. We were both hopeful at first. But despite their similar size, the void spawn was much weaker than the Rat King. As the pair wrestled together, I noticed that the individual rats were biting into Ostorox's flesh.

We only had maybe a minute or two before this thing devoured enough of Ostorox for the spirit summons' form to break down.

"Any ideas?" I asked Hugo.

"I could throw my new bug spirit summon at it?"

I shrugged. It was worth a shot.

"Don't look so skeptical. It's at a good level," he assured me. "This thing will be dead before you can say bingo bongo."

Just as Ostorox was ripped apart and dissipated into mist, Hugo threw his bug spirit summon. It was almost too big to fit into the tunnel and its weight knocked the Rat King over. The bug collapsed on top of it, crushing some of the rats to death.

"Yeah! Take that!" Hugo whooped.

But the surrounding rats that survived began eating the giant bug.

"No! Stay down!" Hugo cried. He had Archer shoot arrows around the bug, but it seemed to have little effect.

Some rats broke off from the mass and attacked Archer individually. Eventually the spirit's form was destroyed along with the bug.

The Rat King reformed itself again and thudded closer to us.

Hugo, however, wasn't done. He flew toward the creature. The sound of a church bell loudly rang out.

It was his Bell Toll ability—a psychic attack that inspired fear in other creatures. The Rat King shuddered and collapsed into individual rats before reforming itself again. We couldn't get past them in time, so Hugo sent out another Bell Toll to keep the creature from attacking us.

"Lucas, what do we do? I can't keep this up for long," he panted.

I thought about what I had left to use. It was only Crimson Domain which might not work. But what did Hugo have left? Some spirit crows and his ghost hand ability?

That was when the realization hit me. We'd killed hundreds of rats. More than enough for Hugo to qualify to use the ability.

"Hugo, use Irascible Dirge!" I yelled.

"What? There's no way that would work."

"Just do it!"

Irascible Dirge was the final ability Hugo had gotten on the last floor. He hadn't been able to make it work there, as it needed certain specifications to activate. Instead of Hugo capturing a single target's spirit to summon and control, Irascible Dirge was a temporary mass summoning of dead spirits. It was designed to be used on battlefields, so we just had to hope that this situation qualified.

A somber horn sound played out and all of the rats we'd killed came back to life. Their spirits solidified and became indistinguishable from the other rats.

I thought Hugo would order them to attack the Rat King, but he did something even better.

The spirit rats were joining the mass, intermingling with it. The Rat King seemed unable to tell the difference at first, though it couldn't control them. Hugo urged his rats to eat. Biting through the necks of rats who died, and then rose again to join Hugo's army. More joined and more died. The spirit rat army kept consuming and growing until only the Rat King was left.

DING! You have slain [Rat King (Uncommon)] Level 120 – Experience Points and Currency Acquired.

Hugo dismissed the rat spirits and, having fought well, they left in peace.

"Man, I can't believe you don't get to keep the rats," I said. That would've been an incredible spirit summon to have at his beck and call.

"I know, right?" Hugo sniffed. "I tasted the power of a Rat King and now they're gone forever. Never even got the chance to name them."

"Are you crying?"

"No, shut up. It's moist in here."

Hugo stopped flapping his wings and settled in the dirty water. It was something he would have only done if extremely tired. I scooped him up and put him on my shoulder to rest. We had to get out of here. We'd only survived due to Hugo's ability, and there was no way he'd be able to cast it again anytime soon.

"Come on," I said. "We should go find our cowardly guide. That Rat King might not be the only monster down here, and I have no idea where we are."

With my heightened awareness ability, I enhanced my hearing to the point where I could hear Gren gasping for breath. He'd tired himself out from running and was hiding behind a corner, trying to catch his breath.

As soon as we got close, I called out to him. "You can come out now. It's over."

Gren sheepishly stepped out and smoothed his rumpled clothes over. "So... I... uh..."

"You still want to get paid?" I asked, cutting him off. He nodded. "Then get us to the city center. We need to find the silver elevator."

He nodded again and took over leading us, though this time he didn't try to make conversation.

Hugo: Damn, that was harsh.

Lucas: Did you really want to stand here and watch him try to justify his cowardice, or did you want to get out of this place and get your feathers dry?

Hugo: The second one. But G-man isn't a Tower Climber. He's a family man. You can't expect him to fight monsters with us.

Lucas: I didn't. I expected him to impotently cower behind us where we could've better protected him.

Hugo: Well, he knows that now. Next time will be better.

Lucas: There's probably not going to be a next time. You were right about us putting him in danger. We'll pay him well for his time and hope it helps with his family situation.

We walked a little farther until Gren stopped at one of the ladders. I looked up, but it looked like any other manhole.

"Are you sure this is it?" I asked.

Gren looked a little offended. "I've been counting my steps. This is right in the city center."

Before I could thank him, he started climbing up first.

"You're coming with us?" I asked, surprised.

He grunted. "The city center is probably one of the safest areas, especially during the day. Grayskins have to protect their investments."

I didn't know what that meant, but he opened the manhole cover and disappeared into the light before I could ask any more questions. Hugo shrugged and urged me to hurry up.

I grabbed the first rung and began climbing up into what I hoped was a better part of the city.

CHAPTER 9
BORNE OF BLOOD

THE LIGHT from the sun blinded me as I climbed out of the manhole cover with Hugo on my shoulder. Shocked gasps nearby followed, which suggested that people emerging from the sewers weren't an everyday occurrence. As my vision adjusted, I saw what the problem was.

Gren had taken us to the city center as promised, but the spot he'd chosen to surface was right next to an outdoor restaurant. The patrons stared at us except for those at the nearest tables—they were covering their noses and looking away.

Considering we were drenched in sewage water, I didn't blame them, but I did linger to observe. Fitting in with the architecture of the city, they were all humans dressed in suits and dresses from the late 1800s. I could tell, not just from the lack of weapons, but from their demeanor that none of them were Tower Climbers.

"Lucas, cover your face," Hugo chastised. He was already hiding his face under his wing. "Our first day in a new place and I'm already humiliated," he moaned. "Creeping out of the sewer like some monster."

Gren stood off to the side, waiting and tapping his foot.

"We're never going to get a reservation there now," Hugo continued. "How are we supposed to fix our reputation? What are we going to do?"

"The same thing as before," I said. "Kill monsters, get stronger, finish the quest, and then move on. Who knows, we might not be here for long."

"Yes! We take the high road. Move on from this place to better things and make them wish they'd had us."

"I'm not sure that's the high road," I said as we followed Gren.

The goblin led us to the elevators. One gold door and one silver door in the middle of the city square. The gold, predictably, didn't open, but the silver dinged and opened at my touch. Other citizens walking around gave us a wide berth, though there were a few stares.

A trade request from Gren appeared, and I paid him his money. "Good luck with everything," I said and held out my hand.

The goblin shook it and said, "Likewise," before leaving.

"Let us know if you need anything!" Hugo called after him. "Don't hesitate, we'll be around!"

"We're not dropping him off on his first day of school. He's going home to his family. He'll be fine."

We got in the elevator and went back to the apartment. Misty was silent when we entered and none of her lights were on.

Maybe she'd switched herself off?

I told Hugo to go wash up first while I did my laundry, or at least attempted to. The door wouldn't open again and none of the buttons I pressed did anything.

"Misty, open the door," I said.

"No," she sullenly replied.

Is it going to be like this every time?

"Don't make me replace you," I warned her.

"I'm not opening up until I've said my piece."

I sighed. "Fine. What is it?"

"Do you have any idea what it's been like? Just sitting here for hours with nothing to do?"

I paused, waiting for her to continue. "That wasn't a rhetorical question," she said.

"I'd imagine it's pretty boring. What do you want me to do about it?"

"I want you to take me with you on your adventures."

"No."

"Give me one reason, why not?"

"I could give you a million reasons. You're too big and heavy for one."

"You're strong enough to carry me."

"Oh yeah, I'll just walk around with a washing machine under my arm. Spend the rest of my time here looking like I just robbed a house that didn't have a TV."

"Wait, what's a TV?"

I almost said something rude, but I stopped myself. She actually sounded sincere there. This could be the solution for both of us.

I went into the living room area and turned the TV on.

"Ohh, *that's* a TV," she said. "It's a little primitive, but... Wait, did that fat man just hit his own lawyer with a chair?"

I nodded. "It's called Fight Court. It's a show that mixes legal cases with trials by combat in the same setting."

"Sounds dumb. Is it popular?"

"Incredibly."

Misty grunted and her door swung open for me to put my clothes in. The silence that followed told me that she was utterly engrossed in what was happening on the screen.

Hugo came out of the bathroom looking fluffier. "Found the hairdryer," he said. "That thing is amazing. Hey, what's with Misty?"

"Nothing. Just solved another problem. People should call me the problem solver from now on."

"That's a terrible nickname. I'm suspending your nicknaming license, pending a review."

"Fine, I'll see you in court," I said as I left for the bathroom.

When I returned, Misty was still captivated by the TV and Hugo wanted to get back out there. I agreed with him, but there were a couple of things left to do. The first being to update our stats after our encounter with the Rat King.

Hugo went first and dumped a lot of points into Intelligence. Suddenly, he received a new message.

DING! You have gained [Bubble Shield (Uncommon)] – This ability creates a small shield around the caster and is designed to block one or two physical attacks before bursting. Note: this does not block magical or psychic attacks and the strength of the shield depends on the user's level.

"Yes! Finally, I can get in on the action," Hugo said.

I appreciated his enthusiasm, but I had to throw cold water on it and caution restraint. The description made it clear the sorts of the situations it should be used for.

"It said it can block one or two hits only," I said. "It's meant to be an emergency last resort measure or something you activate while running away. Or in your case, flying away."

The crow activated it and a clear bubble formed around him.

"Let's test it out," he said.

I rolled my eyes. "This isn't the place for that."

"Come on. Hit me!"

I grabbed the TV remote off the table and hurled it at him. The bubble burst, but the remote had lost all of its momentum and dropped like a stone as soon as it touched the shield. Hugo was completely unaffected and formed a new bubble.

So there's no cooldown on the ability. That was good to know.

"How's the magic cost?" I asked.

"Not too bad," he said.

I couldn't tell whether he was lying or not, so I told him to be careful with it anyway. Not that my words would be heard.

Hugo wanted to leave and try it out on a monster, but I still had my own stats to level. I put most of the points into Dexterity and Perception and received a new ability as well.

DING! You have gained [Magical Awareness (Uncommon)] – This ability is an Aura Sense upgrade that allows you to see active magic that is not perceptible to the naked eye. Note: Certain materials can contain the flow of magic and block your sight.

I activated Aura Sense and noticed several things at once. Misty now had a faint purple glow around her. Was she magic in some way? I then looked at Hugo and saw a golden thread going from his heart to Archer. I was seeing the connection between them—the bond that he controlled them with.

This wasn't the most glamorous of abilities, but if I could see magic coming before it hit me, then I counted this one as a win.

There was one final thing to do, and that was to find out just what exactly the Blood Orchard was. I told Hugo I'd be back in a minute before I went into my domain.

A shallow pool of blood surrounded my feet and darkness surrounded me as the rest of the world fell away. The blood stretched on in every direction, making the domain appear endless, though that wasn't really the case. It was a pocket world that was only a hundred feet by a hundred feet in dimension and was utterly empty until now.

A small tree no taller than myself bloomed in the distance. Its roots sank into the blood, feeding off of it.

I walked toward it for a closer inspection. None of the blood I touched would so much as stain my boots. In this place, it was under my complete control.

The tree was young, but healthy. I could feel its roots connected to the earth of this place. It was as much a part of me as the blood. Something about the tree tingled with the feeling of electricity. It was small. So small that it had escaped my notice until now.

I moved around the tree. Hanging from one of the branches was a single red apple. I commanded it to fall, and it dropped into my hand.

Item Identified! [A Scarlet Apple (Rare, E-Grade)] – Borne from the blood of your enemies. This fruit contains some of their strength. Unlike drinking from your enemies directly to gain permanent power and risk madness, consuming the fruit offers a safer middle ground. Eating a Scarlet Apple will boost all of your stats by 25% for sixty seconds. Note: do not consume more than one Apple at a time.

From the description, it reminded me of the temporary boosts some Climbers got from drinking potions. The apple sounded like something that was worth saving for a rainy day, so into my inventory it went.

I returned to the apartment and picked Hugo up.

"Alright, let's go see what else is out there," I said.

CHAPTER 10
MEETING THE HUMAN ALIENS

When we took the elevator back to the city, we came back out at the same place as before. Even after paying Gren handsomely, we still had a lot of money to burn, and I was eager to spend it. Unfortunately, all of the establishments surrounding us were places to eat and drink.

After a brief exploration, we decided to ask for directions. Most of the people we asked ignored us and kept walking. I guessed I couldn't blame them. Walking around with a sword and cloak with a bird on my shoulder would've screamed 'danger' to me too, not so long ago.

We were about to give up and just pick a direction when a well-dressed, middle-aged man paused to check the time on his pocket watch.

"Excuse me. Would you happen to know where the merchant stores are?" I asked him.

He smiled. "Certainly. They're in the market district. Head that way," he pointed east. "Once you're past the park, you should find them." There was a posh lilt to his accent which I couldn't place, and he even tipped his hat to me before continuing on his way.

That didn't seem like somebody from Earth. Roan did say something about all the residents here being aliens. I went into chat to ask him to clarify that.

Lucas: Where did the humans of the Strand come from?

Roan: This is why you contacted me? Usually when mortals beseech my wisdom, they have better questions.

Lucas: I promise I'll beseech better later. I'm just trying to understand this place. Between the goblins and the Grayskins, it's hard to figure out the dynamics of how the city works.

Roan: Okay, judging from the fact that you're still alive, I'm going to assume you haven't used the word Grayskin in their presence. Don't. They consider it to be a grave insult.

Lucas: So what do I call them instead?

Roan: How about by their names? You racist.

Hugo snickered, and when I looked at him, he tried to turn it into a cough.

Lucas: Can we get back to the humans?

Roan: Right. Certain species have visited Earth in the distant past and took some samples with them. Enough to repopulate another planet or two. Thus, you have humans from other planets.

Lucas: By 'samples' you mean alien abduction. But what do you know about the humans here?

Roan: Very little. This whole thing was set up for this Tower run by the Officiator several years ago. All I know is that the humans are not Earthlings. They grew up with different customs and religions than you did. Be cautious with over-familiarizing. Also, I'm going to be out of contact for a while. Just a little personal business. Nothing to worry about. Is there anything else you need before I go?

Lucas: What can you tell me about the other city faction that isn't goblin or human?

Roan: They're rich, powerful, and secretive. Despite those attributes, they tend to appreciate blunt honesty if you're trying to win them over. You probably wouldn't have much to offer them right now, so you should keep your distance from them too.

The conversation ended there, and I continued down the street until we reached the park. It was lined with a wrought-iron fence and a gate that lay open. The park looked huge and inviting, with lush green fields and trees. Parents were in there playing with their kids and others sat on blankets for picnics.

It was a level of normality I hadn't seen since the System had arrived, and I felt myself being drawn to it.

Hugo flapped his wings to get my attention. "Come on," he said. "That isn't meant for us."

He was trying to gently prod me along, but his words cut deeper than he could've known. Not meant for us. It was frustrating because he was right. We were still on the clock. This Tower Climb had a deadline and if we didn't make it out in time, then we were dead. Neither of us could afford the luxury of a day off right now. But even if we escaped the Tower, I didn't know what kind of life would be waiting for us.

I buried all those questions and feelings and kept walking.

After leaving the park, we walked past a cemetery and a large gothic church. Both also had high iron fences and gates around them. Perhaps as a security measure? Gren had said that the goblins usually left humans alone, but that hadn't been my impression so far. Maybe the other humans here also considered them a threat?

Through the fence, I saw a couple of men in hooded brown robes sitting on the church steps. Gren had mentioned that some of the humans were religious, but I hadn't realized that he'd been talking about monks.

One of them looked up and caught me staring, so I kept walking.

Past the church were these long, connected blocks of three-story houses with rooms to rent. The number of people coming and going suggested this was a well-populated area. But as soon as I set foot on their street, everyone felt the need to leave or go inside.

Lucas: Something's wrong.

Hugo: Yeah, it's like those old westerns where everyone in town clears out right before the big shoot-out.

A group of eight people in brown robes rounded the corner and were heading straight for us. I looked back and saw another ten coming from the other way. Their hands were hidden in their sleeves and they approached calmly.

Lucas: Don't say anything. Just let me do the talking.

Hugo: Oh, because that worked so well last time with the goblins.

Lucas: Let them think you're just a bird. That way, if things turn violent, they'll underestimate you.

Hugo squawked to play along. I rubbed his head to calm him until the monks got close. After that, there was a pause, as if they expected me to say or do something. Me silently standing there seemed to flummox them. But just to be safe, I scanned all of them with Aura Sense. None of them gave off even a hint of magic.

After an awkward moment of silence, one of the monks stepped forward and pulled his hood down. The face was a friendly one. A man in his sixties with a short and well-groomed white beard who beamed at us like we were welcome guests.

"My name is Father Thomas," he said with the same accent as the man with the pocket watch. "The place you are standing in is part of our parish and thus under our protection. We do not allow trespassers. So you must be a wayward soul looking for absolution."

Yeah, I'm not playing that game.

"Nope, I'm new to the city and I just got lost. I'm happy to leave in whichever direction you'd prefer."

Father Thomas gave me a disappointed smile. "Sadly, it can't be that simple. If we just let you go, then everyone will start doing it. Shortly after that, we'd be infested with goblins."

A few of the monks behind us softly laughed.

Hugo: Are we fighting now?

Lucas: Not yet. We don't know how many of the humans in the city are religious. We can't afford to have the entire goblin faction *and* the human faction both hate us.

"Perhaps I could pay for my travel?" I hinted.

Father Thomas was slightly offended. "We are people of God. We have no desire for greed."

Hugo: What about now?

Lucas: No, I'm pretty sure he's still angling for a bribe. You just have to beat around the bush first with these sanctimonious types.

"What about a donation?" I offered. "Surely, that magnificent church of yours requires certain materials and labor to maintain it?"

Father Thomas nodded. "It does, but we are blessed with a wealthy congregation. Perhaps as a Tower Climber you would have something more unique to trade, like that sword of yours?"

Yeah, that ain't happening. I said as much to him and he sighed like a disappointed grandparent.

"You will not leave here unless you comply with my instructions," he said. "If you do not want to give up your blade, then perhaps you have something else worthy of trading?"

Lucas: Summon the bug and throw it behind us when I draw my sword.

Hugo: Got it.

Lucas: Just try to injure them. We'll break their ranks quickly and run until we get out of this area. Much like with Goblintown, something tells me these guys stick to their own territory.

I coldly smiled. "As you say Father, I'm a Tower Climber. Are you sure you want to provoke me?"

Father Thomas whistled, and the monks opened their robes. All of them were wearing armor over their chests. Some carried knives and short swords, while a couple of others carried these lanterns on chains that held a faint green glow.

I drew my sword, but none of the monks moved. It was a group of men and women who stared at me calmly. Just waiting to do their job. Either this wasn't their first rodeo, or they were so devout that they assumed there was no way for them to lose. Neither option was good for me. It meant I'd have to fight to kill and alienate another city faction.

Also, what the hell was Hugo waiting for?

Lucas: Hey, anytime you want to jump in and summon the big scary bug creature?

Hugo: I can't! None of my magic is working.

I used Aura Sense again. The lanterns that the monks were holding were emitting some kind of pulse. I watched as Hugo tried to summon something. A gold thread came out of his chest and the lantern pulsed again, causing the thread to disintegrate.

"You are not the first Tower Climber we've crossed paths with," said Father Thomas. "Our lanterns nullify your abilities and, as you can see, the numbers are in our favor. Why don't you put that sword down and come back to the church with us? I'm sure we can find a reasonable solution. In fact, I think you'd be surprised at what the church can offer you."

I'd met quite a few gods recently, but never any worshippers. It got me curious as to which one they followed.

"What's the name of your god?" I asked, taking a different tack.

Father Thomas was briefly taken aback though his smile remained in place. He seemed to find me taking an interest in his religion flattering.

"It's not just my god, but everyone's," he said. "But I understand that the word of them has not reached everyone. Perhaps that is the very reason why people like me exist in the first place. To answer your question, we worship the Harvest Mother."

I was relieved to hear that they didn't worship a being that already hated me. On the other hand, I had no idea who the Harvest Mother was. Hugo hadn't heard of her either. Her name sounded intimidating, but that was par for the course with gods. Most of them carried a name or a title that was meant to strike fear into the hearts of their enemies.

I tried to contact Roan for advice.

[God Chat Unavailable]

Great. Guess we're on our own.

Lucas: Alright, Hugo, empty your pockets. Let's see what you have.

Hugo: What? We're really not fighting these guys? They seem so suspect. Plus, they're extorting us.

Lucas: I know, but the anti-magic lanterns no longer make this fight a sure thing. Let's see if we have something to trade first. I'd rather stay on good terms with at least one group today.

"I might have something to trade," I told Father Thomas. "But this could take a while," I warned him as we opened up our inventories.

We started with the dead bodies. Hugo and I still had an assortment from our Climb, so I offered the priest a fresh Shrikon corpse to start with. The monks were startled when the dead fishman body was plopped in front of them. Hugo had to cough to avoid laughing.

Father Thomas merely pursed his lips and shook his head.

I took back the corpse, and we moved on to basic weapons, armor, and shields. There was a little more interest in their eyes at that, but most of what we had was junk, or of such quality that it could be called junk-adjacent.

None of it was acceptable to them.

Lucas: Hey, what about your pocket ship?

Hugo: We're in a city in the desert. I couldn't offer it to them without flattening half of the neighborhood. Besides, I lost it on the last floor.

Lucas: Right, I forgot. It's just that I'm getting dangerously close to offering the clothes off my back. At which point, I'd rather just fight.

Hugo: What about potions?

I almost said no, but I did have something that was like a potion. Something Rare that I wouldn't mind parting with.

I pulled out the Scarlet Apple. As soon as he saw it, Father Thomas's eyes were fixed on it.

Lucas: He'd make a terrible gambler.

Losing the Apple wouldn't be a great loss. From what I understood, the Blood Orchard would simply grow more of them as I spilled more blood. This could be a valuable resource that I could keep growing and trading to others for supplies and favors.

I offered the Apple to the priest, and as his hand reached out for it, I pulled it back. Hugo and I couldn't afford to keep doing this song and dance every time we wanted to cross through this district. I needed a guarantee from Father Thomas before I handed over the Apple.

"This gets us permanent visitation privileges," I said. "I don't want me or my bird hassled by your people while we're here again."

Father Thomas nodded. "Very well."

I handed over the Apple and the excitement in his eyes made me think that he was getting away with a much better deal.

The monks moved aside, and we left that district for the part of town that was actually labeled on a sign as the market district.

"That went better than expected," Hugo said.

"Yes, let's see what other problems we could potentially buy our way out of."

CHAPTER 11
DISCUSSING THE QUALIFICATIONS OF AN EMOTIONAL SUPPORT ANIMAL

I WAS FROWNING as we entered the market district. It was almost as large as the city center, with its own square and rows of stores in three directions. The streets and shopfronts looked like they'd just been cleaned. This was a place of wealth that offered premium items, and yet I still couldn't get my mind off our earlier encounter. There was still something about that whole scene that was strange and difficult to put into words.

I stopped and asked Hugo, "Did the monks seem off to you?"

He looked at me as if I might have a concussion. "No, the clergymen carrying weapons and armor that tried to extort us seemed perfectly normal to me."

"Yeah, but that part felt almost expected. It's just that Roan said they'd be more alien. Then the first guy that introduces himself is named Father Thomas? It just seems odd."

"You were expecting the priest to introduce himself as Father Zeepthorp? You think Roan could be lying?"

"No, but he was vague when describing the human faction. Saying that they're more alien than we are could mean a hundred different things. We may have bought access to travel through their territory, but I think we should keep our distance until we learn more. For now, keep playing the simple bird role around the humans."

Hugo: Is that your way of telling me to shut up?

Lucas: Of course not. Companion chat doesn't have a mute button.

Hugo grumbled under his breath as I stopped at the first store. We peered through the large glass windows and saw shelves of potions on display. The finely engraved sign above this place read MIZICK'S MASTERFUL CONCOCTIONS.

A premium potion store was an interesting place to start. Especially if we could find something throwable that could destroy those anti-magic lanterns. Not that I was planning to fight them. It was just good to be prepared.

A bell over the door jangled as I went inside. Hugo silently remained on my shoulder, but he watched everything with open curiosity.

Mizick's potion store was a medium-sized one with several aisles. It appeared to have only a single employee. A tan man in his forties with sharp eyes and flat features. He wore a brown apron over his white shirt to present the appearance that he'd just come out of a workshop. But the pristine white shirt gave him away.

The man, who I took to be Mizick, stared at us with suspicion. His store had no other customers, save for a male goblin wearing a large coat who'd come in before us. The goblin walked down one of the aisles like they knew where they were going and disappeared from sight.

Mizick's hostility seemed unwarranted. I wondered if we'd done something wrong or if he just didn't like Tower Climbers. He didn't say anything, so I ignored him and began perusing the potions on display.

The first ones we came across were these thin green vials with a label underneath, describing them as instant preservatives for making food last longer. Not particularly helpful in our situation, but I had to keep in mind that this was a store for the whole city and not just Tower Climbers.

I was about to move on when Mizick loudly coughed and said, "Ahem!"

I turned and calmly asked, "Is there a problem?"

"There's no need to take that tone, sir."

Hugo and I glanced at each other. "I don't have a tone."

Mizick pointed to the sign beside his cash register. "No pets allowed. You think the rules don't apply to you because you carry that sword?"

Hugo said nothing, but his talons dug deeper into my shoulder. He would continue to play his part, but he expected me to come to his defense. Which, of course, I did.

"He's not a pet," I said. "He's… an emotional support companion."

Mizick frowned. "What's that?"

I guessed that wasn't something they had where this guy grew up. His patience was wearing thin, so I quickly tried to explain why it was important that my bird accompany me.

"It's an animal you own that…" Hugo's talons dug in deeper. "That you care for and look after. An animal that offers companionship and feels good to have around."

Mizick looked unimpressed. "That's a pet," he said flatly. "You are literally describing the reasons why people have pets."

Hugo: Are you sure you don't want me to jump in here?

It was time to switch tactics. I pointed to a one-of-a-kind potion on the shelf behind him. A square bottle with golden liquid inside.

"How much does that cost?" I asked.

"I don't see how that's relevant."

"Tower Climbers earn a lot of money as they descend through the floors."

"So?"

Lucas: Okay, now he's just being deliberately obtuse.

"So," I said. "I am going to peruse your wares and likely spend a great sum of money here. And the only trace left behind by my bird and I, will be the money in your pocket and some empty shelf space. Unless of course, you'd rather I take my business elsewhere?"

He glowered for a moment before giving a stiff nod of acceptance.

Hugo: I can't believe that worked.

Lucas: The power of money strikes again. Let's focus on offensive potions first, before looking at the ones for healing. But before we do that, I want to know what he thinks about the monks.

"As I said before, I'm new to the city and I had a little trouble getting here after I had an encounter with some worshippers of the Harvest Mother."

He snorted. "Those freaks? They like to pretend like all of us humans are a part of their flock, but we're not. Most of us stay away from them."

I noticed a large stock of purple bottles near the front without labels on them and asked what they were.

"They're our most popular seller at the moment," he said. "They dispel curses."

"All curses? How does that work?"

He folded his arms. "It's a proprietary formula."

Hugo: Sounds like a scam.

Lucas: Agreed. Let's move on.

We glanced at the next shelf. This one had large bottles with golden brown liquid inside. There was no label on them, but the goblin from earlier was staring at them too.

"Hey, do you know what this stuff is?" I asked the goblin in a low voice. "I'd kinda prefer not to ask the manager. Already had one negative run-in with him today."

The goblin's hands shook, and he was sweating profusely. He turned to me with a wide-eyed look. "The spirits are restless. I've taken so many of their kind, but the need for more is inexhaustible." He frowned at me. "But you have seen this. You killed one of us." He grimaced. "I must warn the others before I complete my work."

He started to leave when he suddenly yelped, "Ow!"

Above his head was a bottle that was held in a ghostly hand. The goblin angrily pointed at me. "You hit me with a bottle!"

Hugo: No, he didn't. It was me!

The crow used his Spectral Touch ability to swing the bottle down on the goblin's head again. The goblin yelled in pain and tried to grab the bottle, but it floated out of his reach.

Lucas: What are you doing?

Hugo: I'm knocking him out, like in the movies. He's clearly up to no good. We should carry his unconscious body somewhere for questioning.

The goblin sank to the floor and stared off into space. He clearly wasn't all there, but if he knew something about the spirit killer device, then we'd find out.

"Hey, you need to pay for that," Mizick yelled, completely unconcerned about his customers fighting each other.

I forced Hugo to hand the bottle to me and took a closer look at the label. It read, 'Glenmizick whiskey, freshly distilled.'

"You serve alcohol here?" I asked. "And more importantly, did you put Glen in front of your name, thinking it would make it sound fancier?"

He gave a small shrug. "I serve the needs of my customers. Whatever they need, I provide."

"So you're saying it's a *fluid* business?" Hugo asked aloud.

"Oh, nice one," I said.

Mizick frowned. "Wait, your bird can talk?"

Hugo: Damn it, Lucas. I've been made!

Lucas: You just couldn't help yourself, could you?

"I'm sorry," Hugo said. "I'll put the bottle back."

He used his ghost hand to take it off me, but Hugo's offer wasn't good enough.

Mizick shook his head. "No, you have to pay for it now that it's damaged."

Hugo lifted it up to his face to examine it. "It doesn't even have a scratch on it! Really great glass construction by the way, but still, I don't think I should have to pay for this. It's not damaged."

"Just buy the booze, Hugo. We've wasted enough time on this."

The crow grumbled something under his breath and then flew to the counter to buy the bottle, quickly making it disappear into his inventory. I approached the counter and said, "Maybe you can help speed things along. We're looking for offensive potions, you know, face-melting acid in a jar, that sort of thing. Once we've got that, we'll take our green-skinned friend and leave you in peace."

There was a loud crash behind us. The goblin stood and deliberately knocked over several potions. "At last, your people will begin to answer for your crimes," he declared, before opening his jacket. Underneath it was a vest packed with explosives.

I grabbed Mizick and Hugo and dove through the front window just as the store exploded.

The three of us landed hard on the street. I'd gone through the window first and was covered in glass. Mizick lay on the ground moaning, but it didn't appear serious, so I hurried to check on Hugo. My body seemed to have shielded the bird from the worst of it. I pulled a shard of glass out of my cheek and used a few rat corpses from my inventory to heal us both.

Mizick was looking a bit rougher. I handed him a health potion, and said, "Here, drink this. If it doesn't fully heal you in twenty minutes, then go see a doctor."

He drank half of the potion and then said, "But I am the city doctor."

"Man, you're wearing a lot of hats in this town," Hugo said.

"I've had to because of things like these," he replied, raising the health potion. "Years of medical training rendered obsolete by a drink." He sneered and then finished the rest of it. "God, it even tastes good." He stared at the burning wreckage that used to be his store. "My business is gone. I'm ruined."

"Don't you have insurance or something?" I asked.

He shook his head.

"Do you think that was wise, given your proximity to the goblins?" Hugo asked.

Mizick slammed his fist into the ground. He looked up at us, his eyes burning. "This is your fault! You attract trouble. You set the goblin off with your talk and hit him with that bottle. That's probably what set him off in the first place. You need to pay me back for destroying my store."

"How much would that cost?" I ask.

"I think 100,000 gold should do it."

I shook my head. Even combined, Hugo and I didn't have that much money. And even if we did, I wouldn't be eager to give it to this guy.

"Fine," he said. "You're both strong and fast. Maybe you can help me physically rebuild the place?" He saw my expression and then turned his pleading eyes to Hugo.

"I've actually got a lot on my plate right now," Hugo said.

Mizick was about to say something else when four muscular men in suits ran toward us. Only they weren't exactly men. They had gray skin, small tusks, and each one was over seven feet tall. Their appearance instantly made me think of orcs.

Three of them held chrome-plated pistols, while the fourth carried a big metal canister.

I put my hands up and said, "Whatever you may have heard about me. I promise I didn't do it."

They ran past me to assess the fire damage to the store.

"What do you think?" one of them asked.

Another sniffed the air. "Smells like goblin homebrew. Tanite, maybe?"

The one holding the canister lobbed it into the burning store. White foam exploded inside and quenched the flames.

The others nodded in agreement on a job well done before they looked at Hugo and me on the ground.

"Bring them in for questioning," one of them said.

Hugo's eyes lit up as he put two and two together. "Oh, so this is what Gren meant when he said they're Gr—"

I clamped my hand over the bird's mouth before he could finish that sentence.

Lucas: Roan said that word is offensive to orcs or whatever they are. And before you say it, I'm just calling them that as a shorthand instead.

Hugo: Okay, I get it. Don't accidentally throw racial slurs at the gun-toting aliens. Now, can you remove your hand? It stinks of blood.

The orcs grabbed us both and said, "You're coming with us. The boss wants to have a word."

As we were being dragged away, I heard Mizick angrily shout, "Hey, what about my store!"

CHAPTER 12
AN UNDERWHELMING ORC CITY TOUR

THE ORCS CARRIED us further east. I know what you're thinking. But it's okay. I heard them refer to themselves that way. Which was a small weight off my mind, but it didn't really address the larger concern of being taken. Whether we were being arrested for the shop bombing or just plain kidnapped wasn't made clear to us.

For most of the journey, the orcs rarely spoke. When they did, it was usually to complain. The orc that was carrying me had thrown me over his shoulder like a sack of potatoes. He kept one hand on me and one on his fancy chrome pistol. And every once in a while, he'd mutter under his breath about how he should've shot us on sight.

In companion chat, Hugo and I had dubbed him Snappy due to his cheerful demeanor. He had an ugly face to match and burn scars on his hands.

Then there was Lazy, the orc who carried Hugo within one of his dinner-plate-sized hands. He was the heaviest of the group and kept asking to take breaks. He was repeatedly shot down by their leader, Broody. Whenever we did stop briefly, it was so Broody could check his wristwatch and then glance up at the sky. It was unclear why he did this, but the combination of these two things seemed to tell him which streets to go down and which to avoid.

The last orc bringing up the rear was Whiny, the smallest of the group. Though he would still tower over me at six foot six. Unlike Snappy, his complaints were loud, and he often wished that they'd taken an LTV.

Hugo: What's an LTV?

Lucas: I have no idea.

"Enough!" barked Broody. "An LTV is too good of a target for goblin artillery to pass up. We can't risk it."

Snappy and Whiny both grumbled about how unfair that was, but one dark look from Broody and they fell silent.

Getting taken by orcs had not been on my list of plans, but it did expedite things. I allowed myself to be taken without any fuss, hoping that they would lead us to somebody in charge. That way we could try to get on friendly terms with another city faction and ask the goblin's main enemy what they knew about the spirit killer device.

Hugo had been more reticent to agree to my plan.

When we were first captured, he'd unleashed a flurry of insults at them and pecked at the hand that was holding him. The orc didn't seem to mind the fighting. None of his attacks could get through his toughened skin. What all of them did object to was the noise he was making.

I told him in companion chat to calm himself, that we can fight our way out if we must, but first let's see where they take us.

I'd hoped to learn more about this city, but there wasn't a whole lot to see from our positions. Mostly, I tried to keep track of the street names so that I'd have a rough idea of how to get back. The only other thing I watched was the bystanders that we passed along the way.

The humans we encountered had strange reactions to a grown man and his bird being carried through the streets. I expected some shock or disbelief. Instead, it was as if we were unimportant. The humans would either give the passing orcs a respectful nod or turn away to hide their faces. The orcs didn't care one way or the other. They ignored all of them and nobody dared get in their way.

Slowly, we saw fewer humans and more orcs as we moved farther east.

Hugo: Wow, this area seems wealthy. Are we in the Orc district yet?

We had passed through too many streets for it to be a mere district.

Lucas: I don't think they have a district. I think this whole eastern part of the city is theirs.

To hammer this home, the orcs came to a stop in front of a gated checkpoint. There was one large gate for carriages or vehicles and one smaller one to the side for people traveling on foot. Orcs wearing tactical armor and carrying chrome rifles guarded the checkpoint. They allowed people in through the small gate, one at a time, after scanning them with a wand.

Broody cursed. "We don't have time for this." He whistled to get the guard's attention and made a circular motion with his finger for them to open the main gate.

The guards jumped to comply, and there was a buzzing sound as the gate was opened electronically. Despite the gas lamps and cobblestone streets, some future technology was still in play here. I'd have to keep that in mind going forward.

As we were passing, the orc with the wand idly waved it our way. Something on his belt started beeping and suddenly more guards with their rifles came pouring out of a nearby building to block the path in front of us. The ones at the gate already stood at attention. None dared point their guns directly at our group, but some looked like they wanted to.

"I don't have time for this," Broody barked before calming himself. He raised his voice to address everyone present. "Yes, we are aware that the two individuals in our custody are carrying trace amounts of Tanite residue. They are being taken in for questioning."

The orcs in tactical gear glanced at each other. Unsure of how to proceed.

Broody removed his wrist watch and rolled his sleeve up to reveal an intricate brand made of several sigils inside a circle. He showed this brand to them. "Does anyone have a problem with that?"

The orcs shook their heads and stepped aside. Our group continued without a word.

Hugo: Looks like the ones in suits outrank them.

Lucas: It looks that way. Though it didn't seem like there was any love lost between the two groups.

After entering the gate, we passed through several more streets until we eventually reached another square. This one was dominated by a thirty-story building that we should've noticed before now. It towered over everything else. How did we not spot this as we were entering the city?

In front of the building was a large water fountain in the shape of a lotus blossom. It reminded me of hotels back home. But as we entered, the lobby gave off more of a modern business vibe. The place was even air-conditioned, and every light was electric.

Male and female orcs, dressed in suits, were coming and going like it was just another day at the office. It was interesting to note that despite the female orcs being shorter than the males, none of them were under six feet. The other thing I noticed was that all of them looked like capable fighters. I didn't see a single sick or old person in this crowded lobby.

Still, even in this space, Broody was recognized and the other orcs respectfully kept out of his way.

We passed a front desk where the youngest orc I'd seen so far was stationed. His eyes were wide with admiration for Broody as we passed. Unlike the others, his suit looked two sizes too big. Like a kid wearing his dad's clothes.

Broody ignored him and led us straight to the elevators. He pressed the button and waited a moment.

The young orc receptionist leaned over the front desk. "Umm, they're out of service," his voice squeaked.

Snappy sighed. "I miss using the wings. Can we use them next time?"

Lazy shook his head. "They're too big. It's another prime target for goblin artillery."

Whiny nodded in agreement. "You know what would happen if we broke the rules."

Broody opened the door to the stairwell. "Come on," he said. "Job's not finished till we deliver them."

The other three groaned and reluctantly followed us up the stairs. Even with his high level of strength, sweat poured off of Snappy. Halfway up, Broody took pity on him and offered to carry me the rest of the way.

It was an odd experience to be handed off like a child from one big orc to the other. I tried to keep my expression neutral, but Hugo sniggered, making me crack a smile.

"Yeah, laugh it up funny man," said Snappy. "You won't be laughing when the boss gets done with you."

It was obviously a threat, but instead of feeling afraid, I was curious. Being a Tower Climber quickly made one desensitized to such basic threats. Instead, I was hungry for details. I wanted to know what to plan for or use to my advantage.

"What does that mean?" I asked him.

Snappy sneered and opened his mouth, but Broody cut him off. "Come on, we should keep moving. If the boss's meeting finishes early and we're not there, guess who's paying for it?"

Snappy nodded, and the orcs resumed carrying us up the stairs.

When we reached the top floor, Broody opened the door. The voice of a man screaming in pain reverberated down the stairwell. It was the unmistakable voice of someone being tortured.

Hugo: Oh God, is that going to be us?

Lucas: No. But be ready to fight.

Even the orc carrying us grimaced. All except Snappy. He looked at me and grinned. "Guess the boss isn't finished with his last meeting after all."

CHAPTER 13
STRAINED RELATIONS

THE SCREAMS CONTINUED AS we walked down the hallway.

Of course, there's a limit to how much one could scream before running out of breath. So moments of silence followed, and as each one occurred, I prayed for his death. But the moments were always short-lived, and I'd wince every time the screaming started up again.

Now that we were in a confined space, the orcs allowed me to walk on my own. Hugo sat on my shoulder. They said not to make any sudden moves. Not that we could with the orcs sandwiched between us in the narrow hallway.

Broody led us into a fancy office waiting room. There was a small metallic desk to the left and a bench on the right for people to sit on. Straight ahead were double doors with one left slightly ajar.

That's where the screams were coming from. I moved closer to try and see, but a hand roughly grasped my arm. "Wait your turn," Snappy hissed in my ear. He shoved me toward the bench and I sat down.

The orcs now kept their guns holstered under their jackets. I was confident that, barring any surprises, I could take them. It wasn't in my nature to be meek. In fact, I hated it. But much like in a video game, I was committed to exhausting all the dialogue options before killing them.

The screaming suddenly stopped.

It was a relief to everyone. The orcs then stood around us in an awkward semi-circle, unsure of what they could say in front of us.

"Do you know any good places to eat around here?" Hugo asked them.

"Be quiet," Broody said.

Hugo turned to me.

Hugo: Why do they have to be so mean?

Lucas: They are kinda tightly wound. But then again, I'd be too if I worked in an office and had to listen to that tortured screaming.

The door from the hallway opened and a female orc entered. She was my height, dressed in a long trench coat and a large hat that covered her face. The male orcs stared. As far as they were concerned, Hugo and I no longer existed.

"Sorry, I'm late," she said, with a posh lilt. This was the first female orc I'd seen who didn't look like she could rip someone's head off.

"Aria, does he have a minute?" Broody asked.

"His prior meeting is running a little long," she replied.

As soon as Aria took off her hat, her long hair tumbled down. Snappy jumped forward and offered to take the hat from her. She graciously accepted and while his back was turned, she flashed a quick smile at Broody, who gave her one back.

Snappy returned to take her coat and hang it up. She was about to thank him again when she noticed the office door had been left ajar. Aria pursed her lips and closed it before moving to her desk. There was a whir of motors and the desk automatically rose in height. There were no papers, but the desk had a built-in screen that only she could see.

Hugo: Lucas, she has no chair. Does she work standing the whole day? That must be awful.

Lucas: Maybe it's easier for orcs to do?

Broody checked his watch. "Aria and I can take it from here. The rest of you head out."

The other orcs tried and failed to hide their disappointment but didn't argue. As they were filing out, Snappy stopped by Aria's desk to quietly ask her something.

"I'll think about it," she said, loud enough for everyone in the room to hear.

Snappy tightly nodded and left with the others.

"And I thought they'd never leave," she said.

Broody chuckled nervously and then glanced at us. "There're still these two. Do you know how much longer he'll be?"

She shook her head. "Curse magic isn't my thing, and to be honest, I wish he'd never picked it back up again."

Broody stopped himself from agreeing with her. "It's just temporary," he assured her. "Once things are back to normal, it will be set aside like it has been in the past."

"It just feels like... something *they* would do, you know?"

Broody nodded. "It's better to not think about it. Now have you heard anything from Federico?"

Alarmed at the name, her voice became quieter. "You think he suspects?"

"No, but I am wondering when you're going to break the news to him."

"I'm waiting for the right moment."

He put his hands on the desk and leaned over to talk quietly. I couldn't hear what was said, but I noticed her hand was touching his.

Hugo: Should we say something?

Lucas: No, just act like wallpaper and let their office romance play out.

Their whispers became more heated until there was an electronic beep on her desk. Aria silenced Broody with her hand and smiled at us.

"He will see you now," she said.

Before we could stand, the double doors violently flew open. A young man with short, white hair and goat horns strode out with his fists clenched. He wore an old-fashioned navy suit with a vest containing a gold pocket watch. He paused to check the time on it before snapping the clasp shut.

Aria folded her hands in front of her. "I apologize if there was a misunderstanding."

"Tell your idiot boss not to waste my time again!" he yelled.

The goat man made for the door so quickly that Broody stumbled to get out of his way.

Hugo: Who was that?

Hugo was fascinated by seeing another alien.

Lucas: Someone they consider important, judging from their reactions.

Aria favored us with another equanimous smile. "He will see you now," she repeated. Which was her polite way of telling us to get out of the room.

The orc boss's office was a massive space lined with artifacts on small pedestals. If not for the bloodied goblin tied to a chair, it would've felt like we were entering a museum.

The only other "person" in the room was a stout, grizzled orc. He wore the same suit as the others, but had removed his jacket and rolled up his sleeves. Despite these precautions, blood had still made its way onto his shirt.

His flat eyes flicked to us. "Ah good, you're here. Come closer. I'd like you to see something." He tried to sound friendly, but there was no emotion in his voice. It was the flat affect of someone who could torture without feeling a shred of empathy.

I took slow, measured steps to give myself time to warn Hugo.

Lucas: No jokes here. We have to be careful around him.

Hugo shivered.

Hugo: Don't worry about me. Worry about that knife.

I glanced at the orc's hands and was surprised that I'd missed it. The blade was a triangular spiral that ended back in a point. It did not look practical for cutting or stabbing, but its oily black color screamed dark magic.

The goblin did not move or make a sound. I assumed he was dead until I saw his face. Hugo gasped. The goblin's eyes were open and desperately moving around. He was still screaming in pain, but every other part of his body was paralyzed.

My stomach twisted in disgust. "What is this?"

"My name is Enzo, the current patriarch of the De Luca clan. This, as you call it, is ancient curse magic that has been passed down through my family for generations. I'd hoped never to have to use it myself. Though I'm sure my ancestors thought the same. Yet circumstances have forced my hand and here we are."

I pointed at the goblin. "Make it stop," I snarled.

"I cannot. The curse is absolute. Unlike many other forms of curse magic, this one does not attack the outward body. No, instead it attaches itself to the soul first and then eats away at its target from the inside out. There is no cure for it."

I drew my sword and cut the goblin's head off in one clean swing. The head rolled along the floor, but his eyes were still frantically moving. Still pleading for help.

Bile rose in my throat. Shamefully, I had to look away.

"Yes, the curse will even ward off simple deaths in order to prolong its target's suffering. Only complete destruction of the body ends it. I don't suppose you have any Tanite in that Climber inventory of yours? That would melt the body quickly."

I narrowed my eyes. "We're not working for the goblins."

Enzo stared at us and then nodded. "I believe you." He turned to the table behind him and put the knife into a silver box. Next to the box was a vial of green liquid. He took that instead and poured the contents onto the goblin's body and head. The body began to melt.

Hugo and I gagged at the smell and took several steps back.

"But you can understand my suspicion," he said. "We see you entering the city, and the goblin mortar team's aim is worse than usual. Then one of the stores under our protection gets blown up with you two at the scene."

"Trouble kind of follows us around," Hugo said.

"Yes, I've heard that about Tower Climbers. Though you're the first I've managed to actually meet with."

My eyebrows rose. "There are others in the city?"

"A handful at least. They hide in the desert or in the unclaimed section of the city. Whenever one of my people approaches them, they flee. Normally I'd suspect one of them was the cause of the problem, but this started before the Climbers arrived."

"What's the problem?" I asked.

"Orcs and humans have been going missing. Not a lot. Just a few here and there. It's been happening for months and it's put the city on edge. They look to me for answers, yet I have few to give. All we know is that some of the goblins are involved."

"How do you know that?"

He pointed at the melted body. "That one was seen standing over a dead orc with a strange device in his hand. This device." He pulled out the gold cube from his pocket. It looked identical to the one Dratch had, only this one was intact.

"May I see it?"

He handed it to me.

[Item Unidentified]

Well there goes that idea.

"Our technicians couldn't figure out what it's supposed to do. Which is where you two come in. I don't entirely trust the humans and I need someone who can go where my orcs can't. Go back to the market district and find Bartholomew's store. He's a gifted inventor who might have some insights. In fact, he helped design the power system this building runs on."

"So why not go to him yourself?" Hugo asked.

"There was… an incident. Some young upstart orc mouthed off in his shop. It escalated to threats from both sides and then the inventor banned all orcs from his store for good."

"And you allowed that?" I asked.

He shrugged. "We still make orders for certain goods to be manufactured, and he continues to fulfill them. It's awkward, but we've managed to make it work."

"What does he make for you?"

"Replacement parts for our generators, mostly. He's a pacifist and has made it clear that he wants nothing to do with our ongoing conflict with the goblins."

"And how's that conflict going?"

Enzo sighed. "We poke and prod each other in the unclaimed parts of the city in small skirmishes. The goblins are cautious because they don't know the extent of our technological capabilities. And we're the same way, since it's hard to gauge how much explosives they have."

"Why not just stop fighting?"

Enzo's eyes became hard. "Because they keep attacking us. Although the bombing you witnessed was an escalation. They've never attacked that far into the city before." He got lost in thought for a moment and then shook his head. "The goblins aren't your concern. Go to the inventor. Find out what you can about the device and then report back to me."

Hugo: Are we working for him now?

Lucas: No, we are not.

"Why should we help you?" I asked him.

Enzo folded his arms. "It's not a request. Regardless of what the goblins or humans think, this is my city. There are over two thousand orcs in this building alone that will try to kill you if you leave without my blessing, and even more in the surrounding districts. But if you help me, then my organization will assist you in any way it can to help you move on to the next floor."

Hugo: I think we should agree. He doesn't know it, but we have the same quest. Helping him is just helping ourselves.

Lucas: I know. I just hate being bossed around.

Hugo: Let me handle this part.

"We'll assist you," Hugo said. "But first, let's discuss our price."

CHAPTER 14
STONE

WE LEFT the building twice as rich as when we'd gone in. Hugo was proud of himself and recounted what had happened as if I wasn't there. All I could think about was how smoothly things had gone. It never sits right with me when things go well.

"Forty thousand gold apiece!" Hugo said on my shoulder as we walked through the lobby. Heads turned at his outburst and the orcs stared. I picked up my walking pace before one of them decided to try and rob us of the money.

"You know crowing isn't a good look on you," I said.

The bird squinted at me. "Really, crow puns? What's got you so worked up?"

"It was too easy."

"Come on. It's not like I got everything I wanted."

That was true. Hugo had tried to bargain for some of those chrome pistols they carried, but Enzo wouldn't budge. The orcs couldn't risk one of the guns falling into goblins' hands in case they learned how to reverse engineer it. It was the same story with their other technology. So in the end, we settled for cash.

"It was still too easy," I said, keeping my voice low.

"So what do you want to do? Go back in, return the money, and say we can't help even though the quest forces us to help?"

"No, obviously we have to do it. But I think the situation is worse than Enzo let on."

"But why hire us then? Look at this place. He's got an army of orcs at his disposal."

"Well firstly, it's because none of them seem to know what the word 'subtle' means. They're more likely to scare the perpetrators into hiding than find them. The second reason is that he hired us because we're outsiders. No, even worse, we're Tower Climbers. Destruction and mayhem are expected of us. If things go wrong, we'll be the fall guys."

Hugo sighed. "So it's the usual then. Trust no one and be extra cautious."

"That, and we should try to find other Tower Climbers. They might know things about the city that we don't."

Broody was waiting for us when we ventured outside. He muttered something about escorting us out of the orc district. Evidently, Enzo didn't feel that any part of the problem was in the orc section of the city. Of course, being an escort didn't mean he had to answer any of our questions. He walked quickly, taking long strides, and did not look back to see if we were keeping up. I had to jog to keep him in sight.

This time we saw more of what I could only describe as civilian orcs. Men, women, and children all going about their lives. What did they see in this place to risk coming here?

Being here voluntarily was madness.

When we got to the border checkpoint, Broody gestured for us to be let through and then spun on his heels and left us.

"Hey, where was that goblin found?" Hugo asked.

It was a good question to ask. If it was close to where we'd encountered the goblin Dratch, then it could help us narrow things down.

Broody chose to ignore him, which angered Hugo.

"What, you're not going to carry us all the way back to the market?" he yelled.

Broody stopped. He turned back and stomped toward us so fast I thought he might tackle us. We held our ground and regarded him cooly until he stopped just short of us.

"When you fail," he spat. "And you will fail. I'll be the one to pick up the pieces and I'll be the one that saves this city. We found the body in the contested area where most of the fighting happens. Hurry up and die, so that I can do my job."

The contested area was where we'd found Dratch and where Gren lived. We'd have to speak with him again. If this whole thing had been going on for months, then he must have seen or heard something.

Broody walked away, and the gate buzzed to let us out.

"Do you think I did the right thing?" Hugo asked. "I know you wanted us not to antagonize others."

"No, his ego was giving me a headache. He needed to be knocked down a peg or two. Besides, we learned where the other body was found."

It started to rain as we left the orc district. Hugo activated his bubble shield, which kept him warm and dry. It wasn't large enough to envelop anything other than him and where he stood, so every part of me except my left shoulder was getting drenched.

"Do you really have to use that?" I asked.

"You should have brought an umbrella," Hugo sniffed. "Besides, you know how heavy my feathers get when they're wet. I need to stay combat mobile."

"We're just going to the inventor's shop for a conversation, but I'll let you know if I need someone to army-crawl under the shelves."

Enzo told us that the shop was on the outer edge of the market district. We were headed back to the square when I spotted Mizick in the distance. He was standing in front of the burned-out husk of his livelihood, shouting at passersby for help. Though none did so.

I steered us away and went down a different street. "Let's take the long way round."

"Agreed."

When we reached the inventor's shop, we found the door locked. It was dark inside and we couldn't see anything through the windows.

I knocked on the door, loudly and insistently, until a small peephole opened up.

"What do you want?" a voice gruffly asked.

"We were hoping to get your expertise on something we found," I said.

"I'm closed."

"Please, the device is very rare and special. We just need five minutes."

He grumbled to himself and then said, "Alright, show me. Hold it up."

I took the spirit killer cube out of my inventory and held it up to the peephole. Before the inventor could respond, we heard a strange whistle sound like a thin burst of air.

"What is that?" I asked.

It happened again, but this time my eyes caught it. A long metal dart struck Hugo's bubble shield. The shield remained up, but the force of the attack knocked him off my shoulder. He flew backward and hit the ground, bouncing twice before the shield burst.

I ran to check on him. He was dazed but unharmed.

A frustrated screech rang out above us. There on the roof was a small, red gargoyle creature. A needle pushed its way out of its forearm and he threw it at me. My sword was in my hand and I batted the needle aside before picking up Hugo.

"I think I'm gonna be sick," he said.

"Not now, and never on me."

A second gargoyle crept up behind me. It snatched the cube out of my hand and scurried up a drainage pipe to join his friend on the roof.

Beast Identified [Needlepoint Gargoyle (common)] Level 96 – A small city gargoyle that prowls the rooftops in search of treasures. They're attracted to shiny things and bringing them back to their homes. Its body produces needlepoint quills as tough as steel and throws them with precision at anything that comes between them and their treasure.

I didn't like the sound of that.

"Wait here," I told the inventor.

Hugo and I ran after the gargoyles when they turned and fled. We weren't going to let them get away.

Hugo flew up higher while I grabbed hold of a window ledge and climbed the three-story building to get to the roof.

For small guys, the gargoyles were fast as they hopped across the roofs. Hugo flew above them and had summoned Archer, who was firing arrows at them. So far, all of the arrows had missed.

Lucas: Careful. The device is fragile.

Hugo: I know. I remember what happened last time.

The gargoyles hopped to the terrace of a taller building and turned a corner. They were out of my sight, and I hurried to catch up with them while Hugo circled above.

Lucas: Hugo, where are they?

Hugo: I don't know! They disappeared!

Sure enough, I turned the corner and saw nothing but flat rooftops. They couldn't have gone that way, and Hugo would've seen if they'd jumped down onto the street. They must have gone inside.

There was an open window, but it was too dark to see inside.

Hugo directed Archer to climb in first, and then the two of us followed. The window directed us to nothing but a familiar stone set of stairs that led down into the dark.

"You ready?" I asked.

Hugo and Archer both nodded, and we stepped down into the darkness. My eyes quickly adjusted to the dark, but it was still gloomy.

[You have discovered an Isolated Staircase]

New Artifact Identified! [An Isolated Staircase] – This is a sectioned off part of the Tower. When parts of the Tower are in lockdown, this Staircase can let you access another floor. Unlike the Stairwell, an Isolated Staircase is only connected to two floors. This floor could be the next one down, or it could be a random one. Good luck finding out!

[Now entering floor 54]

Huh, so it was the next floor down.

The next floor was a single large room. It was dark and the only thing it contained were rows upon rows of stone gargoyles. The statues varied in size and design. Some featured gargoyles that were taller than me, some only went up to my shin, and many were the same size as those we were hunting.

Okay, this didn't look good. It was obviously a trap.

With the pommel of my sword, I smashed the head of the closest gargoyle. The blow pulverized it in a cloud of dust. I grinned. These things weren't so tough. There was, however, nothing inside of it, and I received no message confirming my kill. That could only mean that some of them were regular statues.

[Rule violation detected]

"What the hell does that mean?" Hugo asked.

[This floor preserves the Gargoyle Stone Army. As a guest on this floor, you will respect its preservation. Failure to do so will have your visitation privileges permanently revoked.]

"I don't like the sound of that," he said.

"Most of them are normal statues. The real gargoyles are hiding among them. We can't just smash our way through or the Tower will kick us out and we'll lose the only tangible clue we have. I hate to say it, but we've got to play their game."

The space between the rows was too narrow for all of us to stick together, so we split up. Hugo and Archer went one way, and I went the other.

None of the statues moved and while they may have all looked the same, they wouldn't be able to hide the device that they were holding.

Eventually, I found a statue clutching the gold cube. The creature had turned itself to stone with its hands wrapped around the device. I tried to pry it loose, but it wouldn't budge.

"Hey, Hugo, it's over here."

I heard a yelp and another crash. I ran over and saw Archer grappling with a gargoyle of the same height. She managed to wriggle loose and fire two arrows at it. The gargoyle turned itself back to stone, and the arrows bounced off the statue.

The gargoyle statue wasn't one of the ones we had seen above. There were more gargoyles in here—much more than the ones we'd chased.

I directed Hugo over to the one holding the device and indicated that we should switch to using companion chat.

Hugo: What do we do?

Lucas: We have to find a way to coax it out. I think if we kill it when it's not a statue, then the penalty doesn't activate.

Hugo: Sounds good.

"Okay, I guess we should split up and keep searching," I said loudly.

"Yes, that is a wise plan," Hugo said unconvincingly.

We turned our backs and moved away. The gargoyle didn't respond, so we were forced to continue our bluff, walking down the rows of statues. I had my sword and knife ready in case another statue sprang to life.

As I passed one on my right, the gray stone rippled. I struck my knife into its belly just as it turned to flesh.

DING! **You have slain [A Needlepoint Gargoyle (common)] Level 96 – Experience Points and Currency Acquired.**

Lucas: Got one.

Hugo: How?! These things are impossible.

Lucas: You gotta hit them as soon as they start to change.

I circled back toward the one holding the cube. Out of the corner of my eye, I saw a gargoyle take two arrows in the chest.

Hugo: Got one! Hey, this isn't so bad.

Soon after he'd said it, three gargoyles attacked me at once. I caught two, lopping off a hand from the first one and the arm of another. The third gargoyle raked its claws across my side and danced away before I could touch it. All three then turned back to stone.

The injury hurt and bled a lot. I almost reached for the gargoyle blood on the floor to help me heal, but then I had a better idea.

I moved down one row and then another. A couple more gargoyles tried to attack me. One took a swipe at my head. But I was able to duck and cast a small Air Slash with my knife. A crescent arc of power blasted out of it and obliterated the creature before it could retreat back to stone. The other gargoyle scratched my arm and got away.

More of my blood dripped onto the floor, but I kept going up and down the rows until I met back up with Hugo at the golden cube statue.

"I got two more!" he said.

"That's great."

"Yeah, I'm feeling a little worn out though. Archer is hanging by a thread."

"Awesome. Now I need you to go back out there and be bait."

"You're not even listening to me, are you?"

"Hugo, I've lost a lot of blood. I can barely stay upright and I'm fighting a serious dizzy spell. Just go out there and give it your best."

"I'll give you my best," he muttered. He stomped one foot on Archer's shoulder. "Go on, mush."

Archer complied and walked down the rows with her bow out, and an arrow nocked. That was fine. We needed to sell this.

From the very back, I could see the entire room.

I watched, and I waited.

A gargoyle tried to attack Archer from behind. But my blood was at its feet. The blood became a weapon, and I drove a spike through the gargoyle's heart. It didn't even see it coming, but the other creatures noticed. The gargoyles tried to use their numbers against us. Four attacked Archer at once... and four died. Now that I'd soaked the ground in my blood, nowhere was safe for them.

Archer and Hugo continued, and I killed another two as they completed a circuit.

"Do you think that's all of them?" Hugo huffed. He was barely staying conscious himself. He needed a break soon, but still had one left to deal with. I pointed to the statue, still stubbornly holding the device.

Hugo groaned. "I can't keep this up much longer. Maybe we should just carry it outside?"

I opened my mouth to argue and then stopped. The rule in this place was about breaking the statues. It didn't say anything about taking one out of there.

I could've slapped my forehead. "I'm an idiot," I said.

"Now, now, that's just the blood loss talking. So how do we do this?"

In the end, I found some rope in my inventory. I couldn't remember where I'd gotten it, but I used it to tie up the statue as best as I could. Archer then picked it up and carried it while we followed close behind with our weapons ready.

It remained stone as we climbed the steps. It never once tried to attack us. Only when we brought it back out into the light did it change back. He used long needles that slipped out of each forearm to stab Archer. Fortunately, he had to drop the cube to do so.

My eyes widened at the falling cube. I dove for it, but a ghostly green hand caught it instead. Archer killed the last gargoyle and then turned to mist.

"Good catch," I said, relieved that his new Spectral Touch ability was proving itself useful.

He handed the device back to me. "At least we're learning from our mistakes."

CHAPTER 15
A SMALL KINDNESS

We RETURNED to the inventor's shop. When we got there, I half expected to have to pound on his door again to get his attention. But to my surprise, he was waiting for us by the peephole. Perhaps he recognized the value of the device.

He opened the door and bid us to enter. "Quickly now," his hand gestured. The rest of him was shrouded in shadow.

That was odd. A shop that was dark and closed during the day. It made me wonder if he was sleeping here or if he was closing the place down.

Lucas: Hugo, pretend to be a regular bird.

Hugo: You mean fly frantically around the room and crap on everything?

Lucas: It's just a precaution.

Hugo: Fine.

I could hear the sigh in his voice. He didn't enjoy acting like an ordinary bird. It was unnatural for him now. He wanted to talk and interact with people. Eat, drink, and live life in a way he never could have before. But there was power in being underestimated. If Hugo had any pressing questions, he could use the companion chat to ask me.

We stepped inside the store, and the shopkeeper immediately closed and bolted the door shut.

"Sorry for the lack of light," he said. "If I keep the shop dark, fewer people try to bother me."

"Sure, who needs customers at a time like this?"

"Actually, I'm just wrapping up with one. Why don't you follow me into the back?"

He started moving before I could answer. So I followed him to the back office, which was surprisingly lit by candles. For someone who worked on a power grid for a whole building, it was a surprisingly low-tech option.

I commented on it and he told me that candles were just cheaper.

In the light of his office workshop, the inventor cast a far less ominous figure. A middle-aged, bearded man with rosy cheeks and kind eyes. He went over to put a comforting hand on the shoulder of his customer. A human boy no older than ten who sat fidgeting on a stool. "Bart, I've been here too long. I should go back," he said.

"You will soon. Just one more moment."

The boy looked up and finally noticed us. He grinned widely at Hugo. "I like your bird."

Hugo cawed once as a thank you, and the boy's eyes lit up. "He can understand me!"

"He's a smart bird," I said.

Hugo cawed again in agreement.

Bart returned with a small wooden crate.

"Here is the water purifier your mother asked for," he said as he handed it over to the boy.

The boy suddenly became serious as he looked through the crate and then frowned. "What's this?" He held up a small metal rod with a ball stuck to the end of it.

Bart smiled. "That's for you. The ball is made of a special metal that bounces and the rod there can be magnetically used to recall the ball."

The boy stared at the toy in wonder and then rushed forward to give the inventor a hug. Bart lowered his voice and said, "Though let's keep this between us. There's no reason your parents need to know."

He nodded vigorously. "This is great! Thank you!" He rushed out the backdoor with the crate and toy under his arm.

Bart was pleased with himself, but I was curious to learn more about the city and why some people might need things like a water purifier.

"What was that about?" I asked.

Bart's smile faded. "Not everyone has the money or the connections to import clean water through the System. The water in some parts of the city is contaminated, so I've been doing what I can to help. The toy is just a small kindness. The reason I told the boy not to tell his parents about the toy is because they'd end up selling it. Though if things get bad enough, the boy will likely sell it himself. He's a good kid. I told him that he should do whatever it takes to survive, except join the church."

Hugo: See, I'm not the only one who didn't like those guys.

Lucas: I don't like them either. I just wanted to get rid of them as fast as possible.

Hugo: You gave them that apple of yours!

Lucas: I can grow more of them. It wasn't a big deal.

"Yeah, I had a run in with them myself," I said. "A strange bunch."

"They're more than strange. Things are bad in the city and they've taken advantage of the situation. It's split the human community of the city in half. One part has joined the church just to support themselves while the other has been pushed to work with the orcs." His face twisted at that last part.

"So you're on the orc side?"

"Unfortunately. But you didn't come here to talk politics. Put the device on the table next to the light. I promise no enterprising little monster will steal it this time," he joked.

I took the cube out and put it down. Bart pulled out a magnifying glass to study it in detail. He murmured to himself as he studied it.

Hugo: What's he saying?

Lucas: I don't know. I think it's just part of his process.

After a few minutes of silence, I prodded him with a question. "Have you ever seen something like it before?"

Bart shook his head. "It's interesting, though," he muttered. The inventor pulled out another smaller rod. He pressed it against one corner of the cube. There was a ping as the bolt flew to the rod. He magnetically removed bolts from each corner and one of the cube's panels slid open. Inside the device were wires and gears. Some symbols had been carved into the gears to enchant them, but I'd never seen anything like it before.

Hugo: No wonder those things are so fragile, with so many delicate pieces and wires packed together.

I grunted in agreement.

"Yes, I see now," Bart said. "This device emits a pulse that attacks spiritual energy. But the interesting thing is that whatever residual energy is left gets absorbed back into the cube." He put the panel back on and screwed the bolts back in. "What you have here is the equivalent of a spiritual hand grenade."

He casually tossed it to me and I half panicked as I caught it. "Not deadly to us, though," he added. "To use it, merely press the circular pattern on the side there."

Hugo: So it is some sort of ghost hunting device?

I repeated the question to Bart.

"You could use it that way. I haven't heard of there being any ghosts around, but now that you Tower Climbers have joined us, I suppose anything is possible."

Hugo: I almost feel like apologizing to the guy for our presence here.

"What about the murders that have been happening?" I asked. "Could the device be involved in them?"

Bart grimaced. "You should be careful how you talk about that. A lot of folks round here still call them disappearances because their bodies haven't been found. They're still clinging to the faint hope that they'll return. As for whether this device was involved? It's hard to say. Once somebody is dead, you could use this device on them to harness their spiritual energy. But these cubes are small. I doubt they can handle more than one use without burning out."

I put it back in my inventory.

"Any ideas on who could have made it or who we could talk to?"

Bart gave an apologetic shrug. "Magic isn't really my area and the other factions are pretty tightlipped about it. I doubt you'd get any orc or goblin in the know to divulge their ancient family secrets. Your best bet, unfortunately, is the church. Some of the clergy practice magic, but they'd probably charge a steep price for information."

Hugo: Yes, let's go knock the answers out of some creepy priests!

"There have also been reports of magic being sighted in the contested zone," Bart continued. "It's where most of the city's monsters spawn, so I'm sure there's a Tower Climber or two there that's using magic. You might have some luck there. Perhaps one of them made the device?"

"I'll be sure to check them out," I said.

I thanked him for his time and we left through the front door.

Once we were a block away, Hugo asked, "So what do you think?"

We had two avenues to investigate. The contested zone and the church. Evening was fast approaching, and I didn't feel like bribing the church again for information.

"I think we should wait till nightfall and see what we can learn about this church without them seeing us."

"Aww yes, reconnaissance time!"

I was glad that we were on the same page. We'd find a good rooftop to stake out our position and watch the church for a few hours. If possible, we'd also try to find a way to get inside. After that we'd move to the contested zone and look for another Climber.

Things felt like they were moving in a positive direction for us. I should've known it would bring trouble.

Suddenly, I gasped and clutched my chest. A sharp pain gripped my heart. It felt like a needle was stabbing me over and over again.

"What is it?!" Hugo cried. He looked around for a threat but couldn't see one. I knew where it was coming from, but it wasn't safe to deal with it on the street.

I gritted my teeth and took off running.

"We have to get to the apartment now!" I wheezed.

CHAPTER 16
REGRETFUL GIFTS AND PRESENTS FROM THE MAILMAN

HUGO PEPPERED ME WITH QUESTIONS, but I said nothing and kept running. I couldn't waste the energy to speak or to type messages in chat. The pain was getting worse. It felt like I was dying. My sole focus was getting back to the apartment. Only then could I make the pain stop.

Halfway there and I stumbled for the first time. Due to my dexterity level, it had been a while since I'd misplaced my feet. It confused me, but I couldn't dwell on it. I had to keep moving. My legs were feeling sore too. What was happening to me?

When we reached the elevator, I lurched inside. My skin was pale and a cold sweat enveloped me. I could barely stay upright. As the doors closed, I felt another shooting spike of pain. I gasped and grabbed the elevator railing for support.

"Lucas, what is it?" Hugo asked.

"Something's... wrong... with... domain."

That was why I had to get to the apartment. After that sneak attack by the gargoyles, I couldn't afford to disappear and leave Hugo alone. I just knew something bad would happen if we weren't in the safety of the apartment.

The doors opened, and I sprang out of the elevator and into my living room, leaving Hugo behind. I activated Crimson Domain. Blood pooled around my feet. I was quickly swept up into the darkness.

In this place, I could heal myself with only a thought. The pain was quickly reduced and receded into a minor ache, but did not disappear altogether. That was when I noticed the source of the problem. There was something wrong with my tree.

The Blood Orchard tree was dying.

Its leaves had turned brown and rustled like the entire tree was being pulled by an invisible force. At the base of the trunk, a black, oily substance was leaking out of it. It smelled like burning rubber.

The tree was dying and because it was inextricably linked to this domain, which was linked to me, I too was dying.

Healing myself had only slowed the problem down. It didn't eliminate it. I tried to heal the tree. Its roots were connected to the blood, so I commanded it to drink and heal itself.

The tree juddered, and the leaves went from brown to black. The more blood it took, the worse it appeared.

What could've caused this?

I tried to contact Roan for advice and only got the same automated message that he was busy. I had to solve this on my own. If this was a magic problem, then maybe enhancing my perception would work.

I used Magical Awareness. My domain looked exactly the same, except for one thing. A golden thread had been stabbed into the heart of the tree. I tried to follow where it went, but it disappeared up into the darkness.

The thread was pulled by an unseen force, shaking the tree again.

I didn't know what had caused this to happen, but I had to make it stop. I grabbed hold of the thread and suddenly my vision changed. Mentally, I was no longer in my domain. I was in an underground room made of stone. The Scarlet Apple was sitting on the floor surrounded by esoteric symbols. Candles were arranged around the edges. I could hear chanting in the background, but I could not see anyone.

I let go of the thread and I was transported back to my domain.

It was the priests. They were using the Apple I'd given them as a conduit to siphon off power from me. I guessed Bart's description of them having magic users was underselling it a bit.

Once again, I grabbed the thread and returned to the scene of the Apple. They may have found a way to steal power and hurt me, but they neglected one thing. Everything in my domain is connected to me, including the golden thread.

With the smallest intention of will, I severed the thread. My vision of the Apple began collapsing. I saw the Apple blacken as it withered and died before I returned to my domain. My pain was now completely gone. And, I'd learned something important. The Scarlet Apples derive their power from their connection to *my* domain. Those priests hadn't created the golden thread. That had existed since I'd plucked the Apple from the tree. They'd merely discovered its existence and found a way to exploit it.

I guessed my chances of growing and selling the Apples were nil.

The Blood Orchard tree was now free from corruption, so I commanded it to drink deeply. Like myself, it healed remarkably fast. The black ooze drained away and its leaves returned to a vibrant green.

I too felt fully restored and returned to the apartment, ready to tell Hugo what an idiot I'd been. I found him perched on top of Misty, who appeared to be offline or sleeping or whatever it was that sentient washing machines did when not in a cycle.

"I'm sorry for worrying you."

"That's okay. We can talk about it later." He shifted a little and glanced away. "There's—"

"You were right not to trust the priests," I blurted out. "They were working some kind of ritual with the Apple to steal power from me."

"Lucas, enough!"

I was taken aback by his tone. "What? I'm trying to explain."

"We have company!" he yelled, looking behind me.

I stopped and turned around, expecting to see Roan. Instead, it was the goat man from earlier, sitting in my chair. He looked annoyed.

"How did you get in here?"

He stood and walked over to me. "You've got mail," he said, handing me a letter.

Frowning, I took it. "That doesn't answer my question. Who are you and how did you get in here?"

He sighed. "My name is Flit. After party chat was removed, the new ruler of the Tower wanted a way for others to communicate across distances. Thus, he created this position and hired me. I am a Postman. You need only call my name and I'll come to take whatever mail you want delivered. Though this only applies to letters. So if you were thinking of using me to mail a bomb to your enemies, then think again."

"But how did you get in here?"

He cocked his head to the side. "Weren't you listening? I'm the Postman. I go wherever I'm requested. Usually there isn't anywhere that's off limits to me, except for you just now. This is the first time I've been forced to wait for someone. I actually appreciate it. This is my first real break in a while. I just wish it had lasted longer."

"What was that with you and Enzo yelling before?" Hugo asked.

"That was a private matter. All I'll say is that he has been abusing my services and my immunity."

"Immunity?"

"Yes, as the Postman, I am untouchable while carrying out my duties. An impenetrable force field forms around me and pushes those aside who get in my way. I warned him that if he keeps it up, every person in his employ or sphere of influence will start experiencing massive delays." He grinned. "That quickly shut him up."

"Wait, so you handle mail for the entire city by yourself?"

He shrugged. "It's not as bad as it sounds. Only Tower Climbers can use my services for free. Other residents have to pay. This cuts down the number of users since they could just walk to whoever it is they want to talk to."

"Still though, that seems tough."

He smiled. "Well, I have my shortcuts and I move pretty fast."

A door appeared on my apartment wall and opened to reveal the market district of the Strand. The Postman waved goodbye and bolted through it at superhuman speed. The door closed and vanished.

"I guess we know how he got in here," I said.

After I recounted to Hugo what had happened, he told me about a new ability he'd gained from spending unused stat points received from fighting the gargoyles. He sounded particularly proud, so I brought up my menu to see what it was.

DING! You have gained [Howling Wind Burst (uncommon)] – This attack generates a focused burst of air with a flap of your wings. It can topple foes and knock stouter ones off balance.

It sounded a little weak to me, but it was something that would let Hugo pitch in directly with fights. He seemed happy with it, so I kept my thoughts to myself.

I threw my own points into Dexterity and Vitality but didn't get another ability this time. Perhaps it'll happen when I next level up.

I thought it was odd that Misty still hadn't said anything or woken up. I pushed a couple of buttons and tapped the screen, but nothing happened.

"I think she's just sleeping," Hugo said.

Perhaps it was for the best. It would give us a chance to read the letter in private. I scanned the letter and my eyes widened when I saw that it was from Daisy.

"Hugo, take a look at this!"

He squinted at the paper and then grumbled. "That's too many words. Just read it to me."

"Wait, you can't read?"

"I can read! But mostly signs or the wrappers of my favorite half discarded snacks. Sometimes I think you forget that I grew up on the streets. I didn't get no fancy book learning school education."

I typed the letter out to Hugo in chat.

Lucas: Dear Lucas and Hugo, apologies for not getting in contact sooner. I am in the Strand and require your assistance. My quest involves investigating a series of grave robbings at the cemetery in the human district. Due to focusing on what we discussed earlier, I haven't had time to work on my quest. I'm asking if you'd be willing to investigate on my behalf and then we can meet up to update one another on our findings. Progress is going well on my end. Signed Daisy.

Hugo: So we work on her quest while she...

Lucas: Yes, that sounds good.

Daisy had promised to free us of our bond to Roan, and while he had yet to ask anything of us, we both knew that day was coming. It was better to be free from any god's control before that day came. Luckily for us, the graveyard happened to be right next to the church. The one that had just tried to kill me. Two birds with one stone.

CHAPTER 17
SPIRIT QUEST

THE HUMAN DISTRICT of the Strand became a different animal at night. One that anxiously waited.

I could feel it in the barricaded homes that we passed. In the tense silences echoing down every barren street. The people were scared. Afraid that they or their loved ones would be taken. Afraid of the dangerous monsters that would appear to test Tower Climbers.

The atmosphere of fear mingled with a cold fog that reduced our sight. It was unnerving. I'd like to say it was because the fear in the place was infectious, but that would be a lie. At night, the city felt haunted, and I couldn't blame those who chose to hide.

But I did question their judgment in coming here in the first place. It was bizarre that people would choose to live in a place like this.

Luckily, their fear was our gain, since it made sneaking around easier. Still, I took precautions. I kept to the alleyways and side streets with my cloak wrapped around me. It broke up my silhouette and to anyone who saw me in the moonlight, I'd look like a passing shadow.

Hugo remained on my shoulder, but had one of his spirit crows watching for threats from above. There would be no more surprise gargoyle attacks this time.

The cemetery that Daisy had wanted us to investigate was close to the church that had tried to kill me. I'd wanted to go there first, but Hugo dissuaded me when we saw the state of their security.

"They've got armed guards patrolling inside the perimeter and the church itself is giving off weird energy. I don't even feel comfortable flying one of my birds over it. It would be detected for sure. The only way we get inside there tonight is if we go in with blades blazing. If we did that though, we'd lose our chance to investigate the grave robbing."

"It's guns blazing. Blades don't blaze." I said, then sighed. "But I take your point. A full-on assault would be too noisy and scare off any would-be grave robbers. We'll take the cemetery first. Revenge will have to wait."

Like the church itself, the cemetery was locked behind an iron gate. Unlike the church, however, there were no guards and the high stone walls surrounding it weren't a challenge for me to scale.

I'd hoped to get a better view of the situation from the top of the wall, but the fog was building up. All I could see ahead of us were a series of mausoleums and narrow pathways.

I quietly slipped over the other side and dropped softly to the ground.

Hugo: This place is huge! I don't even know where to start.

Lucas: We'll have to move farther in. They wouldn't be able to get into these crypts without making a lot of noise and attracting the attention of the church.

Hugo: Unless they're in on it.

I nodded. It would certainly simplify matters if they were.

Lucas: Let's hope we're that lucky.

Hugo asked if he should fly up and scout ahead, but the fog made me wary. There was no way to know what could be hiding in it. I told him to stay close and watch my back as I crept down the path.

There were so many little paths around the mausoleums. So many directions that we could get attacked from. I drew my blades and proceeded with caution.

Hugo remained uncharacteristically quiet, as did the cemetery. If there was ever a place for a monster to pop out and attack Tower Climbers, then this was it. But nothing happened, and I was starting to wonder if we were wasting our time. Then I heard it.

Thud. Thud. Thud.

Heavy footfalls rang quietly in my ears. I'd had Heightened Awareness activated since entering and now I'd finally caught something in the distance. It sounded like a large group moving away from us.

Hugo tightened his grip on my shoulder as I broke into a jog. We had to get to this group before they disappeared.

I rounded the corner, and came to a stop. This was where the mausoleums ended and the graveyard began. In the fog, it looked like a sea of head-stones in an endless green field. Which made it easy to spot the source of the noise.

Two broad, seven-foot figures, cloaked and hooded, stood over a grave with their backs to me. They could only be orcs. But what would orcs be doing sneaking around the cemetery of the human district?

I moved closer for a better look. I must not have been too quiet, and may have startled them. As they turned their heads, I dove behind a large tombstone to hide.

Mentally, I counted to ten and then risked a quick look around the stone. The orcs now held shovels; their focus was back on the grave.

Hugo: What are they doing?

Well, it looks like we found our graverobbers.

Lucas: They're digging up a body.

Hugo: Why?

It was difficult to say at this point, but I took a guess.

Lucas: In some cultures, the family will bury their dead with items that meant a lot to the deceased, frequently the items were valuable. They could be looting the bodies for things like jewelry.

The idea struck me as strange and unlikely as soon as I'd said it. All of the orcs we'd seen looked well-connected and funded. It was difficult to imagine one of them doing this for money.

Hugo: Do you think it's related to our quest?

That was another possibility, but I wasn't ready to assume that it was. The only thing Daisy had said was that her quest involved graverobbing at the cemetery. Our quest was related to the spirit killer device, the goblins, and people disappearing. It was too early to see a connection.

The orcs dug into the gravesite with mechanical efficiency. They did not utter a word. Even their digging was quiet.

We watched as one of them struck down hard with their shovel. Wood cracked and splintered. The other bent down and they pulled a fresh body out of the broken coffin. That body was then deposited into a large sack along with the shovels.

Enzo had told us that live people were being taken, but what if that was just false hope? That in reality, there were rogue goblins and orcs killing and stealing the bodies?

For whatever they intended to do with the body, the sack indicated that it wasn't something they could do here. They needed to transport it elsewhere.

One orc held the sack and waited while the other quickly filled the hole back in to hide the disturbance. Once that was completed, they moved deeper into the graveyard.

Hugo: Where are they going?

Lucas: Maybe they're not done collecting bodies?

Following them proved difficult. The fog was thick, and I was forced to move out in the open among the gravestones.

Halfway across the cemetery, the orcs stopped and turned around. I dove behind a gravestone, praying that they didn't see us.

Hugo: Do you think we were spotted?

Lucas: I dunno. Why don't you take a look?

Hugo: What? Why me?

Lucas: Because you're smaller.

Hugo hopped off my shoulder and took a peek around the corner.

Hugo: They're gone!

Damn it. We lost them already.

I stood up in time to see a meaty gray fist come crashing down on me. I tried to sidestep it, but the edge of his fist grazed my cheek. I rocked back on my heels, stunned. Even a glancing blow packed some serious strength.

Hugo and I backed away while looking around. There was just the one orc in front of us. Had his partner left with the body, or was he lurking somewhere in the fog?

Despite being up close, his hood still concealed his face. I was amazed he could see anything with that thing over his head, let alone fight. Hugo flew up to gain some distance, but the orc didn't seem to notice. He pursued me aggressively, arms swinging wildly. There was no intelligence here. No planning or strategy. Just raw animal aggression.

I knew a direct single hit was deadly, and so I weaved and ducked under his thick fists. I didn't know where Hugo or the other orc was. There was no time for anything other than dodge, sidestep, and... there! I saw an opening and dashed under his swing. My knife slashed his side as I passed, but I felt a lot of resistance. His skin was tougher than a human's. Hell, it was tougher than most Tower Climbers. The cut ended up being too shallow to cause serious injury.

The orc swung his fist backward, and I continued my forward momentum to avoid it.

Out of the fog ahead emerged the other orc with the sack slung over his shoulder.

"Hugo! I could use some help about now!" I called out.

Hugo: Sorry. I thought I saw a third orc. I tried to follow, but couldn't find them in the fog. It might've just been a trick of the light.

A shrill whistle sounded in the distance. The orc carrying the sack stopped and stiffened, while the other ran over to join him.

Lucas: Looks like you were right about there being more of them.

For a tense moment, nobody moved. Then the orcs bent down and touched the ground. The fog obscured their hands. I couldn't make out what they were doing, but as they stood up, a green glow formed on the ground in front of them.

The orcs turned their backs and casually walked away.

"They're leaving?" the crow asked in disbelief as he landed on my shoulder.

The green light lengthened. Bony, gnarled hands stretched out, slowly grasping the air for a foothold. Out of the light emerged three floating skeletons wrapped in tattered cloaks. Their eyes glowed green, and each of them held a lantern on a chain that emitted a glow of the same color. Lots of green.

Beast Identified [Forge Wraith (Rare)] Level 142 – These spirits are the ultimate mindless hunting dogs. But what they lack in brains, they more than make up for in resistance to conventional attacks.

"Hugo, send one of your crows after the orcs before we lose them!"

He nodded. "On it."

He summoned a crow, and it took flight. One of the wraith's lanterns pulsed, and the spirit crow exploded into dust.

Hugo was displeased. "Oh, that is so unfair!"

Meanwhile, the orcs were getting away. I didn't like the idea of us splitting up, but this was our best lead yet.

"Go follow the orcs," I said. "I'll deal with the wraiths."

"But..."

"Go!"

Hugo flew off after them and disappeared into the fog.

Lucas: And don't engage. Only follow them. We need to know where they're taking the body.

Hugo: Understood.

The three wraiths spread themselves out into a semi-circle and began floating toward me. I lunged with my sword, but it just went straight through the apparition and had no effect.

Great, they're incorporeal. Maybe I can just run past them?

One flew in front of me. I swung my sword at its lantern to see if that was their weakness, but it was incorporeal too. A bony hand seized my wrist. It was like being gripped by ice! The cold paralyzed my hand and started creeping up my arm.

I resisted and tried to pull back, but I couldn't break free.

There was still orc blood on the ground nearby. It wasn't much, but I didn't see another option.

God, I hate this part.

I cut off my own hand to break free. The pain almost made me blackout, but I called the orc blood to me. The blood was potent. It shocked me back and kept me focused enough to use Cardinal Arm to close the wound.

As soon as I'd severed my hand, the wraith dropped it in disinterest. I retreated and tried to think of something else. I noticed that as they floated toward me, they would fly around the gravestones instead of through them. The description had referred to them as spirits. Maybe spiritual objects were solid to them?

I still had a working version of the spirit killer device that Enzo had given me. I took out the cube. Bart had called it a spiritual hand grenade, but when Dratch had used it, it had come out like a focused beam. Perhaps the design of this cube was different? In any case, I couldn't be sure of the range of this thing, so I had to get the wraiths closer together.

I decided to lure them away from the open graveyard, backtracking until I reached the mausoleums. There, I searched for a crypt that was the right size. It couldn't be too big or too small. A Goldilocks tomb if you will.

I found one that would serve my purpose. The doors were locked, but I delivered a swift kick and they broke open.

I backed up inside and the wraiths followed. The mausoleum featured a stone coffin in the center of the room and enough space to move around it. I headed to the back of the room and waited for them to float in. Just like with the gravestones, they couldn't phase through anything here.

As soon as they were inside, I raised up the cube and activated the device.

Nothing happened.

I frowned and tried again, but the result was the same. I checked the device over. It looked undamaged. Meanwhile, the wraiths were drawing closer. Maybe I was doing it wrong? I kept touching different parts of the cube, but nothing worked. Damn it! I hadn't set a trap for them. I'd just trapped myself!

In a last-ditch moment of frustration, I threw the cube at the nearest wraith. It passed through its body and hit the wall—exploding into many pieces. As soon as the cube broke, a familiar green glow formed around the fragments.

Oh no.

A fourth wraith was emerging from the debris.

CHAPTER 18
WHO YOU GONNA CALL?

MY OPTIONS WERE RAPIDLY SHRINKING as the wraiths closed in. I considered using Crimson Domain to escape but it would be a temporary reprieve at best. They would be waiting for me when I returned. No, I had to get out of this mausoleum for good.

None of my weapons or abilities would work on them directly, but what about the things in here? The walls in this place were solid to them. They were also moving around the stone coffin in the center of the room. If those things had a physical presence to them, then surely other things in the room must too. Right?

To my left was a simple vase containing flowers. Now, I doubted that ceramic would be their one fatal weakness, but it would serve as a test.

I snatched up the vase and hurled it at the nearest wraith. The object phased right through and smashed to pieces on the wall behind it.

So these creatures didn't consider it a part of this place. Maybe it was too recent. Some new addition that a grieving family member had put here. Or maybe it wasn't considered spiritual or holy enough. Regardless, I had run out of throwable objects in this depressingly sparse tomb.

Unable to fight them, there was only one option left, which was to run past them. There were two on one side and one on the other blocking both paths. So going through the middle and over the coffin seemed prudent. But the mausoleum wasn't that big and if one of them touched me, paralysis would start to set in. I'd have to be fast and at my most agile to make it work.

The wraiths slowly floated along either side of the coffin.

Okay, it was now or never.

I leapt up onto the stone coffin and raced along it. Hands lurched forward, grasping to yank me off. I hopped over one and went into a handstand to launch myself over the others. With much relief, I landed back at the entrance. One good thing about them holding those lanterns was that it limited them to only attacking with one hand.

Of course, I had forgotten about the fourth problem in the room. The wraith from the box I'd thrown had now fully emerged to block my path. It floated menacingly toward me, with one hand outstretched, ready to take my life.

I backed away until I felt my hands touch the stone coffin, the lid shifting slightly. It gave me an idea. I didn't know if I was strong enough to do it, but I had to try.

I grasped the lid with both hands and heaved. The heavy casing came free. My arms shook as I raised it up and swung it at the wraith. The lid slammed into the side of the creature, knocking it into the wall.

The wraith made no sound during the attack and did not appear to be injured. The other wraiths didn't seem to care either and were once again closing in on me.

I used the lid like a board to push them back, before I dropped it and rushed outside. With my sword, I made a double Air Slash attack over the mausoleum entrance. Two crescent streaks of power shot out of my sword and blasted the opening to rubble.

They were trapped inside, and though I dreaded whatever poor fellow might unearth them the next morning, I didn't have time to leave a note. I had to catch up to Hugo and the orcs. After retrieving my real hand from where I'd left it, I reattached it, and contacted Hugo for an update.

Lucas: Hugo, are you there?

Hugo: Yes, I'm still following them. They're at some wall at the back of the cemetery and... Wait, they're moving some of the stones. There's a secret entrance back here!

It was probably easier to avoid detection by coming and going that way. Who knows how many bodies they've stolen using it?

Lucas: Okay, stay with them. I managed to trap the wraiths and I'm on my way.

Hugo: Does trapping them mean...

Lucas: Yeah, I have no idea what to do if they throw more of those things at us. But we'll cross that bridge if we come to it.

I left out the part about how only cemetery items seemed to affect them. I didn't want to worry him now that we were moving away from the graveyard. On the plus side, the city streets made it a lot easier to tail someone without being seen.

Hugo gave me directions to the back of the cemetery. There, at the stone wall, was a section with a large scratch on it. I pushed the scratched area and the section moved inward like a hidden door. Someone had expertly cut out an area of the wall and reinforced it somehow. This would've taken time and tools to accomplish. It was a lot of trouble to go to for grave robbing and it made me more curious about where the orcs were headed.

I climbed through the makeshift door which led me back onto the street. Luckily, there was no one around. I put the wall back where it had been and hurried to catch up with Hugo.

Hugo: Wait, they've stopped behind a shop.

Lucas: Okay.

Hugo: They dumped the body! They threw it down a thing and now they're walking away.

I felt like saying anything else in chat would distract him. So I kept running and waited for his next response.

Hugo: Wait, they're gone too!

I doubled my speed and reached the area where he'd lost sight of them. According to the bird, they'd walked down a narrow side street and turned a corner. By the time Hugo had flown over the buildings, they'd vanished.

Hugo landed on my shoulder with a huff. "They must have ducked into one of the shops," he said.

I retraced the path he had described and studied the storefronts. All of them were dark and many of the doors contained bells to announce when a customer had entered. It was possible, but unlikely that the local cobbler was the orc's secret base of operations.

I looked around and noticed a sewer grate that was slightly askew. I pointed to it and said, "I think they went down there."

The crow frowned. "Maybe?" he offered reluctantly, still annoyed at his failure and losing them.

"It's okay. You did the right thing. They would've heard if you tried to open the grate and follow them."

I got down and put my ear to it to listen. There was nothing.

Opening it up proved equally fruitless once I poked my head down. The grate led to two sewer paths that both went to intersections.

Damn, there was no way of finding them now. They could be anywhere.

I suppressed my irritation and focused instead on the one remaining lead we had. "Show me where they dumped the body," I said. Maybe we could still salvage something from tonight.

Hugo led me around to the back gate of some courtyard that was behind a butcher's shop. The gate had been left unlocked, and the scent of blood still faintly hung in the air. It looked like an area that they used to accept deliveries.

Hugo told me that they'd dumped the body in a "thing," which turned out to be a garbage chute. I opened the chute door and immediately recoiled from the stench. A disgusting mix of death and stale blood wafted up.

Hugo flapped over to the wall to get a respectful distance away from the smell, which left me to investigate. With my hand over my nose, I peered inside. There was only darkness and I couldn't see beyond it. The chute must go down pretty far.

Which begged the question of why a butcher shop in a city of this technological era would require one. Judging from the smell, this was where the butcher threw left over carcasses and other refuse. But why would the orcs dig up a body only to throw it in the trash?

"Can you send a spirit summon down there?" I asked.

The crow shook his head. "There are markings inside the chute that are giving me bad vibes. The same as what I felt from the church."

Odd, I hadn't seen any markings. I switched to Magical Awareness and suddenly saw the sigils.

"How bad is this stuff?" I asked.

Hugo thought for a moment. "I think it's meant to repel spirits. We should be fine."

"*Should* be? Well, that's comforting."

I stared at the chute, unwilling to move.

"You know what this means, right?" he asked.

I made a face. "I do. Have I mentioned how much I hate Tower Climbing?"

"Not specifically, but I think the general sentiment has been expressed."

I climbed into the chute feet first and told Hugo to follow behind me. I held onto the ledge and tried to psych myself up.

"What are you waiting for?" he asked.

"Oh God, the smell is even worse once you're inside it," I groaned.

Hugo summoned his spectral hand and gave me a shove.

I flew down the chute, sliding faster and faster. It was far deeper than expected. I should've been worried, but all I could think about was why would someone go to this much trouble for refuse?

Eventually, I reached the bottom and landed in an enormous stone room. It wasn't a dump at all. The room had high ceilings and carved pillars against one of the walls. A doorway thirty feet high led to darkness at the far end of the room. The city wasn't supposed to be that old, but this looked like an ancient chamber buried under its foundations. Perhaps this wasn't something that was built, but something the grave robbers had unearthed.

The body the orcs had thrown down here lay in the sack just a few feet away. Beyond it were many other bodies, all human, and in various states of decay. Ick! There must have been close to fifty of them all scattered around the room. And given where the chute came out, someone else would've had to have come down here to move the bodies around.

Hugo gracefully landed on my shoulder. "Huh, the smell isn't so bad down here."

Sensing more magic was afoot, I used my other sight. Fiery symbols blazed across the walls and ceiling of the chamber. This whole space was enchanted and something told me it did more than eliminate the place's odor.

I opened the sack. Inside was the body of a recently deceased young woman and the shovels they'd used to dig her up. There was nothing special about the body that Hugo or I could discern. We checked a few of the other bodies, but none of them had any distinguishing features either. They were men and women of various ages and sizes. Even their clothing suggested that their level of wealth varied at their time of death.

"Maybe whoever's doing this is stealing the bodies for an undead army?" Hugo suggested.

"Or it's for some kind of experiment. Remember that Enzo said that live people were disappearing. You wouldn't go to all that trouble when there's an unguarded graveyard filled with bodies."

"It could be two separate crimes. There are supposed to be other Tower Climbers here working on other quests."

That was a good point.

"Let's keep going and see what else is down here," I said, indicating we should go through that giant doorway.

I only made it a couple of steps before a phone started ringing. The sound was muffled slightly. I looked around in confusion until discovering the source. The ringing was coming from inside the young deceased woman's stomach.

While I stared, Hugo was trying to get my attention. "Er, Lucas?"

"What is it?"

I followed his gaze and realized why he was concerned. All of the other dead bodies were stirring.

CHAPTER 19
CLEANING HOUSE

ONE BY ONE, the corpses came to life and stood up. Their eyes dead and lifeless. Their limbs and faces lined with thin blue veins. Something was pumping inside of them and it wasn't blood.

The dead girl by our feet continued ringing. The sound was coming from inside her stomach, but we didn't have time to investigate it. I told Hugo to keep an eye on her in case she moved, and turned my attention to the crowd of zombies. Their movements were slow and stiff, but I wasn't waiting for them to attack first.

I activated two Hemorrhage Gates. Or at least I tried to, but the connection wouldn't form. Hugo was having similar problems with his spirits.

"I can't summon anything!" he cried.

I glanced at the blazing magical symbols on the walls and grimaced. "It's got to be the room's ward enchantment. It's suppressing some of our powers."

I did not feel myself become weaker when I entered the room. In fact, I felt as strong as ever, so perhaps it only affected certain abilities. I had to know what other limitations this place was imposing on us.

I drew my blades and tried an Air Slash attack, which didn't work either.

"We can only use physical attacks," I said.

I was undaunted. This wouldn't be the first time I'd taken on a horde of zombies like this.

"Oh well, that's great for some of us!" he snapped.

The Air Slash attacks were pure magic once they left my blades, but I wondered if magical abilities that generated a physical response were exempt from the wards.

"Try that wind attack of yours."

He said nothing and took off into the air. Part of me suspected that he might have forgotten about the ability, but I kept my mouth shut and watched. Hugo hovered above the zombies, flapping his wings. The flaps got faster and faster until a cone of wind blasted out of him and knocked five zombies to the ground.

"Damn, that felt really good," he said.

I grinned. "See, we can take them."

I cut the head off the one closest to me. Its body remained standing which was slightly unnerving. Then I received a message telling me what it was.

Beast Identified [Cadaver Specimen 082 (Common)] Level 105 – Intruders have been detected and the security system has been activated. All specimens will engage the security protocol.

Okay, that level was a little higher than what I was hoping for such a large crowd, but it was doable. The description accompanying it gave me pause though. Was their coming alive the security protocol?

DING! You have slain [Cadaver Specimen 082 (Common)] Level 105 – Experience Points and Currency Acquired.

That was strange. The headless cadaver was still standing and its hands were twitching. I checked my stats. Killing the cadaver specimen had earned me a single experience point and one gold coin. Far too low a sum for a creature of that level. Something wasn't right here.

The cadavers Hugo had knocked over calmly got back on their feet. There was no hint of aggression in them from being attacked. They merely returned to standing in their original positions.

I backed away from them and warned Hugo not to attack again.

Then, in perfect synchronicity, they all turned to face the doorway.

"What's happening?" Hugo asked.

I didn't know. I could only stare as the cadavers raised their hands and shoved them into their chests. My stomach twisted as I heard flesh being torn. They dug inside themselves and each of them ripped out a palm-sized mechanical device. Small torn tubes dangled from each unit, leaking blue liquid. It looked like a replacement for their hearts.

One by one, they crushed them. A puff of blue smoke was expelled and faded into the air. Then the cadavers collapsed.

Hugo flew over to check some of the bodies and I did the same, looking for clues. "They came back to life just to destroy their mechanical hearts?" he asked.

The ringing in the dead girl stopped, and we froze.

A few tense seconds followed. Then a guttural roar emanated from the darkness beyond the doorway.

"I'm guessing *that's* the security protocol," I said.

The creature stomped into the room. My first thought was that it was an orc on steroids. A giant, muscular brute standing twenty feet tall. It was shirtless and wore nothing but torn shorts and a set of manacles with broken chains rattling as it stepped forward. Cadavers on the floor in front of it were stepped on and squashed into a pulpy mess.

Beast Identified [A Scathing Abomination (Rare)] Level 165 – Another failed experiment, given new purpose as a last resort security system. It will purge all living things within the containment room. A despised creature created from hatred, forbidden spells, and rare chemical compounds. Like its creator, it is infused with rage and will blindly attack any living being on sight.

A glowing barrier formed over the doorway behind it, trapping us inside.

The Abomination had the same blue veins running down its body. This was another corpse that had been brought back to life, only it had been given a much bigger dosage than whatever the cadavers had been given.

"What's the plan?" Hugo asked.

"The cadavers ripped something out of their chests that reanimated them. I'm willing to bet this big guy has something similar in his chest."

"So I distract him while you go for the heart?"

The Abomination fixed its gaze on us and snarled.

"Sure, let's go with that," I said.

Hugo flew left and I went right.

The Abomination picked up a corpse in each hand. He tossed the first one at Hugo, who was mid-flight and didn't have time to dodge it. The bird's bubble shield formed just before he was hit. The dead body slammed into the shield and knocked Hugo back across the room.

I kept running. A body was thrown my way. I jumped over it and sprinted toward the hulking figure. It snorted and snarled, but I wasn't intimidated. Its movements appeared slow, likely weighed down by unnatural bulk. I can take him.

Of course, having fought a regular orc, I knew it wasn't going to be easy. Their skin was tougher than almost anything I'd previously come across, and the Abomination looked tougher still.

I reached for the Blade Weaver ability and felt the enchantment coat my sword and knife with magic that would enhance their cutting power. It took a decent chunk of my energy to use this ability. Had my fight with the orcs in the graveyard dragged out any longer, I would've almost certainly been forced to use it. Now with the Abomination I wasn't taking any chances.

The creature tried to grab me as I got close, its chain swinging in its wake. I jumped up, and plunged my sword down into its chest. I felt the blade sink a couple of inches deep and then stop.

The beast backhanded me, and I flew back across the room. Somewhere along the way, my knife had slipped out of my hand, and I landed hard. Groaning, I spat out blood and laid there trying to collect myself. Being punched by his fist was like being hit by a truck. A big one. The pain was overwhelming. In that moment I didn't want to get up but I had to.

"Lucas, don't move!" Hugo yelled.

Trusting him, I stayed prone on the floor. There was a roar of frustration far behind me. I couldn't see what was happening, but it appeared that the Abomination couldn't see me either. If it had poor eyesight, then I must have blended right in with the other dead bodies.

"Ah!" Hugo squawked.

I heard a sound that could only be described as meat exploding and risked a look behind me.

The creature was now fixated on Hugo and had thrown another body at him. This time, Hugo had used his Wind Burst to push himself out of the way, leaving another body to explode against the wall.

The crow's breathing was getting heavy. He wouldn't be able to keep this up forever.

The Abomination still had my sword sticking out of its chest, but there was no blood. In fact, it didn't seem bothered at all that it was there. It quickly gave up on throwing things and made a blind charge at Hugo with its hands outstretched.

The crow waited until the last second before wind dashing away. The Abomination crashed into the wall, causing it to crack. For a moment, I thought it might break the enchantment and give us more of our powers back, or at least allow us out of this room. But sadly, the enchantment held.

The Abomination grunted and turned, scanning the room until our eyes locked.

I moved first despite the pain, running to the other side of the room. The beast chased after me, stepping on and crushing bodies to a pulp, left and right.

The only card I had left to play was Crimson Domain, providing it wasn't blocked by the wards. I started to activate it. I could feel it building. Finally, some good news. I just needed the beast to get closer so that I could trap it inside.

As the blood pooled at my feet, the creature came to a halting stop. It sniffed the air and turned away from me to focus on Hugo.

I canceled the ability, and the beast turned sharply back to me.

It wasn't out of intelligence. The reanimated creature was running on instinct and whatever blue substance was pumping through its veins. Somehow that instinct had alerted it to my trap, and it knew enough to stay away.

That was good. It saw Crimson Domain as a threat. I just had to get closer and keep it close for the trap to work.

Hugo learned of my plan and got into position. I kept my hands empty and backed myself into a corner until the beast was right in front of me.

"Hugo, now!" I cried.

He flew in from behind, my knife in his beak, and scratched at the creature's head with his talons. It did no damage, but its purpose as a distraction worked flawlessly.

The Abomination reached up to try and swat Hugo away. His reactions were slow, and while his hands were raised, I dashed forward to grab the chains hanging from its wrists. Before it realized what was happening, I ran around it and pulled the chains tight.

On cue, Hugo dropped the knife to me. I caught it, and with Blade Weaver, I nailed the chain to the floor. A second knife was quickly pulled from my inventory. It was nothing special. Just a cheap weapon I'd accidentally picked up while collecting a body. I just had to hope it would hold.

I put the point of the blade through the second chain and stabbed down into the stone. The knife sank in, locking the chain to the ground.

The whole process took less than two seconds and by the time the Abomination realized it had been chained down again, it was too late.

The creature roared and struggled against its bonds.

"You think those chains will hold?" Hugo asked.

"I think—"

Both knives snapped in two. The Blade Weaver enchantment had collapsed shortly after I'd let go of the blades.

The Abomination swung the chains around at me like a nunchucks. I ducked under the first one, but the second one caught my lower legs and knocked me down. As soon as I hit the floor, a giant fist came crashing down. I quickly rolled away and felt the ground tremble as its fist smashed into where I'd just been.

"Hugo, stay back!" I warned.

I tried to get up, but my legs screamed at me to stop. The chain attack must have done more damage than I thought. Its hand was still next to me. I grabbed onto the creature's thick arm as it lifted it up.

"What are you doing?" Hugo cried.

Something dumb. But I had to stay close. Had to keep ahold of him.

It tried to shake me loose from its arm. When that didn't work, it bashed me into the wall. I let out a choked gasp as all the air rushed out of me. The pain was excruciating, but not as much as when it cracked me a second time. Still, I held on.

Suddenly, the Abomination rushed away to the other end of the room while I clung on. It hoped to get away, but it was too late. Blood pooled around our feet and darkness fell as I dragged the beast into my domain.

My body restored itself first to peak health, and then I leapt away from the creature. There was no reason to risk injury now by staying close. I landed fifty feet away and summoned several blood spikes.

They shot up from the ground to attack, but none could pierce its thick skin. It bellowed another challenge and charged at me.

I held my ground and raised my hand. I formed chains of blood this time. They rose from the floor and wrapped themselves around its arms and legs before going taut. Between its running momentum and the chains, the creature crashed to its knees. I cast another chain that wrapped around its throat and squeezed. If I couldn't cut it, then maybe suffocation would work.

Its muscles tensed as it bucked against the chains. One of them broke. I raised both hands, summoning more chains, and redoubled my focus to keep him contained. Even in my domain, I was struggling to hold him down.

That was when I saw it. Symbols faintly burning in the air behind him. Their image growing clearer. The wards on the chamber walls were breaking through. Cracks in the air appeared. My domain was breaking down.

The Abomination struggled again and another chain broke.

It would get free soon. I had to do something before then. I glanced at the Blood Orchard tree, but there was no fruit there yet. The only other weapon I had was my sword, which was still lodged in its chest.

Another chain broke, and then another. It snarled at me... and I snarled back.

I ran madly toward it, and leaped up high while rotating my body to deliver a spinning kick onto the pommel of my sword. The force drove the blade deeper into its heart. The beast's blue eyes flashed brighter and then went dead.

DING! You have slain [A Scathing Abomination (Rare)] Level 165 – Experience Points and Currency Acquired.

DING! Class: [Blood Reaver] has reached level 119 – Experience Acquired.

Woah, I'd gained nine levels for killing that thing. I wanted to divvy up the points, but I had to get back to Hugo first and let him know that I was okay.

I returned to the chamber and wrenched my sword free. I noticed that the wards on the chamber wall were no longer glowing and the barrier blocking our exit was now gone.

"We should leave," I told Hugo. "Whoever owns this place might've been alerted when the security system was activated."

"Shouldn't we fight them too?" he asked meekly.

I appreciated the enthusiasm, but we'd barely scraped through in this last fight and there was another concerning thought.

"We might not be ready to fight whatever was using this thing as a guard," I said, kicking the Abomination's corpse. Whoever owned this place could be worse. The time was right to regroup back at the apartment. Hugo nodded, looking relieved.

I collected the broken knives I'd lost on the off chance one of them could be repaired. The Viper Fang had seen me through a lot of battles, and I was sorry to see it go.

We were about to leave, when the female corpse from earlier started ringing again. In all the confusion, both of us had completely forgotten about it.

We looked at each other and Hugo gave me a 'go ahead' nod. I rolled my eyes. "Coward," I muttered as I went to examine the corpse.

With my sword, I cut her open to reveal a small black phone that was ringing.

Reluctantly, I picked it up and answered. "Hello?"

"Finally," said the Officiator. "I've been trying to get ahold of you for hours now."

CHAPTER 20
A PRIZE-WINNING PHONE CALL

"Which phone reached you?" the Officiator asked.

Both of us stared at the phone.

"You're supposed to be dead," I said.

There was a whirring and clicking sound on the other end of the line before answering. "Yes, the central node was terminated. You are speaking with a backup module in the catastrophic event that my original being was destroyed. Now, which phone did you receive?"

I frowned. "Uh, the one in the dead girl's stomach."

"Thank you. In my current condition, my access to the Tower is limited and so are my prediction capabilities. I seeded phones in several locations designed to go off if they came into contact with you. A phone inside the future cadaver specimen wasn't my first choice, but this information will help improve my future predictions for regaining control."

"So you're aware that Tanver Vhar and Roan have taken over the Tower?"

"I am aware of their *attempts*. Do not be fooled. The partnership between the two is on the brink of collapse and the access that Vhar has over the Tower is minimal. Destroying my central node did not instantly grant him full access. Much of the Tower's security runs passively, and he is continuing to fight with it as we speak."

I looked around, wary of other gods listening in. "Is it safe for us to be talking like this?"

"Yes, no one can see or hear us in the room."

"Is this room yours?" asked Hugo.

"It is not. I merely predicted a scenario in which you would cross paths with the creatures in the cemetery and placed a phone in this body to open up a line of communication."

"Wait, go back to before," I said. "You're saying Vhar and Roan don't have control of the Tower, but I watched him kill all those Climbers at the Golden Door with nothing but a thought?"

"Yes, I'm sure it looked that way to you and the other gods. A stunning display of power meant to cow all of you into submission and cement his new position as owner of the Tower. The truth is that after Vhar had gained unauthorized access to a small part of one of my subnets, he then spent the next several weeks decoding the Tower marks for the people there."

"Tower marks?"

"It's like a unique ID that each Climber is tagged with. It's used to track you and is only removed upon your completion of the Tower."

A companion chat message from Hugo popped up.

Hugo: Well, that's unnerving.

Lucas: Remember, the Officiator is not our friend. He wouldn't care if the Tower killed us. If he's talking to us, it's because he wants something.

"I see," I said, urging him to continue.

"What looked like a simple act of will from Vhar was actually a carefully orchestrated plan that took a lot of work and planning. As I had mentioned before, there were other Golden Doors with other Climbers competing for them. Had I brought any of those Climbers through to you, Tanver Vhar would've been unable to affect them. Frankly, I wish my original self had thought of it first."

"Is that why I couldn't attack him? Because he affected my mark?"

There was another whirring, clicking sound. "You are referring to when you struck him with your sword? No, that was due to his own innate strength as an S+ Grade being. You cannot fight against him at your current level."

"So, what are we supposed to do?" Hugo asked. "Why contact us?"

"Events are conspiring to move against Vhar and Roan. Had I not intervened with this call, you would've both been swept up in its wake. I have a gift for both of you that should help turn things in your favor. Go to the farthest corner of the room on your right. At the base will be a hollow stone with your gifts inside."

I followed his instructions, tapping against the stones until one sounded hollow. I smashed through it with my fist to reveal two small ornate wooden boxes. Inside each was a vial of purple liquid.

As I reached for one, the Officiator interrupted me. "I don't have a lot of time. Use them after our call has ended."

"Is it safe for us to stay here? What if whoever owns this place comes back?"

"I can't say too much about that. But what I will say is that this place is an outpost and the one responsible for it is far from this secret location. You are safe here."

He kept dodging the question. But I wasn't going to let him weasel out of it.

"Again, why help us?" I asked.

There was another whirring sound. Almost like it was processing a response. "You are both considered prospective champions, especially if things go your way during the tribunal. The Tower, despite all appearances, is not meant to be malicious. It is a training ground. It's not my job to ensure all the Climbers die. It is my job to mold the strongest into champions."

"You mentioned the tribunal. What is that?"

More whirring. "Ah yes, I see. I'm too early for that conversation. My current capacity is stretched thin and sometimes I lose track of time. I must go now."

The call ended abruptly, and then an automated message played. "This phone will self-destruct in five seconds." At first, I thought it was kidding, but then it kept going. "Four… three…" I hurled the phone away and braced for impact. "Zero." The phone popped out of existence like it had never been there. I guess that's a more thorough way of hiding his presence here.

"He didn't explain much at all!" Hugo grumbled.

"Only that Vhar's position isn't as strong as he pretends it is. You're right, it's not much. But it's better than nothing. Hopefully, Daisy will have better news for us when we meet up with her later."

We turned our attention to the two potions. I picked up the first one to look at its item description.

Item Identified! [Item Enhancement Potion (Rare: D-Grade)] – This potion can be poured on one item of clothing. It's an alchemical compound mixture that will fuse with the item to permanently upgrade it to D-Grade tier. Note: this potion will have no effect on broken items or items that are already at D-Grade or higher.

The note at the end of the description was disappointing. My sword was already at D-Grade and with my knife broken, I had no weapons to use this potion on. That only left my cloak and clothes, but I wasn't sure if that would be a waste of a good potion.

"Hmm, I'm not sure how helpful this one would be," I said. Hugo didn't respond, despite reading the same message as I did. I guessed the Officiator couldn't have predicted that my knife would break when he left the potions here for us.

I turned my attention to the second potion.

Item Identified! [Ability Potion (Rare: D-Grade)] – This potion, when consumed, will grant one new D-Grade tier ability based around their current Class.

"Now that's more like it," I said.

Hugo still said nothing and looked away.

"What's wrong?" I asked.

He whirled on me. "Do you see me wearing any items, or are you planning to take both potions for yourself?"

Ashamed, I set the potions back down. "You're right. I wasn't thinking. We were left with one potion each and obviously you should take the ability one."

Hugo dipped his head in acknowledgement and then ruffled his feathers. "It's this place. It prioritizes self over others. Pressures people to turn on each other."

"Yes, before people were naturally forming groups. Forming tribes to defend themselves with. It made their groups stronger, but the Tower used that to foster conflict between groups, or maybe that was just human nature. But this city feels different."

"There are other Climbers here," he said, following my line of thinking.

I nodded. "But we haven't seen a single one, which suggests either very small groups or the ones here are running solo."

"Which makes sense. How much better off would you be had you taken both potions for yourself?"

"I wasn't going to."

"I know, but hypothetically speaking."

I thought about it and he was right. Getting new abilities and new gear was thrilling. Even now when I look at the potions, there's a small, almost irresistible thrill whispering what they could offer me.

Hugo noticed my look. "See? You think many others don't feel that way?"

I shook my head and stood firm. "As far as I'm concerned, we started the Tower together and we'll finish it together. Now take your new ability and try not to rub it in my face too much."

"No promises," he grinned, before swooping down to tap the bottle. The liquid inside disappeared and a new message appeared for him.

DING! You have gained [Soul Lance Ability (Rare)] – This ability allows you to harness your soul as a weapon. A lance of power that can be used to attack the souls of others. Physical beings will have some natural defenses that weaken this ability, but spiritual creatures are pure soul and have no such benefits. Note: this ability does carry a heavy toll and should be used wisely.

Hugo and I looked at each other.

"I guess we know who's fighting the wraiths from now on," I said.

The crow hopped up and down with excitement. "This is great! Between this, my shield, and wind abilities, I can finally get in the fight directly."

"I'm happy for you. Now I just need to figure out what to use my potion on."

"Oh, that's easy. You should pour it on your boots."

"My boots?"

"Yeah. You're always using them when running or jumping. Maybe the potion would give them a double jump ability or make them extra quiet?"

"I'd probably prefer the double jump over the other, but I take your point."

I wasn't ready to go with my boots just yet though. My clothing had a self-repair function and was built for stealth. I didn't see how this potion would help unless I had multiple potions for all of my clothes. Sure, it would probably make my pants more armor resistant to attacks, but armor had never really been my thing.

No, the choice came down to my boots or my cloak. The boots were ordinary, and I'd had no problem using them when masking my presence. It felt like a gamble to use it on the boots. It was hard to guess how they'd be improved, so I took my cloak off and re-examined it.

Item Identified! [The Cloak of Umbral Frenzy (Rare: F-Grade)] – This cloak was made by the Shadow Weavers to hunt in darkness. It greatly enhances stealth against F-Grade perception when in shadow and can channel emotional anger into energy to sustain magical abilities.

I'd won the cloak as a prize for completing a challenge room. Ever since then, its stealth capability has been invaluable. It was probably the most important piece of clothing that I owned, and while I'd rarely used its frenzy ability, it was still the obvious choice for the potion.

I set the cloak on the floor and poured the item-enhancement potion over it. The liquid seeped into the material and then faded away. Upon picking it back up, I received a new message.

Item Identified! [The Lord's Umbral Shroud (Legendary: D-Grade)] – An item worthy of the Sanguine Lord. This cloak will reshape itself to a far greater degree than before. It is fire resistant and can absorb minor physical blunt and cutting damage. Stealth is enhanced to the utmost when in shadow, but be warned. The shroud is now more than just a cloak. It is a symbol of your Lordship. Do not let anyone take it from you.

That last part sounded ominous. I wasn't sure what it being a symbol meant, but the cloak felt different when I put it on. I was more intimately connected to it. It felt like an extension of myself, almost like an extra limb.

With a simple mental command, the cloak raised up behind me and held itself rigidly in the air.

"What are you going to do with that?" Hugo asked.

I grinned at the possibilities. "I can think of a few things."

We finished up by allocating our stat points. Hugo focused a lot on Intelligence while I split mine between Strength and Dexterity.

Checking over the rest of the cadavers proved fruitless, and even their destroyed mechanical hearts revealed nothing when I picked one up.

We left the chamber and entered a long stone tunnel. Farther down was the spot where the Abomination would've been chained to the wall, but besides that, the tunnel was empty. It was long though. So long that we couldn't see the end of it.

We lost track of time, but it was over an hour before the tunnel started sloping upward. The climb led us to the night sky, and we stepped outside onto the sand.

The ancient chamber had led us just outside of the city itself. No wonder whoever was using it could come and go without being seen.

"So what now?" Hugo asked.

He wanted to know where we should go next with our investigation. I clenched my fists as I remembered the spirit killer device's function betraying me in the mausoleum.

"The inventor Bart lied to us about the device he examined," I said. "He described it as a spiritual hand grenade. Probably in the hopes that I'd throw it and release the wraith that was trapped inside. I think it's time we pay the humble inventor a second visit."

CHAPTER 21
THE INVENTOR'S WORKSHOP

I SURVEYED the area outside the tunnel entrance. There were no marks in the sand other than my own and there was nothing in sight besides the city. Whoever used this place either hadn't been here for some time, or had taken the precaution of covering their tracks.

So we made our way back toward the city. Back to Bart's shop to confront him.

Hugo: Okay, I'm just gonna say it. That phone call was weird.

I turned to look at him. We'd been walking in silence for the past five minutes.

Lucas: You're just discovering this now?

Hugo: I was trying to work out how giving us those potions would help us avoid trouble with the other gods.

Lucas: And did you figure out?

He sighed.

Hugo: What do *you* think?

I shrugged and then gave it my best guess.

Lucas: I think the call itself was a part of it. He mentioned something about champions and tribunals. Yakeshi had mentioned something about holding one for Roan. So maybe the Officiator believes that we will be free of his influence before that happens.

Hugo: Maybe Daisy really has found something that can help us.

Lucas: Let's hope so.

Entering the city was much easier than last time. I guessed even goblins need to sleep. But then again, maybe they too were afraid of the threats that could be lurking at night. I kept my senses on high alert just in case.

When we reached Bart's shop, my gut told me that something was off. The feeling grew stronger the closer I got to the door. So I kept going and walked past the shop window. Strangely, a mannequin had been placed in the front window that wasn't there before. I watched it out of the corner of my eye as I walked past. The mannequin's head turned, following me with its faceless gaze.

I switched Magical Awareness on. The mannequin now had glowing orange eyes. Wherever it looked, it cast a wide orange haze that stretched out to the middle of the road. It was like a field-of-view cone.

I kept walking past the shop, to Hugo's confusion.

"What is it?"

I hurried past the shop and crossed the road. Once we were well outside of the thing's field of view, I pointed to the window. Hugo watched as the mannequin's head repositioned itself back where it was originally.

He shivered. "That's creepy. What is it?"

The bright orange glow in its eyes faded, like it was powering down, but the haze remained.

"I think it's guarding the shop. Some kind of machine maybe," I murmured.

"Aw man. I was hoping to try out the Soul Lance. Do you think robots have souls?" he asked, his voice hopeful.

"That's kind of a complicated philosophical question that I'm not equipped to answer. Let's just say the odds of having one in this place are low."

"So you're saying there's a chance?"

I knew he was excited to test his new ability, but I had to be firm with him. This thing was motion activated. It was built for a specific purpose. Giving it a soul would only complicate things.

"In this case? No, absolutely not," I said. "Using that new ability of yours takes a toll, so it's probably wise not to test it right now. But I'm sure the opportunity will arise soon."

"What about the wraiths in the cemetery? Didn't they beat you? We could go back and get 'em."

"First of all, they didn't beat me. That was a draw. Second of all, they're buried under a ton of rubble that I don't feel like digging through. Let's focus on one problem at a time."

After watching for a few minutes, we saw no movement in the shop. As an experiment, I picked up a stone and threw it into the orange haze.

The mannequin didn't react.

"It seems to have a limited cone-of-view that we must have triggered when I walked past the window," I said.

Its direction was only pointed outward toward the street, and our voices didn't seem to trigger its attention. If we could find another way inside, then perhaps we could simply avoid it altogether.

"Come on," I said. "We'll find another way in."

If Bart was this paranoid, then he would've put something at the backdoor of his workshop. But that part was windowless. It could be another mannequin or something else entirely. I decided it was safer to avoid climbing the building directly and come at it from another direction.

Hugo noticed we were walking pretty far away from the inventor's shop. "Where are we going?"

I stopped in front of a taller building. It was nothing like the tower the orcs had, but it was several stories higher than the shop and it would serve my purpose.

I climbed up to the roof and looked over the edge. Hugo realized what I was thinking. "Oh, so you finally discovered the best means of travel."

"I figured this was as good a time as any to test the Shroud."

Though now I was having second thoughts, and I found myself wishing the building was much, much taller. At this height, there wasn't a lot of room for any margin of error.

My cloak lengthened behind me, and I could feel my heart beating. I tried to get it under control, but my body wouldn't listen. A direct fall from this height was still dicey if I landed wrong and broke my neck. Even with my healing power, my body knew how dangerous this was.

I had to push those thoughts aside. *This will work*, I told myself.

"It's easy," Hugo said. "Just spread your wings, feel the air current, and then step off."

I spread the cloak out like a wingsuit behind me. There wasn't much air to feel, but that would quickly change as I started to fall. Theoretically, the cloak would help me turn that fall into a gentle glide that I would use to access the roof of the inventor's shop.

Hugo, to his credit, didn't try to push me this time. There was nothing to say or do. He waited until I suppressed the primal part of my brain that was screaming for me to reconsider.

Everything inside became quiet, and I slipped off the roof with my body straight.

Panic quickly took over. The cloak wasn't catching the air, and I began falling like a stone. There was no time to call out for help. I could only watch as the ground got closer.

A blast of air hit me from below. My stomach dropped as I suddenly shot upward.

Hugo: Don't worry. I got you.

He'd bought me a little time. I changed the cloak's shape, widening it and held it firmly in my mind. This time the air current slapped against the material and the fabric held. I'd done it. I was gliding across the city.

It was a strange feeling. I thought that gliding would be exciting, but instead I felt a calm sense of peace.

Hugo came in to fly alongside me and helped guide me back to Bart's shop. I was grateful for that too. I'd completely lost sight of it and many of the buildings looked the same from this angle.

With my black cloak, Hugo was inspired to start humming a theme tune.

I smiled.

Lucas: You saw that show too then.

Hugo: Of course. Every Saturday morning, these kids on the forty-second floor would throw cereal onto the balcony for me during the advertisements.

Lucas: You know, sometimes I doubt that your life on the streets before all of this was as hard as you make it out to be.

I heard a gasp through companion chat.

Hugo: You wouldn't say that if you saw how the kids' mother would try to hit me with a broom. I had to be in and out of there like lightning. I will not be slandered for maintaining pop-culture literacy during my struggles.

I conceded the point to him, mainly because we were almost above Bart's shop and I hadn't figured out how to land yet.

As soon as I got close, I collapsed the cape's shape, and hit the rooftop with a smooth roll.

I couldn't help but grin as I got to my feet. "Okay, that was awesome."

Hugo swooped down and landed on my shoulder. "See? Way better than walking."

There was a skylight over the front half of the shop. Peering down showed us that the door to his workshop was closed and the mannequin wasn't moving. The skylight had a window that could be slid open. I tried to open it but it was deadbolted shut on the inside.

Lucas: A little help here.

Hugo's ghost hand moved through the window and pulled the bolt back. There was a loud creak, and we stopped. I held my breath and stared at the mannequin, but it did not move. Maybe it wasn't designed to hear, but I wasn't taking any chances. Gently, I slid the window open.

Hugo summoned Archer and had her hop down first. I wanted to go down next, but the crow beat me to the punch and swooped down to land on a table. Still no response. Hugo waved his wing at me to come down.

I held onto the edge and slowly lowered myself down before letting go and dropping softly to the ground.

Hugo: I can see the directional view thing you were talking about. I think the robot is only programmed to react to threats coming from the street.

Lucas: We don't know what's waiting for us in the workshop though, so be ready.

There was no sound coming from the workshop, but I could see light shining beneath the door.

I drew my sword, and a summoning circle of light formed on the palm of my other hand as I primed a Hemorrhage Gate.

Archer opened the door, but this time I went in first.

The workshop turned out to be empty except for one immobile figure. As I suspected, there was another machine facing the backdoor. Unlike the thin mannequin, this one was bulkier and made out of a suit of armor. Instead of hands, it had metal clamps which made me wonder if these were more than security. What if they were used to help with production and then repurposed for security? Enzo had said that Bart had changed at some point and sworn off direct contact with the orcs. I wonder what caused it?

"Let's take a look around," I said. "See if there's anything here that tells us where he lives."

There were papers strewn across one of the tables. I skimmed through them but all of them were random sketches of schematics except for the last one. There, under the rest of them, was a sketch of the spirit killer device.

"He was building them," I realized.

"There's more stuff missing over here," Hugo said, pointing to another table. "Sets of tools that have been taken. I don't think he's coming back here."

I took all of the diagrams and put them in my inventory. Hopefully Enzo might have some ideas about where Bart might've gone.

"Maybe he has a house in the city somewhere?"

"Maybe," I said, frowning. "The whole thing still doesn't make sense though. How is he connected to the goblins or the orcs that are stealing bodies?"

We searched the rest of the workshop but didn't find anything of value. We were about to leave when we received a message.

Roan: Hey, just giving you a heads up that I'm back.

Both of us sent him a flurry of questions.

Roan: Yeah, I can't answer any quest-specific questions. Mostly because I don't know, I haven't been following Tower events recently. One thing I will say is to be wary of Enzo. Right now, you're useful to him and his people. The second you're not is when you could be in trouble.

Lucas: I'll keep that in mind. What about the device we picked up before? Could it be used to create more wraiths?

Hugo: You think this is all about building a ghost army?

Roan: That's a strong possibility. Hugo receiving a soul magic attack makes it even stronger.

Lucas: How did you know that?

Roan: Oh, I can see your stats. It's normal for patrons.

That was a little disconcerting. Does that also mean he can see what we've got in our inventories? If that were true, then he would've read the note that Daisy had given me. He could have confronted us about it, but nothing we've done so far technically constitutes a betrayal. He might simply be biding his time and waiting for us to make a move.

Hugo: Hey I was wondering, what's the tribunal?

I shot Hugo a concerned look and mouthed the word 'careful.'

Roan: I'm surprised you're asking about that now. Did you hear something more about it?

There was suspicion in his voice. We needed to tread lightly here.

Lucas: No, it's just that we've finally had time to process what happened at the Golden Door and the comment about a tribunal was something that stood out to us.

Roan: That was nothing but an empty threat relating to inter-god politics. It's not worth concerning yourselves about.

Hugo: And things with Tanver Vhar? How go those?

I closed my eyes and ran a hand through my hair. You're really pushing it, little buddy.

Roan: Things are… ongoing. Can't say more than that, but why did it look like you were about to leave the workshop?

Lucas: We searched it. It looks like he cleared the place out.

Roan: While leaving security as a trap? Mad inventors love secret hiding places. I can't guarantee anything, but I'd suggest you keep searching in case there was something you overlooked.

Hugo glanced at me and I shrugged. It couldn't hurt to be more thorough.

We divided the room in half. Hugo used Archer to search while I pulled drawers out, checking for false bottoms. When I got down to the lower cabinets there were some cans of oil, chemical cleaning supplies, and a few spare tools.

I almost gave up when I spotted a cable tucked away at the back of the cupboard. I followed it and behind one of the cans of oil was a button. I pressed it and one of the walls shifted back, revealing a hidden alcove.

Elation turned to disappointment when I saw that it was empty.

Lucas: Well, you were right. He did have a secret storage space, but there's nothing here.

Roan: It's not a total loss. You now have a target to go after and those diagrams with his signature on them will be enough to convince Enzo to have his people help you look for him.

Lucas: I thought you said we couldn't trust him.

Roan: I said he was using you. I never said you shouldn't use him back.

The alcove suddenly closed shut and iron bars dropped down over the door. I looked in the other room. More bars were covering the front window, the door, and the skylight.

"I must have tripped some kind of failsafe," I said.

Hugo wasn't impressed. "Again!?"

"That last one doesn't count," I muttered while pressing the hidden button. Only now it had no effect. "There must be a way to turn it off."

The large robot suddenly turned, orange eyes afire.

Roan: Whatever you do, don't fight the robots.

There was a table between us and the armor robot. Rather than go around it, it brought a set of clamps up and smashed the table in half.

We started backing away into the other room, only to see the mannequin slowly approaching us.

Lucas: What? Why on earth not?

Roan: At this level of the Tower, power sources small enough to be inside those things are going to be rudimentary and unstable. If you damage them in the wrong way, then they could explode.

Hugo: We've survived worse.

Roan: The explosion would take out half the street.

We backed into the front of the shop, but the mannequin was closing in.

Lucas: So what do we do? We're trapped in here.

Roan: I'm working on it. Just hold on.

The mannequin's hands retracted back and two long, thin blades slid out. It held its arms outstretched as it walked toward us. The arm blades sliced through the wooden shelves like butter.

Lucas: Work faster!

CHAPTER 22
DISARMING

As we backed away, a chair stood in the mannequin robot's path. Much like with the armor robot, it cut through the chair rather than go around it. Fragments of wood exploded and sprayed toward us. A harmless attack, but it was enough to receive an identification message.

Beast Identified [Crude Fashion Mannequin Automaton (Rare)] Level 110 – Retrieved from a dumpster behind a dressmaker and given new life as a security guard. This robot has some interesting quirks. Sadly, you already know about its unstable power core, so that surprise is out. Still, be careful fighting this one. One wrong move and it's ka-boom!

"For the record, setting off this trap is on Roan," I said.

Hugo nodded. "Agreed."

Hugo and I retreated until we reached the metal bars in front of the shop window. The mannequin was slow. We still had time to escape.

With my sword, I used an Air Slash attack on the window bars. The glass shattered, but the bars remained intact.

"Hurry, it's getting closer!" Hugo cried.

"I can't cut through the metal!"

"What about the walls? You said you destroyed the mausoleum before."

I glanced at the wooden beams supporting the roof and frowned.

"I don't know if the building could take it. Blowing through a wall could collapse part of the roof and hit the robots."

"So what do we do?"

Lucas: Roan, can we restrain it?

I was thinking about summoning some chains from my domain to hold it in place until we came up with a better idea. Thankfully, the armor robot remained in the workshop. Maybe because it wasn't programmed to leave that area?

Roan: That's risky. It might injure itself while trying to resist the chains.

Hugo: Well, we have to do something!

Roan: I'm looking for answers. Just avoid it for the time being.

That was easier said than done when the robot was almost upon us. I was about to try and dodge under one of its arm blades when Hugo summoned his giant bug spirit. The creature coiled around us and solidified to give us some cover.

If the robot was smart, it would've realized that the bug wasn't attacking and would simply climb over it. But instead, the robot repeatedly stabbed at the creature. The bug spirit held for now, but it wouldn't last forever.

"Hugo, you can squeeze through the bars and get to safety out on the street."

"What? I'm not leaving you!"

I grabbed him and shoved him through the bars. This was not the time to argue.

"Help me from out there," I said.

Hugo brought Archer back out. She appeared behind the mannequin and tried to distract him, all to no avail. It seemed the mannequin was only interested in living targets.

It continued attacking the bug spirit, and Hugo was growing concerned.

"It can't hold it for much longer," he said.

I figured now was the time to check in with Roan for answers.

Lucas: How's that research coming?

Roan: Slow, and slower still when you keep interrupting me.

What was this, some kind of stalling tactic? Roan should've known right away what this thing was. If this was a test, then we were going to have words once this thing was dealt with.

"It's almost out of health!" Hugo warned.

I put my sword away and prepared to move.

The bug started to dissipate. As it did, I rolled through its smoky echo and got behind the mannequin. The robot blindly spun its arm blades back; one of them catching my arm with a shallow cut. I winced and kept moving while taking care not to re-enter the workshop. It had even less space with a bigger robot inside.

As another test, I tried blinding the robot. First with Heart of Darkness over its eyes, and then by concealing myself in my cloak. Neither seemed to impact its senses as it pursued me.

With its long arm blades, it was easy for it to herd me into another corner. I tried to dash past it, only to receive another cut, this time on my side.

"Oof," Hugo said.

One thing I noticed was that there seemed to be a mismatch with the robot's body. Its legs were much slower than its arms and upper body. Maybe I could use that to my advantage.

Roan: Okay, I think I've got it. Are you close to a body of water?

Hugo: What?! No, of course not.

Roan: Right. Then we'll have to short circuit it with electricity. First get to a lightbulb.

The mannequin's upper body started spinning, its arm blades whirling.

Lucas: There are no lightbulbs! He doesn't use any. There were just some lit candles in the workshop.

Roan: Machines like this would need recharging. There must be an electricity source close by. Think!

I looked around the shop but saw nothing except empty broken shelves. If there was going to be a hidden power source, then it must be in the workshop. I thought about the hidden button I'd pressed that had a cable connected to it. That had to have used electricity.

I ran back into the workshop while praying that the mannequin didn't follow me. The armor robot stood inert between the smashed table halves, like it had powered down as soon as I was out of its sight. Magical awareness showed me the truth. It didn't have a field-of-view cone like the mannequin did. Instead, an orange haze pulsed out 360 degrees around the robot every two seconds. If you were outside of the pulse, then it stopped moving.

"Hugo, use whatever you can to block the doorway."

I couldn't trust that the mannequin was restricted only to the front shop. If it followed me into the cramped workshop space, it would mean disaster.

Archer shifted like smoke and appeared to stand in front of the doorway. A pulse from the armor robot hit me as I approached the hidden button. I froze and watched as the armor robot straightened. It took several steps and then sent out another pulse.

The pulse hit me, but this time it didn't react.

I took a step toward the cabinet with the hidden button and stopped just before another pulse was sent out. As long as I moved between the pulses, I could avoid its detection.

"Hurry, I don't know how much more Archer can take," Hugo yelled.

Lucas: I'm going as fast as I can.

After the next pulse, I made it to the cabinet and bent down before freezing.

Lucas: Okay, I've found a cable that I think has power running through it.

Roan: Great, rip the end of it out.

Lucas: Won't that electrocute me?

Roan: Is there rubber insulation on the cable?

I checked and saw that there was.

Lucas: Yes?

Roan: Great, then only touch that part and you should be fine.

After the next pulse, I grabbed the cable and ripped it away from the button. Sure enough, there were some copper wires that created sparks when they touched.

Lucas: Okay, I've got some electricity. Now what?

Roan: Open the outer protective panel to expose its power source.

Lucas: How do I do that without damaging it?

Roan: There should be a release button somewhere.

It was at that moment that Archer ran out of health and dissipated. The mannequin stepped into the workshop.

Lucas: I don't see a button on either of them!

Roan: It would be subtle. Check the back of it.

Oh sure, easy for you to say.

The mannequin set its sights on me. I tried to move away and pull the cable with me, but it was stuck. I stood there holding the cable as an arm blade tried to stab me. I side-stepped it, but the pulse caught me and the armor robot moved closer.

As soon as the mannequin got within range, I shoved the cable into its chest. Sparks flew off of it, but it remained unharmed. An arm blade swung up high, ready to strike me down. My free hand shot out to grab it before it could cave my skull in.

So much for not restraining these things. I could feel its arm trying to resist me, but that wasn't the problem. The problem was that I'd grabbed it with my only free hand while the other held the electric cable. The mannequin's other arm blade stabbed me in the gut. I gasped and felt my legs shake. They were like jelly and wanted to buckle, but I remained in place.

Lucas: The electric cable didn't work.

Roan snorted.

Roan: Of course it didn't. What part of protective panel was lost on you?

Oh God, I was going to die while someone snarkily critiqued all of my mistakes.

The mannequin pulled the arm blade out of me, and I cried out.

Why do blades always feel worse when they're being taken out of me?

The mannequin pulled its arm back, ready for another stab.

I wanted to retreat, but my legs wouldn't respond. I didn't know what to do. In that moment, I could only stare at the blade.

This is it.

Suddenly, Hugo and several crow spirits flew into the workshop. They danced madly in front of the robot's faces.

"What are you waiting for?" Hugo cried. "Move!"

I dropped the cable and hobbled past the robots. The armor robot's pulse was picking up all of the spirit crows and it didn't know which way to turn. The thing kept turning left and right in confusion. Meanwhile, the mannequin focused solely on Hugo, who danced in the air to avoid its attacks.

Bart had designed one robot for living targets and one robot to repel non-living targets.

This was further proven when the armor robot's clamps hit one of the spirit crows. Enchantment symbols appeared on the clamps for a brief second and the crow it hit vanished into smoke.

Bart was trying to cover his bases with these robots. *But who were they for?* I doubted he could've made them so quickly after our visit. The armor one wouldn't have been for us or Enzo's people. So who was he afraid of?

The mannequin whipped an arm blade at my head, which brought me back to my senses. I ducked and stayed behind to check the back of it. That was when I noticed a small disc shape carved into the back of its right leg. A button that was almost invisible unless the light hit it just right.

I fell to my knees and pressed the button. There was a hiss of air and the front panel of the mannequin fell to the floor with a clang.

I stood up and tried to make a move for the fallen electric cable, but my gut wound was worse than I thought. Hugo saw I wasn't going to make it. He summoned a spectral hand and thrust the cable into the mannequin's exposed chest.

More sparks flew, the robot juddered and its arms grinded to a stop.

DING! You have slain [Crude Fashion Mannequin Automaton (Rare)] Level 110 – Experience Points and Currency Acquired.

Hugo and I let out a sigh of relief, but it wasn't over just yet.

I shuffled over to the armor robot and found a similar button in the same place. Hugo lured it closer to the cable and then shocked it until we received a message telling us it was also dead.

I grabbed a blood source from my inventory to heal myself. It took multiple bodies to do so. That wouldn't do. My stock of high-quality blood was running low. I would need to start thinking soon about how to collect more. Perhaps by seeking out more of those desert bugs?

Hugo flew to the armor robot and grabbed a fist-sized tube. I didn't get a good look before it disappeared into his inventory, so I turned over the mannequin.

The front of it was a mixture of gears and wires that reminded me a little of what the spirit killer cubes looked like on the inside. At the center was a large tube with two smaller tubes inside of it. One contained an orange liquid and the other a blue one.

I pulled on it, and the thing detached from the robot with an easy click.

Item Identified! [Crude Automaton Power Core (Rare)] – A small portable power source that can be recharged with the right amount of power. Use the wrong amount and this thing will blow a big crater into whatever it's near.

I put it in my inventory. It might be useful in the future and, if nothing else, it was further proof to show Enzo of Bart's involvement in all of this.

Roan: You did it. Congratulations.

He'd been evasive and vague about where he'd disappeared to. When he did finally return, he struggled to offer advice on how to deal with an enemy. We needed to know what was going on, if only for our own safety.

Lucas: Once we're out of this shop, we need to have a talk.

CHAPTER 23
SERVITUDE HAS ITS PRICE

AFTER A LITTLE MORE SEARCHING, we found the power generator that Bart was using to recharge the robots. It was buried under some floorboards in the workshop. It was unremarkable in appearance. Just a metal cylinder with tubes and cables attached with different switches on top of it.

I was hesitant to touch any of it, even when Roan assured me it was much safer than the robot power cores. I wasn't putting much stock in his assurances, but we needed to remove the bars protecting the doors and windows.

It was trial and error with the switches that eventually caused the bars to retract.

"Finally, let's go," Hugo said.

"Wait."

I went back to the dead automatons. First, I tried to remove the armor robot's clamps to see if I could use it as a spirit-fighting weapon. Unfortunately, they seemed to be tied directly to the robot. When I did finally remove them from its body, the System message only recognized them as ordinary clamps.

Still, I took them, both bodies, and the power generator under the floor. Everything went into my inventory.

"What are you doing?" he asked.

"Denying the enemy."

I wasn't going to give Bart or someone else the chance to return here and repair the robots.

We left the shop empty and broken. Roan was quiet the whole time. I think he was waiting for me to start.

We found a rooftop a few blocks away that would give us some privacy, and then I began with the most important question.

Lucas: What's happening with you? And since when do you need to research something basic like a Tower enemy?

Okay, that was two questions. I got ahead of myself. I was trying to appear calm, but inwardly I was seething. Both of us could've died while waiting for him to find an answer.

The brand on my hand lit up. The mark I'd received when I'd pledged my allegiance to Roan. He didn't make it hurt like last time, but it tingled and the message was clear. Watch your tone when addressing me.

Roan: Since we last spoke, my access to Tower information has become more restricted. My *research, as you* call it, was me finding someone with engineering experience who recognized the automaton design and then bribing them for the relevant information.

The Officiator was right. Tanver Vhar has cut him out of the loop completely. That wasn't good news for us, since I trusted Vhar even less than I trusted Roan.

Lucas: So instead of backstabbing the other gods and being in charge of the Tower, Vhar backstabbed you and removed your access?

Roan: Yes, that is correct.

Hugo: What does that mean for us? Is Vhar going to come after us?

That was a good point. Having an enemy gain control of the Tower could be a death sentence for us.

Roan: No, he's probably already forgotten about you two. You were merely a means to an end for him.

Lucas: What about the other gods?

Both Yakeshi and Samara wanted me dead. That much I knew, but it was difficult to gauge the mood of the other gods. How many of them were indifferent, and how many of them felt betrayed at the Golden Door when Vhar and Roan made their move?

Roan: That is the reason why I've been absent recently. You asked before about a tribunal. Well in order for one to be called, 70 percent of gods need to vote in favor of calling one. I've been hopping from planet to planet since we last spoke. Shaking hands, kissing babies, and bribing or threatening every lesser god not under another's sway to vote for me. It's exhausting. I came back to check on you two because I needed a break from it.

Hugo: What happens if you fail and one gets called anyway?

Roan: It would be bad. A trial would be held to determine guilt, and if found guilty, that god is then marked for death. You don't just become persona non grata. Every god swears an oath to kill you on sight. Personally, I think the whole concept is a waste of time. It merely allows for cowardly gods to unite and take out the stronger ones. But I was overruled when the original idea was raised.

Lucas: So if a tribunal is called, then they'll kill you?

Roan: No, they'd *try* to kill me and everyone connected to me, which includes you two, in case I needed to spell that out for you. But that's only if a tribunal gets called and if it doesn't go our way. And if that happens, I have an insurance policy.

That sounded ominous.

Lucas: Which is what?

Roan: I won't say, but it's closer to mutually assured destruction than a get out of jail free card, so let's hope I don't have to use it.

Hugo was growing restless. We'd asked about Roan's situation and he'd complied by answering our questions, but none of it helped us right now.

Hugo: So where does all of this leave us?

Roan: The same as before. Forget about Vhar. Forget about the other gods. It's considered bad form to call a tribunal and attack the accused at the same time. Yakeshi will want to do this by the book. None of them will touch you.

There was another question nagging at me. One I'd had since we'd encountered the human faction that belonged to the church.

Lucas: We ran into some worshippers in the city who worshiped a god called the Harvest Mother. Have you ever heard of her?

Roan: Were they Tower Climbers?

Hugo: No.

Roan: Then it wasn't a real god. It's just a story that's tied into some-body's quest line. What's a gothic Victorian-esque city without a dash of horror from a religious cult?

Lucas: So we have nothing to worry about externally, but we shouldn't count on you for help in the Tower either.

Roan: Correct, although I'm working on regaining my former access to the Tower, so I'll be in and out of contact for a while. Is there anything else before I go?

I looked at Hugo, who shook his head. I said that we were good, and the conversation ended there.

We thought about what he'd said. It all sounded plausible, but I couldn't help but feel like we'd picked the losing side. Like everything was tipping against us. I had to hope that Daisy would make contact with a solution soon. This was not a ship either of us were willing to go down with.

The next thing I did was take out a piece of paper and write a message on it. I had to hope this would work.

"Flit, I have a message that needs delivering," I said.

Nothing happened. I glanced at Hugo, who shrugged. Maybe there was some special way to summon him? I was about to ask Roan when suddenly I heard a stone crack.

I looked over the edge to see the goat man scaling the building with only his feet. The stone wall would crack as he skipped up toward us. The way he moved was almost playful, but judging from his glower when he reached us, he was anything but.

"Is there a reason we couldn't have done this on the street?" he gruffly asked.

I apologized and offered him the letter. "Can you deliver this to Enzo?"

He nodded and took the letter, which contained a brief rundown on what I'd discovered so far, but with a few key details left out. It ended with me requesting another in-person meeting, which I believed Enzo would grant.

The letter vanished into Flit's inventory.

He turned to leave, but Hugo was curious about his powers, especially since he wasn't a Climber.

"Is that all it takes? People just call out to you and you appear?" he asked.

Flit stopped and clenched his fists. "No, it's not. When someone makes a request, I'm forced to run to you. I'm not here by choice. I didn't want this life. I'm a prisoner who's stuck in this stupid city until the fighting has ended. Which will be never, by the way. Even when the Tower is finished and the city and all its inhabitants are returned to their original location, I'll still be stuck here ferrying messages between the warring factions."

"I'm sorry," Hugo said. He hadn't meant to touch a nerve with his question.

"How'd you end up here in the first place?" I asked.

Flit suddenly looked tired. His ears twitched, and he sighed. "That's a long story. Now I've got to go. I can't stay in one place for too long. There's always another letter or package to be delivered."

I thought he'd jump down to the street, but instead he hopped from roof to roof. Skipping across the roofs with a speed and grace that I'd never match on my best day.

"He's trapped here like we are," Hugo said.

I nodded and while I was sympathetic, there was little we could do for him now.

Dawn was also breaking, and I beckoned Hugo to my side. I knew where we should go next, but we had to hurry before the sun rose too high.

CHAPTER 24
BUG HUNTING

WE SLIPPED OUT of the city and into the desert undetected. There was a close call near the east gate with a goblin patrol, but luckily, they'd moved on after a few minutes. Leaving the city this way was a risk. We could have simply reused the hidden tunnel where we'd fought the cadavers, but I wanted to see how parts of the city woke up. I wanted to gauge the responses of its inhabitants.

The way they began their days was slow. Which was odd at first glance. But then again, if they were importing food through the System and nobody was starving, I guessed I'd be laid back too. Those who worked security, whether they be human or goblin, were the first to rise. Then the tradespeople slowly followed without a care in the world. As the sun rose, all the fear that had been so palpable at night seemed to fade away.

I took it to be a form of resilience. These people were adaptable. They knew what they were signing up for with the Tower and so they rolled with the punches.

It was admirable, and it made me wonder if I'd gotten too complacent. Too comfortable with these brushes with death. The Tower was supposed to challenge Climbers, but lately every fight felt like a close call. Something had to change. I just wasn't sure what.

That was partly why we were out here in the sand searching for bug monsters. It was a chance to experiment, as well as stock up on blood and train. All things I felt had been sorely neglected lately.

We moved away from the city and deeper into the desert. Though not far enough to lose sight of it on the horizon. Getting lost out there was the last thing we needed.

The farther out we got, the more we encountered these steep rolling hills of sand dunes. It was only after climbing to the top of one that we spied our first monster of the day.

A flame red, five-foot-long centipede-like creature with large mandibles was in the valley below us. It was picking at the bones of a bird and hadn't noticed our presence yet.

"So who goes first?" I asked.

Hugo's spectral hand appeared with a coin. "Call it," he said.

"Heads."

He flipped the coin, and it landed tails.

I gestured. "Alright, have at it."

"Do bugs have souls, I wonder?" Hugo asked himself. "I guess now's as good a time as any to find out."

He left my shoulder and swooped down into the valley below. The bug heard the flap of his wings on approach and turned to cover the bones protectively. It reared up, screeching a challenge to Hugo, who hovered in the air. A faint purple light formed in front of the crow's chest. The color grew stronger, like it was charging up.

Beast Identified! [Baby Blightfire Centipede (Common)] Level 78 – Identified by their red exterior, these small creatures are left to fend for themselves quickly after birth. In this inhospitable environment, they're forced to become scavengers or engage in sneak attacks until they're mature enough to fight for their food. Their preferred method of hunting is to hide in the sand until prey is near. They then use their

forcipules, two stinger like front legs, to inject Blightfire venom into their prey for an easy kill.

The Blightfire Centipede sensed danger and went on the offensive. It scurried toward Hugo, but it was too late. A pulse beam of energy shot out from the crow and hit the monster squarely in the head. The bug's body absorbed the blow with seemingly no damage, but the creature was stopped in its tracks. All of its past aggression had disappeared. It laid down on the ground like it had given up on living.

The creature wasn't dead though. We'd received no message of that, and there was the occasional brief twitch that showed it was still alive.

Hugo landed while breathing heavy. Using the Soul Lance had taken a lot of energy out of him, but he wasn't helpless. He summoned Archer to go over to the bug and investigate. She kicked the centipede, and it merely rolled over onto its side and curled up.

I went down to join Hugo.

"It's like it's given up," he said.

"Seems like your ability is more of a depression lance, at least when it comes to the living. It might cause more damage to purely spiritual beings though."

He looked disappointed. "So it's just going to lie there?"

"That, and have recurring thoughts blaming itself for not moving."

"Well, now I feel bad."

Four more bugs of the same type crawled out of the sand up ahead. They were hungry. They'd sensed food, and they were crawling past their apathetic kin to get it.

Archer fired an arrow at one as it passed her by, but the arrow bounced off of its carapace.

"You want me to…?" I asked, seeing the trouble that he was having.

"No, no, I got it."

He summoned his Dune Pincer spirit. It was massive compared to the bugs coming toward us and should still out level them, providing they were the same level as the first bug.

"Go get 'em, Milton," he said.

I frowned, trying to think of an action star with the name Milton. Maybe that was part of their real name? I mean, if John Wayne's real name was Marion, then I guessed it was possible that a Milton could've slipped into a Hollywood blockbuster without me noticing.

"Milton, huh?" I asked, looking for clarification.

"Yeah, there's no backstory for that one. I just like the name and think he looks like a Milton."

I shrugged. "Fair enough."

Milton silently surged forward and its pincers grabbed the closest bug. Two of the others attacked Milton from the sides, while the remaining one scuttled past. It was heading straight for us.

I raised my sword to prepare. Hugo's spectral hand appeared and put it over my blade to lower it.

"It's still my turn," he said.

I nodded, lowering my weapon but not putting it away.

He flew up into the air and used a Wind Blast to knock the creature back into Archer's arms, where she wrestled it to the ground. The bug was helpless on its back as its many legs kicked the air. Archer drew an arrow and stabbed it in the soft underbelly. The bug squealed and tried to wriggle free, but she continued stabbing it. Plunging the arrowhead in and out until the creature bled out.

It must have taken over fifty stabs. The spirit had looked in control the whole time, but she'd still taken some damage. Archer wobbled as she stood up and was favoring one leg over the other. Hugo saw that she was completely spent and dismissed her.

There were three bugs left to deal with, but luckily Milton was having an easier fight. He cut two centipedes in half with his pincers. The final one tried to attack while his pincers were occupied, but Hugo saw it coming. Using Milton's greater size and weight, he smashed his body down on the last enemy bug and crushed it to death.

Incredibly, by not moving and staying huddled on the floor, the centipede Hugo had used a Soul Lance on was still alive. The crow seemed almost hesitant to kill it.

"Think of it as a mercy killing," I said. "Besides, if we don't kill it now, then something else will. You might as well do it for the experience, if nothing else."

Hugo sent Milton to finish it off, causing him to level up.

All in all, it was a good start to the day. We hadn't been out here for too long and already Hugo had captured the spirits of the five bugs, gained enough experience to level up, and now knew how much of a toll using his new ability could take.

I bent down to touch the blood of one of the bugs. It was hot out here in the desert. I hadn't realized it, but as soon as I made contact with the blood, I felt a slight amount of dehydration within me recede.

Yeah, their blood would work just fine for my purposes.

I added their bodies to my inventory and received two more System messages.

Item Identified! [Baby Blightfire Centipede Venom Sac (Common)] – While smaller than the ones that reach full maturity, these sacs can still carry enough venom to put down targets several times greater in size.

Item Identified! [Blightfire Venom (Uncommon)] – A particularly brutal and clever toxin. This venom works in two stages. The first is a dormant stage of quiet replication. Once it enters the bloodstream, it spreads quickly, but without any ill effect. The second stage is when it ignites. A full Blightfire Venom sac burns the victim completely from the inside out, leaving only the bones in which to suck out the marrow.

The venom sounded perfect for some of the tougher targets I'd gone up against recently. While I missed my Venom Fang knife, this Blightfire might prove to be a great substitute.

I was about to ask Hugo to fly up and look for more bugs when we heard a noise. It was coming from another dune, and it sounded like running.

I focused my attention on it.

"He's over here!" a voice yelled out.

I raised my sword and waited for an attack that didn't come.

"Yeah, this way!" shouted another voice, a little more distantly.

"They're hunting someone else," I murmured to Hugo.

Curious, we kept low when climbing up the tall dune and peered over the edge. Six men and two women in brown robes, holding weapons, were running up another dune and away from us.

"What do you think?" I asked.

"That it's way too hot out here to be running in robes?"

"That goes without saying. I meant, are you up to following them?"

The crow scoffed, mildly offended that I'd even ask the question. "I can still fly faster than you can pump those meat appendages. Now come on. I want to see what it is they're chasing after."

They disappeared over the next dune, and we hurried to catch up to them. It took several more hills until they'd stopped running.

Over this next dune, the desert flattened out and up ahead was an oasis with lush palm trees ringing around its edges. A bearded man wearing nothing but pants stood in the shallow end of the water, refilling a flask. His back was to the cultists, completely oblivious to the danger. They pointed at the man and silently closed in.

"We have to do something," Hugo whispered.

"Stay here," I said.

This was my turn.

CHAPTER 25
DEFILING A STOUP

THE CULTISTS WERE QUICKLY CLOSING in on the man in the water. I had to get their attention. The thing is, it's tough to make a loud approach when walking in sand. So, as I walked down the hill, I repeatedly banged my sword against my knife. The clanging of metal caused them and the man they were hunting to turn in my direction.

The cultists were shocked. They murmured amongst themselves and spread out with their weapons, ready to face me. The man they were after had a different response. He grinned at me and flopped backward into the water, floating in the oasis without a care in the world.

He didn't look surprised to see me or the cultists. Was he drawing them here for a trap?

I continued cautiously down the hill. There seemed to be no sign that anyone or anything was lurking nearby for an ambush. But there were a lot of bugs that could burrow under the sand and remain there undetected. Still, I was confident that I could handle whatever was waiting for me.

Hugo: What are you doing?

He was surprised by my approach. I could've snuck up and taken out at least three of the eight before they even realized what was happening.

But I had a good reason for my loud entrance.

Lucas: I'm introducing myself.

Hugo: Should I be sitting down for this?

Lucas: Probably. I am hoping for a little conversation first.

The cultists were two women and six men. All of them were relatively young and fit, which made sense. You wouldn't send more senior people out chasing down threats. They held their weapons in front of themselves protectively. A mixture of short swords, axes, and one crossbow. They were being cautious and weren't sure what to make of me yet.

I didn't know whether they were involved in the apple ritual that had almost killed me, and I didn't care. I just wanted to know why they were chasing this man.

As soon as I'd made my presence known, the cultists ignored the man in the water. The one holding the crossbow stepped forward to announce himself as the leader of the group. Dark-haired, and with a square jaw, he looked like someone who should be doing TV modeling rather than running around for religious zealots.

Crossbows are tricky. Even with all the points I'd put into Dexterity, I wasn't sure if I was fast enough to dodge fire from one. But there were good things about facing it too. I wasn't worried.

"What are you doing here?" he asked me.

"Hey, that was going to be my question to you," I said.

He glanced back at the others. Their mouths hardened and the grip on their weapons tightened, but they still didn't make the first move. There are eight of them and one of me. The odds should be in their favor, but they know I'm a Tower Climber. They aren't sure if they can take me. I wonder what level these people are at?

I put the knife and sword away in my inventory. This relaxed them a little.

It shouldn't have. The weapons were just a diversion—I never had any intention of fighting with them. My sword was for more serious threats and besides, I wanted to try something new.

"You need to leave. This doesn't concern you," he said while hefting his crossbow.

He didn't directly point it at me, but the implicit threat was clear. I chose to ignore it and ask my main question before things got bloody.

"Why are you after him?"

The leader clenched his jaw. Not used to being questioned, that one. Perhaps he was a rising star within his church? Though I doubted he was too high ranking. They wouldn't send someone that important to run out into the desert like this.

One of the women put a hand on his shoulder and whispered something. He nodded and relaxed slightly. I didn't hear all of it, but the gist was that they thought they could talk me into walking away.

The leader sighed and said, "he has repeatedly broken into our church despite numerous warnings to stop."

That's it?

I looked past them to the bearded man who was doing the backstroke in the water. He noticed me looking and gave a lazy wave before continuing to swim.

"He defiled our stoup!" yelled another cultist.

"Your what?" I frowned.

A flicker of disgust passed over the leader's face. "He urinated in the holy water," he said. "We've tripled security, and yet he keeps finding ways inside. We need to know how he's doing it, and then he must answer for his blasphemy. But none of this has to concern you. You can walk out of here alive right now."

I smiled, flashing my teeth. "I'd say the same to all of you, but then I'd be lying."

The leader raised his crossbow and fired. It was the smartest thing he could've done, and had I been someone else, it might have caught me off-guard. But I'd been waiting for it.

I darted left and felt the bolt cut through my lower side and fly out the other end. Damn, still too slow. Luckily, the guy was a terrible shot. He'd aimed far too low. The bolt was also a through-and-through, which causes less damage. Though it was hard to feel grateful when there was a hole in my stomach.

I spat some blood out onto the sand and straightened up like the bolt was no big deal. "The reason why you won't be leaving here alive is that my friend and I are out here experimenting," I continued. "I've spent so much time worrying about appearances that I'd neglected one of my better powers. But I don't have to worry about that anymore. The time for holding anything back is over."

"The Harvest Mother herself protects us," he insisted. "We are her faithful. Her chosen."

"No. You're practice."

I opened two Hemorrhage Gates in front of me and activated Cardinal Arm twice. Blood flowed out from the portals to coat my forearms and hands. It hardened, giving me armored gauntlets that ended in razor-sharp claws.

The leader quickly realized his mistake. He scrambled under his robes to reach for another bolt to reload with, but by the time he does so, it will be too late.

I sprang forward, closing the distance with a few short bounds. He was too distracted to notice, still busy fumbling with the crossbow's mechanism instead of dropping it or using it as a club.

I sliced open his throat with one swipe and begin to drink. A System message popped up, giving me his name and telling me he was level 115, but I didn't care. There was only one message I was looking for.

DING! **Class: [Blood Reaver] has reached level 120 – Experience Acquired.**

Distantly, I felt something poke me in the back. Looking over my shoulder revealed another cultist. He'd cut me with an axe and I hadn't even felt it. The cultist pulled back for another swing, but I ignored him and kept drinking. He hit me again and the wound healed almost instantaneously.

"Do something!" another cultist screamed.

"Go for his head!" shouted another.

He listened to his friends and raised the axe high above his head. No fancy decapitation, just a straight swing down to split my skull in half.

I kept drinking, though there wasn't much left.

[Sanguine Lord Bonus from Blood Consumption Activated]

DING! Class: [Blood Reaver] has reached level 121 – Experience Acquired.

That was strange—I'd never seen that message before. This wasn't an ordinary level gained from killing. The System was explicitly telling me that drinking the blood would net me extra levels.

The axe swing came down. I abruptly let go of the leader's lifeless body and sidestepped it. The man's overcommitted swing caused it to hit the sand, putting him off balance.

My claws ripped across his back. I felt his spine break and watched him fall. He was still alive but paralyzed. I left him like that and turned my attention to the others.

The two female cultists and one male muttered a prayer. Their eyes were wide and their hearts raced as their tongues tripped over the words. With my face covered in blood and my claws, I must have looked like a demon to them.

Another two held swords and were praying over them. Their faces were hard and angry. They wanted to fight.

I almost joined them until I realized I was missing a cultist. I looked around and saw one of them fleeing. He was running back toward the city, but first he'd have to make it up the steep sand dune.

A Hemorrhage Gate appeared, and I drew out enough blood to form a javelin. A high Dexterity stat had helped hone my aim with throwing weapons into an art form. I watched the fleeing cultist. I measured his stride and speed before pulling the weapon back for a throw.

Wind blasted around me as I launched the javelin with all my strength. It flew up high in the air.

"Go! Keep running!" one of the men shouted.

The one fleeing didn't look back as he sprinted up the hill. None of them realized that it wouldn't matter if my aim was off. I controlled where the javelin went.

It arced down and pierced through the man's chest as he reached the top of the hill.

"No!" one woman cried.

Using the javelin as an anchor, I dragged his body back toward me and tossed it in front of the others.

This pushed the two with the swords into action. Only their blades were glowing purple now. The other three cultists had joined hands. They continued to pray and were somehow empowering the blades.

The swordsmen sneered at me with unearned confidence as they approached. They thought a god was on their side. I would tear that delusion away from them as I took their lives.

I summoned the javelin and twirled it in front of me like a staff. Their eyes focused on it. So much so that they missed the Hemorrhage Gate open below their feet. Blood spikes erupted, impaling them both.

A level 110 and a 112. A few days ago, they might've been a serious threat. Now they were just fodder that was in my way.

Even after they passed, their bodies still twitched. I could feel the blood still inside them calling out to me. But it would have to wait.

The final three cultists were the most scared of all. They'd dropped their weapons but did not try to run or fight like the others. They merely held each other and continued to pray with their eyes closed.

"What can you tell me about the ritual with the apple?" I asked them.

They ignored me, but my words made their legs shake. Their bodies desperately wanted them to run screaming. It wasn't just faith keeping them here. They were leaning on each other for support.

If this was a strategy, then it was a clever one. It made them look innocent, and it made me want to spare them. I've still got blood from the other bodies to collect. I doubt I'd miss what clearly looks like the three weakest members of the group. They could also run back to the church to warn them of the threat I pose. That could potentially get the church to leave me alone, or it would make them double down and come after me.

Decisions, decisions.

"They're not innocent," the man from the water said. He was suddenly standing right next to me.

How had I not seen him or heard him coming?

A hollowed-out coconut appeared in his hands with a bendy straw sticking out of it. He took a sip and a Hawaiian shirt formed on his body.

"A week ago, these three, along with another, tracked down a girl from their congregation. She had missed the church's service for several days in a row. They broke into the girl's house while her parents were away. They thought she was a sinner who'd abandoned her faith. Instead, they found a sick girl laid up in bed. Of course, that was just confirmation that the Harvest Mother had turned her back on the girl. They killed her and threw the body down into the sewers."

It was an interesting tale, but I wasn't particularly moved by it. Especially since his whole appearance undercut the seriousness of the allegation.

"Why should I believe you?" I asked.

The man shrugged. "I'm just telling you why I started pissing in their stoup."

"Doesn't seem like much compared to murdering a child."

His eyes twinkled. "And yet it was all I needed to bring them here."

What the hell kind of powers did this guy have?

"You've seen the kind of company these three keep," he continued. "Decide quickly. We can't stay here for much longer."

He had a point there. I wanted to ask why we couldn't stay much longer, but when I turned back, the man had returned to the water.

Deciding to finish this quickly, I tried to summon another Hemorrhage Gate. An explosion of pain burst through my brain and I cried out.

[Magical Exhaustion Imminent]

State Identified! [Magical Exhaustion] – When you use too much magic so suddenly, you overburden your soul. This leads to spiritual and physical pain. Pushing even further in such an exhausted state can be fatal. Magical Exhaustion cannot be cured with conventional healing potions or blood healing. Time and rest are the most common ways to recover from this condition.

Right, this was new for me. I'd focused primarily on fighting with a sword and knife while only using magical abilities sparingly. By using only my magic, I'd pushed myself close to my limit. I also knew that if I used another ability right now, the pain in my head would be far worse than before.

Still, I didn't regret testing my limits or drinking the blood. I would gain levels far quicker this way, and I needed as much power as possible for the fights ahead.

My blood gauntlets had fallen away as soon as the Magical Exhaustion message had appeared. So I took out my sword and quickly dispatched the last of the cultists.

DING! Class: [Blood Reaver] has reached level 122 – Experience Acquired.

DING! You have gained [Consume (Legendary)] – Blood and all of its inherent power can now be absorbed by touch alone on those you have slain.

CHAPTER 26
THE FOOL

I CLOSED my eyes and focused on my senses. Their blood, their power, was all around me. I could feel it in their bodies and the places where it had leaked onto the sand. All of it was still alive. Still pulsing with energy.

I held my hands out and activated Consume. The blood rushed to my hands. All of it was being magically absorbed.

DING! Class: [Blood Reaver] has reached level 123 – Experience Acquired.

DING! Class: [Blood Reaver] has reached level 124 – Experience Acquired.

DING! Class: [Blood Reaver] has reached level 125 – Experience Acquired.

[The Tree has been Sated]

This new ability was incredible. It'd been a far easier fight than the automatons or the Abomination and yet I was able to squeeze far more levels from it. I'd also gained another Scarlet Apple to collect once we got back to the apartment.

The power of Consume was amazing, but it did appear to have a trade-off. If I consume the blood, then it gets converted into levels. But that leaves me without any blood to heal myself with, outside of fights. I needed to make sure not to overdo it with Consume.

Just to be thorough, I added their bodies and weapons to my inventory. It all carried little value, especially since all of the bodies had been exsanguinated. But you never know what you might need in the Tower.

My stats were the next priority, and it was a massive haul. Altogether, I had 6120 stat points to allocate. The first thing I did was add 2500 points into Vitality to expand my magic capacity. I still liked using my sword, but my abilities offered me a greater degree of flexibility in how to approach threats. It would mean that Vitality was now my second highest stat behind Dexterity, but I was okay with that.

I then buffed up some of the lesser stats. Throwing 500 points each into Willpower and Intelligence. You never know when I might need them and it made me uncomfortable keeping their numbers so low.

Next, I put 1000 points into Perception. Another slightly neglected stat. There had been a few too many surprise attacks for my liking, so 1000 points felt like a good number to reduce the chances of that happening again.

Finally, the remaining points were split equally between Dexterity and Strength at 810 points each.

Stats
Name: Lucas Hudson
Race: Human (Grade: E)
Evolution Path: Reign of the Sanguine Lord
Class: Blood Reaver Level 125
Currency: 20920 coins

Strength: 4318 > 5128
Vitality: 2875 > 5374
Intelligence: 965 > 1465
Constitution: 3126
Dexterity: 5490 > 6300
Perception: 2445 > 3445

Willpower: 861 > 1361

Free points remaining: 6120

I clicked accept and felt a rush of power course through me as my stats increased. This was what I need to beat them and ensure that we survived. This was the path forward.

Hugo flew down to land on my shoulder.

"So that was… interesting," he said.

"We can't hold back anymore. I don't care how it looks. We have to fight back with everything we've got if we want to get out of this place alive."

He cocked his head to the side. "What prompted the change?"

"There've been too many close calls. I've tried to be accommodating. I've tried to do what others say is the right thing, and where did it get us?" I clenched my fists to try to contain my boiling rage. "Almost all of our friends are dead. I don't want to join them, and I don't want it to feel like luck when we survive an encounter."

"I miss them too," he said. "It felt easier being in a group. Psychologically, I mean. You just feel safer surrounded by greater numbers. Now, that's gone and the challenges we're facing are getting harder. I get that you sometimes have to go to a meaner place to fight. I just want you to come back afterward and be the person that argues with me on whether a hotdog is a sandwich or not."

I put my hand around him and pulled him in for a hug.

"It's in the sandwich family," I said quietly.

We both laughed.

The man from before got out of the water and walked slowly toward us. I knew that he was either extremely fast or had some kind of stealth power, so this approach was purely for our benefit. But despite his power, I strangely didn't feel threatened by the man. He felt safe and friendly for reasons that I couldn't explain.

"Who are you?" I asked.

He grimaced. "Don't have a name. Or if I did, I've forgotten it. Most people just call me 'Fool' or 'The Fool.' Then again, most people are idiots, but the name seems to have stuck."

That didn't sound right. I knew as soon as I saw him that he was from Earth. In fact, he'd been the easiest Tower Climber to identify thus far due to his tattoo. It was a very distinctive yellow cartoon sponge character. Why he'd chosen to have that permanently marking his stomach I couldn't say, but it did feel good to meet another Climber again. To talk to someone who truly understood what we were going through.

I had a million questions, but The Fool had seen my frown over his name. Before I knew what was happening, he appeared right in front of me and gently pressed his finger against the tip of my nose. "Boop," he said.

I tried to shove him away, but instead found myself slipping and falling over.

Me slipping on sand? That doesn't make any sense.

Player Identified [The Fool, Class: The Fool, Level: 1]

Hugo sucked in a breath. "How have you survived this far into the Tower at level 1?"

"It's related to your Class, isn't it?" I realized. He had some kind of luck power. That's why I couldn't touch him before and why I slipped. Reality literally bent in his favor to prevent me from shoving him.

The Fool grinned and looked away. "Couldn't say. One of the conditions for picking it."

"But why give up your name?" I asked.

His mouth twisted, and his expression of mirth vanished. "Because this whole place is a fucking joke. So I am going to bumble and fumble my way to the finish line to prove that the joke is on them." His grin returned, and he slapped me on the shoulder. "But enough about that. You thought you were saving me from those robed idiots, and I suppose it's the thought that counts, right?"

There was still anger behind his eyes. I got the sense that he wanted us to move past it, and I wondered if that was another condition of his Class. The System calls him The Fool, so maybe he's supposed to act that way in order for his power to work.

"What were you even doing out here in the first place?" Hugo asked.

The Fool's eyebrows rose, and he lightly slapped his forehead. "Ah, thanks for reminding me. Another Climber I met in the city asked if I could get them some oasis water. Not sure what they wanted with it. Forgot to ask. Good excuse for a stroll though."

"And what did they offer in return?"

The Fool looked at Hugo like his question was strange. "Nothing," he replied. "I was just bored. Figured I'd do it just to see what would happen. And look! I suddenly meet more nice people." He glanced at where the bodies had lain. "And some not so nice ones."

Hugo and I tried to play it cool, but both of us couldn't ignore that he had met another Climber. I had to know everything about them.

"Who was the Climber you were doing the favor for?" I asked.

He scratched his beard as he tried to recall. "Dunno. They never gave a name. They had some kind of shadow power obscuring their appearance and voice. I think it was supposed to be intimidating. Usually I would've ignored someone that up themselves, but as I said I was bored."

Hugo: That's got to be Daisy!

Hiding herself was strange, but it tracked with her only communicating with us via letter. She's being extremely cautious, but given what she's working on, I couldn't blame her. Who knows what god a random Tower Climber might work for? Still, if Daisy was expecting this oasis water, then it made sense to go with The Fool to meet her. Once he'd delivered her what was promised, we could share what we've learned so far.

"Hey, would it be okay if we tagged along to meet this person?" I asked.

The Fool's eyes lit up. "Yes! The more the merrier! You lead the way."

"Uh, I don't know the way," I said.

The Fool nodded like I'd said something deeply thought provoking. "No, you're right. The strongest should lead the way. Come along, and keep an eye out for any model trains. I think I lost part of my collection on this floor."

He took off walking at a brisk pace while whistling something cheery.

Hugo: He's a strange one.

Lucas: Just stay close. We've suffered unholy monsters and Abominations. We can handle being locked into an awkward conversation with a strange guy.

The Fool stopped and looked back. "You guys should stay close. This area won't be safe once I leave. There's a range limit and once I'm too far away, I won't be able to hold back the big bugs anymore."

Hugo: What the hell does that mean?

Lucas: I don't know. But I'm pretty sure asking follow-up questions about it won't help.

We hurried to catch up. I had a million more questions about how his powers worked, but once we were by his side, he ignored us and resumed whistling as he walked.

CHAPTER 27
THE UNINCORPORATED ZONE

I BECAME nervous as we approached the city gate. The sun had been up for hours now and the goblins would definitely be looking for intruders.

The Fool was completely at ease though, strolling through the gate like he owned the place.

What kind of magic would his Class employ to allow us inside undetected? Would we sneak through the sewers? Would some accident happen nearby to divert a group's attention so that we could walk by? There were so many ways his power could manifest that my nervousness was slowly being replaced with curiosity and excitement.

Hugo was of a similar mind.

Hugo: What do you think is going to happen?

Lucas: I don't know. Maybe the artillery the goblins had launched at us before blows up in their faces, or those that try to chase after us keep falling over? If his power works as he said it does, then it could be anything. Let's keep close and watch.

As we turned a corner, we spied two lightly armored goblins holding spears and guarding the path ahead. They noticed us as soon as we noticed them, but they didn't react or raise the alarm.

So far, so good.

The Fool walked up to them and nodded. "Sup, Fizz. Sup, Klutch." He tossed them a pack of cigarettes that the goblin on the left caught. Both of them nodded back and stepped aside to let us pass.

We passed on through without complaint. Hugo waited until we were out of earshot to voice his disappointment.

"Wait, that's it?" The crow was underwhelmed.

The Fool smirked. "It's best not to always overthink it." His stomach then audibly rumbled. "Hmm, maybe we should swing by the human district for food first."

I didn't like the sound of that. It would cause unnecessary delay and we had to reconnect with Daisy.

"Do we have to?" I asked. "Perhaps we could deliver the water first or grab something nearby to eat?"

The Fool arched one eyebrow at him. "Have you ever tried to find a non-smoking section in a goblin restaurant before? Trust me, it's not as easy as it sounds."

Hugo: Is that even a real thing?

Lucas: Careful. If it's not, his power might will one into existence.

Hugo: There's no way he's that powerful. Look at everything he's used it for so far. Other than the coincidence of you showing up to save him, it's just been him bribing goblins and you falling over. Maybe he doesn't have grand powers. Maybe you just slipped.

Lucas: I did not slip. But you're right. We assumed he was strong from his words and the fact that he got this far as a level one. He might've just been lucky. Still, Daisy trusted him enough to give him a task. We just have to keep him focused on taking us to her.

"Let's see if we can find something to eat on the way," I said. "If not, I'm sure Hugo could steal some. He's an excellent food thief."

"It's true. I am," he replied with zero modesty.

The Fool gave a half shrug and kept walking in the same direction we'd been heading before, so I took it as a positive sign.

We kept walking until an argument could be heard from one of the windows above. A goblin couple on the second floor were fighting about something, and The Fool stopped to eavesdrop.

"And I'm so sick of you always bringing apples back from the market! Buy something else next time!"

An apple flew out the window, presumably thrown by one of them. It bounced off the wall and fell into The Fool's outstretched hand. He took a big bite out of it and while chewing said, "Never mind. Let's go see your shadowy friend."

Lucas: See, I didn't slip.

Hugo: Oh God, just let it go! Fine, he's telling the truth, but that doesn't mean we're completely safe.

I think a part of the reason he disliked the power that The Fool had was because of how unpredictable it was. I told him we could handle any problems that arose, which didn't calm him down very much. It was only when I pointed out that The Fool's power seemed to only work in his favor, and that he seemed to like us, that he loosened his grip on my shoulder.

Instead of heading east, we went north into what was known as the unincorporated part of the city. I knew this because there was a literal sign hanging up ahead that the goblins had erected. The words 'WAR ZONE' were on it scrawled in blood.

The Fool had finished his apple and explained it to us like this. Before the Tower took the Strand, this was the industrial heart of the city. A place filled with productive factories and warehouses. All now abandoned as everything the people needed was now imported by the System.

There was always fighting between the factions, but it increased once the Tower moved them here. Each faction struggled to hold on to territory here and so it quickly became known as the unincorporated zone. A place where battles could take place without the risk of civilian casualties.

As soon as we passed under the war zone sign, explosions could suddenly be heard nearby.

"What just happened?" Hugo asked.

The Fool looked around and scratched his chin. "It's some kind of containment field the orcs developed. It keeps the bombs, debris, and such from accidentally falling outside the zone. The goblins don't mess with it because it benefits them as much as it does the orcs."

He paused to listen as a few more explosions went off farther away.

"Huh, it's actually kind of mild right now," he said.

"What about the humans?" I asked. So far, they hadn't been mentioned at all in regard to this area.

"They typically steer clear of this place, although the zone stretches across the entire northern part of the city, so it's connected to every district."

I was surprised that The Fool was telling us all of this since I was under the impression that he either didn't like to or couldn't answer questions. He saw me frowning and the question I had on my mind.

"My power ebbs and flows," he explained. "In the ebbs, it's easier to be a little more serious and answer questions. I just can't rely on it too much or push things too far."

"What happens then?" Hugo asked.

"Bad things. There's a limit to how insightful a Fool should be."

We continued walking until we heard orcs. Three of them near an intersection up ahead, talking and getting closer. They sounded happy about something.

The Fool ducked behind some crates and gestured for us to follow. We crouched down next to him and waited for the orcs to pass.

Once they did, Hugo asked The Fool, "Couldn't we have just walked past them?"

"Yes, but it would've been loud and sometimes trying to flaunt the power causes it to backfire. I'm The Fool, remember? I'm not an omnipotent jester."

Hugo: Wait, what's the difference?

I shrugged.

As soon as we left cover, The Fool broke into a run.

Lucas: He's on the move. Come on.

Hugo held onto my shoulder as I walked briskly next to him. It turns out my fear of him getting away from us was unfounded. A level 1 running was nothing to me, but to him, he was huffing and puffing after ten minutes.

He stopped in front of a factory to catch his breath. The big iron sliding doors lay open, but inside it was too dark to see, as all the windows were too covered in dirt and grime to let any light through.

I guess this is the meeting spot. I almost walked past him to go inside when he threw his arm out to block me.

"Don't. I have to clear them by going first."

I wasn't sure what he meant at first. It turned out that the warehouse was loaded with traps. The open doors hadn't been from neglect or laziness, they were a trick. A false invitation to thin out enemy patrols.

We stayed close as The Fool pointed out the traps. The first was a tripwire that was so thin, I almost didn't believe him when he told me. I mimicked his movements when stepping over it and saw just past it was a bundle of poison-tipped needles that were spring-loaded.

The Fool looked around while rubbing the back of his neck. "You know, this reminds me of a place I used to work at. You know, in the before times."

I nodded, though truthfully this place looked a hundred years out of date for our society.

"What kind of work did you do?" Hugo asked.

I shot him a look that said not to encourage him to go down this tangent, but it was too late.

The Fool grinned. "Well, mostly I goofed off. Used my smoke breaks to smoke weed in my car around the corner. The boss never knew."

He absolutely 100 percent knew. I gave an encouraging smile and kept listening. I didn't know if this was part of his power or not, so it was best to just keep him comfortable.

"Huh, is that an actuator?" he asked himself, staring at some dark corner of the room. He started walking toward it. I hurried after him until I felt my foot press down on something. I froze. The floor tile my left foot was standing on was slightly lower than all of the others around it. Must be some kind of pressure-sensitive trap.

"Um, Fool, could you come back here?" I asked loudly. And yes, I felt silly saying that out loud.

To his credit, The Fool came back and squatted down to inspect the tile. He squinted at it for a few seconds.

"What is it?" I asked.

He shrugged. "How should I know? It looks bad though."

Fuck it. If I lose the foot to an explosion, I should have enough blood in my inventory to heal myself. Still, it would be better if Hugo and The Fool got some distance before I set off the trap.

"Is there somewhere safe that Hugo could fly to?" I asked.

The Fool looked around. "No...?" He said it like he wasn't sure.

"Wait, you mean you don't know?"

"Look man, I don't know what's in this place. My power works on vibes, and the vibes are telling me that you shouldn't move, even though you were thinking about it."

Damn, how did he know that? If his power could account for my healing ability, then maybe the trap was worse than I thought? We're over halfway into the factory now. So maybe the traps get more intense the farther in we go? The explosion might be bigger than I was imagining. Instead of losing a foot, I could lose my life. Maybe even Hugo's too, if he stays on my shoulder.

Lucas: Would you fly onto The Fool's shoulder at least?

Hugo: I'm not letting you set that thing off. We're figuring a way out of this together. Now relax. You're sweating and it's kind of gross with me so close to you.

Lucas: Of course I'm sweating, there's a bomb under my foot!

"I did not tell you that you could bring friends," said a deep, alien voice that echoed around the factory. "You were to tell no one of our arrangement."

The Fool shrugged. "Yeah, well I got bored. Besides, it's not like you're paying me. Now can we get this over with?"

"By bringing others, you've compromised this location. What makes you think you or your friends are leaving here alive?"

Hugo gave The Fool a panicked look. "Quick, do something!" he cried.

The Fool looked embarrassed. "Hey, so remember when I talked about my power backfiring if I push it too hard?"

Inwardly, I cursed. Somewhere in the near future, countless beings across the galaxy would receive their update on events within the Tower. And I could hear all of them laughing over the fact that I trusted a fool.

CHAPTER 28
THE FICKLENESS OF LUCK

"LEAVE the water and then leave this place!" the voice snarled.

Shadows swirled like strands of silk at the edges of the light. They strained against it in all directions. Their voice bounced around the space—alien and unrecognizable.

Hugo's eyes turned white, signifying that he was about to summon something.

"No, don't!" I cried. "Think of the traps!"

For all we knew, this whole place could go up from one wrong move. We had to tread very carefully here.

Hugo backed off, but he still wouldn't leave my shoulder. I kept my foot forward on the trap and looked to The Fool, hoping that he would help get us out of this. He has a prior relationship with the Climber, so maybe he could talk him down.

The Fool pulled out a potion bottle filled with water. "You mean this?" He held it aloft smugly. His face quickly turned to dismay as the bottle slipped out of his hands. We watched as it hit the floor and shattered. The Fool frowned at the remains. He appeared genuinely puzzled by what had happened, like his own power had acted against him.

"Leave and don't come back!" the voice repeated.

All of us were unmoved by the threat. In my case, literally so.

"Not until you deactivate this trap," The Fool insisted.

The shadowy voice went quiet, which struck me as strange. They were trying to affect an air of menace, and yet the longer we stood here like this, the weaker they seemed. Maybe the traps weren't just an extra security caution. Maybe they relied on them to fight. Either that or they were wary of The Fool's power and hesitant to test him.

After a few tense seconds, I heard a clicking sound beneath my foot.

"There, it is done," the voice said.

I glanced at The Fool who shrugged. "Feels like it."

Great. Not exactly a ringing endorsement.

Slowly, I raised my foot while bracing for an explosion. When none came, I had to ask about this shadow person to learn more about them. We hadn't come all this way for nothing.

"Who are you?" I asked. "Have you met any other Tower Climbers on this level? So far you and The Fool are the only ones we can find. Please, I'm looking for a friend."

"You know this place pits Climbers against one another," the voice said. "It's not wise to group up anymore."

"Does that mean you were in a group before?" Hugo asked.

"Once," they replied, sounding bitter about it. There were several more clicking sounds around us. "There, I've deactivated the rest of the traps. You're free to go now."

But I wasn't done. This was the best lead we had to learn about what was happening in the unincorporated zone. If they weren't willing to listen, then I had to find a way to make them.

I reached for my shroud's power. This was a cloak made by the shadow weavers and with it I leaned into my Heart of Darkness power. Suddenly, I could feel the shadows around the factory. They felt alien and slippery, like eels. Mentally, I grabbed hold of some of them and pulled them toward me.

"What are you doing?" the voice asked.

My own shadow lengthened. The deeper into shadow I was, the stronger I felt and the tighter my grip became. I pulled more of the factory's shadows toward me, claiming them as my own, adding them to my shadow. It kept building behind me, growing larger.

"Enough!" the voice roared. All the shadows I'd taken were ripped away from me. I tried to get them back, but I could no longer sense any of them.

A figure stepped out of the natural shadows of the factory, holding a cross-bow. His eyebrows rose at the sight of me. "Lucas?" Damian asked.

I was surprised too, but Hugo was pissed. "What the hell, man?"

Damian lowered the crossbow. "Sorry. My darkness power obscures me, but it also obscures other people too. So I only get outlines of people and distorted voices. Useful for hiding or stealth attacks, not so useful for identifying people."

"Why so paranoid in the first place?" I asked.

He looked at The Fool who had wandered off and was currently drinking a beer and trying to get one of the machines to start running again. The place had no power, so he was just pointlessly pressing buttons and messing with some cables.

"I'm not affiliated with any of the gods," he said quietly. "Which means I'm more of a target."

That was surprising to hear, especially after encountering him on that other planet working for Roan. I asked him about it.

"That was a one-time thing. He said he already had a Climber with shadow powers and he didn't need another."

He was referring to Daisy, but I doubted they'd ever met before, so he couldn't have known about her.

"Have you met any other Climbers on this floor?" I asked.

He shook his head. "Not really. Heard or saw glimpses of fighting that might've come from one of them, but I never got close enough to know. If there are others here, then it's only a small handful."

Hugo and I frowned at each other. "That's not what we wanted to hear," I said.

"And all of them are keeping their heads down," Damian added, before pointing at The Fool. "Except that one, but I suspect he's not allowed to. In some ways, his power carries the greatest cost that I've ever seen in the Tower."

The Fool was still playing with the machine. Oblivious to our conversation. I wondered if Damian was right, but it was all disappointing to hear.

"Damn, we came here for nothing," Hugo said.

"Hugo!" I admonished him.

"Sorry. It's nice to see a familiar face, Damian, but we were hoping to learn more by coming here."

"Oh, I didn't say I hadn't learned anything. Follow me upstairs to the office."

Now that the only shadows remaining were natural, my eyes adjusted as we followed him to a set of metal stairs. Strangely, The Fool had silently decided to join us.

The stairs led up to an almost empty office. There was nothing in it except a table covered with papers and a sleeping bag in the corner. Damian pulled back the curtains to let some light into the room. The window gave a view of one of the larger streets that ran right past this side of the factory. The road was empty at the moment, but I was still wary of lingering too long in front of it in case I was spotted.

"Things have been quiet the last few days," Damian said. "It's making me anxious, and is yet another reason why I've been so cautious lately."

The Fool nodded. "It's like they're planning something."

"Who?" Hugo asked.

"All of them," Damian replied.

He moved over to the table and pushed aside some of the papers to reveal a hand-drawn map of the city. He pointed to a section in the north. "See, we're here in the unincorporated zone north of the goblin territories." He then moved his finger across to the upper middle part of the city. "A lot of fighting between orc and goblin happens over here in the center of the zone."

"Why's that?" Hugo asked.

"Neither side wants to overextend themselves. But as I said before, that stopped a short time ago and now they're just consolidating resources for something."

"I think I might know something about this," I said. "Have you heard about the disappearances?"

Damian looked puzzled. "Other than The Fool here, you're the first people I've talked to since coming to this floor."

Hugo: Wow, that's depressing.

Lucas: Yeah, although most of our conversations with the locals haven't exactly been great.

"Well, Hugo and I have spoken to members of each faction and we believe there's another group at play here."

I went on to explain the disappearances, the stolen bodies, and the experiments we found. That the factions were losing people and becoming even more insular. Both Damian and The Fool took my words seriously. They were especially interested in the part about the hidden tunnel that led out of the city. Unfortunately, when I asked if there was anything out there besides monsters, both admitted that they'd spent very little time in the desert and were unsure if there was.

But due to the way the tunnel was built I had to think that there was more to it. There had to be something out there.

Damian warned me about going out there blind. The desert could be more dangerous in some ways than the city. He was right, but I didn't like staying still. I needed a new direction to move things forward. We'd talk about different ideas, go round in circles, take a break, and then talk again. At some point The Fool brought out chairs for us to sit on and we ate together. None of us felt like saying much then. I guessed mentally we all just wanted a rest.

Afterward we resumed going over the map, marking our respective encounters, and talking about what to do next. I wanted to go after the church, especially after my last few encounters with them, but Damian thought that the goblins were hiding something. He argued that they were also closer and easier to investigate. So I countered by saying that we should split up to cover both. Damian agreed.

The sun was beginning to set at this point and we were about to leave when a small canister smashed through the office window. Smoke gushed out of it, quickly filling the room. Coughing, I ran over to the window. A group of robed cultists were circling around to the factory doors while others were across the street, lurking in the shadows. Perhaps they were hoping we'd jump out of the window to avoid the smoke.

"It's people from the church," I said. I could also hear an engine roaring and getting louder. Something was driving down the street, but I couldn't see it.

The Fool pushed me aside. "Let me see. This is probably all my fault. I pushed my luck too hard earlier."

As he stuck his head out of the window, his feet slipped and he fell over the edge. I rushed over to try and grab him, but it was too late. I thought he was dead. Until... a goblin truck sped by. The Fool lay in the back of it, waving at me, before the truck turned a corner and disappeared.

"Is he okay?" Hugo asked.

"Yeah, he's doing better than we are right now. How are we getting out? This factory doesn't have a back door."

Damian nodded. "It's fine," he said matter-of-factly. "I can get us out of here."

Shadows spread out around him, suppressing the smoke, but as they tried to reach beyond the office they faltered and disintegrated.

Damian cursed and picked his crossbow up off the table. "They have anti-magic batteries," he said. "So I'm open to ideas."

I drew my sword and waited for the first one to come up the stairs.

"That's easy," Hugo said. "We fight. They lose."

Damian smirked. "Fair enough."

CHAPTER 29
THE RIGHT TOOL FOR
THE JOB

SMOKE STILL HUNG in the office, obscuring much of the space. Damian was a shadowy outline shuffling papers into his inventory. I even watched the table disappear into there as well. I couldn't see what was happening outside or down in the factory below. At least not without sticking my head out and making myself a target. But we could all hear them moving around. Their boots slapping against stone and concrete as they moved into their positions.

"What are they doing?" Hugo asked.

"They're securing the building to make sure there aren't any other ways out," I said

"They're also confiscating my traps," Damian groused.

"Why?" the bird asked.

"They know we're stuck up here," I replied. "So they're taking their time getting ready. We can't stay here. If they want us dead, then they'll just throw something nastier than a smoke bomb in here."

Hugo looked longingly at the window. "You sure we shouldn't just go out that way and escape?"

I shook my head. They were hoping that we'd try that, and had something set up and waiting for us. I wasn't sure what it was exactly, but I could feel it. Someone fast, agile, and small might not have the same problem as me though.

"I've changed my mind. Hugo, why don't you go play outside?"

For once, he didn't argue. I think he knew that the magic batteries that blocked abilities would hurt him most of all. At least on the outside, he had a chance to fight back.

He flew out the window and disappeared.

Lucas: You good?

Hugo: Yeah, I'm on the roof. I'll take care of the ones outside, but it might take a few minutes.

That was okay. Damian and I would need some time ourselves. The batteries that drain magical abilities might've diminished some of our greater powers, but we were still formidable in more traditional ways.

We readied our weapons and made for the doorway when something arced in the air and fell toward us. A green vial hit the foot of the door and shattered, releasing a green noxious gas. It ate the regular smoke as it rose and began to encroach into the room.

"That's one of mine!" Damian yelled, angry at himself for letting them get their hands on it. He shoved a potion into my hand. "Drink this!" There was a wild look in his eyes as he pulled a potion out for himself and drank it in one big gulp. Spurred on by his worried state, I quickly did the same.

The green gas cloud grew weaker. Its color fading before completely disappearing.

"What was that supposed to do?" I asked.

"You don't want to know," he muttered, before manually sliding a bolt into his crossbow.

Thud. Thud. Thud.

Heavy steps rattled against the metal stairs. The rusted iron work groaned, straining under the weight. A robed figure, tall and almost too wide for the doorway appeared. His face was covered by some kind of black cloth and in his hands was a large metal pipe.

As he ducked his head down to enter the office, Damian fired his crossbow. The bolt hit him squarely in the chest, and hung there. Damian and I glanced at each other with a knowing look. He's wearing armor under his robes.

Now it was my turn while Damian reloaded. I rushed forward and went low with my sword. I slashed at the back of his legs, aiming to hamstring him—yet I too felt resistance. Was he covered from head to toe in the stuff?

It was too late to ask him.

He violently jabbed the end of the pipe into my gut. All the air whooshed out of me and I gasped and stumbled back. Damian fired his crossbow again. The giant cultist had to duck to avoid taking a bolt to the face.

Maybe his head isn't armored?

My stomach was in pain. Part of me wanted to vomit, but another couldn't stop wheezing to catch my breath. Without thinking, I pulled a body out of my inventory to drain it of blood. Only when I placed my hand over it, no connection formed. As long as those batteries were active, I couldn't access blood healing either.

I put the body back and reappraised our new friend. He was faster than he looked. That pipe attack had come out of nowhere. The scars on his pale hands suggested he was tough, too. Had I not seen those hands, I might've considered him an orc.

Enemy Identified [Senior Abbey Enforcer, Level: 139]

At least he didn't have a name. Not that it would have stopped me, but a little extra dehumanization was always nice in a fight to the death.

I moved forward cautiously and threw out several feints, baiting him to swing the pipe and give me an opening. But he never gave me one. Instead, he remained in front of the doorway blocking it.

I backed up to Damian.

"What do you think?" I asked.

"His head is unarmored, and he doesn't want us leaving this room. Could be waiting for even more reinforcements to come and help capture us. How's it look outside?"

I peered out the window. The smoke had fully cleared now, but the street below was pure chaos with the cultists fighting the spirit summons.

"Magical," I said, to which he grunted. "But also crowded. Perhaps we should stick with Mr. Pipe for now?"

The cultist slammed his pipe onto the ground and bellowed in rage. It was meant as a challenge to us, but it ended up sounding more like an agreement.

"I think he's saying he wants to continue," Damian said. "He must be special if he's the first one they send to us."

"Plus, he's got a pipe. They don't just hand those out to any old religious fanatic."

Damian went left, and I went right. He could still see both of us, but the farther apart we were, the harder it would be to follow our movements. I'd engage him with my sword, and Damian would wait for an opening to take his head.

Mr. Pipe wasn't stupid though. He saw what we were planning and so he suddenly dashed toward me, swinging the pipe. I tried blocking it with my sword, and a jolt of pain shot through my wrist and up my arm as I struggled to hold on. He was too strong to block, but it had served as a distraction.

Damian, to his credit, took the shot while Mr. Pipe's back was turned. The bolt bounced off the back of his head.

I cursed. His head was armored too. He'd dodged the earlier one to make us think of it as a vulnerability.

Clever.

I cursed again. I hated fighting clever enemies. Give me dumb drooling idiots and I'll happily cut them down for days. But clever enemies? Those were tougher to walk away from unscathed.

He swung his pipe in these wide, heavy swings that I could only dodge. Each one forced me a little farther back. I couldn't let this guy corner me.

I launched into a series of shallow sword cuts all over his body, slicing through the soft fabric of his robes. If I could just see what kind of armor he had on, then I could find its weak spots.

The robes lay in tatters. When I reached forward to rip them free, he kicked me. It was a low, vicious strike to the knee. My leg buckled, and I looked up to see the pipe flying toward me. I brought my arm and sword up. Heard the crack as my arm broke and felt the sword fly out of my hand across the room.

I was stunned. The pain in my arm was shrieking at me, but I still forced myself to stand. Mr. Pipe hit me again and again. I tried to shield my face and get away until my back hit the window. I'd run out of space. He knew it too and took pleasure in pulling the pipe back for a big baseball bat-like home-run swing. The kind of swing that could take my head clean off.

Damian lobbed a potion at his back. It shattered, and there was a hiss as it ate through the fabric and armor. Mr. Pipe grunted in pain and jabbed the end of the pipe into my gut. I doubled over in agony. Then, he swung upward at my chin. The blow rocked me back, and I tumbled out of the window. Down, down, down.

No soft truck saved me as I slammed into the pavement. My vision danced with stars as I was sprawled there groaning.

Hugo: Lucas! Are you okay?

It took me several moments to focus long enough to read the words in front of my eyes.

Lucas: Yeah, never better.

My mouth was full of blood. I wanted to spit it out, but everything hurt so much that I couldn't move.

Hugo: I can't get to you right now. Just don't move.

Lucas: What about the cultists outside?

Hugo: They're all busy. Just stay where you are.

But I couldn't do that. The damage to my body was extensive, and I was already feeling faint. If I didn't move soon, then I knew I'd blackout. At which point, it would be too late.

I grit my teeth and took stock of the situation. One arm was broken and one knee was severely injured. There was some internal bleeding from those pipe jabs. It also hurt to breathe, which suggested a couple of cracked ribs. And some smaller injuries barely worth mentioning, like the glass I cut myself on, falling out the window. My cheek was bad too on one side of my face.

I tried to open my eyes, but the right eye wouldn't open all the way. It was a slit that I could barely see out of. I guessed I should be lucky it hadn't swollen completely shut.

There was fighting going on behind me across the street. I could hear running, shouting, and people dying. Spirit crows flew nearby, attacking cultists. Hugo was right. They were too busy fighting to even notice me.

I dragged myself to my feet and leaned against the wall for support. I had to get back inside the factory and disable the battery.

Every hobbled step made me wince. Walking was hard. All I focused on was the next step in front of me. Just one step.

Eventually, I made it back around to the front doors of the factory. They were still open. I spied a group of cultists inside with their backs to me.

Idiots. Anyone could just walk in.

There were six of them, but the one that caught my attention was the one standing in front of the magical battery. A metal-cased hollow cylinder three feet long that held some kind of spinning gyroscope with a blue glowing gem in the center. There was even a handle on top of the battery to make carrying it easier.

Was this something Bart had made for them?

I shook my head. It didn't matter how the thing worked. Only that it appeared fragile and hopefully could be destroyed.

I looked around for something to use and found an old open toolbox on the floor containing a pair of screwdrivers. I picked one up with my good hand and steadied myself. I only got one shot at this, but if I could hit that blue gem from here, then it might disable the battery.

I hurled the screwdriver at the battery's core. The screwdriver went spinning across the room. I watched it go wide and clang off the side of its metal casing.

The cultists turned toward the sound. They seemed startled until they saw the state of me. Bloody and broken, with one eye almost swollen shut. One of them laughed as he approached. So I picked up the second screwdriver and waited.

The laughing cultist was a young man with a mocking grin and empty hands. He couldn't see the other screwdriver hidden against my wrist. He grabbed my shoulders and pushed me back outside. I let him steer me away from the battery and away from his friends. He probably wanted to take me back to the church himself and claim credit for capturing me. I stabbed the screwdriver into his neck. His grin slowly vanished and his mouth formed a shocked O-shape… as he died.

But letting him pull me away from the factory actually helped. I was outside of the battery's range. I called his blood to me, drawing it to my hand, absorbing its healing property.

After draining him, I was left disappointed. Everything still hurt, especially my arm and knee. On the plus side, there was no more internal damage and I could see clearly out of both eyes.

I wrenched the screwdriver free and hobbled back toward the factory.

CHAPTER 30
THE STRENGTH OF FAITH

THE REMAINING cultists watched me re-enter the factory. Their wide eyes darted to the bloody screwdriver in my hand. They knew what I'd done and what I was planning to do to them.

All of them moved closer to the battery. Guarding it, but also seeking its protection. Clutched to their bodies was an assortment of whatever makeshift weapons they could get their hands on. It was mostly chains and pipes, though one of them did find a wooden two-by-four that they held in front of themselves like a sword.

I could see their faces. Just ordinary middle-aged men and women that could've been shopkeepers I'd walked past without even blinking. Now they were scared. Now they were quietly trying to pray their fear away. Their mouths moved quickly in a whispered frenzy.

I couldn't make out the words and didn't much care to. They were the enemy. Anything else after that was a moot point.

I limped toward them with the bloody screwdriver. They stopped praying and tensed up. They expected me to fight, but instead I headed left and found one of Damian's deactivated traps. The tripwire for it had been cut away, but the rest of it was still taped to the lower side of a crate. Thirty poison-tipped darts in a cartridge, spring-loaded, and poised to shoot out when the trigger was pulled.

Carefully, I peeled the cartridge off of the crate and slowly walked back to face the cultists. They knew I was holding something, and though they couldn't tell what it was, it unnerved them. Rightly so.

"You'll never defeat us!" one of them yelled. "The Mother always protects her faithful," another spat.

I looked at each one of them in turn. "You should've prayed harder."

I pulled the trigger. The darts shot out with a quiet hiss in a wide spray pattern. Three cultists fell down screaming while the other two dove for cover.

Not wasting any time, I hurried over to the undefended battery. Twisting the handle caused the gyroscope to stop spinning and the glow surrounding the gem to fade. There were still waves of residual heat coming off of the battery, but I could sense that it had been deactivated.

Three of the cultists were still writhing on the floor from the poison. I summoned a Hemorrhage Gate and shot a blood spike into each of their hearts. They died instantly and I was able to replenish my health back to its peak state.

As I stretched and enjoyed having the full range of motion in both arms again, I heard feet scuffling across the floor. The two cultists who'd survived the darts had crawled to opposite ends of the room and gotten to their feet. Their fearful eyes flickered from me to the battery. A long second passed before they made a break for the door.

They didn't get far.

Two more blood spikes shot out and hit them in the back. Their bodies dropped in front of the door.

As I moved in to consume their power, I saw a crowd of cultists in the distance heading my way. I counted at least thirty members, with two at the front holding active magic batteries. These battery bearers were flanked by cultists wielding crossbows. I was outside of their range for the batteries, but that wouldn't be the case for long.

The cultists spotted me before I could hide. Their bolts started flying in my direction.

I hid behind the door and ran behind the factory's machines. I had to get Damian and Hugo, and then get us out of here. The defunct battery had my attention, though. It was out in the open. Maybe I could make a run for it and put the thing in my inventory.

I decided to go for it. I broke cover and rushed toward the battery. Before I could get there, a bolt hit the gem, causing it to shatter. Another bolt cut across my arm. I was forced to keep moving to avoid further attacks.

The stairs to the office would leave me exposed, too, so I drew blood left over from the dead cultists to me. Using Blood Leash, I threw it out like a whip to wrap around the top stair railing. With a mental command, the blood yanked up into the air and, like a magnet, pulled my body toward it.

I hit the stairs with a rough thud. A little bruised, but otherwise okay. What I saw in the office wasn't what I expected, though.

Mr. Pipe held Damian up against a wall and was actively choking him. Damian appeared unarmed and was struggling to break free from his grip. I frowned at the scene, confused.

"Why are you toying with him?" I asked Damian.

"Want... to beat... fairly," Damian wheezed.

I had to struggle not to roll my eyes. He could have killed Mr. Pipe as soon as the battery was deactivated. Instead, he held his other powers back. He wanted to be able to hold his own if he got hit with another battery. Admirable, but short-sighted.

"We don't have time for this," I said. "Reinforcements are coming with more batteries. Either you do it or I will."

Damian reluctantly nodded.

Shadows suddenly poured out of his mouth. They flowed toward Mr. Pipe's head, where it appeared they were being absorbed. The giant cultist let go of Damian and stumbled back. He ripped off his face covering, and his entire big head was covered in a roiling smudge of shadow. Now it was his turn. He was being choked by them.

Damian casually walked over to his fallen crossbow and picked it up. The bolt loaded on it magically changed to a different bolt.

"So the window?" he asked, just as Mr. Pipe collapsed.

I nodded. "Let's steer clear of the street though."

I leapt out of the window and threw out another Blood Leash to grab the edge and swung myself up onto the factory's roof.

Lucas: Hugo, we're leaving.

Hugo: Do we have to? I'm getting so many levels off of these guys.

Lucas: More are coming. Right now there are too many for us to fight head on.

I stood on the roof waiting until Damian climbed up the old-fashioned way, with the crossbow slung across his back.

"You took your time," I said.

"I had to set something up. Speaking of which, we should keep moving."

Hugo joined us as we jumped across to the roof of a neighboring building. We ran along the rooftops until we were a few streets away when Damian asked us to stop. He turned around to look back the way we'd come just as the factory exploded.

"What was that?" I asked.

Damian smirked. "Remember that trap you stepped on? Well, I reactivated it and put it on a timer. It was all mechanical, so there was no magic for them to block."

"I stepped on that?!"

"That does seem rather extreme," Hugo said.

Damian shrugged. "It was meant for orcs. I've never fought one, but I've heard they're tough."

I confirmed that they were and suggested that we keep moving. I wanted us out of the unincorporated zone as quickly as possible. That explosion was a lightning rod for trouble, so the farther away from it we were, the better.

The walk back to the human district was uneventful. Thank God. Any time a patrol got too close, the three of us would blend into the shadows. The fact that it was now nighttime made that a breeze.

Once we'd crossed over into the somewhat safer human territory, Damian explained that it was best we part ways here. He still wanted to check out Goblintown, and he knew that I was even more dead set on heading to the church.

"I'll come find you if I uncover anything useful," he said.

We nodded to each other, and he turned and disappeared down one of the alleyways.

Hugo was less than enthused with my plan however. He wanted to go back to the apartment but the night was still young. Plus, I wanted to take full advantage of investigating the church while so many of their members were distracted. Hugo argued that he was tired from fighting and wouldn't be at his best if we ran into more trouble. Birds.

"I could share my healing power and pour some blood on you?" I offered sweetly.

The crow ruffled his feathers in disgust. "Bleh! I'll pass."

"Are you sure?" I pressed. "It's better than coffee."

Hugo looked at me with disappointment. "You know I'm more of an energy drink bird."

"Right, it was the one where the label has a guy on a dirt bike riding over a mountain."

His eyes lit up. "That's right! Do you have some in the apartment?"

"No."

He lowered his head, crestfallen.

"But I'm sure that I could make something similar," I added, trying to cheer him up.

"Really?" he asked, his voice full of hope.

I nodded. It was refreshing to have someone around who could be thrilled by the simplest of things. Maybe it had to do with how he lived before the Tower came. That when you struggle to survive each day, the smallest of pleasures matter the most.

I wasn't lying about making it either. I had some caffeine pills that I could crush up and put into a soda. It should emulate the effect quite well.

We were about to cross one of the main streets when a horse-drawn carriage pulled up beside us. It was finely painted with blue and gold and looked like something a king might use. A male orc wearing a cloak sat up top, holding the horse's reins. He did not look down at us, merely stared at the road ahead.

The carriage door opened and a female orc stepped out. She was about my height and wore a black suit without a tie. Her dark hair was tied back in a long braid that reached all the way down to her lower back.

She cleared her throat and pulled out a scroll of paper from her jacket to read. "To the Tower Climbers, Lucas and Hugo, you have been cordially invited to attend a party at Mr. Enzo's estate this evening."

This couldn't have come at a worse time. We had to get to the church while the cultists were distracted.

"Yeah, we're busy," I said. "Why don't you reschedule us for an appointment for tomorrow?"

The orc flashed her teeth. "While this invite is politely worded, my boss was emphatic about how much he wanted you there. This isn't a request. Get in the carriage before I make you."

Hugo remained silent, which meant he was letting me make the call on this one. I glanced around. We were alone on the street, but if these orcs didn't come back, Enzo would know it was us. I also didn't feel like fighting with another faction, so we got in the carriage.

CHAPTER 31
AN INTERESTING ESCORT

ONCE WE'D SAT DOWN, the carriage lurched forward, speeding us down the empty street. Most of the road was paved, but occasionally we would hit a pothole and we'd feel the carriage rumble. After the second bump, I had to tighten my fists to resist the urge to flinch. The driver either couldn't, or wouldn't, slow down no matter how many of them she hit. Evidently, we were in something of a hurry to get to this party.

The carriage itself was meant to elicit a feeling of luxury for its passengers, with its satin pillows and decorated interior. A comfortable mode of transportation for someone of a high station in life. Loaning the carriage out to others like myself was probably considered a privilege that one was expected to feel grateful for.

Well, I hated it.

We were in a big rolling wooden box with two tiny windows limiting our view, and loud horse hooves shouting our presence to anyone with working ears. It could very well be our coffin if we were ambushed.

Our orc chaperone didn't seem to share my concern though. She sat across from us with her hands in her lap. Her body language was relaxed, but her stare wasn't. She peered at me with an intense focus that I found unnerving.

"Can I help you with something?" I asked her.

She slowly studied me up and down. "They say that those who survive the trials of the Tower are great warriors."

The term 'great' was pushing it. I wouldn't trust half the Climbers I'd met to successfully run a McDonalds, let alone anything in the Tower. Hell, I was pretty sure Hugo and I didn't qualify for that label either.

I was curious to know whether she was talking about those who'd survived the entire Tower, though. The information imbalance between us bothered me, but I didn't want to look too eager for answers. So I met her gaze and waited for her to elaborate.

"Well, are you?" she asked.

I decided to hedge. "It's a work in progress."

Hugo: Speak for yourself.

The crow had nestled himself on top of one of the pillows, despite me warning him to bail out the window at the first sign of trouble. He chose not to join the conversation, so I let it be and focused on our orc escort.

She seemed disappointed with my answer. Her interest in me was waning. That was fine. I didn't feel like bragging about my skills, especially when there were better things to talk about.

"So what's this party we've been invited to?" I asked her.

She stared out of the window and glibly replied, "You'll find out when you get there."

I suppressed a wave of frustration. I'd played it too cautiously and now she found me boring. If I wanted to keep the conversation going, then I had to reignite her interest.

"Do you ever actually use the knife you keep by your ankle, or do they make you wear it as part of the uniform?"

She turned back to me, surprised and elated that I'd spotted it. The fact that it had become second nature to search for weapons when meeting someone should've troubled me. But it was that kind of paranoia that had kept me alive. So far.

"It gets more use than you'd think," she said as she pulled back her left pant leg to reveal the blade that was strapped there. The placement seemed awkward. It wasn't something she could quickly get to in a fight. It would've been easier to get a shoulder holster and wear it under her jacket. Maybe carrying it wasn't so approved after all.

She took the knife out and handed it to me. I tested its weight and casually flipped it in my hand a couple of times. It was a nice piece of craftsmanship that made me miss my own knife.

I reluctantly handed it back to her and said, "Very nice... Uh...?"

"Chiara," she replied.

"I really hope that's your name and not the name of your knife."

"Do Climbers name their weapons?" she inquired, part fascinated and part horrified.

I shook my head. "Not if they can help it." Though I was sure there were some out there that did, and technically, the inventory had a naming system for every item. "What about that pistol you keep under your jacket? Does that have a name?"

Chiara grimaced. "Not one that I can remember. The person who invented them named it something long and pretentious. Most of us have taken to calling them Gats. And no, you can't hold it. Strict orders from above on that front."

Hugo suddenly opened his eyes. He'd seemingly been trying to get a nap in before we reached the party, but between the bumpy road and our conversation, it had proved fruitless.

"And what exactly were your orders surrounding us?" the crow asked.

Her mouth tightened as she looked at Hugo, clearly annoyed at him for interrupting our conversation. She seemed far less interested in Hugo despite the fact that he was also a Tower Climber, and had only wanted to ask me about my fighting skills. Perhaps she valued physical feats over fighting with magic?

"The boss told me to get you and bring you to the party as soon as possible," she replied, sounding bored.

"And he's fine with me coming to his fancy party dressed like this?" I asked, gesturing at my dirty clothes.

She shrugged. "Tower Climbers are known for their eccentric fashion sense. If anything, it will highlight you among the crowd and improve his standing among the guests."

By looking like he's got a couple of Climbers in his back pocket. I didn't like the presumption of ownership, but I'd swallow it for now. He could still be of use to us.

Chiara caught something in my look. "It doesn't bother you?" she asked. "Being summoned and taking orders from my boss?"

She was probing, probably to try and determine how much of a threat I was to Enzo. I decided to be aloof. She hadn't attended our meeting with her boss and I doubted all the information from it was shared with her.

I relaxed my body and smiled. "I don't take orders from him. We have a mutual agreement."

I was hoping it would bait her curiosity, but instead she burst out laughing.

I tried not to let it bother me, but Hugo was offended and took the bait. "Hey, what's so funny?"

"If you truly think that, then you're in for a surprise. My boss doesn't share power. He doesn't do partnerships. Whatever you're thinking right now is what he wants you to think."

Now it was my turn to laugh. "In a few days, we'll have moved on from this place to the next floor down. A week from now and we'll barely be able to remember his name. So he happens to be the biggest fish in this small pond. That means nothing. There are oceans beyond this place.

We've swum with monsters greater than your boss and likely will do so again."

Rather than being angry or offended at my words, she seemed excited by them. She looked like she wanted to ask a question when the carriage suddenly came to a stop.

We had arrived at our destination.

At the farthest southern corner of orc territory was a long, tall hill. At the top it overlooked most of the city, except for the tower Enzo also owned, and a second peak where he had built a large mansion surrounded by manicured bushes and trees.

Ahead of us, orcs and humans, dressed in expensive suits and dresses, were stepping out of identical carriages and going inside.

"Anything else we should know before heading in there?" Hugo asked.

Chiara nodded. "I possess several methods of disabling you both should you misbehave or run before the meeting occurs."

She tried to be threatening, but that sparkle in her eye told me she was having fun. I met her gaze and let out a bored yawn. The rest of her body remained composed, but her mouth opened a little to bare her tusks. The prospect of fighting a Tower Climber excited her. There was a part of Chiara that wanted me to try something.

I didn't take the bait, instead settling into my seat to wait. I'd noted that attendants were coming to open the carriage doors for the guests and I decided that we should do the same—ideally it would emphasize our importance. There could be others at this party with pertinent information. I couldn't have them thinking that I was below them or they'd never talk to me.

Hugo: Any advice?

His eyes were bouncing between the crowds on the grounds in front of the house and the practiced servants milling between them with drinks. It was almost too much information.

Lucas: Don't talk unless we're alone with Enzo. I may need you to spy on some people.

Hugo: Fine, but any canapés you come across are mine later.

Lucas: Agreed.

Hugo: I'm serious. I want to see you take an obnoxious amount of food and put it in your inventory. I'm talking quantities that will cause people to throw you dirty looks.

Lucas: Fine.

After an awkward minute of waiting, a human attendant dressed in a fine servant's uniform rushed over and opened the door for us. He was a bald man wearing a pair of white gloves that didn't have a speck of dirt on them.

"So hard to find good help these days," Chiara muttered as she stepped out first.

The attendant bristled at the remark. "Apologies. We did not realize it was you who had decided to procure a carriage so abruptly. I'll have the search called off."

My eyebrows rose. "You stole this carriage? And here I thought you were just a loyal soldier following orders."

Chiara grinned. "It was somebody's orders. I just thought it would be more fun to pick you up myself."

"And is it?"

"I haven't decided yet."

Another human attendant rushed over to us. This time it was a woman with short, red hair. In fact, all of the servants at this party seemed to be humans that were either bald or had extremely short hair.

This attendant was red-faced from running as she approached me. "My master apologizes for the suddenness of this invitation and that he cannot see you just yet. You are encouraged to enjoy the party until his prior meetings are concluded." She then turned to Chiara. "Miss Accetta, your father is waiting for you in his study."

She nodded and walked away with the attendant without so much as sparing a glance back at us.

Hugo: Wait, what just happened?

Lucas: Chiara is Enzo's daughter.

Neither of us knew whether that was a good thing or a bad thing.

We stood at the entrance, watching others enter Enzo's mansion. Every guest tried to sneak looks at me and Hugo as they passed us. Some were subtle about it, while others openly stared. I paid close attention to the human faces despite not recognizing any of them. That didn't mean there weren't cultists hiding among the guests. Just that they were being careful.

After all the funny looks, I was starting to feel more exposed just standing out here. There was no use putting it off any longer. I walked toward the mansion's entrance. It was time to join a party where we don't know anybody and half the people probably wanted us dead.

CHAPTER 32
TRUST ISSUES

GUESTS CONGREGATED in small groups within the foyer while still leaving room for the servants and other visitors to move around. Thankfully, no one announced our presence as we entered the mansion. In fact, no one seemed to notice us at all, now that we were inside. Not that we wanted the attention, but this felt deliberate.

Hugo: This feels weird.

I nodded. Several times, people would glance at us and then look away.

Lucas: It's like they're trying to pretend we're not here.

Hugo: On Enzo's orders?

Lucas: I doubt he'd care.

I made eye contact with one woman and her head turned away so sharply I thought she might've given herself whiplash. That's when I understood why they were acting so strangely.

Lucas: It's fear. They're afraid of us.

This sentiment didn't extend to the orcs though, who could be split into two groups. Group one were orcs in suits working security. They stood at the edges of the rooms like statues while they watched everything.

The second group, in fancier garb, were orc merchants and their partners. They were the most jovial orcs that I'd seen thus far, as they laughed and drank.

One thing was clear though. None of the servants were orcs. A not-so-subtle display of power by Enzo to remind people of their position within the city.

A quick scan of the crowd told me that they were only here for the party. None of them would have useful information for us.

I moved through the foyer and out through an open side door. It was a warm night and a lot of guests had chosen to congregate in the garden grounds behind the mansion.

Lucas: This looks like a good place for you to eavesdrop.

Hugo: Alright, I'll see what I can find out.

He took off without another word and I ambled around looking to find someone who seemed like they'd be worth talking to. Enzo struck me as a practical person, and so while there might be a lot of vacuous people attending this party, there also had to be those of importance too. I just had to discover one of them.

Moving around the side of the house led to a large terrace with a balcony overlooking another garden below. I stepped to the edge of it and was surprised by what I saw.

There were goblins at this party as guests. There were eight of them split equally into two groups, keeping their distance from one another. The group to the far left just stood there glaring at anyone who dared walk near them, while the other group was laughing and smoking. Strangely, this actually unnerved people more and they gave the laughing group a wide berth.

"It's an old ambassador practice," Gren said as he stood alongside me.

I tried not to look surprised to see him here. "What is?"

"When one clan goes to negotiate with another, they send two groups of representatives. One sober and one high on Serenity Leaf. Then both groups return home and make their report to the clan chief."

I guessed that explained why everyone was keeping their distance from them. None of the other guests wanted to risk getting accidentally dosed by secondhand smoke. It was odd to see them here though, since they seemed to be at war with the orcs. And with all the disappearances, I'd gotten the impression that the city's factions were isolating themselves. Yet here they all were, enjoying a party together.

"What are they doing meeting with the orcs?" I asked him. "Matter of fact, what are you doing here at all? Last I heard, the goblins weren't big fans of you."

Gren coughed awkwardly. "That part is still true. I didn't come here with the clan's ambassadorial team. When I heard about this party, I bribed a human I knew for his ticket. My brother Vrog is on the team, and this might be one of my only chances to see him without risking his reputation."

"Which one is he?"

Gren peered over the balcony and then turned away. "The sober one with his arms folded."

I looked and saw the one he was talking about. He looked exactly like Gren, but wore a fine black tunic with gold around the edges. While the other sober goblins looked angry, Vrog looked bored. He also kept checking a fancy silver watch on his wrist.

"Nice watch," I said.

Gren grunted. "He's an engineer by trade. Built it himself. He probably wishes he was back home right now tinkering with something."

An engineer? Now that was interesting.

"I don't suppose he ever mentioned something about magic-draining batteries, spirit capture devices, or the people disappearing?"

Gren gave me a flat stare. "No, somehow those topics never came up at our family dinner."

"Right, sorry. What about why they're here?"

He shrugged. "I have no clue. I was never well connected to the political scene of the clan, even at the best of times."

I thought about what the orcs might do if they learned someone uninvited had acquired a ticket and crashed the party.

"Is it risky for you to be here?"

Gren took out a Serenity cigarette and lighter. He almost lit it, and then changed his mind and stuffed it back into his jacket pocket. "Nah, this isn't Goblintown and the others won't make a scene while they're guests of the orcs. Still, it won't look good if I just walk up to him to talk."

"*Are you* going to talk to him?"

He shrugged again. "I dunno. I've seen him. He looks healthy. Talking to him now in front of the others will just make things worse for him. You know, guilt by association and all that."

"But you're still here."

He sighed. "Yep." A passing servant with a tray of drinks stopped. Gren grabbed two glasses of champagne. I reached out to take one. I downed the glass and then a second in quick succession. "Right now, I'm just waiting to see if he'll break off from the group to take a piss."

Being on piss-watch duty sounded like a poor way to spend an evening, but the pain in the goblin's eyes told me that words wouldn't dissuade him.

"What about if I got him away from the others so that you could both speak freely?"

Gren's eyes narrowed. "Why would you do that for me?"

"Hey, you escorted Hugo and me to safety."

"Yeah, but you paid me for that."

"Then consider this favor a downpayment in case I need your services again."

The goblin nodded and rubbed his chin as he thought for a moment. "They wouldn't have dared arrive in one of those gaudy carriages. They would've driven here. Tell him that the goblin truck is leaking fluid. Vrog will jump at the chance to fix it if it means getting away from the party."

I nodded and clapped Gren on the shoulder. "Good luck with your brother."

There was no way to avoid being noticed coming down the stairs. So I grabbed a drink from one of the servers and unsteadily stumbled down them. Pausing every so often to sway, I walked over to the goblins and scrunched my face up in disgust.

"You know the contraption you came here in is leaking fluid? It was disgusting having to wade through it to get here. I don't know what they were thinking inviting your kind here."

One of the goblins stepped forward like he wanted to hit me, but Vrog grabbed his arm.

"Ignore him," he said. "I'll go check on the truck."

I finished my drink and walked off, pretending to search for another. Luckily, none of the goblins followed me. I could, however, feel their eyes boring into the back of my skull until I was out of their sight.

I was about to fill Hugo in on what had happened when a flicker of shadow caught my attention. A pale woman in a black dress, with dark hair, was moving away from the party and deeper into the garden. I couldn't see her face, but her build and hair reminded me of Daisy.

She walked fast toward some tall decorative hedgerows that could easily hide a person. I had to hurry before I lost sight of her.

The voices from the party started to fade the deeper into the garden I went. But by the time I'd reached the hedges the woman was gone. Multiple paths now lay in front of me. Choose incorrectly and I might never find her.

I tried enhancing my hearing and heard only silence. The same thing happened with Aura Sight. It was like she'd vanished.

"You need to be more aware of your surroundings," Daisy said behind me.

She had led me here so that we could talk alone.

"Good thinking, luring me here," I said.

She gave me a strained smile, like she was trying to be playful, but her heart wasn't in it. There were dark circles under her eyes and her skin was paler than usual.

"I almost didn't think we'd meet," I said.

"I would've sent another letter detailing a time and place. Other things got in the way. Where's Hugo?"

That was a good question.

Lucas: Hey, where are you right now?

Hugo: I'm trailing some merchants who knew people that died in the factory explosion. I don't think they're cultists, but they might be related to them. They keep alluding to next steps but haven't said anything specific. Why? Did you need something?

Lucas: No, stay where you are. I found Daisy.

Hugo: What?! I'm coming over.

Lucas: No, you're better off where you are. Look, we'd just ask the same questions anyway. It's better this way. I promise I'll update you when I've learned something.

Hugo: Fine, but we're swinging by the kitchen to clear this place out before we leave.

Lucas: It's a deal.

"Hugo is elsewhere on another task," I said.

Her smile dipped at the vague answer. "I see. So you don't trust me now?"

I hesitated about how to answer. Being paranoid has kept me going this far. Plus, Daisy had secrets. She claimed that Roan had stolen her memories and didn't know why, but she also claimed to know of a way to beat the gods.

"You know, I didn't much care for mysteries before everything went to hell. So you can only imagine how much I hate them in this place."

"What is that supposed to mean?!" she snapped.

"Oh, you want a list? You were the only other survivor from the Golden Door massacre. You didn't get in the elevator with us, and nobody seems to have noticed or cared about the message you handed me."

Even with delays to broadcasting what Tower Climbers did, someone must have seen me read it by now. At the very least, Roan should've said something.

The anger drained out of her. She sighed and in a quiet voice said, "It wasn't an ordinary message and I couldn't go with you. I had to make my own way down for my own reasons. As for surviving? That one's easy. Our connection to Roan. *Our brands* had saved us despite being the very thing keeping us shackled. You want to stop working together? Fine. I'll leave."

She turned to go.

"Wait! I'm sorry," I said. "Life in this place has been… intense lately. But we still want the same thing. We can still help each other. Please tell me what you've learned."

Daisy stopped. There was some lingering anger in her eyes over not being trusted, but she was willing to stay.

"You first," she said. "Did you investigate my quest like I asked?"

I told her about the two orcs in cloaks that I'd found and how they were stealing bodies from the human cemetery. None of it held much interest for her until I explained the part about the hidden tunnel entrance outside of the city.

"So it's somewhere in the desert," she muttered to herself.

"What is?"

She waved my concern away. "Just the next part of my quest. I can take it over from here. Now let's talk about why we're really here," she grinned. The very topic excited her, and I had to admit it made my heart rate spike up a bit too.

First, we get rid of the gods. Then we get free of the Tower and save whatever's left of our world.

It sounded simple and enticing. But we had to be cautious, because one wrong move and the gods would crush us like bugs.

I looked around. "Is it safe to talk about that out in the open?"

We appeared to be alone in this space of the garden, but you're never truly alone in the Tower. Someone was always watching.

A large square of metal with strange writing on it materialized in her hands. She laid it on the ground and began unfolding it. These square sheets of metal then locked into place, forming a mat.

I used Magical Awareness and instantly regretted it. The mat was like white fire. I grimaced and looked away before it could blind me. Whatever this thing was, the magic behind it was intense.

"Step onto it," she said.

I bent down and poked it with my finger first.

[Error!]

[Item Identification Not Found]

Figures.

Daisy didn't say a word and just watched me. She wanted me to go first as an act of trust. Well, I could do that.

I stepped onto the mat and frowned. I didn't feel anything.

"Relax, it's not active yet," she said as she stepped onto the mat. A vial of blood appeared in her hands. With the utmost care, she uncorked it and let a single drop fall onto the mat. The writing and symbols blazed to life.

"Okay, we have a few minutes of privacy. We're blocking every signal except the Tower itself."

"Why not the Tower as well?"

"Because then we'd die. The only way I know to remove the mark of the Tower is by walking out the exit of level one."

"So it's like the brand gods use when they patronize a Climber?"

"Funny you should mention that. I'm close to a breakthrough. One that will allow us to remove our brands and be free of Roan for good."

"How is that good news? Considering the fact that he's the only god that can enter the Tower now. Even if we did remove our brands, he'd just kill us the old-fashioned way."

"Wrong on both counts. You see, our brands are his direct link to the Tower. When that link is cut, expelling him will be easy."

Yet another reason why Vhar killed all those Climbers at the Golden Door. It was to make sure the other gods couldn't return here directly. Something about what she said stuck with me though.

"You said both counts. What's the other?"

"It's the other gods. I don't know how, but some of them have found a way to sponsor new Climbers. There's at least one or two in this city, and I think one of them might be connected to the church."

"How do you know all this?"

"I have my ways." Judging by my frown, she knew that wasn't a good enough answer. "Look, the less you know, the less risk there is of Roan finding out. There are a lot of eyes on you right now. Just be patient. I'm sure I'll know more soon."

She tried to step off the mat, but I grabbed her and pulled her back.

"That's not good enough!" I shouted. Hugo and I didn't nearly die in that tomb just to hear that she was still working on it.

"Well, it's all I have!" Daisy yelled back.

"Where are you getting the information?"

"I can't tell you. If you were captured and the information got out, it would hurt more than just us. Look, Roan made me tag along on a lot of trips to a lot of not so nice places. When he wasn't around, I spoke to some of the locals. I made connections, and I learned things."

"Why did Roan leave you those memories? I thought he took them all."

"He did. One of those connections contacted me and I've been trying to earn my freedom and build my memory back, piece by piece, ever since. Now are you going to let me go?"

I didn't break eye contact, but I knew there were tendrils of shadow lurking beyond the mat ready to stab me a dozen times over. She knew about my healing, so she'd probably go straight for my heart and head. What she didn't know was that I'd had Crimson Domain primed since stepping onto the mat. At this distance I could pull her inside of it before her shadows reached me.

But I didn't want that, so I let her go.

"I'm sorry."

"I'll contact you again when I know more," she said, all business.

I nodded and left with more questions than when I went in. Hugo was going to be pissed about Daisy's lack of progress. All I could do, as I returned to the party, was hope that he'd had better luck than I had.

CHAPTER 33
TWO THIEVES PASSING IN THE NIGHT

HUGO WAS WAITING for me in a tree when I returned to the party. He swooped down onto my shoulder just as I walked past it.

"Please tell me you've got good news," I said.

"That was about to be my line. What happened?"

I filled him in on what Daisy had said and, to my surprise, he took it better than I had.

"At least we know what the goal is now and we no longer have to work on her quest. I think we should return to focusing on the church."

"Sounds like you did learn something," I said.

Hugo sighed. "Not much. The people I overheard weren't cultists, but they talked about something going down in a few hours tonight at the church. Wouldn't say what it was though."

"What makes you think they weren't cultists?"

"Because they were afraid of them. They wanted to leave the party early and barricade themselves in their houses, type of afraid."

Whatever was going on with the church tonight sounded like something we couldn't afford to miss. We'd stop by the apartment to grab some stuff and then head to the church. But by the sounds of it, time was against us. We needed to leave this party. Now.

"Okay, let's see if we can force a meeting with Enzo and get it over with," I said. "We've been here long enough."

We walked back into the mansion. I was about to turn down a hallway when Hugo cleared his throat and looked to the left where the kitchen was.

Right, I had promised him. Time was a factor. But we could spare five minutes.

"I don't know why you just didn't go by yourself to steal the food," I said.

Hugo scoffed at the idea. "A bird flies into a kitchen and everyone screams murder. Objects are thrown and best-case scenario, the bird is chased out of there. However, if a bird enters a kitchen with a human bodyguard to steal the food for him, then they'll target you first, since you're bigger."

"Gee, thanks. I love being bait."

"That's great. It's good to take pride in what you're good at."

Some servers walked by as I approached the kitchen. All of them eyed Hugo, but said nothing. Probably because they were instructed not to. All the servants gave off a very 'seen but not heard' vibe, and nobody stopped us from entering the kitchen.

Inside the kitchen was a maelstrom of frantic work. My face was blasted with hot air as soon as I entered. All I could hear were cooks shouting at one another. I was worried that our presence would be a factor, but everyone was too busy working at their stations and yelling at each other to pay any attention to us.

To the side were serving trays of food on a table, ready to be picked up by servers and taken out to the guests. I tapped several trays with my finger and one by one they and the food disappeared into my inventory.

After our sixth tray, I was ready to call it a day and find Enzo when I saw another familiar face that I never expected to see.

The Fool was slowly walking through the kitchen from the other end and toward us. He too was stealing, but it wasn't food he was after. Instead, it was random objects that seemed to have almost no value. A dirty dish towel, a saucepan, a wooden spoon, and even a pair of one chef's reading glasses that he'd kept in his front pocket.

His efforts in thievery were even more overt than our own and yet no one seemed to notice that he was there. Another effect of his power perhaps, but why wasn't it working on us?

As he drew near, I opened my mouth to say something, but he put his finger to his lips and indicated that we should talk outside. I nodded and we followed him out, down a hallway, and into an empty sitting room.

The Fool closed the doors so we'd be alone, and then said, "You should've just ignored me. We could've just been two thieves passing in the night."

I frowned. "I don't understand."

The Fool threw his hands up in exasperation. "Acknowledging me in the kitchen while I was working changes things!"

Hugo and I glanced at each other, unsure of what to say.

The Fool turned away, muttering to himself. "Gotta fix it. Just make some adjustments."

His eyes began roaming over the room, and he resumed stealing things. To us, the choices looked random, but to him, every object was heavily considered before being taken. Although that seemed to change when he stopped putting items in his inventory. Instead, he grabbed an antique sword off of the mantelpiece and dropped it on a couch. Then he took an empty wine glass, a dry wooden log from the fireplace, and finally, a portrait of Enzo standing behind a younger female orc. It looked like a painting of him and his daughter. The girl had a small scar on her chin. It was interesting that the painter had included it, but that didn't mean it was worth taking.

These items sat in a pile on the couch while The Fool looked at them with pride. "Sometimes I even amaze myself."

Hugo cocked his head to the side. "What are you going to do with them?"

The Fool looked surprised. "Me? Nothing. My inventory is full. I need you to hold on to these items for me until I can collect them."

Hugo: His inventory is full?

Lucas: Sounds like a lie. Plus, what if this gets us into trouble? The painting might have sentimental value, at least.

"I don't know if I want to steal from the orcs right now," I said.

The Fool insisted. "Come on, I'll owe you one. I just need you to hold on to a few things for me until I offload some of this junk I've collected."

"So you do know it's mostly garbage?" Hugo asked.

"Of course. I just take what my intuition tells me to take. It works out in the end. Usually."

Reluctantly, I took the items and put them in my inventory. The Fool seemed relieved.

"What brought you here?" I asked. "It can't be just for this all stuff."

The Fool shrugged. "There Are only two places worth being in the city tonight. Here, or the church. The latter gave me a bad vibe, so I chose here where there's lively conversation, and free drinks."

"And how many of the guests have seen you?"

"All of them will vaguely recall my presence. It's sort of a passive effect of my power that comes up sometimes. Doesn't work on Tower Climbers though, obviously."

"What does your intuition say now?"

He gave us an apologetic smile. "That this conversation has run its course. Sorry, but I gotta go."

He started walking away, and I panicked. He might know more about what's going on with the church, or maybe he'd be willing to help. His power was impressive and certainly something I wouldn't mind having on our side.

"Wait!"

I grabbed his jacket and the piece of clothing just slipped off of him as he kept walking.

"I'd really advise against following me. The effects are unknown, but usually pretty bad."

I nodded and didn't try to stop him from leaving.

"Well, that was odd," Hugo said.

"Isn't it always with him?"

"At least you gained some artwork out of the deal. You could hang it up in the living room or your bedroom."

"Great, I could have Enzo's stern orc face staring down at me as I sleep. It'd probably give me nightmares."

A man behind us politely coughed. It was one of the servants.

He wrung his hands together and while staring at the floor said, "Apologies, but Mr. Accetta will see you now."

Hugo: You think he heard the part about you insulting his boss?

Lucas: Maybe? Who cares? I've said worse.

Hugo: I just don't want to jeopardize what we've got going with him.

I smiled.

Lucas: Feeling a little possessive over the deal you negotiated with him?

Hugo: Maybe a little.

He flew to my shoulder, and we followed the servant down several hallways until we were as far away from the party, without leaving the mansion, as possible. Two orcs in suits stood guarding one hallway and stepped aside to let us pass. The noise of the party was completely gone now. Enzo had called everyone here for a celebration and then isolated himself away from it. Not that I'm surprised. It was likely just an excuse for him to conduct business anyway.

Upon reaching a set of doors, the servant politely knocked, and another orc opened the door from the inside.

We were led into a large study filled with books on the walls and comfortable leather couches. Enzo stood in front of a large fireplace watching the flames dance, while Chiara lay on one of the couches, idly flipping her knife over.

The servant who'd escorted us silently bowed their head and left.

"Aww, I was just about to tip him," I said.

Enzo turned to face us with a stony expression. "Are you saying my staff are not well compensated?"

He kept his voice neutral, but some offense was clearly taken. I thought about how best to address the situation when Chiara laughed. "He's clearly joking, Father."

I took another look at her and saw that she lacked the scar on her chin. She wasn't the girl from the painting, which meant Enzo probably had another daughter.

Enzo nodded tiredly at Chiara and then fixed his eyes on me. A long, quiet moment stretched between us. I didn't appreciate the power play of just silently staring at someone until they spoke.

"Interesting party. It's not the day of your daughter's wedding, is it?" I asked.

Chiara winced and Enzo gave me a flat stare. "No, one of my daughters is a delinquent who'd rather act tough on the street than follow orders. The other is dead. Now can we get to business or do you have more jokes that no one laughs at?"

He gestured for us to sit and we did. I noticed that he remained standing, but I kept quiet about that part.

Hugo: He seems mad. Maybe he's right about the jokes?

Lucas: Are you serious?

Hugo: Well, you are kind of an acquired taste.

Lucas: We're not his servants. I'm not going to let this guy push us around just because he holds a lot of power on this floor.

"So, let us begin," Enzo said. "This party that you referenced was in part due to your involvement with the shop attack. A goblin suicide bombing in the human district made a lot of waves. Goblintown sent word denying their involvement, and considering the target, I think they're telling the truth. I'm meeting with their delegation here tonight to smooth things over."

My eyebrows rose. "A peace plan?"

"The beginning of one, potentially anyway. They'll want to know what's being done about the disappearances. Apparently, they too have experienced them. It would help me in the meeting if I could bring something to the table."

I basically laid out everything we'd uncovered thus far, from the inventor Bart's involvement, to the two orcs that were stealing bodies.

Chiara suddenly sat up. "I'm sorry, did you say orcs? What did they look like?"

"They wore hooded cloaks," I replied. "I never saw their faces."

She folded her arms. "How do you know they were orcs then?"

I rolled my eyes. "Seen a lot of seven-foot-tall human bodybuilders in this city, have you? Or maybe they were just really tall goblins with gray skin?"

Enzo punched the side of the fireplace so hard that the stone cracked. "Enough! If you have nothing worth contributing, then say nothing," he yelled at her. He then turned to me with gritted teeth. "Continue."

I then recounted about the pit and the reanimated bodies. Enzo took a moment to process all of this before asking, "And what is your current best guess on what is happening?"

Everything that had happened thus far was too organized to have been done by a simple monster on this floor. A Tower Climber with the right Class could have the power to do it, but the kidnappings started happening before this floor even opened so that rules them out.

"The most likely scenario is that a resident of the city gained some kind of power over the dead," I said. "It's either Bart or someone that Bart works for. They might also be connected to the church, but I'm not sure how yet."

Enzo looked surprised at hearing the church connection. "What makes you say that?"

I then told him about the cultists, their magic batteries, and how they attacked us in large numbers at the factory.

Enzo shook his head. "That doesn't make sense. You said they attacked in great numbers, so why would they recruit orcs to steal bodies for them? More to the point, why dump them elsewhere when the church is right next door to the cemetery? No, I think it's more likely that you stumbled upon church business in the unincorporated zone, and suffered for it. The church isn't the problem, focus on finding Bart."

"I still can't believe he'd do it," Chiara said.

"This isn't the time for sentiment," Enzo snapped. "Bartholomew has made his choice and we must make ours."

Chiara stared daggers at us. "Provided they're telling us the truth."

I pulled all of Bart's sketches and paperwork out of my inventory and dumped it on the floor between them. They moved closer and stared at the sketches of the spirit box device.

"This is his handwriting," Enzo said, pointing to some notes in the bottom corner. His gaze softened, and he put a comforting hand on her shoulder. "I know you liked him, but he's not the same as he was. Even you must admit that he's changed. Think of those who've been taken. Remember the children?"

Chiara closed her eyes, trying not to show emotion.

Enzo carefully scooped up all of the documents and nodded to us. "Thank you for your involvement, but I think it's best that my organization takes over now. Stay away from the church and do not look for Bartholomew."

Unfortunately, that wasn't an option. We had business with both, considering we'd be stuck on this floor until our quest was resolved. The investigation would have to continue, whether Enzo liked it or not. Still, sometimes you just need to make the person acknowledge the threat out loud.

"And if we refuse?" I asked.

"Then you'll never leave this floor alive," he replied with no anger or malice. It was the flat tone of a person who'd ordered the deaths of many without blinking.

Enzo turned back to the fire. It was his way of ending the conversation and dismissing us. I looked to Chiara for guidance, but she was still lost in thought over the inventor's betrayal.

Lucas: Let's go.

I knew Hugo wanted to argue, but it was clear that Enzo had made up his mind. The crow followed my lead, and we left the mansion behind.

An attendant offered us a carriage to take back, but I declined. Instead, I opted to hike down the long hill and through the orc territory.

"I'm feeling very used right now," Hugo said. "We're not seriously going to drop this, are we?"

I snorted. "Of course not. We'll pick up some supplies at the apartment and then see what this big church meeting is about."

Enzo should've realized that we don't respond well to threats. Unless of course, he'd planned to cut us loose knowing what we'd do next. That way, if things went wrong with the church, he had complete deniability.

Hmm. Plans within plans, and we still didn't have the full picture. I didn't like it, but we'd do what we've always done and improvise.

"Come on," I said. "It's time to arm up for the midnight mass."

CHAPTER 34
ARGUMENTS ABOUT THE WARDROBE

HUGO and I returned to the apartment. When I said that we were there to collect supplies, I was mainly talking about myself. I'd spilled a lot of blood recently. So I knew that if I went into my Crimson Domain, there'd be a Scarlet Apple waiting for me.

It was something I'd planned on saving for emergencies. After the last few battles, I doubted that I would need it. As long as I remained cognizant of those batteries and took them out manually, then the cultists wouldn't be an issue. Still, it was better to have it and not need it.

Once we were inside, Misty was up in arms over our absence. Well, as up in arms as one could be without possessing them.

"Where have you been? The TV stopped working hours ago!" she said.

"We were at a party," Hugo replied.

I suppressed a groan.

Lucas: Damn it, Hugo. Why did you have to tell the bored and high-strung sentient washing machine that? It makes it sound like we were having fun while she was trapped here alone.

Hugo: It's fine. The party was boring for us. We'll just tell her what we did.

"Look, the party was strictly for business meetings," Hugo began.

The front door suddenly locked, making us jump. I didn't even know the thing had an electronic lock on it. The air in the room changed as well. I thought it was my imagination at first. I wiped some sweat from my brow. Was it getting hotter in here?

Misty struggled to contain her anger and find the words. "You... you went to a party dressed like that?"

Hugo looked at me and whispered, "I think she's talking to you." He then hopped away to the other side of the room. The coward then looked away like he didn't know me.

The temperature in the room kept increasing. I pretended it didn't bother me. I just wanted to resolve whatever this was as quickly as possible.

"Why? What does it matter?" I asked tiredly. This wasn't a conversation that I had much interest in having. I'd hoped to be in and out of here in less than two minutes and we were already getting past that. I worried that if we stayed too long, then we'd miss whatever was going on at the church tonight.

"When you walk around in clothes cleaned by me, you are representing me," she said. "I have a reputation to think of."

Part of me wanted to check the back of the machine to see if there was a reset button. The other part of me recognized that having clean clothes again felt really good, so I had to salvage this. I couldn't go back to walking around in ten layers of dried monster blood. But I also couldn't let Misty dictate terms and push us around either.

"Look, I'm sorry your feelings got hurt," I said. "But we just came back here to grab something from my domain. We have another appointment to get to, so maybe we can discuss all of this another time?"

"And when will that be? After another day of me sitting here in silence? After..."

She kept complaining, and I started to tune her out. My domain was ready.

I wanted to get the apple, and who knows? Maybe Hugo could talk some sense into her.

Misty saw the blood pooling around my feet. "Don't you put this conversation on hold, Lucas Hudson!"

Hugo stared at me. His eyes pleaded with me to stay. More for his sake than anything, but I knew I wouldn't be gone long.

I disappeared from their sight as I entered my domain. A feeling of peace swept over me. Without even looking, I could feel how healthy the tree was now. Feel the new fresh red apple hanging from it that was ready to be plucked.

With a single thought, the apple disconnected from the tree and fell into an open hand formed of blood. The hand carried the apple to me where it went into my inventory.

With that out of the way, I took a minute to think about how I wanted to handle the Misty situation. She was stuck in the apartment alone for periods of time. She had control over other apartment functions like the locks and the thermostat, so we were unlikely to leave the apartment without her permission. And ultimately, all of this stemmed from her being bored and lonely.

I returned to the apartment and was hit in the face with an icy blast of air. Misty had turned the air conditioning to a setting that shouldn't be possible. Whatever enhancements had been made to the apartment?

"Look who decided to come back," she said.

Hugo was perched on top of the couch, shivering. "Do something!" he begged.

"How are you doing this?" I asked. "I thought you were a sentient washing machine. How did you gain access to other apartment functions?"

I didn't want to say it out loud, but Misty had been a gift from Roan. I didn't think she'd been put here to spy on us, though it was extremely difficult to hide anything from him unless we were in a place that was cut off from the Tower. But having greater access to the apartment, including the ability to lock us inside, was truly troubling.

"Oh, that happened when I needed to change the channel on the TV," she replied. "But now I can't get the thing to work and I'm sick of being ignored in this place."

I walked over to the TV and peered behind it. One of the cables had become disconnected. It must have been loose and finally fallen out. Hence the lost connection. Not that it should've mattered since I'm pretty sure the TV, like all electronics in here, run on magic rather than electricity. But the apartment was an imitation by the Tower of Earth normalcy. An attempt at being a safe, familiar refuge.

And it had been somewhat successful until Misty showed up. Still, I plugged the cable back in and the TV returned to life.

Misty made a clapping sound through her speaker. "Great, you fixed it! But we still need to discuss this wardrobe situation."

"I'd love nothing more," I lied as easily as I breathed. "But Hugo and I need to get going."

"I think you're forgetting that I can control the apartment," she threatened.

"I think you're forgetting that I can do this," I said, pulling out the TV's power cable.

"It's fine," she sniffed. "I can just turn the temperature back up and wait you out."

My sword appeared in my hand. "And I could see what washing machine scrap metal goes for in the city."

"Alright, enough!" Hugo yelled. "Lucas, stop acting all murdery."

He stared at me until I put my sword away. The crow nodded in appreciation and turned to Misty. "Look, I know it sucks that you're stuck alone in this apartment a lot of the time, and you barely get to wash anything."

"And when I do, it's always the same set of clothes," she groaned. "Why do you only have one outfit, Lucas? Are you a cartoon character?"

276 SCOTT W. JAMES

I ignored her jab and let Hugo continue.

The crow cleared his throat. "But, despite your situation, you need to look at it from our point of view. Every time we leave this apartment, we're fighting for our lives. When we come back here, it's because we're looking to rest and recover, even though every minute we spend in here is a minute lost out there. Time is against us, and if we don't find a way out of this Tower, then we'll all die."

"Wait, even me?" she asked, shocked at the prospect of her own mortality.

"*That's* what you took away from this conversation?" I asked incredulously.

"I just need a minute to process the doom I've learned is hanging over my head."

We waited for her to wrestle with the concept of death until we felt the temperature return to normal and heard the door's lock turn.

"I guess we all need to learn how to live together and be mindful of each other's needs," she said. "But I still think you should wear a wider variety of clothes."

"I'll think about it," I muttered as I grabbed Hugo and rushed out the front door.

"Thank you for being understanding," Hugo yelled back over my shoulder.

Misty silently closed the apartment door. Perhaps the situation hadn't been fully resolved but progress had been made thanks to Hugo. I've really got to let him negotiate more. Although that's a lot easier to do when you're calm. Maybe all the stabbings, beatings, and dismemberments over this past month have made me grumpier?

As we got in the elevator, Hugo wanted to discuss our next steps. The important thing we both knew was getting close to the church without being spotted. For that, I had the perfect idea in mind.

CHAPTER 35
UNDERCOVER

"I DON'T KNOW why you insist on checking every window before we leave, Harold," the woman said as she stepped out of the house. She adjusted her long brown robes and checked to make sure there wasn't a spot of dirt on them. They were a symbol of her devotion, after all. Plus, what would her neighbors think if she attended mass in a dirty robe?

"Sometimes I worry about your faith," she said, before readjusting her gray hair.

Harold, a bald man in his fifties, was wearing an identical robe as he stepped out of the house behind her. "I'm not worried about our *health*, Edith. I know the Mother protects us. I just think she has better things to do than protect our house from water damage if the wind knocks the windows open again."

The married couple had no children and left an empty house behind as they walked down the street. They were heading to the church for the big meeting. Meanwhile, cultists from other houses were doing the same in different parts of the human district. The difference between them and this couple was that they lived more on the outskirts, in a less favorable part of town. Which meant the pair had a longer walk to the church and saw fewer of their fellow parishioners while doing it.

"Do you think this will run longer than usual?" Harold asked. "I'm starting to wonder if I should've brought a snack with me."

"I told you to eat before we left," she chastised.

Hugo: Maybe we shouldn't do this. They seem like a nice, old married couple. Maybe they just got swept up in the religious fervor that's going through the city? They could be innocent.

"I hope there's a sacrifice this time," Edith said. "It feels like we've gone too long without spilling the blood of the faithless."

Hugo: I'll take out the one on the left.

We crept silently along the rooftops, following their movements. Walking alone at night should've made them paranoid. Yet they walked with complete confidence, never looking up or over their shoulder. Blind faith had made them zealots, and I had no sympathy for them.

Once they turned down a small side street, Archer and I dropped softly to the ground behind the pair. It was important not to make a sound or draw blood. So as agreed, I grabbed the head of Harold on the right and broke his neck in one swift movement. Hugo, while controlling Archer, did the same to Edith.

The System didn't even bother to recognize his name when I killed him. It was all but saying that these people were just meant to be fodder.

I put the body in my inventory and saw that the robes had been put in a separate slot. I selected the robes and they appeared over my armor. They felt a little loose when I moved. Harold had been a little heftier, but I'd make do. Plus, once I pulled the hood up, I'd be indistinguishable from any of the others.

Hugo saw me moving around in the robes and sighed. "The usual then? I'll fly above to spy on them?"

I shook my head. "I think we can do better this time." I pointed to the second body and told Hugo my idea. He laughed and immediately got to work on it.

———

"How's it feel?" I asked. We were getting close to the church. So if there were any kinks in the plan that needed to be ironed out, now was the time.

"It's a little awkward, but I'm getting the hang of it."

Hugo moved Archer forward with several halting steps. He was under the robes inside her body and using her eyes to see. I didn't quite understand how he was doing it, but he assured me that he was perfectly safe in there.

"This was genius," he said. "I should've been a mech pilot ages ago!"

His control became more stable as we reached the church gates. I doubted he'd be able to fight like that, but I was hoping to avoid a direct confrontation anyway. We were here to spy and gather information.

Other cultists were already heading inside the church, but there was a group of them with weapons standing guard by the gate. They looked like they were expecting trouble.

We kept our heads down as we passed them.

"Come on, get a move on," said one of the guards. "You should be the last of them."

Iron creaked behind us as the gate was closed. We were now locked in the church grounds. I glanced at the fence of iron bars surrounding us. They were high, but easily climbable. The only problem would be exposure to crossbow bolts when I did it.

If. If I did it, I reminded myself.

We joined the procession of cultists who were slowly making their way into the church. At first, I thought it was about being respectful, but the closer I got, the more I realized the truth. There were just too damn many of them.

Hundreds of them were densely packed into the church, all looking straight ahead to a stage at the back. Even the pews had been removed to make room for everyone. Three large boxes sat on the stage. Each one was covered with a white sheet. Cages perhaps? I couldn't hear anything from them over the sound of the crowd murmuring to one another.

A door at the back of the stage opened, and the crowd fell silent. Two men walked out. The first was Bart, wearing black robes. There was some kind of metal device on his hand, but it was difficult to make out the details of it. Behind him was a weathered old man in a set of white robes. A pendant with a red jewel hung from his neck. I took him to be the man in charge. Though I did wonder at the significance of Bart's black robes.

"Welcome," said the man in white. "Thank you all for coming on such short notice. There has been an exciting new development that needs your attention." He gestured at Bart. "Our partnership has borne fruit. I will allow him to explain. I'm excited to tell you all that I have heard from the Mother directly and she says to tell you that the harvest is close at hand."

"The harvest," everyone around us solemnly chanted.

Luckily, no one seemed to notice that Hugo and I hadn't said anything.

We watched Bart step forward. He wore a serious expression and looked like he'd rather be someone else.

"I have several items that may be of interest to your group," he said in a flat voice.

Bart pulled the sheets back on the cages. The first one contained an orc. It sat hunched up in the cage, with glassy, dead eyes. It only wore torn pants, so we were able to see there were injection marks along his arms. The second cage contained a wraith. It floated in the middle of the cage and was anchored to some kind of stasis field emanating from a cube that sat below it.

When I looked at the final cage, my breath caught in my throat. It was another Abomination. Though a little smaller than the last one I'd seen, the design was unmistakable. It appeared to be sleeping.

Again, I glanced at the cages themselves. They didn't look like much. Any one of these monsters could rip through this crowd, and if one were to get loose, chaos would ensue.

Bart clapped his hands together. "So, who wants to bid first?"

Hugo: What's going on?

Lucas: We were wrong about Bart being a member of the church. He's selling them monsters.

Hugo: How would they even go about using wild monsters?

I told him that I didn't know. Nor did I understand why he'd go against the orcs if he was looking for money. They were the wealthiest faction by far. Alienating them didn't make sense.

The leader in white coughed politely. "Perhaps a small demonstration first to ease any lingering doubts."

Bart nodded. "An excellent suggestion, High Priest." He raised his hand. The device on it was made up of metal fingertips on wires. It led to a small circular device on the palm of his hand. A blue crystal sat in the middle and faintly glowed. "This is a control device," he explained, before opening the cage containing the wraith.

There were a couple of gasps from the crowd, but nobody moved. Bart aimed the control device at the cage and the wraith flew out of it and up over the crowd. He made the creature spin in circles and dance all the way up the church's high ceiling before sending it back into its cage.

Bart locked the cage door and said, "So, who wants to go first?"

The cultists broke out into applause, and Hugo and I quickly joined in to avoid standing out. Once the fervor of the crowd had died down, Bart repeated his request for the bidding to start. The cultists within the crowd happily obliged and started throwing out offers. The numbers they gave meant nothing to me, so I tuned them out. Though I did wonder what these people wanted with the monsters in the first place.

Hugo: Maybe it has something to do with the harvest that their leader mentioned?

Lucas: Whatever that is. It sounds like something we have to put a stop to.

We ended up spending the better part of an hour standing there. It turned out that Bart wasn't just selling three monsters. The ones on the stage were just the show models. Apparently, he had more stock tucked away somewhere else.

One thing that stood out to me was that Bart refused to haggle on price when it came to the Abomination, and nobody seemed eager to buy it. It had the highest price out of the three, but that wasn't the only obstacle. I think its presence naturally unnerved them and so they were shying away from it.

Once the bidding was over, the High Priest led the group in a prayer before the meeting ended. It concluded with the High Priest saying, "May the Mother protect us all."

"May the Mother protect us all," the crowd chanted back.

With everything finished, Bart descended back down the stairs while the High Priest left the stage to talk to some of his flock. The majority of the crowd were beginning to trickle out of the church, so I figured that our spying was over. That was until I saw some regular cultists climb the stage steps and descend into the basement.

Lucas: Wait up here.

Hugo: We're splitting up?!

Lucas: I need you to listen in on the High Priest while I see what Bart has been up to.

Hugo: What happens if you get into trouble?

Lucas: There aren't any batteries up here. Summon everything you have and go to town.

I followed another cultist onto the stage and down the steps. It led to a long underground stone hallway with several doors and rooms. Lit torches lined the walls, and I caught a glimpse of Bart's black robes as he entered the room at the end of the hallway and closed the door behind him.

None of the other cultists followed him into that room. So when the hallway was clear, I opened the door and went inside.

The room was a tiny office space. Bart was sitting with his back to me, hunched over a small writing desk. A knife slipped into my hand. It was time to get some answers.

I grabbed his shoulder and spun him around. "Scream and you die," I snarled.

But the face in the black robes wasn't Bart's. It was a reanimated cadaver. It opened its mouth and green gas spewed out. The gas hit me in the face! I coughed and tried to warn Hugo, but the room was spinning, and my vision blurred…

The last thing I felt was my head hitting the floor before the darkness took me.

CHAPTER 36
SIX WORDS

I JOLTED AWAKE IN A PANIC! My body was upright but I couldn't move. My wrists and ankles were bound to a metal chair. Struggling was useless. Even with all my strength, the restraints wouldn't give.

Breathe, I said to myself. *What's the last thing I can remember?*

Images of the cadaver spewing poison gas came roaring back. It had knocked me unconscious in the church basement. A trap set by Bart. Had he known I was there the whole time? If that was true, then a second trap could've been waiting for Hugo. I have to get out of here.

I opened my eyes and took in my surroundings. This room was different. I was in some kind of underground cave. Electrical lights dangled from a cable running along the wall and there was medical equipment stored nearby. Further ahead, a plastic curtain hid the rest of the room, but there were lights back there too. A human shadow flickered past the curtain.

The necromancer was back there. Although I had to say, this space was a lot more science-based than magical. Bart must have used his expertise as an inventor to combine the two. Though for what purpose I couldn't even guess.

"You're finally awake," Bart said from behind the curtain. "That's good.

Though if you're trying to summon your familiar to save you, it won't work."

That's when I saw the battery. It had escaped my notice till now because it was a different design than the others. This one was rectangular shape with three sides covered in black metal. The gem side was pointed at me like it was directionally focused. If I could get past it or knock it over, then there was a chance I'd regain access to my powers.

Wait, what did he mean by familiar?

I reached for my inventory. With a knife in hand, I could cut myself free and be on him in less than a second.

[Inventory Request Failed]

[System Interference Detected]

I tried to contact Hugo and got a similar message.

"It's an interesting creature you made though," he added. "I could see the utility in it."

Bart stepped out from behind the curtain. He'd ditched his black robes for a conventional shirt and pants with a leather apron that held several small tools in its small front pockets. With the glasses he wore, he looked much more like the friendly inventor everyone had taken him for. I guessed it wasn't theater. He was just wearing what was practical for his work.

Bart looked me over. "So you're the one everyone has been getting worked up about over the factory explosion," he said.

"So you're the necromancer. The boogeyman that makes people disappear and has got half the city scared."

Bart's face screwed up in disgust. "Necromancer?" He shook his head. "What an ugly name."

"Well, what would you call someone raising an army of the dead?"

"An army of the dead?" he chuckled. "That's a good one. No, they're merely experiments. My true goal still remains out of reach. But I'm close. I just need a few more resources and it'll work."

He said it like it was a foregone conclusion. He's overconfident. I have to keep him talking to buy time and see what I can learn.

"Is that why you're selling those creatures to the church? For money?"

"That and it helps keep the orcs off my back. The church's arrival was quite fortunate for me. It's empowered the human faction and now half of them are no longer the orcs' lapdogs." There was venom in his voice on that last part. It sounded like he despised them.

"And so, in the chaos, it makes collecting bodies that much easier?"

He nodded. "See, you understand."

"What I don't understand is why am I still alive?"

Bart sighed. "I've been experiencing some... unusual setbacks recently. I need to know how much you've told Enzo, along with the names of your associates and where I can find them."

I knew where this was going. We were about to go through the usual bluster where he threatens to torture the information out of me, and I swear to never say a word. But before we could get to that, there was a knock on the door behind me.

Bart recoiled in shock. He wasn't expecting company. We were supposed to be alone.

Startled, he grabbed a control device and slipped it onto his hand. Past him lay two orc bodies. One female was at the back in a glass case and a male exposed on an operating table.

He moved past me to a wooden door. I thought about shouting for help until Bart opened the door and visibly relaxed. "Oh, it's just you," he said.

He walked back over to the table and put the control device away. I heard footsteps behind me and looked over my shoulder.

Flit stood there looking uncomfortable. He winced when he saw me tied to the chair. "Sorry," he said to me. "I can't interfere."

I nodded and pretended like it didn't bother me.

Flit handed a letter to Bart, which he quickly read, then dismissed the mailman.

Flit turned to go. Maybe he couldn't help me get out of here, but that shouldn't keep me from being able to use his services.

"Wait! Can I send a letter?" I asked.

Flit looked at the restraints around my wrists and then at Bart, who shrugged. "I don't see why not. Most who end up down here are dead before they get the chance to write final words."

He picked a scalpel up off of a tray and an orc pistol.

There goes my chance of fighting him off.

Bart handed the scalpel to Flit. "Cut only one wrist free, whichever one he writes with."

The mailman approached me cautiously, like I might attack him as soon as I was free. My body remained still as I calmly informed him that I was right handed. He cut the restraint free, and my eyes darted to my other wrist. Flit shook his head. He could do no more than this. Only what was absolutely necessary to write a letter, which thankfully included pen and paper. He held the paper while I considered what to say.

Bart said, "Fair warning, you should know that we're not under the church. In case you were thinking of warning someone to come and rescue you. I figure if I'm going to let you write your last words, then you shouldn't waste them."

I thanked him and stared at the page. Despite what he believed, I wasn't going to die in here. But if I didn't know where I was, then asking for help was pointless. Luckily, I'd just learned a very important piece of information, and if I was getting out of here, then it was prudent to plan ahead.

The letter was short. I only needed to write down six words along with who it was addressed to.

I nodded to Flit that I was done, and he folded the letter up and put it in an envelope. He didn't so much as glance at the contents. He couldn't care less what any of us write.

Another thought occurred to me as he slipped the letter into his jacket. "Hey, is it possible for you to hold on to that for a while?"

"You mean not deliver it right away?" he asked, frowning. "I guess there's no rule against it. I can hold on to it until you need it delivered. When you're ready, call my name and I'll come to you."

I thanked him, but before he could leave, Bart ordered him to re-tie my wrist to the chair. Even with a battery pointed at me, the inventor was smart enough to keep his distance.

Flit did as instructed, and silently left. He was no help to me now, but if I was right, then that letter would prove useful in the future.

Bart tsked and gestured to the body of an orc strapped to the table. "You know you've interrupted my work. I have a schedule that I'm trying to keep to, so your interrogation will have to wait a moment. Until then, why don't you think about all the things I could do to you if you don't tell me what I want to know."

A large audio recording device was wheeled out and turned on. Bart placed it near the orc body before approaching a circuit breaker with a series of cables. These cables had needles on the end that were inserted into different places on the body. Once they were in place, he threw the switch and electricity coursed through the orc body. The body started shaking with steam rising off of it.

Bart turned the device off and grumbled, "The voltage was too high. The body is tougher than a human body. Apparently, upping the voltage in order to get through just causes the body to overheat. Subject 17-O is a failure." He glanced at me. "Subject 1-C possesses rapid regenerative healing when exposed to blood. A potential avenue if the trait can be isolated and transferred."

He put me on that table to be his next experiment. I had to get out of here. But then I heard a thud upstairs and decided to stall.

"You know, I have some expertise in what you're doing. I could help you," I said.

Bart nodded without turning around. "Sure, you could," he said, not believing a word I'd said.

"What about my associates? I could tell you about the factory!"

He saw my frantic state and his mouth tightened into a flat line. "Looks like I'll have to sedate you to get you on the table."

He kept the orc pistol in one hand and picked up a syringe with the other. I resumed struggling as he got closer. I felt the chair tip over as I fell onto my side.

"This is pointless," he said. "You're only wasting energy."

I whispered something too quiet for him to hear.

"What?" He stepped closer.

I looked up into his eyes and shouted, "Now!"

The ceiling exploded, missing Bart only by a few feet. Still, he was hit by debris and knocked down. The syringe and gun both flew out of his hands. The explosion had pulled down the battery. My ears were ringing so loudly that I couldn't think straight.

I looked up at the giant hole in the ceiling. As the smoke cleared, I saw Hugo and Gren peering down. Hugo flew down and summoned Archer to cut me loose.

Bart unsteadily climbed to his feet. A thin trickle of blood was running down the side of his head. His eyes were a little unfocused until he saw Archer begin to rise out of the ground. Desperate, he looked for his gun but couldn't find it. It was lost somewhere in the debris. Bart decided to cut his losses and fled through the door.

Archer cut me free, and I replenished my health from my inventory. Gren, not wanting to be alone upstairs, hopped down into the hole with us. He was carrying a satchel that rattled when he moved. He looked like he wanted to be anywhere else than here.

"Come on, we have to go after him," I said.

Bart was too dangerous to let escape. Rather than follow through the door where a trap could've been set, I pointed back up to the hole. Gren cried out in alarm when I picked him up and ran toward Archer. I jumped at her, and she caught my foot and boosted us out of the hole.

We were now in a basement with another set of stairs leading up and out. The door up there had been left slightly open, with a sliver of light peeking through.

"Thanks for coming," I said to Gren.

"Hugo was very insistent."

"How did you find me so fast?" I asked the bird.

Hugo puffed up his chest. "I saw Bart leaving the church. He had one of his minions carrying your unconscious body. So I followed them here and when I realized I couldn't get in by myself, I went back for help."

"How long was I out?"

"The sun is almost up if that helps."

Damn, a few hours at least.

There was a crash upstairs!

"Lucas, get your sword out," Hugo said. "He's got more of those battery things upstairs."

Now I understood why he needed to bring Gren. A battery wouldn't have any effect on goblin engineering.

With my sword in hand, I went first up the stairs. Hugo dismissed Archer and sat on Gren's shoulder. If a battery hit us directly, then neither one of them would be much use in a fight. Thankfully, they both knew it, and followed me at a respectable distance.

We were in the heart of the necromancer's lair. There could be all sorts of monsters or traps waiting for us. So I braced myself for the worst when I reached the door.

I jumped out the door, blade in hand, to find… sunny-yellow-painted walls with picture frames, but no pictures. There was a coffee table with little knick-knacks on it, and a giant wooden spoon and fork on one of the other walls for decoration. This wasn't a lair. It was a family home.

Gren and Hugo joined me in the hallway. I was about to ask which way we should go when Bart stumbled around the corner. There was rage in his eyes. He wanted to kill us but his legs were shaking.

"What's he doing?" Gren asked.

"He's trying to stay conscious," I replied. "Considering the head trauma, we might get lucky and he'll pass out on us right here."

Bart reached into his apron pocket, pulled out four small cubes, and threw them at our feet.

"Or not," I sighed. I put my sword away. "Run!"

CHAPTER 37
FIGHTING WITH SPIRITS

WE FLED DOWN ANOTHER HALLWAY, away from Bart and the impending wraiths. I had no idea where I was going. All I knew was that we had to get out of this house and get back to either the cemetery or the apartment. Whichever was closer would work.

Eventually, we found a back door and stumbled out onto the sand. I cursed. We were in the desert.

"How far away is the city?" I asked them.

"It ain't close," Gren replied, indicating that we'd never make it on foot in time.

An ear splitting screech hit all of us. We clutched our ears and cried out.

Beast Identified [Wailing Banshee Wraith (Rare)] Level 142 – These spirits can pack quite the punch with their voices, but the same weaknesses apply to them as to the other wraiths. Good luck!

That was great to hear, except for the fact that we were nowhere near a cemetery.

"Lucas!" Hugo cried, pointing to Gren, whose ears were bleeding.

He'd be the first to die from the banshee attack and then it would be Hugo and myself. We couldn't run. There were some tall sand dunes behind us, but past that would just be more desert. We couldn't fight. I didn't have anything to trap them with and I bitterly regretted not stealing some gravestone. It would've cost me nothing to have it in my inventory.

There was one option left. Hide. I'd never tried it before, but in theory, we should all be perfectly safe.

Gren collapsed to the floor, screaming in pain as the four wraiths floated closer to us. The screaming got louder with their proximity.

I kept all of us close and activated Crimson Domain. Blood pooled around us. For me, entering the domain was a subtle transition from one place to the other. For Hugo and Gren, it was more like being violently yanked into another dimension.

They both fell into a shallow pool of blood. I healed myself and Hugo through our bond, but Gren needed a health potion. He was barely conscious, so I had to force him to drink it. When he finally recovered, he looked around and grunted. "Did we die? Is this hell?" He sounded almost resigned to it, but when I explained that they were in my domain, he just gave a tired nod.

"Why's it so creepy looking?" Hugo asked.

"I don't know," I replied. "I didn't design the place."

Hugo held his wings up in surrender. "Hey, don't get snippy. It's a very nice dimension of blood and darkness."

"We should be safe here for a while. The wraiths won't be able to get in."

"What about Bart?" Hugo asked.

I thought about it. Technically, to the human eye, it would've looked like we just vanished. If Bart had magical senses, then he'd be able to see the thin thread that connected my domain to the place in the Tower. He could then point a battery at that thread to cause the domain to break down. But he didn't have the sight, and he didn't know everything a Tower Climber was capable of.

"He can't hurt us in here either," I said. "But given his level of caution, he'll keep the wraiths around for security. As soon as we leave, they'll attack us."

"So we're just stuck here?" Gren asked.

"I'm going to make a call," I said.

Lucas: If you're there, I'd really appreciate some advice on how to deal with wraiths.

Roan: Of course. What kind?

Lucas: Wailing Banshees.

Roan: Wraiths are remnants of spirits. Something has to die in order for it to become a wraith. This causes things that remind them of life to repulse and hurt them. Gravestones are a good example of this, but so are the raw primal elements. Running water is also a good one.

Lucas: We're in the middle of a desert. Not a lot of water out here.

Roan: Ah, then I'd go with fire. It's a classic and it should work on them.

Fire was something we might be able to do. I told the others what Roan had said and had Gren check his satchel. It was disappointing to learn that he was out of explosives, but he did offer his lighter. I had that expensive bottle of liquor in my inventory that I'd been forced to buy. Grabbing that and a rag allowed me to make a Molotov cocktail, but it was only good for one target. And even if we somehow took out the other three, we were still stuck in the middle of nowhere.

"Wait, how did you guys get here?" I asked. Hugo I could see flying, but there was no way he'd carried the goblin here.

"We drove," said Gren. "I've got a bike parked over the dune."

"How quickly can you get it started?"

Gren smiled. "Immediately if it gets us out of here."

"Stay close," I said, and pulled out a Scarlet Apple. A prompt came up asking if I wanted to consume it. I said yes, and it told me to take a bite.

I bit into the apple.

[Temporary Reduced Scarlet Beast State Active]

[Mental State Unchanged]

[Speed, Strength, and Toughness Temporarily Enhanced]

I collapsed the domain. The wraiths were waiting for us on the other side and began their screeching. Hugo and Gren cried out in pain, grasping their ears. For me, the pain had dulled thanks to the apple. I lit the Molotov cocktail and hurled it at the closest wraith.

There was an unholy screech as it burst into flames. The other wraiths recoiled in shock and floated away from the fiery wraith as if they were afraid of it.

Not wasting any more time, I grabbed Gren and sprinted up the hill and over the other side. Gren's motorcycle was right where he said it would be.

He hopped on the front, and I sat behind him with Hugo on my shoulder. He turned the key, and the engine stalled. I nervously looked back up the hill. There was no sign of the wraiths, but something in the sand to our right shifted.

"Come on!" I yelled.

"I'm trying!" Gren yelled back.

He cranked the ignition again. This time, a large bug burst out of the sand. It skittered toward us.

I skewered it with a Blood Spike from a Hemorrhage Gate.

DING! You have slain [Diving Sand Beetle (Common)] Level 132 – Experience Points and Currency Acquired.

More sand shifted around us. They were attracted to the sound of the bike's engine. Twelve more bugs crawled out of the sand. I fired off more spikes, but some of the bugs had hardened shells and the spikes bounced right off them.

"They're getting closer!" I warned.

"Come on, you piece of shit. Work!" Gren cursed and slapped the side of the bike. He turned the key a fourth time, and the engine roared to life.

"Yes!" Hugo cheered.

We sped off away from the bugs, tearing across a flat plain.

DING! You have slain [Wailing Banshee Wraith (Rare)] Level 142 – Experience Points and Currency Acquired.

DING! Class: [Blood Reaver] has reached level 128 – Experience Acquired.

I updated my points and received a new message.

DING! You have gained [Weak Blood Ignition (Uncommon)] – Blood is a form of energy for you. With this ability, you can use that energy to make the blood you control combustible. Congratulations, you can now make blood fire. Well, a small amount of it anyway. Like a small packet of matchsticks worth. Wait, did your people still use matchsticks at the time of the integration? Never mind. I'm sure you'll figure it out.

The System must have reacted to me using fire to take out that wraith and was rewarding me accordingly. This was good information though. You never know when I might need to set something on fire.

Riding across the desert was strangely peaceful. The sun was up and it should've been hot, but with the wind in our faces, we never felt the temperature. Of course, the loud engine made conversation impossible for Gren. Not that he would've participated anyway. He was entirely focused on the path ahead, only pausing occasionally to glance down at the compass that he'd attached to the bike. This was how we'd find our way back to the city.

Lucas: I dunno about you, but I could use a break.

Hugo: You? Weren't you asleep for hours? I'm the one that was up all night worrying about you.

Lucas: I don't know if chemically induced unconsciousness really gives someone a restful night's sleep. Besides, I wasn't talking about that. Just a nap back at the apartment before we decide our next move.

Hugo: Oh yeah, that sounds good.

After an hour of travel, we finally made it back to the city. But Gren hadn't slowed down, and we were fast approaching the city gate.

"Hey, you should slow down and take us around to the side," I said.

"What?" Gren shouted, not hearing me.

"There's a secret entrance," I shouted back.

Gren didn't understand, and we plowed right through the open city gate. A few surprised goblins dove out of our way as we sped toward them. Gren turned down a side street, but underestimated his speed. He tried to brake too late, and we crashed into the side of a stall.

Only minorly bruised, I looked around. Gren had driven us right into Goblintown. Before we could get up, a group of spears was pointed at our throats, with even more behind them holding unlit sticks of dynamite.

Hugo took one look at the group and shook his head at Gren. "And you told me that you were motorcycle certified!"

CHAPTER 38
COMING TO TERMS

THE GOBLINS HAD FORMED into teams and surrounded us. The ones with the spears argued that they had caught us trespassing first, and so they were the ones who were entitled to kill us. But the group holding the dynamite argued that it was they who had caught us. This back and forth went on for some time while we sat there, awaiting our fate.

Hugo: What do you think? Can we take them?

I shook my head. The ones with the dynamite were a little concerning, but they were nothing compared to the artillery I'd glimpsed them set up on some of the roofs. They had mortars aimed at us. Something told me that they were itching to use them regardless of the potential collateral damage.

"Alright!" one of the spear goblins shouted.

The other goblins fell silent.

"Let's just stab 'em a bit with the spears and then you lot finish 'em off with the fireworks?" he suggested.

The goblins all began grinning and nodding. They liked this plan a lot. They were about to close in when Gren's brother, Vrog, came running around the corner. "Wait!" he yelled.

The goblins froze, recognizing that Vrog outranked them. He stopped to catch his breath and then said, "These prisoners are with me."

There were a few moans of disappointment, but most of the other goblins backed off. Only one leered at us and asked, "Do you need help securing them?"

Vrog gave us a look asking us to play along.

"We surrender," I said.

"Yep, we give up," said Hugo.

Gren looked at the ground and said nothing. I noticed that Vrog hadn't looked at him this whole time, either. He just kept his eyes on Hugo and me.

We got to our feet and let Vrog march us out of there. Once we were alone, Vrog angrily rounded on Gren. "What were you thinking coming back here?"

Gren shrugged, looking defeated. "It was an accident."

Vrog put his fingers to the bridge of his nose like he didn't want to have this conversation. "Okay, fine. Just go. I'll make up some excuse about how you escaped. These two will have to come with me though."

"Come where?" I asked.

"To meet the clan chief. She'll decide what to do with you."

"And if we say no?" Hugo asked.

"Too many goblins saw you blatantly enter our territory. At this point, if I don't bring you to the chief to try and de-escalate things, then it'll be open war with the humans. So will you come with me to make your case, or will you choose war and save yourselves?"

Hugo and I looked at each other.

Hugo: Come on. Half of the human district are cultists. It's not like they don't have it coming.

Lucas: Yes, but the other half are innocent. They don't deserve to have goblins bombing their houses. Plus, this could be an opportunity. Who knows how much security Bart has put in place since we left his lair? There might be a way for us to get the goblins on our side.

Hugo didn't look like he was sure that it would work, but he was willing to go along with it.

"We'll go with you," I told Vrog. "But Gren comes too."

"What?!" Vrog replied.

Gren looked up in shock as well. "That's a death sentence!" he exclaimed.

"Gren is our goblin witness," I said. "He has seen the lair of one who's responsible for all the disappearances that have been happening in the city."

Vrog absorbed this new information quickly and grimaced. "Fine, but let me do all the talking."

He marched us into the heart of Goblintown. Some stared at us in surprise while others were enjoying it and treated it like a show. They knew there was drama due to our presence and shouted questions at Vrog for answers. He merely told them that it was chief business and kept us moving. I did my best to keep my head bowed and to look as non-threatening as possible. Most of them were more interested in the fact that Gren was here. A banished exile being forcibly brought back excited them.

Past the market stalls—and what Vrog called the munitions factories—was a series of large tents. It surprised me to see tents, of all things, in a city and I said so to Vrog.

He grunted. "It's traditional. Our clan used to move around a lot, but that got harder and harder to do on our old planet. Too many wars and too few resources. We were forced to adapt and took a part of this city that had been abandoned, for ourselves."

We were pushed forward toward the largest tent. Something that could easily hold over fifty people comfortably. As we entered, my guess turned out to be accurate. There was a small crowd on either side of the entrance.

The way they jeered and booed at us made me feel like we were entering a courtroom. Which, if Vrog was to plead our case, was close to the truth.

At the back of the tent several ancient looking goblins sat on chairs. One chair larger and more special than the others was in the center of this group. An old female goblin sat in it wearing a simple gray homespun dress. This was the clan chief.

We stood in front of them and waited. The clan chief raised her hand and everyone in the room stopped talking.

"Why have you brought two outsiders and an exile here?" she asked Vrog.

"They claim to have information about our people who have been taken. I thought if there was any truth to it, then we should hear them out."

The chief sighed. "Very well." She turned to me. "You stand accused of trespassing not once, but twice on our territory. Not only that, but you have brought one who bears great shame back into our midst. So be quick with your words."

I swallowed. Okay, this might be a harder sell than I'd first thought.

"The one responsible for the disappearances is a human inventor named Bart," I told them.

"Yes, we know that already," she replied.

Taken aback, I froze for a moment and was unsure of how to continue.

"Is that it?" she asked, raising her hand as if she were about to call some guards forward.

"No, there's more," I said. "I know where Bart is hiding. It's not in the city. He has a house out in the desert."

The crowd of goblins laughed and even the chief smirked. "Child, nothing can sustain itself out there, save for the bugs that call it home. We know this... this thief," she spat. "This thief is with the church of the Harvest Mother. They are protecting him inside their church."

"That's not true!" shouted Hugo. "He sold to the church, but his true lair is in the desert."

The goblins in the crowd started stomping their feet. Their way of calling for our heads.

"Tell them, Gren!" Hugo pleaded.

Gren chewed his bottom lip and then took a step forward. He raised his hand for recognition to speak, and to his surprise, everyone complied.

"On my honor…" he began.

"Your honor means nothing here," said the chief. "If you wish to speak, then it will be on your brother's honor and his family's honor."

Vrog's eyes widened. He wanted to speak out, but the chief silenced him with a look.

Gren solemnly nodded. "On my brother's honor, I swear to tell the truth. The human beside me isn't lying. Sixty miles from here, I traveled by bike and discovered a large house that belonged to the inventor Bartholomew. He has a lab there where he runs experiments on the dead bodies of orcs, humans, and goblins. He controls dangerous spirits, wielding them like weapons."

"We do not doubt his crimes," said the chief. "Only his location. Still, the fact that you would risk your brother's honor for this makes your claim worth considering." She turned and looked behind her to a gap in the tent. "What do you think?"

The tent flap opened, and Enzo strode inside flanked by three orcs, including his daughter.

"What is this?" I asked.

Enzo's cold eyes regarded me. "We have come to an accord after going through the documents you provided, which included detailed notes on goblin experimentation. We are now certain that the goblin faction had no hand in Bart's crimes."

"That's good?" I hazarded a guess.

He gave a stiff nod. "But I do not believe you have been entirely forthcoming. You were seen entering the church wearing the church's robes. I think you are protecting Bart and that you are trying to lure us away from the church and into a trap out in the desert."

"What about Gren's testimony?" Hugo asked.

"I care not for what some banished goblin says. Such creatures would say anything if it served their own interests. I say we execute them."

He checked with the clan chief as a sign of respect, confirming that it should be a mutual decision as part of their new accord. The chief nodded and two male orcs beside Enzo pulled out their pistols.

This was it. I had to use my insurance policy. Man, I really hoped that this would work.

"Flit!" I shouted.

The orcs paused.

"Do you really think that will help?" asked Enzo. He gestured for his men to raise their weapons and continue.

They'd fired their weapons at us! It sounded like two thunderbolts crackling, but nothing touched us. I opened my eyes and saw Flit standing in front of us. Smoke curled off his body from where he'd blocked the shots. He was so fast that it took a second for everyone to register that he was even there.

"What is this?" asked Enzo.

"You can deliver the letter now," I said.

Flit walked up to Enzo and handed him the envelope. The orc boss read the note and then let it slip through his fingers. His body shook with rage, but his voice remained calm. "What is that supposed to mean?" he asked us.

Chiara picked up the note and read it. "Father, is this true?" she asked, her voice rising. "You told me we buried her!"

"Her body is in Bart's laboratory in a glass coffin," I said. "I saw it myself."

"How would you even know what she looks like?" Enzo countered. "She died well before any Tower Climbers showed up here."

I went into my inventory and produced the painting that The Fool had given me. It depicted Enzo with his other daughter. Chiara looked like she was either about to cry or punch someone.

"Will someone explain?" asked the clan chief, looking annoyed.

The note I'd written was simple. The words were 'I know where your daughter is.' She was older in the glass coffin, but the scar on her chin was too unique to not recognize.

The effect on Enzo was greater than anticipated. He stared at the painting. "I'd always hoped it was something ordinary that had gotten her. Something quick. To think of her lying in the hands of that monster."

The clan chief sensed that the meeting was spiraling out of control. "This is something we must discuss in private," she said and ordered everyone else to wait outside the tent.

Everybody awkwardly shuffled out. Most of the goblin crowd was ordered to move on entirely while the rest of us waited nearby. Despite everything that had been said, nobody wanted to be near the three of us. Our fates were still undetermined and we were seen as contagious.

Flit walked up to us though and handed me a note from Daisy.

"Thank you," he said. "Once things with the church are settled, I'll finally be able to be free of this job."

"Don't thank me," I replied. "It seems like everything is happening on its own right now."

Flit shook his head. "You found the one responsible for the disappearances and finally ended this city's paranoia once and for all. With cooler heads, a truce was struck thanks to the both of you."

Flit left and despite his words, we both knew that the quest wasn't over until we stopped Bart for good. That was the only way we'd be able to continue on down to the next floor.

I read the note from Daisy. It said that she'd run into trouble and was forced to move on. She said she'd see us on the next floor, down near the elevator, with better news.

I showed the note to Hugo.

Lucas: What do you make of this?

Hugo: Hmm, doesn't feel right. It's vague. Could it be from someone else?

Lucas: You think it's Roan setting a trap for us?

Hugo: It sounds like something he'd do. I guess it doesn't matter. We'll have to check it out, anyway?

Lucas: Right, but the necromancer is first.

Enzo and the chief stepped out of the tent together.

The chief said, "We find your story plausible, but we cannot risk leaving the city undefended. We also cannot spare any of our people, but we offer these instead."

She snapped her fingers. A goblin and an orc both came forward, each carrying a small box. They opened them up and offered them to Hugo and me. One contained a black orb, and the other a knife made of black metal.

It must've looked weird to the others, but as a sort of Climber tradition, Hugo and I poked both items for their stats.

Item Identified! [Spirit Orb of Kelstus (Rare)] This orb contains a curse ability that can imbue other spirits with curse magic. The perfect weapon for ghost-on-ghost violence that's been plaguing this fair city.

Item Identified! [Ceremonial Dagger of Kelstus (Rare)] – A knife enchanted with Kelstus's own death curse. Deadly to spirits and the living alike. It will destroy the souls of anything C grade and below (Note: a living body will act as a barrier, and greatly slow the curse magic down. Not recommended for quick living deaths unless used as a conventional knife.)

The choice was obvious. I took the dagger while Hugo absorbed the orb's power. We thanked them for their help, but there was still one last thing to discuss.

"What about Gren?" I asked.

The chief looked weary of conversation at this point and merely nodded. "Yes, you may take the banished one with you for assistance."

Vrog stepped forward and handed Gren a fresh satchel filled with explosives. It wasn't exactly what I'd meant, but Hugo saw what I was getting at.

"Can he be unbanished?" the crow asked.

The chief shook her head. "He'll need to do more than act as a delivery driver to redeem himself. That said, his wife and six children will fear no reprisals or recriminations if they choose to visit Goblintown again."

She turned and left.

Hugo looked at Gren in shock. "You've got six kids! Why the hell are you running around with us?"

The goblin ignored him. "Let's just get this over with," he grumbled.

"It's just so irresponsible," Hugo said to me.

I tried to keep my face neutral, refusing to take a side as we went back to the motorcycle. By the time we got there, Chiara was sitting on a second bike waiting for us.

I opened my mouth to speak, but she held up her hand. "I don't want to hear it. It's my sister and I'm going."

I closed my mouth and nodded.

We got on the bikes and rode back out into the desert to see the mad inventor one last time.

CHAPTER 39
CONFRONTING THE TRUTH

RETURNING to the lair was more straightforward than I'd envisioned. No bugs attacked us during the entire trip. And even when we climbed up the tall dune overlooking the house, there was nothing to see. It was eerily quiet.

"Do you think he's still in there?" Hugo whispered.

"He's got nowhere else to go," I said. "People in the city know what he's done. This is the end of the line for him."

"There's no way for us to approach the house without being seen," said Chiara, who was crouched beside us. "There are too many windows."

Gren had bravely chosen to wait by the bikes, but had assured us that at the first sign of bug activity, he'd run up to join the fight. Truthfully, I was glad that he was staying out of it. It was one fewer person to worry about. Though, I did put one of his dynamite sticks in my inventory because you just never know.

Hugo stretched his wings out. "This time, I'm going first," he said.

Archer and Milton crawled out of the sand and made their way down to the house. Chiara and I followed closely behind while Hugo circled in the air.

Wraiths came pouring out the door, followed by shambling cadavers.

None of the wraiths were screaming which was good, but they were moving fast. Hugo engaged them with his summons. Archer's arrows were imbued with curse magic, as was Milton's pincers. The curse magic seemed to damage them. And when one of the wraiths got too close to me, I swiped at it with my dagger and it fell apart.

I looked back and noticed that Chiara had pulled out an orc pistol and her knife. This time her knife was giving off the same cursed black energy as my own.

She shot some of the cadavers before they even had a chance of getting close. All headshots. None of them got back up after that.

This was good. It felt like we were winning until I heard a series of thuds behind the house.

An Abomination lumbered around the corner. Chiara fired several shots at the creature, but they only singed its outer layer of skin.

I glanced at the house's doorway. The way to Bart was clear, but I didn't know whether the Abomination would follow us inside. The last thing I needed was a roof collapsing on top of me.

Chiara saw my predicament and made a decision. "Go!" she said. "We'll hold them off."

"But..."

Hugo: Lucas, she said go!

Right. With Hugo and the others occupied, it was up to me to finish this.

I ran inside and cut my way past several cadavers that were still lurking in the house until I reached the basement. It was empty, but that didn't lessen my caution as I approached the door that would lead to his laboratory.

I wasn't stupid. He had to have something set up down there for whomever tried to come down. Luckily, I'd brought a welcoming gift.

I lit the stick of goblin dynamite, threw the door open, and tossed it inside. As soon as I slammed the door shut behind me there was a tremendous boom. I waited a few more seconds, then I took my sword and knife out and ventured in.

Part of me expected to see the wreckage of the laboratory and Bart's charred corpse. Instead my heart sank. The place had been untouched by the blast.

Bart stood there, holding a gun and smirking at me. "You like it? It's a new forcefield I installed after my last goblin visitor."

"It's over," I said. "Even if you kill us, more will come. You can't fight your way out of this. Enzo knows what you did. I have to admit though, it was pretty ballsy of you. Stealing his daughter's body for your experiments."

"You know nothing!" he shouted, suddenly switching from jovial to angry.

There was a control device on his other hand and he pointed it at a table. An orc cadaver sat up and slowly climbed off the table.

Huh, looks like he finally figured out how to make the orcs work. Strangely, something else caught my attention. Next to the glass coffin containing Enzo's daughter was a large glass jar. In it, some white light and black light were melting together and repelling one another. The effect was so mesmerizing that I almost let the dead orc take a swing at me.

Beast Identified [Orc cadaver experiment 19] Level – 149

It was slower than a regular orc, for which I was grateful. The downside was that Bart was controlling this one directly, and I'm pretty sure its strength hadn't diminished at all.

"What's the point of this?" I asked, before dodging another punch. Bart still had the gun and the batteries. He could've just shot me.

"Because I'm not going to get the chance to say this to someone else. Once my work is finished, I'll be leaving this place and going farther away to somewhere much deeper in the desert. Somewhere green where we can live peacefully. I'll never get the chance to say this to Enzo, and nobody else would care to listen."

"But I'm a captive audience, so I'll do?"

"Yes, although I'll have to kill you too. Otherwise, you'd try to stop me from completing my work."

I tried to shove the orc back, but it was like pushing against a solid wall of meat. A thick, gray hand lurched out to grab me and I darted back.

There were always the stairs, I thought. Run away and grab more explosives. There had to be a limit to that forcefield of his.

"I guess you fleeing would be the second-best option for me," he said. "Of course, I'd just put the forcefield back on and leave it up permanently. You'd never make it back inside. But I'll leave that decision up to you."

I cursed. I didn't like running away, and I especially hated leaving things unfinished. So I decided to stay and moved around the orc.

Bart raised his gun, but I knew he wouldn't fire unless I got too close to him.

On one of the tables was another control device. Bart had been so confident that he'd completely overlooked it.

I snatched the second device and slipped it onto my hand. Bart sensed what I was going to do and fired just as I dove behind the orc. A beam of plasma shot out and burned a smoking hole right into the cave wall.

I put the second device against the orc to try and control it. Instead, a sharp feedback pain hit both of our heads. We both cried out, but I had a tougher constitution than he did.

The orc cadaver collapsed. Whatever connection Bart had to him was temporarily severed.

With my idea to control the orc gone, it was time to go to plan b. I ran toward the glass case containing Enzo's daughter. Bart fired his gun wildly until I got close to the body.

"No, don't touch her!" he cried.

He was protective of her. The only body with a glass case to preserve it. This one was special to him. Bart feared that I was going to destroy it, but that had never been my plan. I was going after the glass jar. I'd used

Magical Awareness and seen the truth. There was an aura inside the jar. That was somebody's soul trapped in there.

Bart rushed forward to stop me, but he was too slow. I slapped my control device against the jar containing the soul.

Suddenly, the cave vanished, and I was standing in a green meadow on a sunny day. There was an orc woman in a summer dress, picking a flower when I arrived. She looked at me with curiosity.

"Who are you?" she asked.

She was Enzo's daughter and looked exactly like she did in the coffin.

"Er, my name is Lucas… and I need your help."

She smiled warmly, but there was sadness in her eyes. "I can't help anyone. I'm dead."

Okay, I'm glad I didn't need to have that conversation. But I was still very much alive, and if she was special to the inventor then maybe she could help me.

"Well, there's a man named Bart who thinks that he can change that. He wants to bring you back to life, and is currently trying to kill me."

"Bart? Oh, he wouldn't hurt a fly."

"Wait, you know him?"

"Of course. He's my husband. I'm Alessia, by the way."

Now it all made sense. The animosity Bart had with the other orcs. All the secrecy. Nobody would have approved of an orc and human marriage. I'd seen the way Enzo treated other humans. He considered them to be servants or problems to be dealt with, but never equals.

At the edges of the meadow, the grass caught on fire. It spread rapidly toward us. I tried to run and to warn Alessia to do the same, but she just stood there. The fire hit her first and spread up her entire body. She screamed as it consumed her, yet even then, she did not move. But when the fire reached me, the flames harmlessly flowed past me.

312 SCOTT W. JAMES

I blinked and suddenly the green meadow had returned with Alessia standing there, same as before.

"It comes more frequently now," she said.

"The curse magic?"

She nodded. "It was an accident. He'd grabbed a curse knife without realizing it. I panicked and tried to take it from him. He accidentally cut my hand, and that was it. I tried to tell him that it wasn't his fault, but he wouldn't hear of it. Instead, he'd just read books on curse and death magic until my time ran out and I succumbed to the curse. Bart must have found a way to keep the curse from consuming my soul after it took my life. But he doesn't know how to get rid of it. If he'd talked to my father, then he'd know that it's impossible."

Oh my God. She's been trapped in here this whole time, being tortured by the curse. It must be agony.

"Do you even want Bart to save you?" I asked.

Her smile became sad. "Like I said, that's not possible. Could you pass a message on to him? Please tell him to let me go. The time we had together was special, but it's time to let me go."

The meadow disappeared, and I found myself standing back in the laboratory. The only difference this time was that Bart had pressed the muzzle of the pistol right against my forehead.

"At this angle, there's zero risk to my wife," he said. There was a manic look in his eyes now. The thought of me injuring her was threatening to destroy his sanity.

"She wants you to let her go," I said, hoping to get through to him.

"I know that!" he snapped. "Don't you think I've spoken to her?"

"But the fire…"

"A temporary pain she must only endure for a little longer."

"You've lost it. What you're after is impossible. She told me so herself and her family knew curse magic. You're never going to cure her. But you could still save her."

Bart grunted. "Are those your last words?"

I almost said yes until I remembered something. "Do you mind if I have one last cigarette before I die?"

The inventor shrugged. "I never cared for the habit, but she would want me to be reasonable. She'd want me to let you."

She'd probably prefer you freed her from the nightmare you put her in, I thought.

I took out the Serenity Leaf cigarette Gren had given me and smeared a drop of my blood on the end of it. I used Blood Ignition to light it and prayed that I didn't fully inhale. With the cigarette lit, I sucked in as much smoke as I could and then blew it directly into Bart's face.

He coughed, and for a moment I thought his finger on the trigger might twitch. But after a few seconds his features softened. The anger melted away and a warm smile spread across his face.

"What is this?" he asked.

I tamped the cigarette out and took a couple of steps back before saying, "Something to help you reconsider your life choices."

"I feel warm, and oh no!" He frantically looked at me and the jar containing his wife's soul. Tears rolled down his cheeks as he raised the pistol and shot the jar. With the glass broken, the black light and white light both quickly faded away.

Bart sank to the floor sobbing. "Why did I do that?"

I remained silent. There was nothing that I could say. The question was to himself. In this altered state, he'd finally grasped how much pain he'd put everyone through, and it was breaking him.

Suddenly, he looked up at me and smiled again. "Thank you, but you should go now. It's finished. It's all finished."

I nodded and started heading back up the stairs. It was over. He had nothing left to fight for and would turn himself in. I doubted that Enzo or the others would kill him. A brilliant mind like his would be put to work in some form or another.

Halfway up the stairs, I heard a pistol shot and stopped.

DING! You have slain [The Necromantic Engineer Bartholomew] – Level 168 Experience Points and Currency Acquired.

DING! Quest Completed – Congratulations! You've solved this floor's primary quest and have now gained access to the next floor down.

I fucking hate this place, I thought to myself as I marched up the rest of the stairs.

CHAPTER 40
IT NEVER RAINS BUT IT POURS

"THIS IS SO FUCKING STUPID," said Gren.

"Shh, it's gonna work," I whispered. "Also be quiet. Your voice is scaring them away."

We were lying under the bodies of some dead goblins out in the desert. This time though, the city walls were still within sight. Earlier today, a group of goblins had gone out to fight some bugs as part of a training exercise. The bugs had overwhelmed them and they'd perished.

Some goblin onlookers stood on a nearby hill, watching for more bugs. They wanted to go down and collect their dead, but they were wary of more attacks.

This had presented us with an opportunity. It had required me to force Gren's hand, and he eventually agreed. For understandable reasons, Hugo sat this one out as Gren and I crawled under the bodies. We pretended to be dead in order to enact my plan of turning Gren into a successful corpse piker. With the crowd of goblins watching, this was the perfect way for him to regain his honor.

"Like I said, fucking stupid," he muttered, trying hard not to gag.

The bodies around us stank, and we'd been lying in them for nearly an hour. I could tell that he was close to giving up. Frankly, the thought had crossed my mind too. But I reminded him to be quiet, and we waited. Gren held a short spear in his hand, and I had my sword lying next to me. Whatever bugs had attacked the other goblins might be too strong for Gren on his own. But with my help, I was confident that we could put on a good show for the goblins watching on the hill.

After more waiting, we heard the sound of mandibles clicking somewhere nearby. That was another frustrating part about playing dead. The lack of being able to see. Luckily, we had a spotter.

Hugo: There's one beetle looking bug getting close to the edge of the corpse pile.

Lucas: Which way?

Hugo: Your left. Get ready.

One bug was perfect. When it was almost on top of us, I shouted, "Now!"

Gren and I shoved the bodies aside. The beetle reared up in surprise, making itself taller. Gren took the initiative and jabbed his spear into its belly. The beetle screeched in pain and skittered back. The stab had been shallow, but I was impressed with his courage.

"Is that enough?" he asked.

"No, we have to kill it and avenge your fallen comrades."

"But these weren't—"

He was cut off as the beetle charged at him. I slammed into its side before it could progress farther. The beetle was knocked off balance, so I followed it up with a small cut from my dagger. A little curse magic coursing through its body should help slow it down.

I backed away, pretending to be tired while Gren stood there looking uncertain.

"Come on," I encouraged.

Gren hesitated long enough for the beetle to recover and prepare for another charge. Unfortunately, it had deemed me the greater threat and was racing toward me.

I waited for it to get near and then dove to the left. The bug passed right by, one of its legs stumbling. The curse magic was beginning to take effect. It was happening quicker than I'd anticipated. I had to get Gren back in the fight before this thing collapsed.

But the goblin's knees were shaking. The onlookers on the hill would be too far away to notice, but I could tell that Gren was right on the edge of running away.

I ran over to him and held my sword up like we were making a desperate last stand.

"You can do this," I told him. "That spear has more range than my sword. Stab it as soon as it gets within range, then run to the side of it."

Gren nodded vigorously. "Stab then run to the side. Got it."

The beetle came at us again. This time, I was ready with a little trickery. Right before it came within range, I threw a knife at its feet. One leg was sliced clean off. As it lumbered toward us, Gren lashed out with his spear. The bug stumbled head first onto the spear and died instantly.

With the beetle vanquished, a few of the goblin onlookers applauded, while others rushed down to congratulate Gren.

"Everyone will hear of this!" one cheered as he ran up to Gren and clapped him on the shoulder.

I quietly recovered my knife and slipped away from the group to let Gren have his moment. Our eyes met one last time, and he nodded to me in appreciation before showing off his spear to the other goblins.

He might not be the greatest goblin warrior, but at least he could now return with his family to Goblintown. He didn't always think the best of himself, despite the fact that he'd saved my life multiple times. So part of this was about paying him back and helping him redeem himself. But I wanted more than that for him. I wanted this to mark the start of a new, positive chapter in his life, and I believed it would.

Hugo flew to my shoulder, and we hiked back into the city.

"That was a nice thing you did," he said.

I nodded. "Yeah, for once it really feels like we're leaving a floor better than we found it."

"Yeah, it feels good to improve things. We made a positive difference to the people here."

As we entered the market district, we heard a voice call out, "Potions! Get your potions here! Anything and everything to cure what ails you!"

It was Mizick holding a small tray of bottles. He stood on a street corner, shouting to any passerby. His clothes were worn and dirty.

Hugo and I tried to do a U-turn when he spotted us. "You!" he pointed an accusatory finger. "You owe me a new shop!" He angrily stomped toward us, the potion bottles in his tray rattling.

"What do we do?" Hugo asked.

There was only one thing we could do.

"Run!" I yelled.

We took off down another street, his angry shouting getting quieter and quieter.

"Okay, so maybe not everything was better," Hugo admitted.

"Hey, we were just in the wrong place at the wrong time. We can't be held liable every time a mad bomber decides to end their life in our presence."

We reached the elevator, and as the doors opened, we found Roan waiting for us.

"Get in," he said.

We stepped inside and waited. This could only be serious.

The doors closed, and Roan pushed the button to take us back to the apartment.

"Now we can speak," he said. "The chat I have set up with you should still be secure, but I couldn't afford to take any chances. I had to see you in person to warn you."

"Warn us?" Hugo asked.

"It's about Daisy," he said.

"What… what did she do?" Hugo asked in the most suspicious sounding voice possible.

I couldn't help but tense up, but Roan waved our concerns away.

"This isn't about her note promising to free you or beat the gods. I've known about that from the start."

"And you're not upset?" I asked.

"No. In fact, we expect it. Lots of Climbers and former Climbers have tried to take a swing at us. Now every god reacts to it differently, but I would've been a little insulted if you hadn't tried something at some point. Neither of you are cut out to be meek and submissive. Just blindly following authority. Now, with that being said, I need you to follow my authority on what I'm about to say."

Here it comes.

"Daisy is trying to recover her memories. Normally, this wouldn't be a problem. She's tried to do this several times before. The difference this time is that after the Golden Door fiasco, I'm public enemy number one with the other gods. One of which, and I don't know who, is trying to help her recover her memories."

He paused to see if we understood.

"I feel like you're building up to something," I said. "Can you just say it?"

"Fine. I'm not saying this is my fault. But Daisy's lost memories, if recovered, would risk wiping out this entire galaxy."

There was dead air for a second as we tried to process that last sentence.

Hugo cocked his head to the side. "Huh?"

"I can't go into details, but you need to find Daisy and stop her."

I folded my arms, not liking one bit where this was going. "You mean kill her?"

"What? No. We need her alive. Without her, we lose our potential doomsday device and the protection that entails. No, just find her and convince her that her lost memories are overrated."

Oh, that sounds simple enough, I thought to myself.

The elevator doors opened back to the apartment hallway. Flit was there, holding a black envelope. He handed it to Roan, who instead of opening it, just incinerated it as soon as he took it from the Flit.

"I thought you were free from all this?" I asked Flit.

"I am," he replied. "I got a new job with better benefits."

Roan sighed and stepped out of the elevator. "It never rains, but it pours."

Flit raised one eyebrow at the god. "Your response?"

"I still have time," Roan growled.

Flit politely nodded just as a new door formed in the hallway, and he disappeared through it.

"Are we going to talk about what just happened?" Hugo asked.

"Not yet," Roan replied. "Just focus on keeping Daisy safe." The elevator doors were closing, which meant we weren't getting any rest before heading to the next floor. "Oh, and if she's changed her name again, stay away from her. She'll kill you if she learns who you are."

The doors closed, and we began our descent to the next floor.

"What the hell does that mean?" Hugo asked.

"Well, he said it best. It never rains, but it pours."

END OF BOOK 3